She felt his touch and suddenly, unexpectedly, the pieces of memory and the shadows of darkness were gone—gone with the simple touch of his hand. Words and thoughts ceased when he ran his hand over her shoulder with an infinite slowness. Her breath caught in her throat as his fingers traced her neck before he cupped her cheek, searing her with sensation.

ℬLUE 𝒲ALTZ

An unforgettable novel of the power of passion by the author of *Wild Hearts*

Praise for Linda Francis Lee's *Wild Hearts*:

"Sexy . . . brilliant break-out book for the ever talented Linda Francis Lee."
—*Affaire de Coeur*

"This tale of those battered by life who manage to keep their WILD HEARTS will entertain and delight."
—*Romantic Times*

Titles by Linda Francis Lee

BLUE WALTZ
WILD HEARTS

Blue Waltz

Linda Francis Lee

JOVE BOOKS, NEW YORK

BLUE WALTZ

A Jove Book / published by arrangement with
the author

PRINTING HISTORY
Jove edition / January 1996

All rights reserved.
Copyright © 1996 by Linda Francis Lee.
This book may not be reproduced in whole
or in part, by mimeograph or any other means,
without permission. For information address:
The Berkley Publishing Group, 200 Madison Avenue,
New York, New York 10016.

ISBN: 0-515-11791-9

A JOVE BOOK®
Jove Books are published by The Berkley Publishing Group,
200 Madison Avenue, New York, New York 10016.
JOVE and the "J" design are trademarks
belonging to Jove Publications, Inc.

PRINTED IN THE UNITED STATES OF AMERICA

10 9 8 7 6 5 4 3 2 1

For Michael,
     who offered me the dance
          of my long-held dreams

ACKNOWLEDGMENTS

I would like to express my sincerest appreciation to . . .

Amy Berkower, my agent, for her wisdom, her kindness, and her ability to make great things happen.

Gail Fortune, my editor, for her insight, her enthusiasm, and her tireless efforts on my behalf.

Liana Cassel, for her good cheer and constant encouragement.

And last but never least, to my dear friend Kathy Peiffer, for her endless help and support during the writing of *Blue Waltz*.

CHAPTER
ONE

They were dancing again. She could feel it.

The plaster wall was cool against her cheek, hard against the collarbone beneath her long velvet gown, unrelenting against her outstretched arms.

Winter was fast approaching with clouds thick in the sky, turning back the light, while rain tapped the mullioned windows with merciless repetition. The long, endless days were cold and dreary. Chilling her to the bone. Making her ache. Though at night the music came through the wall, warming her like a lover.

Pressing closer, she rolled her head slowly against the painted surface, across her forehead to her opposite cheek. The swirls of long-dried plaster, frozen for all time in faint, hard-edged relief, bit into her skin as she sought the music, sought the sound. She longed for the melody to seep deep inside her, deep into her soul. Making her complete.

She rolled her head back, again and again, even slower, in cadence with the waltz that drifted through the wall that separated her town house from the next. Pushing away, her lips parted with a smile, faint and dreamy. She ran her hands down the plush velvet of her gown, relishing the feel. She loved the dress. It was the first thing she had purchased after moving to Boston, before buying this house.

Soft silk undergarments brushed over her skin when she moved just so. She wore no corset or stays, never had. In fact, until she had come to Boston five months ago and visited a dressmaker for the first time, she had been blissfully unaware that women wore such things.

The music grew louder and she knew her neighbor had opened a window, or perhaps it was French doors, in spite of the cold, or perhaps because of it. They were dancing, after all. In pairs most likely. Arms entwined. Waists encircled. Warm breaths caressing reddened cheeks.

Frequently, she tried to picture the crowd, what they wore, what they looked like. If they had long hair or short. Fair skin or dark. If they were happy or sad. Each night she imagined them as something different. One night they were princely gentlemen with perfect ladies dressed in corsets and stays; the next, heathen religious deviants forsworn by their Puritan neighbors, performing some pagan ritual dance. The thought always amused her. Somehow breechclouts and feathers were far more intriguing than perfection and propriety.

The notes soared. Her favorite part of the melody was approaching—the part where she allowed herself to dance—carefully, slowly. Practicing. Always practicing.

Only practicing until he arrived.

Her heart raced with excitement and anticipation. It wouldn't be long now, or so she had been telling herself since arriving in Boston. But what if he didn't come?

The thought seared her, leaving her feeling empty and alone. Doubt rushed in, trying to fill the void. But then the music peaked, filling her mind—saving her. And after a slight bow of her head, she attempted a curtsy to the grandfather clock that stood against the wall, then began to dance. In time to the music.

Carefully. Slowly. Practicing.

She dipped and swayed, her long skirt sweeping the floor. Twirling, twirling, round and round, though her movements were not so quick and not so round. But still, the music was mellow and surprisingly sweet, drifting through the wall and along to her house on the crisp late fall breeze. Warming her.

At least for a while.

"One day I'll take you to Boston, my Blue . . ."

The words leaped out of memory, startling her, ceasing her turns as quickly and efficiently as if someone had reached out and grabbed her arm. The despair hit her instantly, unmercifully, as it always did. Pressing her eyes shut, she took a deep breath.

The music seemed to grow louder, less sweet. She glanced around the room, seeking refuge in her surroundings. The ceilings were high, the floors made of wood, and the windows plentiful. She could see the world by day and the heavens at night. She had learned many years before that she could exist no other way.

The minute she had seen the town house she had known it was perfect. It didn't matter that clearly it was only one tall, narrow section of what had once been a single great town house which had been divided into two houses. No other would do. She had told the solicitor she had hired to make the owner an offer. When he had protested that the property was not for sale, she refused to be daunted. She had stared at the finely wrought front door, painted blue amidst a sea of black and brown, and determined she would have it. At any cost.

"We will dance, little one, on St. Valentine's Day . . ."

Her body flinched. The words infiltrated her mind darkly, filling every corner and crevice, pushing at everything else.

"No!" she insisted as she looked up at the crenelated crown molding, concentrating.

". . . in the grandest of ballrooms . . ."

Her eyes fled from the molding to the fluted door casings and carved marble colonnades. She did not want to remember. Not now—not ever. She wanted him to arrive and make all his promises come true. And he would, she told herself, her finger circling endlessly on her velvet gown. Everything was perfect. Everything that he wanted was here in this town house on Arlington Street. Everything was ready.

"Under chandeliers with huge dripping crystal teardrops . . ."

She stepped back toward the wall, her stiff leather shoe catching on the edge of the Aubusson rug as she sought the music, sought its escape.

"Every person there will stop and stare in awe at your beauty . . ."

"No!" She pressed her hands to her ears, trying to block the words from playing over and over again in her mind. Round and round. In time to the music.

"With hair like waves of creamy dark chocolate . . ."

She began to hum.

". . . and eyes almost painfully blue . . ."

Her humming grew louder.

". . . wearing a gown of lavender silk . . ."

". . . with miles of the finest ruffled petticoats and flowers in your hair," she whispered into the room, finishing the old familiar words like a memorized poem.

She faltered then, her ability to fight waning against the onslaught of memories—fragmented memories, only fragments. She slumped back against the wall.

The muffled music played on, wrapping around her, making her dizzy. A strange strangled cry sounded deep in her throat as she began to roll her head from side to side, ever so slightly, her eyes pressed closed.

"But you will dance with me, my precious Blue Belle, sweeping across the floor, as elegantly as a queen . . ."

"Liar!" she shouted, taking up the cane that had fallen by her side and banging it against the wall, just where she had pressed her cheek, carefully, longingly, only minutes before.

"Be quiet, you fools!" she cried as she pounded the wall. "Be quiet this instant!"

The music ground to a crazy discordant halt as violins and cellos ended on different notes. The dancers wheeled to a stop. Laughter trailed off to a muffled buzz.

"It seems your new neighbor, the Old Widow Braxton, is at it again, eh?" a young gentleman asked with a chuckle.

"So it would seem, Lewis." Adam St. James shook his head slowly and stared at the adjoining wall. A lazy lick of blond hair fell forward on his forehead, nearly to the narrow blue eyes that stamped him as a proper Bostonian Brahmin as clearly as his genealogy chart ever could.

It was all he could do not to hang his head and groan his frustration. Good God, what had he done? he wondered in dismay, not for the first time. How could he have possibly succumbed to the beady-eyed little solicitor and sold that woman his home? But he was not one to spend long intervals mucking about in the stagnant pools of regret. What was done, was done. He could do nothing about it. Thank God he had been able to move into this place, though he doubted he would be able to stay for very long.

After a moment he pushed the wayward strands of hair away, then turned back to his guests. With a wry grin he raised his glass for a toast. "To the Widow Braxton. May her sweet temper bring her nothing but happiness and joy."

"And hearing less keen!"

The revelers cheered and tossed back great quantities of the finest French champagne. The musicians packed away their instruments, knowing there would be no more dancing this night.

A woman dressed in a long gown of taffeta and lace swished toward Adam, her myriad jewels glistening beneath the crystal chandelier. "What does she say to you about it afterwards?"

Adam's blue eyes danced with amusement as he studied his guest. *Nouveau riche,* some were inclined to call her. *And glad of it,* he knew she would respond, as she had been heard to say on more than one occasion that the Puritans had come an awfully long way to merely set up shop and mimic the very country they had risked life and limb to flee. Adam was inclined to agree. "Nothing, Clarisse, she says nothing," he answered simply, and started to turn away.

"Nothing?" she exclaimed, grabbing his arm.

Adam looked down at the tiny bejeweled hand which looked so fragile and pale against his black coat. There was no doubt that Clarisse was beautiful and, more importantly, reasonably wealthy. For one startling moment he thought he might just take her up on her offer of marriage. She could use his good name. He could use her money. A fair trade, it would seem. Certainly it would solve a great many of his problems. But as always, he couldn't do it, couldn't imagine the life he would have to lead married to one of the Clarisse Websters of the world.

"You mean to tell me she bangs your wall down at night, then ignores it the next day?" she persisted.

Someone had wound up the gramophone, a source of music, while not so rich and textured as the orchestra, was not nearly so loud and never brought the wrath of the Widow Braxton down on their heads.

"Ignores it?" Adam glanced back at the wall. "Perhaps, perhaps not. I don't know. I've never spoken with the woman."

Several of the guests sounded their disbelief. A few of them, losing interest in the discussion, began to dance around the polished parquet floor.

"How can that be?" a short man named William Henry asked.

"You sold her your home, for God's sake!" Lewis added. "How is it possible that you've never spoken with her?"

"And now that you've moved in here, you've lived next door to her for almost three months."

Adam looked back at his guests, aware more of the couples who danced slowly to the music than the others who badgered him with questions. "Three months or a lifetime, I've neither met her nor seen her, or if I have I didn't know it was she. The woman has refused all overtures of neighborly friendship, and she hasn't received me when I've gone over to apologize for the noise." He shrugged his broad shoulders. "After a while, a person stops trying."

"Apparently the Widow Braxton has yet to hear of your famed charm," Lewis said with a laugh.

"Once she hears," William exclaimed, "she'll be banging down your front door instead of your wall!"

The group laughed, all except Clarisse. She touched her plumed fan to her cheek, seeming to consider. "Come to think of it, I don't know of anyone who has seen her, except her solicitor—"

"And mine," Adam finished as he threw the last splash of champagne down his throat.

"What did he say she was like?" someone asked.

"Old and fat?"

"Old and mean?"

"Old and hideously unattractive?"

"Actually," Adam replied, pouring another glass, "he said nothing at all about her looks, ugly or otherwise. Though I got the impression she wasn't really all that old. Either way, all I know for certain is that her bank, or perhaps her mattress, is stuffed with a great deal of money." He held the champagne glass up to the light. "At the time I had little interest in anything else."

"Well, she must be hideously unattractive not to come out or receive a single soul," Clarisse stated. "I know for a fact that she has been sent invitations to the best houses in Boston. Proper Bostonians, it would seem," she added, her eyes narrowing, "are attempting to embrace her with open arms."

"Great huge bags full of money go a long way toward gaining entrance to the finest drawing rooms and dining rooms in town. And ugly or not," Lewis continued, "she's obviously rich as Croesus. . . ."

". . . and crazy as a loon," Clarisse added heatedly.

"Who's crazy as a loon?"

The simple question, spoken in a deep, rumbling voice, brought everything to an abrupt halt. One guest after another turned toward the doorway, until they all stood silently, frozen in place, the only sound coming from the gramophone that played softly in the corner.

"Stephen!" Adam blurted out, his swagger suddenly gone, his champagne glass nearly slipping from his fingers. His voice grew nervous. "What are you doing here?"

Stephen St. James stepped into the ballroom. He was a tall, elegant man with black hair swept back from his forehead, and dark eyes that scanned the crowd. His jaw appeared to be chiseled from the same hard granite with which the house was built, and his necked carved from the marble that covered the entry hall floor. The only flaw on his cold implacable form was a small half-moon scar just below his left eye.

At length he turned his attention back to Adam. "Last I heard, I live here."

A murmur of unease rippled through the room. William glanced between his feet and his host, as if he was not quite sure what to do. Even Clarisse appeared uncertain. Lewis, however, crossed his arms on his chest and watched with amused interest.

Stephen's gaze never wavered. His fingers curled around black kid gloves as he scanned the length of Adam's ruffled and brocade-clad form. "A better question might be: What are *you* doing here?"

Adam forced himself to relax as he set his glass aside and stepped forward. "Of course, of course. I'm sure you *are* wondering what I'm doing here. And we'll get to that, all in due time, all in due time. But tell me, brother, what brings you back from London so soon? I wasn't expecting you for another two, maybe three months."

"Obviously." Stephen grasped the bottom of an up-ended champagne bottle from a bucket of ice. "A *Montagne de Reims Grande Cuvée?*"

Adam blanched.

"From my cellar, no doubt," Stephen said, dropping the bottle back into the watery ice.

"I'll restock! I'll go out first thing tomorrow."

Stephen turned to his brother and gave him a look of

barely held patience. Several of the guests shifted nervously, eyeing the door.

"Well, time to depart," Lewis finally said into the uncomfortable silence.

No sooner had Lewis set his glass aside than the remainder of the revelers followed suit and practically ran one another down in their haste to be gone. There was not a person in Boston who had not learned, either firsthand or second, that to cross Stephen St. James was tantamount to committing social and financial suicide. The crowd in attendance this night could afford neither.

Adam watched them go, his eyes both wistful and leery.

"Who is crazy as a loon?" Stephen asked again in a voice both soft as velvet and unrelenting as steel.

Adam cringed, casting about in his mind for an expedient prevarication. Finding nothing suitable, he opted for the truth. "Your new neighbor."

It took a moment for Stephen to absorb the import of his brother's words. And when he did, his somber countenance darkened even further.

The Back Bay of Boston consisted of perfectly ordered streets, lined with elegantly designed town houses built in long neat rows. Stephen's house was at the end of a row. A house, in fact, which had once been the entire row before his father had years earlier divided it into two town houses; one smaller, one much larger, where Stephen lived to this day. The only "neighbor" he had was Adam who lived in the smaller town house.

"If I understood you correctly," Stephen said finally, "there is someone I am unaware of living in your home. This could only mean two or three things." He stood perfectly still for a moment without speaking. "You've either taken on a boarder, gotten married," he looked away and took a step toward the wall, "or you've sold the only thing of worth you have ever owned." He glanced back. "Tell me you got married, Adam."

The gramophone needle skipped, then caught the thick groove of the next piece and music flared once again. Mozart. Piano Sonata No. 17 in D major. Adam listened to the beginning strains of the first movement, the keys striking the notes so beautifully, and he considered taking up piano lessons. He had always wanted to play. It was the practicing that put him off.

"Adam! Answer me," Stephen said.

Adam pursed his lips before he pushed the music from his mind and dragged his attention back to his brother. With a shrug of his shoulders, he forced his most charming smile. "I'd be happy to tell you I got married, but then at some point I'd be forced to produce a wife. That might prove difficult."

"Not if you would bother yourself to marry any one of the numerous eligible and wealthy young women who prostrate themselves at your feet."

Adam held back a shudder of distaste at the image that loomed in his mind. "An exaggeration I assure you, dear brother. Regardless, once *you* have 'bothered yourself' to marry, get back to me with that complaint."

Adam ignored Stephen's clenched jaw and forged ahead. "As to the boarder, he or she might be easier to produce, but in the end, when I have to leave the warm and safe—" he eyed his brother "—relatively safe confines of your splendid home, I'd have no place to go."

Stephen visibly tensed.

"So I guess I must admit that I . . . sort of sold my home."

A moment passed.

The tension was almost palpable when Stephen finally spoke. "You 'sort of' sold your home!" His voice was low and deep, tight. "How can a person 'sort of' sell their home? A house, I might add, which I gave you after you badgered me to death about needing a home of your own."

Adam tilted his head and grimaced. "Living alone wasn't all that wonderful, I suppose."

"You suppose?" Stephen took a slow menacing step forward.

Adam's eyes opened wide. "But God knows how much I appreciated the house—loved it, in fact," he murmured more to himself than his brother, his voice melancholy. "But it's not all that bad, really. You're obviously concerned about that little remark you overheard about the woman being crazy as a loon. Well, I for one am sure it's all an exaggeration. I'm certain she'll turn out to be a very good neighbor. Nice, sweet, no bother. Much better than me." He tried to laugh. "And since you never have parties or make any noise of any kind, I'm sure she'll never have need to bang on the wall again."

Stephen's eyes widened, then narrowed in turn. "Bang on the wall?"

"Only when the music became too loud," Adam explained, suddenly engrossed in picking lint from the sleeve of his jacket.

Stephen groaned, the sharp edges of his anger seeming to ease as he looked at his younger brother. "Good Lord, what have you done?"

Adam dropped his arm to his side, the lint forgotten. "I really hated to sell it," he admitted finally, "really I did."

"Then why did you? Why did you sell something that, despite your remarks to the contrary, you loved and cherished more than anything? Or need I ask?" Stephen sighed and ran his strong chiseled hand through his hair. His voice became dry. "What did you need the money for this time?"

French doors, leading to a balcony at the front of the house, stood open in the ballroom. A late fall breeze drifted in. When everyone had been dancing, the breeze had mingled through the room like a welcome guest. Now it was simply cold.

Adam walked over and shut the doors, clutching the handles, his head slightly bowed, as if unwilling to let go. He knew he should have been used to disappointing his brother by now. But somehow each time it happened it was as painful as the first. Years of trying to be like Stephen had only managed to convince Adam of the futility of the act. And that was something, he knew, his brother would never accept. Adam wasn't certain he could accept it, either. "I'd rather not talk about it now."

"Well, I would!" The words exploded through the high-ceilinged ballroom, echoing against the walls and hardwood floor, drowning out the strains of music that still played on. "What did you need the money for? Are you going to tell me you broke another axle on your carriage and you needed money for repairs? Or gambling debts, perhaps? Woman trouble? Let's see, what was it last time? An investment gone awry? What?"

This time it was Adam's jaw that clenched, Adam's eyes that grew unfathomable. "Leave it alone, Stephen."

"Like hell I will. I'm sick and tired of bailing you out of trouble!"

Adam sighed as he looked out into the darkened night. The remnants of his tattered defiance fled, leaving him defeated. "Yes," he said. "So you've told me."

Stephen looked up toward the ceiling as if seeking

guidance. "Why, Adam? Why does it always come down to situations like this? Have I done so poorly by you?"

Adam turned to him and started to speak, wanting so much to tell him why, wanting so much to talk to someone as smart and logical as his brother about all that was wrong. But before the words would come, a crash from belowstairs suddenly sounded through the house. Loud shouts and banging followed.

Both men turned toward the door, their anger and frustration forgotten as they tried to make sense of the noise that was fast approaching, ascending the stairs from the first floor.

"What the devil—"

"There you are!" a man jeered from the doorway in drunken disarray, his words slurred, a gun in his hand, his eyes trained on Adam.

Stephen started to step forward, but was stopped when the gunman turned his attention and the pistol in his direction.

"Who the hell are you?" the man spat at Stephen.

"Now, Tom," Adam interjected, his tone calm but cautious, "you have no quarrel with him."

The man named Tom glanced back at Adam. "You're damned right, you bastard!" he hissed. "My quarrel is with you. You tangled with the wrong man, St. James. I'll not be bought off. Not this time. Not me." The muscles in his face worked and strained. "You're not going to do this to me! You're not—"

"Tom," Adam said quietly. "Give me the gun. Then we can talk about this silly misunderstanding."

"There's nothing more to talk about, do you hear me? Nothing! You're not going to get away with it!"

"Now, Tom," Adam repeated, stepping forward.

"Adam," Stephen said, the word a demand. "Get back."

Adam, however, took no notice. "Give me the gun, Tom," he continued, taking another step forward, his eyes imploring.

The fury in Tom's eyes seemed to waver for the first time. The crease in his brow eased and he looked down at the gun. "You shouldn't have done it," he whispered.

And then Adam lunged.

At the movement, Tom tensed and his eyes widened, before his indecision vanished, his anger bursting forth unchecked as his finger pulled the trigger. Only it was Stephen who ran forward and got there first. Stephen who made the vain attempt to stop the events from unfolding. And Stephen who jerked back at the impact when the bullet struck.

Time hung suspended. Smoke from the gun barrel rose in the air. Adam tried to force his brain to work, to make sense of the unimaginable. Staring across the room at Stephen, he didn't notice when Tom slipped out the door.

"Stephen," Adam breathed, the single word snapping him out of his stupor, and he ran forward.

Stephen leaned back against the wall, blood seeping through his fingers where he held his chest.

"Dear God, I'm sorry," Adam cried. He reached out, but flinched back in surprise at the wet heat of blood. Reality washed over him. "God, I'm the one who deserves to be shot!"

Stephen's breath hissed through his teeth when he tried to move. "Don't say that. It's not true." He took a deep, labored breath. "You're a St. James, Adam. A St. James."

And when Adam pressed his eyes closed against the

truth of his brother's words, and the inevitability of what that meant, Stephen slumped to the floor, red streaking the wall behind him, just as the gramophone needle began to beat softly against the center of the record, announcing the music was at an end.

CHAPTER
TWO

Silence. Long nights of frustrating silence. No music. No dancing. Nothing more than silence since she had heard that haunting shot three weeks before.

Belle Braxton pushed angrily away from the wall. She stood very still before turning her attention to the grand-father clock, her eyes set and determined. At length she clenched her teeth and curtsied, then started to dance. One, two, three, as best she could. One, two, three, with all the grace she could muster. Across the hardwood floor. Trying. Yearning. Feeling instead only the dark heaviness in her mind.

With a groan of frustration she jerked to a halt. It was no use. The music was gone. Dancing was impossible.

If she had not heard the shot herself, she would have doubted it had happened at all. There had not been a mention in the paper or a word of rumor from any of the servants. It was as if the incident had never occurred.

A fire burned in the grate, casting the room in golden light. She paced back and forth, the only sound coming from the bells of Arlingon Street Church as they tolled the hour. Her leg was sore, had been for weeks. For a while she had relied on her cane. But she had spent too many years learning to walk without it to take it up again because of a little pain. She had to keep walking. She had to work out the stiffness. It was the cold weather and the fact that she hadn't been out of the house since she moved in that her leg was becoming so stiff now. But the streets were crowded with people and carriages, making her uneasy, making it difficult to go out.

She glanced toward the window, the mullioned panes turning to murky mirrors against the night. It was hard to fathom that so many people existed, much less in one place. And always outside, rushing here and there. Good heavens, where were they all going? she wondered. Did people really have so many places to go?

Belle glanced over at a pile of invitations she had received. Maybe they did. And perhaps she should accept one or two of the invitations herself. She really needed to get out. She could wait at dinners and parties as easily as she could wait in the house for her father's arrival.

Her heart leaped in her chest. Her father. Browning Holly. He was coming for her. Any time now. She knew it.

At twenty-nine years of age, she was a widow, her husband dead five years now from rheumatic fever. She had more money than she knew what to do with. And after leaving her lifelong hometown of Wrenville, Massachusetts, she had traveled the sixty miles to Boston to purchase the home of her father's dreams. It had everything from the moldings and castings to the carved marble colonnades he so desired.

And here, in the city he so loved, he would come for her, she told herself firmly, pressing her eyes closed against the familiar ache in her heart.

The wind was growing stronger, buffeting against the windows, preceding the storm that was said to be imminent. She could just make out the muffled clank and scrape of pots and pans two floors below in the basement kitchen, reminding her that supper would be ready soon.

Thursday night. Roast and potatoes, no doubt. Delicious roast and delicious potatoes, but roast and potatoes nonetheless.

Running her fingers along the mantel, she sighed. She was tired of eating the same thing on the same night every day of the week—just as she was tired of waiting.

Unexpectedly, she wished for chicken and dumplings on a Thursday night, and clear skies with stars shining in the icy blackness of night. And she wished for a new life. An ordinary life, she thought, as a milkmaid or mother, or even a young maiden woman in Boston with nothing more in her head than a long list of parties and the names of beaux who surrounded her with flowers. A life of no more dreaming. No more waiting. But most of all, no more fragments of memory, no more dark heaviness that she had found since moving here hovered relentless at the edges of her mind.

The feeling welled up in her, all at once, the pain and longing almost choking her. The music was gone and she had learned no other escape, however temporary even that had always proven to be. She would have left the city weeks ago had she not been certain her father would come for her, here in Boston.

The memories that so often plagued her started up again in her head, as if to punish her for willing them extinct. But she would not have it. She would not allow the past to ruin tonight.

She walked to the door and threw it open, ignoring the pain in her leg. She took the stairs as quickly as she could, down and around until she reached the first floor and the cupboard that held her heavy outer wear.

Her butler, Hastings, raced up a flight of stairs from the kitchen and down the hall, his normally impeccable attire slightly askew, his coat gone, a dishrag in his hand. "Madam, where are you going?"

Belle paused as she pulled on a new, fur-lined, long black cape. Her eyes surveyed the length of the butler. Belle was tall for a woman, taller than Hastings; formidable, when she wanted to be. She had learned that dubious skill over the years.

Belle glanced down at the rag he held in his hands. Cotton, she thought, a smile pulling at her lips. Just like the towels her mother used to use. With alternating lines of blue and red against the white, lines that ran the length then continued on, down the other side, never ending if the towel was flipped end over end, again and again.

"Uhm, you see," Hastings began self-consciously, "I was . . . helping Miss Maeve with supper."

Belle blinked, before forcing her mind back to Hastings. Her smile grew luminous. Without warning, she reached over and squeezed his arm. "Good for you, Hastings, she deserves the help."

The man tensed at the touch, which clearly made him uncomfortable. But Belle's smile only broadened as she dropped her hand away. "Sorry, Hastings. I forgot. Forgive me. Lesson number one: Never be too familiar with the staff. I'll get it yet. I'm really rather bright." Her deep blue eyes danced with amusement. "Especially for a woman. And with you here to teach me the way of things, before you know it your efforts will pay off and I'll walk right past you and Maeve and Rose without even acknowledging that you're there."

Hastings straightened, pulling his shoulders back, and despite the rag in his hand and his missing coat, he looked every inch the proper butler once again. "Most definitely, madam."

It was all she could do not to roll her eyes as she stared at the man, wondering why in the world he wasn't insulted. But he wasn't. In fact, she had learned that the only time he *was* insulted was when she wasn't acting the proper lady of the house. Belle almost snorted out loud, but held it back. Barely. Just barely.

"Well, fine." Belle pulled her cape securely around her. "I'm off, then."

"Off, madam?"

"Yes, Hastings. It's high time I get out of this house. Fresh air and a crisp breeze will be good for me."

"But a storm is coming," he reminded her.

She pulled open the door. A gust of wind and dried leaves rushed in. For a moment she didn't move. She stood in the doorway, wind whipping her hair from its pins, as she stared off into the distance, sounds teasing her mind. *What if he doesn't come?*

Her smile deserted her and her brow creased. "Can you hear them, Hastings?" she whispered without turning back.

Neville Hastings stepped closer, coming to stand behind her, just off to the side, and listened. "Who, madam?

The nearness startled her and she jumped, which in turn startled Hastings.

Belle laughed loud and true, relieved. "We're a pair you and I," she said with a shake of her head. "You listening to voices of propriety, me listening to voices in the wind. How do things like that come about, do you think?"

Hastings shifted on his feet, staring curiously at his employer, but was saved from comment when a short, plump woman with gray hair and rosy cheeks bustled up from the kitchen.

"What, pray tell, is going on around here?" the woman demanded, her words laced with a thick Irish brogue.

"I'm going out, Maeve," Belle responded with a

laugh and a toss of her windblown hair. "I'm getting out of this house."

"Out?"

"Yes, out, out into the wind."

"But surely you're not. Not when supper's almost ready."

Belle's eyes filled with regret. She liked Maeve, and had since the day the solicitor had sent Maeve and Hastings over with letters of recommendation in their hands. "I'm terribly sorry, dear. But I thought I'd go out for supper this evening."

"Out for supper? You? A lady alone?" Maeve asked suspiciously. "It's unnatural." She glanced at Hastings. "Isn't that right, Mr. Hastings? Unnatural, I tell you. I've never heard of such a thing in all my days!"

"Well, you've heard of it now, for I'm taking myself out to supper, and not you or Hastings, or the impending storm, is going to stop me."

The wind was harsh, but Belle hardly cared. It felt good to be outside. When first she arrived in Boston, she had spent days working her way up and down the grid of streets that comprised the Back Bay, looking for just the right house. She had always walked, not caring if people looked at her oddly or if little children snickered at her awkward gait. Having spent virtually no time in a carriage before journeying from Wrenville to Boston, by the end of the sixty-mile trip, Belle had come to hate the closed and cramped confines of the carriage, not to mention the great whooshing speeds at which it traveled. *That,* not taking one's self out for supper, was unnatural as far as she was concerned.

And of course, no matter where she turned, there were those great huge crowds of people who lived in the city. But she would survive. Eventually even become used to the bustling hives, she was certain. But get used to a carriage? Never.

This night, however, she need not worry about crowds or carriages. The streets were deserted. She walked alone up Arlington Street, leaning into the wind. The Public Gardens stood to her right, its spiked black wrought iron fence looking angry and unwelcoming.

She was on her way to Charles Street. The Bulfinch House was there, stately, elegant, impressive—or so her father had always told her when she was a child. Tonight she was determined to find out.

Her head tilted back and she took a deep breath. She felt good and vibrantly alive. One minute she was fighting off demons, the next she had kicked them away. A ready palliative, it would seem, was simply to venture outside.

The public house loomed, stately, yes, but imposing as well. Her excitement abated. She had never been to a public eating house in her life. Standing alone in the privacy of her home, she had given no thought to what going out to supper actually entailed. She hadn't thought much past simply getting out of the house. Suddenly she wondered how a person went about going to such a place? Was there a certain way one entered? Something special one said?

The heavy wooden door looked as angry and unwelcoming as the spikes surrounding the park. Maybe she should come back another night. But that would leave her with nothing to eat except the very thing that had sent her on this journey in the first place.

On that thought, before her courage could desert her completely, she pulled open the door and walked inside.

"May I help you, *madame?*"

When her eyes adjusted to the dimly lit room she

found a man, French she guessed, dressed in formal attire, his features harsh with disapproval. She glanced into the inner sanctum of the restaurant, dark wood and red velvet everywhere, and noticed that there was not a single unescorted female in sight, and very few escorted ones at that.

"May I help you?" he repeated, his tone brusque.

"Yes." She drew herself up, clutching her cape tightly around her body. "I'd like to be seated."

Thick bushy eyebrows rose at her statement, and when he started to speak, she cut him off. "Is there anything wrong, sir?" she asked in a tone filled with hauteur and self-importance.

She had learned the tone during her stay at the Hotel Vendome, while she waited for the previous owner to move out of her house. Sitting in the lobby, among the statuary and potted plants, she had watched men and women of apparent importance go about their business. Belle had always been a quick study, and during that time she learned just how people got what they wanted— whether they deserved it or not. It had been a deplorable display if ever she had seen one.

She started to turn away, disgusted with herself that she could even think of acting the same way. But suddenly the memories swelled in her mind, always there, always lurking, making themselves felt, and she tossed conscience aside, shamelessly willing to use whatever means necessary to gain entrance into this bastion of what she hoped would be culinary forgetfulness.

"My good man," she said straightening still further, pulling her shoulders back, much as Hastings had done earlier. "You seem to be unaware of who I am."

Unaware hardly described it, she conceded to herself. There was no reason for this man or anyone else in the establishment to be aware of who she was. For in truth, she was no one of importance in a town filled with important people.

"I will overlook the impertinence this time," she continued, her voice deep and dry. "It is a cold and dreary night and I'm sure you would much prefer to be at home, which undoubtedly has caused your good sense to flee. Just don't let it happen again."

She turned toward the main dining room, her spine stiff and her heart pounding. "Over there, my good man, that table will do nicely."

With that she tossed her cape into his arms, then proceeded toward the table in question, her gait slow and careful, regal, she hoped. Only when the man followed and actually pulled out her chair, did she start to breathe again.

The menu was filled with entrees she had never heard of before.

Cornish pigeon with rice dressing.

Tangerine dressing cockaigne over squab.

Squid in cream sauce.

Good Lord, roast and potatoes were sounding better by the minute.

At length she settled for onion soup, endive salad, and something called Paté de Foie Gras. It was obviously French, sounded exotic, and certainly had to be delicious. Weren't French chefs known for their culinary prowess?

Her meal arrived with amazing swiftness. Belle suspected the speed had less to do with efficiency than the maître d's desire to see her gone.

The soup was good, the salad edible, but the foie gras . . . Perhaps she should have asked for roast and potatoes instead. The only item that had been truly delicious was the bread.

With a sigh she lifted the cloth covering the silver bread dish to peer inside. As expected, there was not a roll to be had. And not a waiter in sight. Leaning back in her chair, she pushed at the paté with her fork until she caught sight of an entire dish of bread not two feet away on the table next to hers.

The table was occupied by a man who sat with his back to her. He was firmly engrossed in the *Boston Globe,* which lay flat and folded on the edge of his table.

"Excuse me," she said.

The man didn't move.

"Excuse me," she repeated, leaning slightly closer.

She saw his head rise just a bit. For a second, when he remained perfectly still, she thought he would ignore her, simply go back to his paper and pretend he hadn't heard. But just when she was about to say excuse me once again, he turned, slowly, not quite all the way around.

He was large and imposing, with dark hair, cast darker by the faded light in the room. On closer inspection she noticed a thin, half-moon scar just below his left eye. Without a word, she studied him, straight forward, without flirtatiousness, summing him up.

His bearing was calm and confident—a man used to getting his way, she concluded. Instinct told her he was not someone to cross lightly. Someone dangerous, someone she'd do well to steer clear of. Someone, she thought unexpectedly, who could dissuade her from her path.

She nearly slipped off her chair when she started to turn away, suddenly apprehensive.

He reached out and steadied her. "Are you all right?"

His voice surprised her. The sound was smooth and deep, mesmerizing. A voice a person could drown in, become lost in and never find her way out.

For a moment she forgot why she had gained his attention, or that she would do well to steer clear of him. She had the fleeting desire to ask him to say something, anything, whatever he pleased, just so long as he continued to speak and allowed her to listen.

"You have a beautiful voice," she said simply. "Has anyone ever told you that?"

Her words seemed to catch this dark, dangerous pirate-man off guard. The thought pleased her immensely and she laughed, delight mixing with her relief, making her careless. "Either the answer is no," she continued, when he didn't respond, "or you don't hold great stores in having anything about you called beautiful."

One slash of dark brow raised slightly, but still he gave no response.

"No, you don't look to me to be a man who would like to be called many things at all, much less beautiful." She glanced over his attire, or at least what she could see of it, since he still hadn't turned completely around.

"Black coat, black trousers, black boots. Unrelieved black. Intimidating," she determined, her apprehension forgotten entirely as her eyes slid over his somber clothing. "And obviously intended to be that way."

She pursed her lips. "I have a book on fashion that discusses the vices and virtues of wearing the color black. Let me think. Austere, unapproachable, forbidding." She laughed. "Though I'm not certain which are the vices and which are the virtues."

He leaned back in his chair somewhat, his chiseled features cast in sharp relief by the flickering candlelight. "Have you gained my attention simply to criticize my clothing, or is there something I can help you with?"

His tone startled her, dispersing her delight as quickly as it had appeared. She couldn't tell from his expression if he was angry or sarcastic. Either way, she concluded, finally remembering the initial reason for their encounter, she no longer had any interest in sharing a portion of his meal. But when she started to offer her apologies and settle for the foie gras, their eyes locked and held.

Her pulse slowed. And after a moment the dark heaviness that always lurked at the edges of her mind dissipated. As if she had come home.

The soft clank of silverware on china and muted voices sounded around her. She didn't understand this feeling, didn't understand how it had happened, or from where it had come. She studied him more closely, trying to find some explanation. She saw that the confidence was still there; it was unmistakable in this type of man. But there was something else that she had failed to notice before. Something both repelling and oddly familiar.

She didn't know him, she was sure of it. But somehow it seemed if she scoured the recesses of her mind she would be able to recall him, as if indeed she knew him after all.

But that was absurd, she admonished herself as soon as the thought wafted through her head. She didn't know anyone in Boston, especially not this man with his icy reserve.

"Why is it you have gained my attention?" he asked again, looking at her as if he, too, was trying to determine if he knew her.

"Your rolls," she replied without thinking.

His brow furrowed and his head cocked slightly to the side, and she knew he was trying to determine if he should be outraged or insulted.

"My rolls?" he inquired.

"Yes, your rolls. You asked if there was anything you

could help me with." She glanced at the food item in question. "Yours appeared to be going to waste. And silly me, I thought perhaps you wouldn't mind sharing."

After a moment he looked over at the bread which sat on his table, then turned back. He studied her face for an eternity, before his eyes traveled down the length of her velvet gown.

She felt the blood rush to her cheeks. Never in her twenty-nine years, neither while she was married nor anytime after, had anyone looked at her in such a way. Blatant. Perusing. Intimate, as if she wore no clothes.

She started to turn away, cursing herself for the impulsive behavior that never failed to get her into trouble.

"Help yourself," he said.

His voice wrenched her loose from her thoughts. She nearly flinched back when he held the dish out to her, a silver edge catching her reflection and casting it back.

"Have them all, if you like."

And then she saw it. The sling that held his arm. Black and pristine, just like the rest of his attire, but a sling just the same.

The man had been wounded.

It hit her all at once why he seemed so familiar, why she felt she knew him. Because he had been hurt. Maimed.

In a manner of speaking, she did know him. Perhaps not the man himself, but she knew the look in his eyes that said he had experienced a moment in his life that was so indisputable and consequential that it never stopped mattering. One incident—not a lifetime of incidents—just one that changed the way he looked at the world, and changed the way the world looked back.

She didn't know if for him the incident had anything to do with the sling. But somewhere, sometime, some-

thing had happened. A quirk of fate undoubtedly, an
anomaly in what had been a perfect world, that changed
his life forever. She took a deep breath. Yes, she knew it
all too well. She recognized the despair, glossed over with
the same indifference that she saw when she looked in
the mirror.

Breathing deeply, she started to hum. Slowly. Softly.

Could he remember his moment of change? she wondered. Could he put a name to it, could he see it in his
memories—whole and complete? Or did he see only bits
and pieces, the missing fragments always threatening in a
dark murky place in his mind?

Her leg began to ache, but still she hummed, the
sounds shaping into a tune. She began to rock gently in
her chair—slightly—the movement barely noticeable.
Her tune grew louder and she tapped her finger against
the white linen tablecloth, looking away.

She saw herself back in her room, attempting to
dance, the bits and pieces of memory trying to comman-
deer her mind. Her heart began to pound. Sounds rushed
through her head like wind howling in a storm, ceasing
the tune.

Without taking the rolls or responding in any way,
she turned further away from him, pressing her back
against the chair. Seeking, searching, grasping for something solid, something firm. But still her heart pounded.
The palliative had failed, evaporated at the look in his
eyes.

"Is something wrong?" he asked.

His deep voice wrapped around her like a thick, soft
blanket of concern. It sounded as if he truly cared.

Her throat tightened. She didn't reply, couldn't reply.
What would she say? Yes, something is wrong. Everything
is wrong. Never. She would never say such a thing.

She had to get out of there. Escape—outside, into the open air. Where she could breathe.

Pushing back from the table, her chair snagged on the thick carpet. She tried to reach out and catch the wooden frame. But her hands fumbled like a clumsy schoolgirl's, and the chair tumbled to the floor. A few heads turned in her direction. The pirate-man started to stand.

"I'm fine," she finally managed, tossing coins onto the table that she pulled from her reticule. "Really, I'm fine."

The maître d' appeared at her side, and when he touched her elbow, she whirled around, her eyes wide.

"I've got to go," she stammered. "I've really got to go." Then she turned on her heels and fled as quickly and as carefully as her maimed leg would allow.

She hurried out into the night. The wind was blowing harder than before. The sky had opened up, spilling great torrents of frigid rain over the earth. She had forgotten her cape, didn't think of her cape, as she began to make her way toward home.

The memories pressed in on her, the words wreaking havoc with her mind. She began to walk faster, her limp more pronounced the faster she went. Instead of taking Beacon Street to Arlington, she veered off through an opening in the black wrought iron fence onto a path that cut across the Public Gardens, which she had learned led to her house.

The rain was driving now, hard and cold against her face and body. Her dress stuck to her skin, her hair ran in dark rivulets across her head. She walked and walked, her leg aching. The trees and benches began to look the same, the paths becoming indistinct. She had no idea where she was. Following whichever path she came to, she moved as if she were trapped in a maze, unable to find her way out. Frantic. Desperate.

"I love you, Blue."

The words loomed in her mind.

"I love you, my sweet child."

"Oh, Papa," she murmured, the words carried off with the wind.

She was hardly aware of the chatter of her teeth, her body's violent shivers that tried in vain to keep her warm, or the lights that glowed in the window of her home not fifty yards away.

"I love you, my sweet Blue Belle."

"Oh, Papa," she cried.

Her foot caught on a bulging tree root. Reaching out in vain for something to steady her, her knees gave way and she fell to the ground.

"Papa," she whispered as she sank down into the mud. "Oh, Papa, where are you?"

CHAPTER
THREE

"I'm home!"

The door slammed, shutting out the bitter February cold that blew in on its wake, making the tiny log house shudder.

"Mama, Mama! Papa's home!" Belle cried out, her mop of brown ringlet curls bouncing crazily on her head.

Running as fast as her chubby little legs would take her, she raced across the rough-hewn floorboards and rag rugs to her father, wrapping her tiny arms around his leg.

He was a big bear of a man, with a full head of thick, coarse brown hair, and gray eyes which he joked used to be as blue as Belle's before they faded due to all the pond swimming he had done as a child.

"There's my Blue Belle," he said, removing his heavy leather gloves and rubbing the top of her head.

His hand was large and calloused, the weathered skin catching in her hair. But Belle didn't mind, just as she didn't mind the feel of his coarse woolen trousers against her cheek, or the smell of hay and hard work that tickled her nose when he came home at the end of the day.

He tilted back his head and sniffed. "Mmmm, mmmm, mmmm. Smells good in here. What's your mama cookin' tonight?"

"You know! You know what it is! It's your favorite!"

A teasing smile parted his lips. "Don't tell me we're having beef stew . . ."

". . . with little baby onions!" Belle finished for him.

"You're right, darlin'. Next to you and your mama, that is my favorite. All that thick juicy sauce . . ."

". . . smuttering all the carrots and potatoes!"

He chuckled. "Smothering, sweetheart, smothering all the carrots and potatoes."

Gently, he grasped her shoulders and pulled her away, then leaned down until he looked her straight in the eyes. "And why, I wonder, are we having such a special treat tonight?" He seemed to ponder the· question with great deliberation.

"Don't you remember, Papa?" she asked, her voice suddenly breathless.

"Let's see," he teased with the utmost seriousness. "Could it be we're having company?"

"No," she replied hesitantly.

He screwed up his lips. "Could it be Sunday and I forgot?"

"It's Wednesday, Papa. Wednesday, the fourteenth of Feboorary."

"February, darlin'," he said chuckling. "And could it be," he added, grasping her chin between his thumb and forefinger, "that it's your birthday?"

"Yes!" she cried, jumping up and down. "You remembered! You remembered!"

"I also remembered something else." He reached into his coat pocket as he straightened. When he stood in the small house, his head nearly touched the ceiling, the months of dry winter air causing his hair to stand on end when he walked through the room.

She watched wide-eyed as he pulled both hands behind his back. The muscles in his shoulders and upper arms moved as he did something she couldn't see. Finally, when she thought she could stand it no longer, he presented both fisted hands out to her like a magician.

"Which one?" he demanded, his giant frame towering over her in the tiny house.

Belle stared at his hands with great deliberation. "That one," she blurted out, pointing to his left hand.

With a devilish smile, he opened it with a flourish.

"Empty!" Her nose wrinkled as she considered his other hand. She looked up at him again with those blue eyes and tilted her head.

Her father threw back his head and laughed. "Such a darlin' you are, Blue Belle." He opened his other hand.

"Peppermint!" she squealed, snatching the stick away, then hugging him tight.

"Browning Holly, you'll ruin that child's appetite giving her candy before supper." Madeline Holly stood in the kitchen doorway, a smile on her lips that belied her exacting tone. She had dark brown hair and deep blue eyes, making it easy to see where Belle got her looks.

Belle immediately disengaged herself and ran to her mother. "Mama, Mama, look. Peppermint!"

Madeline reached down and traced the back of her flour-covered hand down Belle's cheek. "Yes, love, peppermint, a special treat. But save it until after supper."

Glancing up, Madeline met her husband's eyes across the room. Her dark hair was pulled up and away from her face. "You're a devilish man, Browning Holly," Madeline said, her smile softening.

"How could I refuse those big blue eyes and a smile as sweet as her mother's?" he asked roguishly. "Especially on her birthday. Besides, I've brought you a surprise, too, my love."

One delicately arched brow rose. "You can't charm me with sweets, husband, as well you know."

Browning laughed as he removed his coat and hung it on a peg by the door. "Then I guess I'll just have to throw yours away."

"Give it to me! Give it to me!" Belle said, jumping up and down.

"No, Blue," he responded, though his eyes, filled with a deep, gentle love, were locked with his wife's. "This is a surprise only for your mother. One I'll just have to see if she will reconsider later tonight."

Madeline's eyes grew intense as she returned his heated gaze. At length, she turned away and headed toward the small kitchen at the back of the house.

Browning closed the distance that separated them with a few bold strides. Pulling her back into his embrace, he nuzzled her cheek. "Ah, Madeline, my love. I missed you today."

Madeline started to laugh and slap at his hands. "Mr. Holly, behave yourself. Supper's nearly ready," she said, pulling away, but not before she pressed one graceful finger of promise to his lips.

"Tonight, then, my dearest love," he whispered after her.

They sat before the fire, a rare pot of stew and a freshly baked loaf of bread on the table to celebrate Belle's sixth birthday. The small family laughed and talked and sang a few songs. When the last song was finished, a contented hush fell over the table.

"I take it all went well at the farm today," Madeline said, an earthenware cup held delicately in her hand.

"As well as any day. He wasn't around much. Had things to attend to in town."

"If only he would spend *more* time in town," Madeline replied, her tone suddenly harsh.

Browning reached across and grasped his wife's hand. "Soon, love," he said, his eyes intense. "Soon, I'll take you back to Boston, just as I promised."

Belle looked on, her tiny face screwed up with worry. "You don't like the farmer, do you, Papa?"

Forcing a smile, Browning reached over and ruffled her hair. "Don't you worry your pretty little head over such things."

"Then tell me the story about the Boston place," Belle demanded. "Tell me about the cobbled streets and tall houses built all close together, with grand ballrooms and huge candle tears."

"Chandeliers, darlin'," Browning corrected with a laugh.

Madeline shook her head, her lips parting with a whimsical smile. "The tales you've filled this child's head with, husband."

"Not tales, love, the truth, as well you know."

With that Browning became animated, regaling his audience with details of the life they would lead once they moved to Boston.

It was always the same, the same stories, the same fairytale life. And Belle loved it, always had. She couldn't wait until it started, for though she knew the stories sometimes made her mother look sad, they also made her smile in a soft, dreamy way that Belle loved so very much.

Belle ate her meal, the smells of herbs and fresh bread filling the room, the fire crackling, keeping the small family warm and cozy, far removed from the bitter cold outside and the hated farmer who made her mother and father so very unhappy.

"Tell me about the house," Belle pleaded, when her father's words began to trail off.

He stared into the fire, and for one nearly panic-stricken moment Belle was afraid he wouldn't go on, would keep that horribly sad look on his face that she hated so.

"Well, let's see," he said, blinking at the flickering flames.

Relief washed over her. "The crenelated crown moldings!"

"Ah, yes, the crenelated crown moldings." He turned back to the table, a sigh escaping his lips. "With fluted door casings. Carved marble colonnades. And a huge fireplace that has a finely wrought portrait hanging over the mantel."

"Of who?" she asked, as she always did.

His lips curved up on one side with a hint of a smile. "Your mother, of course."

"No, sir," her mother said as always, her milk-white complexion filled with adoration and pride. "Of you, Browning Holly. Tall and proud. Dressed in fine clothes. A man to contend with."

And when her mother said the words, Belle knew her father was pleased.

Browning laughed and pushed his empty bowl away, then leaned back. Pulling a pipe from its pouch, he filled the bowl with tobacco, tapped it down, struck a match, then clamped the stem between his teeth.

Belle loved the smell of tobacco, the rich aroma wrapping around her, telling her everything was all right. She loved as well what she knew came next.

"We'll receive invitations from everyone of importance," he continued. "And your mother will wear dresses of lavender chiffon with sheer scarves of gold, settin' off her delicate complexion, and silk laces so soft they could only be spun from the most exquisite of threads."

Madeline giggled like a debutante. Browning took her hand and squeezed lightly, briefly.

"She'll have mountains of bonnets with feathers and frippery no one could match, and furs by the finest furriers in the city." He looked back at the fire, pulling thoughtfully on the stem of his pipe. "Just as she had before she married me."

Madeline reached across the table. "And I'll have them again. I believe in you, Browning Holly. Just as I have since the day we met."

Browning looked at his wife, and Belle saw all the love he felt for her mother. A twinge of panic flashed through Belle. She loved her mother dearly, but sometimes she felt so sad and alone when it seemed her father loved her mother so much more than he loved her. She pulled in a deep breath. Belle knew from experience that if she didn't prompt him again, she would be left alone at a table covered with a half-smoked pipe and empty dishes when her parents went off to their room.

"And what about me?" she demanded, forcing a laugh.

Her mother pulled her hand away, red rushing to her cheeks, but her father simply continued to gaze at his wife. Tears burned in Belle's eyes when she determined that she had failed. The stories were at an end.

But then her father's face shifted and he smiled.

"We will dance, little one, on St. Valentine's Day," he stated, turning his attention to his daughter.

Belle leaped up from her stool and began to dance. "Twirling, twirling, round and round," she chanted, relieved. "On my birthday."

"Every person there will stop and stare in awe at your beauty."

Extending her arms, she twirled, her skirts billowing about her tiny legs.

"With hair like creamy waves of chocolate," he continued, "and eyes almost painfully blue, you'll dress in a gown of lavender silk, with miles of the finest ruffled petticoats and flowers in your hair."

She ran her hand over her hair and twirled once again, her movements exaggerated, playacting all that he described.

"Every man there will try to claim your first dance," he said, pushing up from the table, his lips spread in a grin. "But you will dance with me, my precious Blue!"

He swept her up into his arms and she squealed her delight. Round and round they went, sweeping elegantly across the floor.

They danced about the room for a few more minutes before her father set Belle down. "There it is, the fine story of Boston and even a dance on Valentine's Day. Just the first of many."

He turned her in the direction of the thin ladder that led to the loft where she slept. "Now, off to bed with you, young lady."

"Happy birthday," her mother added with a smile and a gentle kiss.

Up in the loft Belle slept secure on her straw-filled mattress. Burrowing deep, she pulled the covers up to her chin. A small window had been built into the side wall. Belle loved her window and kept the curtains tied back. When she lay in bed, on clear, cloudless nights she could see the moon and the stars. During the day, if she stood just right, she could see the very edge of the farm on which Papa worked.

Even though her father grumbled constantly about the old farmer, he said the man paid better than anyone around. But still her father hated him, and as a result so did Belle. But one day, one day soon, they would move to Boston, just as her father always promised, and get away from the awful man.

And until that time she had the nights. Summer, spring, winter or fall, it was always the same. Her father by the hearth, smoking his pipe. Her mother with a needle and thread, sewing or darning, or simply leaning back, losing herself in Papa's tales. And afterwards, as Belle drifted off to sleep, she listened to the sound of her mother's gentle voice humming a waltz as her parents danced across the rough-hewn floor. In time to the music. Twirling, twirling. Round and round. Just as she would dance one day, in the grandest of ballrooms, held secure in her father's arms.

CHAPTER
FOUR

BOSTON 1893

The room was nearly empty. The other patrons had already finished their meals and left. Only Stephen remained among the tables, one long, strong finger slowly running along the edge of the silver-plated bread dish. Around and around. Again and again. A subtle heat emanating against the tip of his finger.

His dark eyes looked at the plate without seeing it. He sat off-center in the chair, his elbow resting on the linen-covered table, his legs crossed in a way that on almost any other man would have seemed effeminate. Stephen St. James, in his perfectly pressed black coat and trousers, crisp white shirt and stark black tie, only looked at ease.

A snifter of brandy sat before him. A cigar lay to the side. It was his favorite part of the evening. Normally. A good meal finished. One brandy and one cigar to savor as he reflected upon his day, before he said good night, then, depending on the weather, took his carriage or walked the short distance to his home. There the house would be quiet, the servants, except his butler, Wendell, up in their rooms or gone for the night. Everything would be in order—everything as it should be.

But this night, as Bertrand, the maître d', hovered close by, clearly anxious to get home to family and friends of his own, though unwilling to hurry such an important man, Stephen thought not of his day or of the quiet solitude that awaited him, but of the woman who had interrupted his meal.

An angel. Perfect and lovely. With dark brown hair, almost black. Porcelain white skin, unpowdered. Lips full and red. Cheeks a dusty rose. And her eyes—an astonishing shade of blue, like the late afternoon sky when the sun is almost lost to the horizon and the heavens glow deep and rich. His head jerked slightly as he took a sharp, shallow breath.

When she had first entered the room, a clearly disconcerted Bertrand following in her wake, the tangle of thoughts that had crowded his head dropped away. He forgot about the dull ache in his arm and shoulder. He forgot about Adam and the yet-to-be apprehended gunman. All he could think about was the sheer mesmerizing force of her eyes when she gained, no, demanded his attention and asked to share his bread. Even now, more than an hour after she had fled through the door, that tangle seemed unimportant and distant. He thought only of the striking beauty who had sat herself down at the table next to him with a look and a manner that even Bertrand had apparently been loath to question. A slight smile tugged at his lips.

Who was she? he wondered. Where had she come from? When asked, Bertrand had known nothing more about her than he did. She had appeared without warning, and had left the same way, providing no name or any clue to who she was. Though now that she was gone, Stephen wasn't altogether certain he wanted to know. A woman, unescorted, in a public house, interrupting his meal and asking him to share his bread? No, he had no interest in knowing who she was. Or so he had been telling himself, again and again, as his finger slowly circled on the silver dish.

"Is something wrong with the brandy, Monsieur St. James?"

Stephen's finger stilled. He glanced between the crystal snifter and the maître d', who leaned down, concern creasing his forehead. "No, Bertrand. The brandy is fine." He pushed the chair back and stood. "But I've kept you long enough."

"Ah, no, monsieur. I am in no hurry."

Stephen smile, a tired smile. "Of course you're in a hurry, and I hardly blame you. A wife and five children, isn't it?"

Bertrand straightened proudly. *"Oui, monsieur.* How kind of you to remember."

Stephen's smile faded. "I'm not kind, Bertrand. Not kind at all. Just ask my brother."

Once outside Stephen instructed his driver to go on without him. "The rain has stopped and the walk will do me good."

"As you wish, sir," the man replied before pulling away in the black-enameled landau Stephen used in winter, the black lanterns on either side swaying in the night like beacons to the netherworld.

Buttoning his sealskin coat and pulling his top hat low on his head, Stephen stepped through the opening in the black wrought iron fencing and onto the path that meandered through the Public Gardens toward his home. Indeed, the rain had stopped, but the now bright night was still filled with a bitter chill. Massive billowing clouds, like mounds of newly sheared wool, scudded across the black sky, sometimes obscuring the moon and stars. A bone-numbing wind came up to wrap around him. And

just when he began to regret the impetuousness that had
bade him walk the distance across the park, he saw her. If
he had taken the landau, or even walked along the road,
he would have missed her—lying in the mud like something discarded. Motionless and forgotten. Unwanted.

. He knew it was her with a certainty, as if he had
expected to find her there, had suspected she would
never make it to her destination on her own. In the darkened public house she had seemed strong, though oddly
weak, invincible but strangely vulnerable. Now all her
strength was gone.

He dropped to one knee beside her.

"Madam." His deep voice resonated in the darkened
winter night. No response, just the secret whisper of the
wind through the long, delicate limbs of willow trees.

"Madam." With his good hand he took hold of her
shoulder and shook. When she still didn't move, he
cursed and glanced about for help. With one useless arm,
he didn't know how he could move her on his own.

"Madam!"

Her eyes fluttered, but didn't open.

"Madam, please!" He shook her again, something
akin to frustration growing within him—or perhaps it was
panic. But that was absurd. He never panicked, and certainly not over a woman he didn't even know. "Madam!"

She stirred and groaned, a faint distant sound, before
her eyes slowly opened. Through half slits she looked up
at him. A moment passed, a long moment as clouds
drifted by, and then she smiled, a slow, secret smile as if
she didn't lie in a puddle of thick, grasping mud, her full
lips, once so red, now blue with cold. "Hello, pirate-
man," she whispered.

Stephen's brow furrowed, and he nearly forgot their
predicament. Nearly. "Are you hurt?"

"Hurt? Who can say?" She tried to move, the effort making her grimace. "We've all been hurt, my pirate-man."

He hesitated, studying her curiously, then unwilling to chase that particular hare down a path he had no interest in traveling, he simply asked, "If I help, do you think you can stand?"

"Of course I can stand." Her smile widened, but her eyes fluttered closed.

"Madam, please! You've got to help me. I can't do this by myself."

With effort, her eyes opened again. "Help you? How can I help you?"

"By trying to get up, then telling me your name so I can see you home."

The wind swirled around them, catching the brim of his hat, tugging it from his head. But he didn't notice, didn't care that the silk hat raced through the park, pushed on by the wind like a whirling dervish gone out of control.

"You've lost your hat," she murmured faintly.

"No matter. Just tell me your name."

Her smile grew soft and dreamy. 'Mmmm. My name. Don't you know my name?"

"Of course I don't know your name," he said. He glanced around again in hopes of finding someone, anyone, to help. But the park was empty. "Tell me your name, madam."

"Blue Belle." She tried to lift her arm from the mire, but it wouldn't let her go.

"Bluebell? Your name is Bluebell?" *What kind of a name is Bluebell?* he questioned silently, wondering if he should believe her.

"Yes," she said, the simple word slurred. "Blue Belle.

That's what my father calls me. Blue Belle Holly. It's a pretty name, don't you think."

He racked his brain, trying to think of any Hollys he knew or had ever heard of. But he neither knew of nor had heard of any. And he knew almost everyone in town.

"Where do you live? Where can I take you?"

"Boston. I'm going to Boston. To the Back Bay." Her eyes rolled back. "Where they have the grandest of ballrooms and tall houses all lined up, playing sentinel to the street." She giggled. "Imagine that. Houses as soldiers. Poetic, don't you think?"

Stephen groaned. If he hadn't sat next to her and seen that she'd had nothing alcoholic to drink, he would have sworn she was drunk. "Where in the Back Bay?" he demanded, his concern growing.

But her giggles had ceased and her mouth had gone slack, her lips much too blue. This time, when he called her name she didn't respond. And no matter how hard he shook her, she failed to stir. He had to get her out of the cold, and quickly. Knowing there was no help for it, he slid his good arm underneath her shoulders. He set his teeth against the sharp stab of pain that ran down his side. A lesser man would have faltered. But Stephen St. James was not a lesser man, hadn't been since he was seventeen years old.

Holding her securely with one arm, he carried the woman the rest of the distance to Arlington Street and up to his house. Only seconds after he kicked the front door with his muddied boot it opened. Instantly, he was relieved of his burden when his butler, Wendell, took the woman in his arms without a word of question, and called out for help. Servants appeared in braided hair and nightcaps, suddenly wide awake with purpose. In spite of himself, Stephen followed as they scurried about, carrying the woman upstairs, starting a fire, bringing hot water, saving her from the ravages of cold.

When Wendell tried to entice Stephen away from the scene with a brandy and roaring fire of his own, he shook his head and did nothing more than step out of the room while the maids removed the woman's clothes. Once the servants were through, they dashed out with mumbles of cleaning the clothes, drying them by the huge kitchen fire, then returning them posthaste. After what seemed like hours, though in reality was only a few minutes, Stephen was left alone in the wood-paneled hallway outside one of the many guest bedrooms in his home. Ignoring the persistent ache in his shoulder and side, he stepped back through the doorway to make sure all that needed to be done had been accomplished. If she needed a doctor, he would send for one.

The woman who called herself Bluebell Holly lay in the huge four-poster bed, curled on her side, nearly hidden beneath the sheets and covers. The mud had been washed away and color had returned to her cheeks. Bluebell Holly would be all right. A doctor wouldn't be needed.

The house had grown quiet, only the occasional clang or muted voice from the kitchen wafting up the stairs. Pressing back against the wall, Stephen felt the smooth plane of plaster covered by fine paper solid against his spine. He stood silently, mesmerized. His heart pounded in his chest, hard, and he felt a stab of longing so deep that it took his breath away.

He knew he should leave, seek out the brandy and fire that Wendell had suggested.

Like a thirsty man seeking water, he took a step forward instead.

He was drawn to her in a way he didn't understand. It

wasn't just her beauty—he had known some of the most beautiful women in the world. And it certainly wasn't her manner—Lord, he had never encountered anyone so outlandish. Then, what was it? he wondered, taking in what he could of her sheet-covered form.

His heart beat oddly as he looked at her—this strange woman who had come into his life so unexpectedly, twice now. He moved slowly, almost reluctantly, as he took the steps that separated them. Closer and closer. Step by step, the movement filling him with something that at any other time he might have termed hope. He nearly laughed out loud at his own melodramatic thoughts. But he didn't want to wake her, so he held his laughter back. He wanted to look at her. Just look, as if by doing so it would give him some clue as to why unwanted thoughts of her circled in his mind.

Her breathing was shallow and steady as she drifted in that place she was seemingly reluctant to leave, as if that place, that dark and obscure haven, gave her respite.

A red brocade, high-backed chair with a gilded frame stood to the side. He pulled it close. Too close. But he wanted to see. Had to see. Before she woke, before she left, and he never saw her again.

Never saw her again.

The thought was reassuring. He *wouldn't* see her again. He would discover what about this outrageous woman had so intrigued him. Then he would learn her address and send her home. Mystery solved. Case closed. All loose ends tied up neatly. Yes, that was reassuring.

Her breathing was even, and her lips were no longer blue. Her eyes remained shut as she murmured and stirred. And when she turned, the bed sheets shifted, not much, but enough to provide him with a glimpse of skin as white as froth on a turbulent sea.

He knew he should adjust the covers then leave, and he started to do just that. But when he went to move the sheets, up over her shoulders, she moved again, and the sheets fell further away.

He sucked in his ragged breath. Her breasts were full with rosebud nipples, soft and pliant. Unexpectedly, his fingers longed to make them rise and harden. To caress. To cup, gently. The desire was intense as something he could only call reverence or awe wrapped around him.

He should have left immediately and called a maid. But he didn't. It was wrong, he knew it. He had never done anything like it in his life. He could have almost any woman for the asking, but just then, and never again, he thought fleetingly, he didn't want any other woman, couldn't think of any other woman. His mind was filled with her.

If another man had done such a thing, he would have shown no mercy. But another man hadn't done it. He had. As he knew he shouldn't. But something in him, something deep and primal, something foreign in his well-ordered world, caused him to stay.

She murmured and stirred, the sheets falling lower, revealing a curve of hip as gentle as a still night in spring. He desperately wanted to touch, to feel, the satiny smoothness of perfect skin. To nip. To taste.

He reached out slowly, almost timidly, as if he were no more than a schoolboy, knowing he was breaking every gentlemanly rule he lived by, his hard-carved hand suspended mere inches above her skin, not touching, only desiring. But then she turned, rolling over onto her back, her eyes pressed closed in delirium, or perhaps just sleep, leaving his hand suspended not over satiny skin but the triangle of dark hair between her legs.

Sensation radiated through his body. He felt his

body's instant, nearly painful, response. Never had a woman, any woman, affected him so. Everything else in his life paled, grew distant and hazy in the face of this woman, this strange woman with her alternately laughing then haunted blue eyes.

Images of raising her knees and spreading her gently washed over him. His tongue longed to lathe her secret core, to taste her on his lips. His jaw tightened with the restraint he placed on himself. The urge to ease his need, to impale her sweet body, again and again, until he felt the hidden recesses of her womb, nearly overwhelmed him. He wanted her. Badly. He wanted to wake her. Look into her perfectly blue eyes and make her want him, too.

But then the sheets fell even further away, falling to a pile of white linen and woolen snow beside the bed.

"No," he breathed, emotion flashing in his normally fathomless eyes.

She was laid out before him, as if sculpted from marble, breathtaking, perfect—except for her leg.

His mind reeled. An unfamiliar tightness pulled at his throat, stung at his eyes. And where he hadn't touched her before, he touched her now, on the leg so obviously and brutally broken, then clearly never repaired.

Intense, biting sorrow washed over him. Barely, carefully, he ran his palm over the uneven surface, so unlike its twin, which was shapely and perfect. His fingertips drifted up her leg and over to her hand, so fragile as it lay against the bed sheet, curved in sleep, trusting—of him— as he sat beside her naked body.

Guilt and shame pushed the sorrow away. He looked around, suddenly startled to find himself there, to find her there. To find the perfection of her body. No, he amended, the near perfection. And he wished as he had never wished for anything before that he could make it right, set it straight, make her whole.

The thought startled him, as much as finding her there had startled him. He didn't even know her, didn't even know from where she came. She was no business of his, whoever she was. He would do well to remember that fact.

He started to go then, to escape the unfamiliar things she made him feel—things he didn't want to feel. But unexpectedly her fingers curled around his. When he looked back, her eyes fluttered opened. "Don't leave me," she whispered, with a look he couldn't define. Fiercely happy? Infinitely sad? Deeply afraid? He wasn't sure.

"Please don't go," she said.

He glanced down at their fingers, entwined like lovers, hers nearly lost in his. At length, in the quietness of the elaborately appointed room, the fire casting luminous shadows against the walls, he eased back into the chair.

She didn't let go. With effort, he pulled his hand free so he could cover her body with the bed sheets from the floor, no easy task one-handed. But when he finished, she still moaned quietly in distress. He stared at her for one long moment before he sighed in resignation, or perhaps in fear—what if he could never let her go? But that was foolishness, he told himself firmly as he took her hand again, lacing her fingers with his.

Her grip was surprisingly strong, as if she held on for dear life. And as he gazed down on her, he wondered if perhaps that wasn't exactly what she was doing.

Not until he leaned back in the chair, his head resting against the cushioned back, her hand secure in his, did she seem to ease.

Who was this woman, this Bluebell Holly? With the

face of an angel and a leg so badly damaged that it was easy to believe the gods, jealous of what they had created, had dashed her against the rocks to even things out. How had it happened? he wondered. A spill from a horse? A tumble in the woods? A fall from a tree? No, he whispered to the red and orange flames that leaped and swayed in the fireplace, it had been nothing so simple, of that he was certain.

CHAPTER
FIVE

Belle woke with a start. She was cold, very cold as she became aware of a clock tolling the hour. Midnight.

Her brow furrowed, and when she looked around she realized she had no idea where she was. Where were her paintings of flowers and sketches of trees? Where, for heaven's sake, was her favorite overstuffed chair?

With a sudden, quick movement, she turned her head in the opposite direction, and what she saw made her mouth drop open in a silent gasp. A man, sound asleep, sat in the chair next to the bed. On closer inspection she realized it was the same man she had spoken to at the Bulfinch House—though, unlike then, now his hair was disheveled; his hard, relentless mouth was soft, even approachable; his penetrating eyes were obscured by sleep.

She rolled back against the pillow and pressed her eyes closed. *Dear God,* she pleaded silently, *say it isn't so.* But when she looked again, she found the man was still there, sound asleep, comfortable as you please.

She dropped back again and pressed her eyes closed, tightly, trying to think. To remember. Bits and pieces came back to her. Running. Cold. Very cold. But why, she couldn't remember. And then the man, the pirate-man, leaning over her, making her warm. She groaned when she realized she remembered nothing else. But her groan turned into a squeak of distress when she became aware of the state of her dress—state of undress, she amended.

She was as naked as the day she was born. Good heavens, what had she done? What had transpired in this strange room with this virtually unknown man?

But then she calmed, if only somewhat. Surely if anything had transpired of a nature she was disinclined to name, she would have remembered. How could a person . . . do those unforgivable types of things and not remember? They couldn't, she reasoned, they couldn't at all. She might be there for reasons that were not altogether proper—the fact that a man was sitting next to her while she wore not a stitch of clothing was certainly improper—but she hadn't been there doing . . . having . . . making . . . uhh—*Good Lord, you're a grown woman, Belle Braxton, just use the word*—she had not been copulating! Surely!

But then she wondered about something else, something in her mind that was a great deal worse than having . . . mated. What if he had seen her leg? Her head swam. Maybe that was why she was so certain nothing improper had happened. They might have been well on their way to the heights of sinful ecstasy, writhing with wicked pleasures, moaning in immoral delight, until he would have undoubtedly caught sight of her leg, bringing . . . things to an abrupt halt. The end. Finished. *Fini.* She knew firsthand how such a sight could dampen the mood, snuff out the candles of desire so quickly and thoroughly that one would be disinclined to believe that any had ever been lighted at all.

But then Belle looked back at the man, remembering as she did the very stiff and proper way he had acted at the public house. He appeared to have had his sensibilities abused by her merely asking to share his bread. Good heavens, she couldn't imagine what he would have done had she asked to share his bed! She giggled at the thought, but sobered quickly enough when she remembered her unfortunate circumstances. Nevertheless, she was reassured that this man hadn't seen her leg or any other part of her unclothed body. No doubt he sat there now to protect his precious domain. It was a maid who had disrobed her, surely, though why, she couldn't imagine. But understanding was the least of her concerns just then, departing was.

She took a deep breath, then let it out slowly, quietly, doing her best not to wake the man. She had to get out of there, preferably without him knowing, wrapped in the sheet, if that was all that was available. But when she looked around the rest of the room, she found her clothes neatly folded before a fire that burned low in the grate.

With a stealth that would have made a dime novel detective proud, Belle slipped from the bed, her long, dark hair cascading down her slim form. She grimaced only once when her bad leg hit the floor, then she tiptoed across the room, threw her dress over her head, not bothering with the nuisance of undergarments, pulled on her shoes, bundled the rest of her clothes under her arm, before she snuck out the door. She made it through the semi-dark hallway, then down the long curving staircase, without laying eyes on a single soul except for the frozen-eyed gazes of what must have been ancestors to this household whose portraits lined the walls. Not until she turned the knob and pulled open the massive front door did it occur to her that she was barely dressed, with no cape in sight, and she had no idea how far away she was from home.

But her concerns proved unfounded when she stepped outside onto an elegant, polished brick walk of what was clearly an expensive home. In the Back Bay. On Arlington Street. Across from the Public Gardens. Good

Heavens! She was no further away from her own house than twenty yards!

Twenty yards away from home!

She staggered back a step before catching herself on a granite pilaster when she realized she had just been in the house of the man whose music she had heard through the wall, and whose myriad guests had danced long into the night.

Good Lord, she had just slept naked, for reasons unknown, in the bed of the dark, dangerous pirate-man who lived next door.

CHAPTER

SIX

"You really should take it easy on that arm, Stephen."

Stephen glanced out the window of a room that stood just off the foyer, overlooking Arlington Street and the Public Gardens. For most people, this space would have been used as a receiving room. Stephen had turned it into his study, with thick red draperies, plush Oriental rugs, dark woods, and row after row of leather-bound books.

His doctor stood beside the heavy, finely wrought mahogany desk, the man's wire spectacles perched on his nose. "Really, Stephen. You have to be careful."

Stephen didn't bother to tell the doctor that he had been extremely careful—until last night. "I heard you the first time, Harold."

"Well, it's just that if you're not cautious, the shoulder will never heal."

"I didn't ask about healing, I asked about movement. Will I or won't I ever be able to move my arm again?"

The doctor appeared to grow uncomfortable and became absorbed in arranging his medical instruments in his black leather satchel.

"Harold?"

The doctor's heavily lined face creased further in consideration. Harold Mayfield had been Stephen and Adam's doctor for as long as Stephen could remember, and their father's before that. It had been Harold who had come to the house twenty years before and told the boys of their parents' death.

The memory was shrouded in a haze of cold and pain. An icy winter night. Slick, frozen roads over an old, narrow bridge. Swerved to miss an oncoming carriage. Crashed through the wooden railing. Died instantly.

What Stephen remembered most clearly of all was being seventeen years old and trying to comprehend the fact that his parents were never coming home.

Adam had only been twelve at the time and had never been the same again.

Stephen had taken over. He had tried to fill his father's shoes. But at seventeen or twenty-seven, and even now at thirty-seven, more often than not he knew he fell short—at least where Adam was concerned.

John St. James, Jack as everyone had called him, had been a big man, a happy man, a man who knew everyone's name and used them frequently. He had loved life, and it had loved him—at least until that night so many years ago when his luck ran dry, pinching out the flame that had burned so brightly and intensely that, when it was gone, many were left alone in the dark. Even now, twenty years later, Stephen missed the man as much as he had that first day, perhaps even more.

Harold finally snapped his bag shut and sighed. "Well, if I'm to be straight with you, Stephen, I don't hold much hope for your shoulder to be of much good to you any longer. At least not in the way you're used to. You'll get accustomed to it, though. I've seen it before. The body adjusts. Amazing thing, the body. Just like a three-legged dog gets along just fine without that missing leg."

Stephen looked on, his face tight in stony silence.

Harold seemed to realize that comparing Stephen's condition with a three-legged dog was not the most reassuring of comparisons. He hemmed and hawed, then added, "You should be thankful you aren't dead, son. A couple of inches lower, and that bullet would have gone right through your heart." His head bobbed up and down. "And we both know what that would have meant. So don't go dwelling on not being able to use the arm any longer. Just be thankful you're alive."

Stephen considered the words, putting them at a distance, unwilling, or perhaps unable, to deal with the reality of what the doctor had said. He had already experienced the impotent anger of weakness last night in the park. How would he ever be able to get used to living without the use of his arm?

"Stephen?"

He focused and found the man staring at him. "Thank you for your honesty, Harold," he said, his tone clipped. "Now, if you've poked and prodded your fill, I have work to do."

Harold stood nonplussed for the moment, seemingly uncertain as to what he should do. At length, he only shrugged his shoulders, gathered his bag, and departed.

Stephen turned back toward the window. The day was brisk and cold. Winter was here to stay. No more teasing days of fall, only harsh bitter cold that would wrap the city in its unforgiving grip until April—March if they were lucky. He watched, very still, as Harold heaved himself into his carriage before the driver snapped the whip in the air, and the ancient brougham rumbled off down the cobbled street. Just when Stephen started to turn away, a hired hack pulled up. It was Adam who stepped out, paid the driver, said something that made the man laugh, then headed for the door.

Since the night of the shooting, Adam had rarely been around, unavailable when Stephen had wanted to question him. Now, as the front door quietly opened, then very carefully closed, after which Adam headed straight for the stairs, it appeared that he would try to avoid the issue, or at least Stephen, again.

"Adam!" Stephen barked, his frustrations seeping through, his normally iron-clad control strained.

Adam hesitated at the bottom of the staircase, before he turned toward the study with a sigh. He crossed the marble foyer in a few reluctant strides, then walked into the study. His sandy blond hair was disheveled, looking as if he had used his fingers rather than a brush to comb the strands. Even his smile was tired. Without a word, he dropped down into a casual sprawl on the leather sofa. "Comfy, is it new?"

"You look like hell!"

Adam raised an eyebrow. "You don't look much better yourself, dear brother." But as soon as the words were out, he seemed to wish them back. His poise became less relaxed, and his handsome face became strained.

"No, I suppose I don't." Stephen's laugh was harsh.

Pushing himself up, Adam said, "I'm sorry. I shouldn't have said that. It's no wonder you don't look—"

"Tell me about this house situation." Stephen cut him off, having no interest in discussing his arm any further. "I've been waiting two weeks to learn the details of the sale."

Adam sighed, running his hand through his hair. "It's done, Stephen. The house is gone. Signed, sealed, and delivered. Forget it."

"I will not forget it." The words were laced with steely resolve. "Why did you sell it?"

For a moment it seemed that Adam would simply push himself up from the sofa and leave. Instead, he ran his finger along the seam of the cushion. "I needed the money."

"Again?"

"Yes, again, damn it!" Adam stood abruptly and came to stand toe to toe with his brother. "I needed the money! Again! Always again!"

Stephen's eyes narrowed and his full lips thinned in anger. "Who drew up the papers?"

Adam jerked away with a curse. "You won't give up, will you?"

"I think we both know the answer to that."

The clock ticked the minutes away as Adam simply stood there. At length he sighed. "Her solicitor drew up the papers."

"What was his name?"

"Wilkins. Or maybe it was Walker, Waller." He shrugged, the fight along with any traces of good cheer finally and completely gone. "Damn it, I don't know."

Stephen's good hand fisted at his side as he strained to keep himself under tight control. "Who took care of your side of the transaction? Nathan?"

Adam scoffed. "Your assistant wouldn't give me the time of day, much less help me with the sale of my house."

"Because he knows I wouldn't have approved."

"What, of giving me the time of day?"

"Your insolence is not appreciated."

"Nor has it ever been," Adam snapped.

This time Stephen ran his hand through his hair. "Just tell me who represented your interests."

"Jesus, Stephen. Why can't you just leave it alone?"

Stephen's jaw clenched. "Who represented your interests?"

With a dejected bow of his head, Adam said, "Peter Maybry."

"Peter Maybry! He's a crook."

A dry smile etched Adam's face. "My kind of guy."

Stephen pursed his lips, hating this, hating that the only interaction he had with his brother, his only living relative, always turned out like this. But he had learned that hating the problem did nothing to solve it. "I'll have Nathan look into the matter. There isn't a contract written that can't be undone. And if Maybry was involved, all the better. He is notorious for bad contracts."

Stephen turned away and walked over to his desk.

"Is that it?" Adam asked, his tone insolent. "Am I dismissed? Sir?"

Turning back, Stephen looked at his brother. "Yes," he said finally, not knowing what else to say, what else he could say. But just when Adam got to the door, Stephen spoke, trying for a conciliatory tone. "What time are you leaving for the Abbots' dinner party? Perhaps we could go over together."

Without turning around, Adam said, "I hadn't planned to go."

Then silence.

"What do you mean, you hadn't planned to go? Elden and Louisa are lifelong friends. Their parents were friends of our parents, and our grandparents were friends before that. I don't believe I understand."

"Well, let's study this." Adam's voice dripped with sarcasm. "What part of that sentence don't you understand? The 'I hadn't planned' part, which should cause you no problem since you're always telling me I never make plans; or the 'to go' part, in which case you need English grammar assistance, which I am in no position to provide."

"What is wrong with you?" The words exploded into the room, Stephen's restraint finally gone.

Surprise flashed across Adam's face, then turned almost instantly to resignation. "What do you want from me, Stephen?"

"I want you to be the man you are capable of being! That's all, and you know it!"

"But therein lies our problem, dear brother. I'm not a man who can direct a seventeen-fleet shipping line, or knows which buildings to buy and which to sell. I'm a man capable of little more than running through his inheritance in a matter of years, then living off the largesse of his older and clearly smarter brother. The man you want me to be and the man I am truly capable of being are two very different individuals. When are you going to accept that?"

"Never! Do you hear me? Never. I will never accept the fact that you have grown into manhood as a lazy, worthless, spendthrift who has no respect for who he is, or for the obligations a man of your stature is expected to fulfill."

"Then you're never going to accept me. Face it, Stephen, I am all those things you say, and more."

If it hadn't clearly been the middle of the day, with faded winter light falling through the window, Stephen would have sworn it was night—those hours in the darkness when everyone else in the world is asleep, though he lay awake, the promise of day beyond reach, his thoughts crowded by uncertainty. "What is wrong? You used to seem to care. What is it that you want?"

"What I want has nothing to do with honor and duty —something you could never understand. I'm not perfect like you! Everything I do is not perfectly proper, totally with honor."

Without warning, a glimpse of naked white skin flashed through Stephen's mind. Silky smooth. Infinitely touchable. For one oppressive moment, the room stood silent. Still.

"You would never dream of doing anything that didn't fit into your strict sense of what is proper and honorable."

But Stephen hardly heard. He stared at his brother without seeing. He saw instead the image of himself, wrongly, sitting silently, not moving away. He sucked in his breath.

"They could write a book about propriety based on the way you live!"

His hand, extended above milk-white skin, longing to feel, as she slept, her mind in some safe nocturnal haven, unaware of his actions.

"No one can live up to your expectations. No one!"

Full breasts, slender waist, delicately rounded hips. Desire. Hard, aching desire.

"Least of all me."

Beautifully perfect—except for her leg. Stephen pressed his eyes closed and turned away, turned to his desk. When he opened them again, he saw the simple piece of ribbon he had found on the floor of the guest bedroom. He had awakened, stiff and disoriented. At first, he'd had no idea why he was sitting there in a hard-backed chair, in a room that he had given no more than a fleeting thought to in all the time he had lived in the house. But then he saw the rumpled sheets, and he knew, he remembered. Bluebell. Bluebell Holly, with eyes so blue it was almost painful.

Practically jumping up from the chair, he had scanned the room, looking for her. He expected to find her looking out over the park, or curled up in a chair waiting for him to wake. But the park below remained unwatched and the chair across the room sat empty. She wasn't there. She was gone.

Frigid cold seeped into his soul. He had been alone for so many years, but he had never felt as lonely as he had when he found Bluebell gone. But that was ludicrous. If he had felt cold, it was due to the fire dying out, and if he had felt alone, it was because the household had yet to awaken and fill his home with smells of freshly baking bread and respectful laughter. He should be thankful the woman had slipped out of his house on her own so he didn't have to deal with her that morning. Yes, he was thankful. He wanted nothing to do with Bluebell Holly, he reminded himself just as he had the night before. She was absolutely no business of his.

He grabbed up the ribbon from the desk top and crumpled it in his fist, ready to throw it in the fireplace when Adam banged his fist on the desk.

"When will you accept that, Stephen? When will you accept the fact that no matter how hard either one of us tries I will never be another you?"

Stephen focused his gaze on his brother. He could hardly remember what they had been talking about. "Did I tell you they have a lead on the gunman?"

Adam's eyes widened and his body tensed. "What are you talking about? I thought you weren't going to pursue it?"

"Whatever gave you that idea?"

"No authorities. No reports."

"I didn't want it all over town. I'm not interested in having that little debacle talked about over afternoon tea by everyone in Boston. I'll not be fodder for the gossip mill. But I hired a man to look into it. He doesn't have much, but with little more from you than the name Tom to go on," he eyed his brother suspiciously, "he has his work cut out for him. Are you sure you don't remember who he was?"

"I told you," Adam replied, his voice tight, "I met him briefly, in a pub. All I know is his name is Tom. We had words over a card game."

"I thought it was over a horse race."

The two men, of equal height, though of two very different appearances, stood staring at each other.

"Leave it alone, Stephen." Adam's voice was laced with stern resolve. "Just leave it alone. It's been taken care of."

"Someone barges into my home, tries to kill you, shoots me instead, and I'm supposed to act as though it never happened?"

"Leave it alone," Adam repeated.

"Like hell I will!"

"Like hell you won't!" This time, it was Adam's control that exploded. "You may think I'm worthless and can't do anything right, but I will do whatever it takes to make you leave this alone!"

One slash of dark brow raised. "Is that a threat, brother?"

Emotions scudded across Adam's classically carved face like so many storm clouds in an otherwise flawless sky. With a sudden curse, he turned away. "There are times when I wish we weren't related. You're dead inside, Stephen. You have no feelings. You are cold and hard, ruthless. You know nothing about living or caring for people, really caring for people. You only care about propriety."

The words hit Stephen hard. Another day he might have been angry. How many times had he tried to explain to Adam that it wasn't propriety he cared about, rather responsibility? But this day too many other emotions churned in his mind to make room for this discussion. Suddenly, he was tired, though it was a fatigue that went beyond mere lack of sleep. And no matter what Adam believed, the fact remained that Stephen had been given little choice in his responsibilities. He had performed them to the best of his abilities. Nothing more, nothing less.

A tiny ray of sun, faded and weak against the thick clouds in the sky, peeked through. It caught in a pool of water that lay on the ground outside the window, sending a hint of multicolored rainbows out into the world. Stephen suddenly thought of rainbows and pots of gold, precious jewels in buried treasures. He had given up his belief in such things long ago. But suddenly he remembered a time when he did believe.

"Do you remember Sutter's Hill?" Stephen asked suddenly, his voice strong but quiet.

"Sutter's Hill?" Surprised echoed in Adam's voice.

"Yeah, you know, up on—"

"Old Man Wilbur's land."

"Yes, Old Man Wilbur." He chuckled. "He was a mean old man."

Adam smiled slightly, tentatively. "You used to say he was a mean old coot."

Stephen's laughter rang loud and true. "Me?" Had he really?

"Yes, you," Adam replied, still looking out the window.

"Do you remember," Stephen continued quietly, "the day we climbed up into Old Man Wilbur's tree?"

Adam shook his head and grimaced. "My backside is sore just thinking about it."

Laughter laced with words as Stephen spoke. "I

couldn't sit down for a week. He was as mad as I've ever seen after he caught us tossing berries at him."

"He probably never would have figured it out if the whole blasted bucket of berries hadn't fallen out of the tree."

Both men laughed softly. But their quiet laughter trailed off when they both recalled standing at their front door, on either side of Old Man Wilbur, his dirt-covered fingers attached to their ears.

Stephen grimaced. "Father didn't think it was quite so funny."

"No, I don't suppose he did. But you know," Adam seemed to consider, "I've always wondered if Mama wasn't trying to hold back a laugh."

"No!" Stephen hesitated, thinking. "Really?"

"Sure. Where do you think I got the idea to gather the berries in the first place?"

"From Mother?" Stephen's voice rang with incredulity.

Adam nodded.

"She *told* you to drop berries on Old Man Wilbur's head?"

"Well, not in so many words, Stephen. But one day she told me about doing the same thing when she was young." He furrowed his brow. "I believe her victim was an Old Man Cabot. She, however, didn't get caught. Or if she did, she left out that part of the story."

"I can hardly believe it," Stephen said with a shake of his head.

"Don't you remember how after Papa gave us whippings then left for the office, she had Cook make us hot cocoa with an extra dollop of whipped cream?"

Memories of long ago shimmered in Stephen's head. He remembered his mother as she smoothed first Stephen's then Adam's hair, before placing cups of cocoa on the table for them. Stephen hadn't given it much thought at the time. He only remembered feeling miserable at having so disappointed his father. But now that he thought back on it, he did remember his mother and her smile, and the special gift of cocoa with extra whipped cream.

Adam had always been closer to their mother. Stephen shouldn't be surprised that she would tell him such a story. A pang of regret washed over him. His memories of his father were vivid, but his memories of his mother were virtually nonexistent. His father had been a dominant force in his life; his mother only floating in the background. Perhaps Adam was correct.

"I guess I do remember," Stephen said finally.

"Do you remember the plays we used to put on?"

Stephen groaned. "How could I forget?" Though in truth, until that moment, he had forgotten.

"The laughter and the fun," Adam said.

"Before Mother and Father died."

Adam sighed. "That seems to be how time is divided for us. Before they died, and after."

They didn't look at each other, but stood side by side, looking out through the mullioned window, looking out across the street and into the park, their large, strong hands in their pockets, except for the one that hung in a pristine black sling. But standing there as they were, side by side, shoulder to shoulder, someone might have noticed the resemblances between the two men. The different skin tones and hair colors wouldn't stand out so much as to override any recognition of the similarities. The same height. The same chiseled cheekbones and jaws. Necks strong. Shoulders broad. So many similarities in men who had grown to be so different.

"So, what do you think about the Abbot's party?" Stephen asked finally.

Adam's broad shoulders rounded for a moment, before he shrugged and gave his brother a rueful smile. "I guess I could make the time to go."

"Good," Stephen said simply with a brisk nod of his head, wanting to say so much more but having no idea where to begin, or how.

But before Stephen could utter another word, the mantel clock chimed the noon hour, disrupting the quiet.

"I'm beat," Adam said, turning away from the window. "I think it's time I got some sleep." He laughed, his characteristic good cheer restored. "I'll need all the rest I can get if I have to spend the evening with Louisa Abbot and her friends."

Stephen didn't respond. He merely smiled and watched his brother go. Suddenly the thought of spending the evening with the likes of Louisa Abbot appealed to him as much as it apparently appealed to Adam. Not at all. Stephen nearly laughed. How strange to agree with his brother. But he realized it wasn't so much that he agreed with Adam as it was that he found himself thinking once again about the woman. About Bluebell Holly.

Where was she? he wondered. What had happened to her? And strangely . . . would he ever see her again?

CHAPTER SEVEN

The dress was stunning, Belle decided. Perfect for a party —the Abbots' dinner party, specifically, which she had decided in a weak moment to attend.

She tried to twirl around in front of the framed cheval glass that stood in the corner of her sitting room, but contented herself with simply swaying gently from side to side.

The dress was made from a rich lavender satin, with long puffed sleeves, a fitted, short-waisted bodice, and a full, petticoat-padded skirt. Over the dress she wore a shimmery gold girdle with designs made from light and dark lavender strands woven into the cloth, which fell gracefully about the skirt, and was caught up on either side by catches of solid gold.

Belle hardly recognized herself. It seemed impossible that the woman in the mirror was the same person she knew herself to be. She reached out and touched her reflection. Like a whisper, she ran the backs of her fingers down the glass from her cheek to her neck. She was going to a party, in a dress that was stunning, just as she had always known it would.

Leaning forward she pressed her cheek to the mirror, her breath frosting the silvered glass. When he finally arrived, her father would be so pleased, so proud. Yes, when he arrived. For their dance. On St. Valentine's Day. Just as he promised.

A shiver of excitement raced down her spine. First the house, then the dress, and now the party. The pieces of her life were coming together with the exactness of a nautical chart. She was navigating the sea and was avoiding the rocks as best she could. Tonight she would sail into the harbor of society. Hopefully she would gain a mooring.

Rose walked in just then with Maeve right behind her. Rose was as tall and slim as Maeve was short and squat. At the sight of Belle's dress, Rose's eyes opened wide. Maeve gasped.

"*That's* the dress that was delivered today?" Maeve demanded.

"Yes, it is. Isn't it lovely?"

"Lovely?" Rose's widened eyes softened and grew indulgent. "Well, yes. In it's own way it is lovely."

"I explained in precise detail just what I wanted. And precise detail is what it took. Good heavens, you'd think that seamstress had never sewn before."

"You asked someone to make that dress, that dress specifically?" Maeve seemed incredulous.

"Well, of course. I described everything about it from the high-buttoned neckline down to the billowing petticoats beneath. Billowing. Such a word, billowing," she added, before she gave a quick shake of her head. "I didn't want to take any chances that the dressmaker would get it wrong. And even then I had my doubts. I'd say, full skirt, and she'd stare at me dumbfounded, before repeating what I had just said as if she had not a lick of sense about fashion." Belle laughed. "Not of course that I have any sense about such things. In fact I have none. But this is one of the dresses I have dreamed about for ages."

"But missy," Maeve began, using the endearment she

had begun calling her employer, "the dress . . . is . . . well . . ."

"What is it, Maeve? Spit it out. I've never known you to be tongue-tied."

"You see," Rose interjected, "it's just that . . ."

"It's just that the gown," Maeve stated, her shoulders back, "beautiful as it may be, is hopelessly out of fashion."

Belle's eyes widened and she turned with a start back to the mirror. "What do you mean, the gown is hopelessly out of fashion?"

"Just that, missy. The seamstress was dumbfounded, I'm sure, 'cause this type of dress has been out of style for a good twenty years."

"Thirty," Rose clarified with a nod of her head.

"Thirty years?"

"Yes, lovey."

"That can't be!"

"It's true," Rose said.

"That's impossible."

"Mr. Hastings will tell you," Rose said.

"That's a grand idea." Maeve raced to the door, her arms chugging like side rods on a train, before she hollered down the stairs. "Mr. Hastings! Mr. Hastings!" When she stepped back in, she smiled. "That'll get him here in a hurry."

And sure enough it did.

"What has happened?" Hastings stood in the doorway breathing heavily, his gray hair falling forward. "What's wrong?"

Belle looked at him in the mirror, her porcelain features creased. "Is this dress out of fashion, Hastings?"

"What?"

"The dress, Hastings. Is it outdated?"

Neville Hastings glanced from his employer to Rose then to Maeve, with a look that said as clearly as words that he couldn't believe what he was hearing. But to his credit, he merely smoothed back his hair, studied the gown, then said, "Yes, madam, hopelessly outdated."

Belle scoffed at this and studied herself. Screwing up her lips, she debated. In the end, she simply tilted her head and shrugged. "It's timeless, not hopeless. Yes, I have on a timeless gown that will never be out of fashion because of its sheer beauty." She nodded her head, convinced.

Rose, Maeve, and Hastings glanced at each other, clearly unconvinced.

"Missy?" Maeve began hesitantly. "Ya know, the gown is a mite short in the front."

"I want my shoes to show."

"Well, yes, and no doubt they do, but . . ."

"What now, Maeve?"

"I was thinking, that if you took away some of the petticoats . . ."

At this, Hastings, if possible, snapped to greater attention, cleared his throat, turned on his heel, and headed for the door. "If you'll excuse me, I have things that need attending to."

The women watched him go.

"Poor man," Maeve said fondly. "Obviously isn't used to a household full of women."

"Might not be used to women," Rose interjected, "but it'd be obvious to a blind man that he'd like to get used to you, Maeve."

The older woman blushed, waving her hand in the air as if slapping the words away.

Belle looked on with interest, the dress for the moment forgotten. "Maeve? You and Hastings?"

"There is not a lick of truth to that, Mistress Belle. What would that fine man want with a little nugget like me? Oh, no, I'd never be so bold as to have my eye on the butler. I'm a cook, yes I am, and I know my place."

Belle glanced at Rose, then back at Maeve. "You may be a nugget, but a nugget of gold, and while you might not have your eye on Hastings, the more I think about it, I believe Rose is right. Hastings must have his eye on you. Why else would our perfectly proper butler help you in the kitchen?"

"Do you think—" Maeve said quickly, too quickly for her liking it seemed, for she immediately washed her face clean of emotion and added, "Nonsense. The two of you are talking nonsense. And as I was saying before such nonsense was spewed forth, if ya didn't have on all those petticoats, the front of the gown would just barely touch the floor . . . as it should."

Belle and Rose exchanged a knowing glance before Belle smiled, then leaned forward and studied her shoes.

Rose smiled as well, then tapped her finger to her lips as she returned her attention to the matter at hand. "Maeve is right, Miss Belle. The dress would look *even* lovelier if it was a bit longer."

"Hmmm. Do you think?"

"Yes," the two women replied in unison.

Belle considered her reflection in the mirror. "Maybe you're right," she said with reluctant nod of her head. "And I suppose the petticoats don't really matter so much."

But whether their mistress was reluctant or not, Maeve and Rose took charge in an instant, and in only an instant more they had removed three of the four petticoats. The result brought a slight, crooked smile to Belle's lips.

After Maeve left Rose to work on Belle's hair, she found Hastings waiting at the top of the stairs.

"How did it go?" he asked.

Maeve shrugged her shoulders. "Without all those silly petticoats she looks fine enough."

"God love her," he muttered with a shake of his head.

"She's a strange one, that's God's own truth," Maeve said as they took the stairs to the lower floor. "But it's hard not to love her like she was me own daughter."

Hesitating, Hastings turned back and glanced at the door which led to Belle's room, his normally stern brow lined with emotion. Then, without ever uttering a word, he turned back and continued on his way, though a fond, almost reluctant, smile curved on his lips.

Carriages lined the length of Commonwealth Avenue nearly as far as the eye could see. Broughams, five-glassed landaus, clarences, light rockaways, even a hired hack mixed in here and there, all waiting patiently to deliver their passengers to the palatial entrance of the Elden Abbots' French Victorian mansion—all for a seated, intimate dinner of eighty. And no one, it seemed, had thought to walk to the festivities no matter how beautiful the night had proved to be. No one, that is, but Belle, who walked the distance as easy as you please and was standing in the foyer in front of a liveried footman before the long line of conveyances had managed to cut itself in half.

For all her excitement, Belle was slightly nervous. Joy mixed with trepidation. She couldn't help but notice that, just as Maeve and Rose had predicted, she was dressed differently than everyone around her. But what did it matter if she was different from everyone else, she quickly reasoned. She didn't care what people thought about her. She didn't.

A liveried footman gained her attention by asking her name.

"Belle Braxton?" the footman repeated, scanning his list. "Would that be Mrs. Hershal Braxton?"

The name surprised her. Belle inhaled sharply and she nearly pressed her eyes closed. She wondered if it wasn't too late to turn around and return home. How long had it been since she thought of herself as Mrs. Hershal Braxton?

"Madam? Are you, or are you not Mrs. Hershal Braxton?"

She cleared her mind and looked him straight in the eye. "That is my name, yes," she replied, handing over the cape which Hastings had so discreetly, and without question, retrieved from the Bulfinch House.

Thankfully, the line moved slowly, for she was swept up a long, curved flight of stairs built of hard, slick marble. She clutched a bannister made from the same white marble until she reached the top of the grand stairway and was introduced to the host and hostess for the evening.

"Mrs. Braxton," Louisa Abbot enthused.

The woman spoke a little loudly, Belle was inclined to think, especially considering the muted tones in which everyone else spoke.

"How good of you to join us for our little gathering," the woman added.

Little? It was all Belle could do not to glance incredulously down the long line of guests still waiting to be received.

"Thank you for inviting me, Mrs. Abbot."

"Louisa. Please, call me Louisa."

"All right," Belle replied. "And you must call me Belle."

"Splendid, how simply splendid. I know we are going to be marvelous friends."

Belle looked at her, startled. "How can you tell?"

Louisa's radiant smile faltered and she looked confused, but then she giggled. "A sense of humor! How divine. Have you met my husband Elden, yet? Of course you haven't."

Belle was duly introduced then swept along into an ornately appointed drawing room without ever receiving her answer. Would they be friends? She thought she might like that.

The guests stood about, talking and laughing, in small groups or intimate couples. The men all looked the same in black pants, waistcoat and jacket, with white ties, shirts and gloves—crisp and clean, elegant. But the women, in contrast, were bedecked within an inch of their lives in more ruffles and bows and jewels than Belle could imagine. She wasn't altogether certain how a single one of them had made it up the stairs.

Still, no one spoke to Belle, though several glanced over at her curiously. But Belle was content to stand alone and take in the scene that was proving to be more interesting than she had imagined.

Minutes passed, however, and somehow, someone learned her name. "That's Belle Braxton," the person whispered to first one person then another. And before too long everyone in the room knew that the Widow Braxton had made her first social appearance of the season.

"How do you think Louisa got her here?" a short woman asked.

"No one has been able to get her to accept a single invitation since she arrived."

"No one has been able to get her out of that house." The women laughed.

"I wonder if the rumors are true?"

Stephen and Adam took the steps to the Abbots' Commonwealth Avenue home. They were the last guests to arrive, and by the time they reached the top of the stairs the drawing room was full. Elden had already stepped away from his wife and was mingling with the guests. Louisa had just begun to turn away herself when she saw them.

"Stephen," she gushed. "How wonderful that you made it." She squeezed Stephen's hand before she leaned over and kissed the air on either side of Adam's head. "Adam, you scamp. You grow more handsome every day. The woman who lands you will be a lucky woman indeed. In fact, I believe it's time I made it a point to match you up with just the right woman."

Adam's smile didn't reach his eyes. "I'm not certain 'lucky' is the word, Louisa. And don't put yourself out on my account."

"Adam doesn't have problems finding the women, Louisa," Stephen interjected as he scanned the crowd. "He simply loses interest in them once he has them."

Louisa twittered her laughter. But then she sobered and leaned forward conspiratorially. "Your neighbor is here."

Adam's eyes narrowed in question. "Neighbor?"

"Yes, the Widow Braxton."

"Really?" Adam said, surprised.

"Yes, really. And everyone is talking about her."

"What are they saying?" Adam asked.

"Well, nothing that hasn't gone around already. But from all accounts she has a great deal of money."

"That I already know," Adam added dryly.

"Oh yes, we heard about that unfortunate little incident with the house."

"Yes," Stephen added, still looking over the crowd, "haven't we all."

"Thank you, dear brother, for your ever inspiring contribution to this conversation. But tell me, Louisa, where does the woman's money come from?"

Stephen stood by, listening with half an ear.

"Well," Louisa began, "it is said that her husband, a good puritan man from Wrenville, had a fortune. Inherited. Timber money, I believe. All of which she apparently received upon his death."

Adam whistled softly. "So it's true."

Louisa giggled again. "Widowed or not, you should consider marrying her, Adam!"

"At least you'd get your house back," Stephen added, his tone dry.

Adam clenched his teeth.

"Now, now, let's not get into a huff," Louisa said, placing her hand on Adam's forearm. "I know how the two of you can be. I never should have started it. It's just that she really is perfectly marriageable. She's beautiful, rich, and has a good name. She's a Landford, you know."

"A Landford?"

"Yes, Adam, on her maternal side." Louisa leaned closer. "It's said that her mother ran off with the groundskeeper. Never heard his name, and of course it was ages ago, but I remember something going on over at the Landfords'. But I was younger than the Landford girl. And it was kept quite hush-hush."

"Really," Adam said, his face lighting up with a devilish smile. "The widow has plenty of money and, thankfully, a fine old name, making it easy to disregard the fact that her mother ran off with a gardener, and her husband is from a rural farm town."

"Adam! She's a Landford. What do you expect me to do?" Louisa asked uncomfortably. "If you weren't such a dear friend, I'd think I was being insulted."

Adam draped his arm around her shoulders. "Louisa, I would never insult you. Besides, I don't blame you for inviting the Widow Braxton." He laughed. "What with all the industrial and banking money going to New York and new buildings needed to house museums and more money needed to keep up the old ones, most everyone here would be willing to disregard the fact that the woman's good name is tarnished and her husband probably couldn't spell *society* much less move within it."

"You forget, Adam," Stephen said, surprising them both, for they had practically forgotten he was there, "Boston society is made up, not of blue bloods who brought their coats of arms across the ocean, or even purebred pilgrims as we are wont to believe, but of hardworking, moneymaking merchant adventurers who carved out a place for themselves on this shore." He looked back at his brother and his hostess with a devilish smile. "We are nothing more than descendants of . . . pirates, so to speak."

"Stephen!" Louisa exclaimed, scandalized.

Stephen offered her a charming smile. "You know it's true. Have you forgotten that not-so-long-ago episode involving the illustrious Miss Mary Baker Eddy?"

"The founder of the Christian Scientists?" Adam asked.

"Yes, the very same."

Louisa looked on uncertainly.

"She awarded herself a Scottish crest—"

"As was the trend of the time," Louisa interjected, conveniently remembering that detail.

"Of course, but unlike the rest of the good souls who were assuming coats of arms as they saw fit, hers was scraped off her doorway by the very clan who truly bore the right to it—after they had sailed all the way from Scotland to do it."

Louisa muttered and Adam laughed out loud.

"Stephen," Adam admonished, looking at his brother in amused surprise, "you're making our hostess uncomfortable."

"My apologies. I was simply making a point. The Widow Braxton has every bit as much right to society as we do." Though as soon as the words were out of his mouth, Stephen could hardly believe what he was saying. Not that it wasn't true. But what did he care what people thought of the woman—a woman, in fact, whom he planned to divest of her house. Legally, of course. Certainly he would never simply dump her out in the streets. No, he was going to have Nathan nullify the contract then find the woman another home. There were plenty of houses in the Back Bay that he was certain people would be willing to sell. And if he had to, he'd build her one himself on a new parcel of land.

He turned back to the crowd—but stopped abruptly before he completed the turn.

Houses, and widows, and coats of arms wrongly assumed fled from his mind, chased away by the mind-numbing sight that met his eyes. For there she stood, every detail remembered precisely. The woman who had plagued his mind. "Bluebell," he whispered.

"What, dear?" Louisa asked.

The roar in his ears was deafening. She was here. He

had imagined her in a thousand different places. In the North End, one of many in a large family; in the South End, as the daughter of an Irishman. But never here. He had never imagined her here in the very midst of his world, standing with an ease that said she belonged.

"Stephen," Louisa persisted. "What is it?"

"That woman." Stunned, Stephen nodded toward the woman he had met at the Bulfinch House. "Who is she?"

Louisa peered through the crowd. "Who, Stephen?"

Adam's eyes followed as well. "Yes, who?"

"The woman, standing alone, in the lavender-and-gold gown. Who is she?"

It took a moment for Louisa to find the woman in question, but when she did, she gasped her delight. "Oh, my stars, that's the Widow Braxton, Stephen. Your neighbor."

CHAPTER EIGHT

It took a moment for the words to register, but when they did, Stephen hardly believed it. Bluebell Holly was the Widow Braxton—the crazy Widow Braxton?

Louisa laughed, clutching her feathered fan to her breast. "You really *haven't* met her, have you, darling?"

"My word," Adam breathed. "She's beautiful. Stunning, really."

"I think so, too," Louisa responded. "As does every man in the room. Even the women are hard-pressed not to admit that she's striking. After all everyone has heard, you can imagine what we expected."

But Stephen hardly listened—and cared even less. He already knew the woman was beautiful, he already knew that her eyes were magical, and her lips enough to drive a man to distraction. What he hadn't known, however, was that she had lied to him. Bluebell Holly, indeed.

"Good God, Louisa," Adam said. *"This* is the daughter of a Landford and a gardener?"

"Groundskeeper, dear. There's a difference, you know."

"Of course, of course." Adam continued to stare across the room at the widow. "But tell me, what else do you know about her?"

She glanced between Stephen and Adam, seeming to debate if she dared go on, before she said, "I don't know much more to tell. As I said, it was all kept very hush-

hush. You can imagine that Raymond Lanford rued the day he ever allowed that man onto his estate to tend a single blade of grass. He died, you know, Mr. Landford that is, not too long after the daughter ran away, with his wife to follow him to the grave soon after." Louisa shook her head. "Such a shame. Neither the Landford girl nor the groundskeeper were ever seen again. And not a word about them was uttered to my knowledge until their daughter, Belle, showed up a few months ago."

Stephen turned away from Louisa with a start. He scanned the crowd, searching. "Belle," he whispered. "With eyes so blue it was almost painful. Not Bluebell, but Blue Belle. Blue Belle. That must be it."

"What must be it, Stephen?" Adam asked.

Stephen seemed surprised to find his brother standing there.

"What are you talking about?"

At length Stephen focused on his brother. "Nothing. I was just mumbling to myself." He turned back. Just then a knot of people broke up, revealing her. She hadn't lied about her name. He was irrationally pleased.

He watched. Her smile was soft, at ease. She took in the room, seemed to study a Chinese vase, find enjoyment in a Chippendale chair. She appeared content to stand alone. But then a woman he had known his whole life, but whose name he couldn't recall, approached Belle and began to speak with animated gestures. Soon Belle was joined by another woman, then another, until a circle of women surrounded her.

Stephen watched as her smile faded and her body visibly tensed. He could see that she felt cornered. He had thought she looked so at ease, as if she belonged. He was wrong, or at least partially, because just like the night he met her—only last night, if that was possible—she appeared once again to be invincible, but strangely weak. And like last night in the Bulfinch House, he felt the sudden need to go to her—to protect her. But before he could move, the women stepped away. It was then that their eyes met.

Emotions leaped in her eyes like so many flames in the nearby fireplace. They stood forever, neither moving, lost in each others' gaze.

He expected her to feel many things when she saw him. Guilt, shock, embarrassment, panic. She had slipped from his house, after all, no better than a common scullery girl. But he was totally unprepared for the dazzling smile which she offered him like a gift. No guilt, no discomfort, only surprise and perhaps pleasure at seeing him there.

"Louisa," Stephen said, never turning away from Belle, afraid to look away for fear that she would disappear yet again. "Perhaps you'd be so kind as to introduce me to my neighbor."

"That's a grand idea," Adam interjected. "I'd love to meet our neighbor."

Stephen eyed his younger brother for a moment, unsure of what he felt. Could it be that Adam was interested in this woman out of all the women he had run across? Was it possible that this woman was the one woman who could capture his brother's imagination and make him happy—this woman who plagued Stephen's mind at every turn? Was Adam as mesmerized as he?

"Come along, fellows. What fun! I'm going to have the pleasure of introducing Boston's two most eligible bachelors to the newest and most intriguing lady in town. The girls will all be atwitter."

Stephen watched Belle as they approached. She stood very still, her porcelain features washed clean of emotion. Common sense told him she would be nervous. But he was learning rather quickly that common sense failed to apply when dealing with this curious woman.

"Belle, dear," Louisa began, "I have the pleasure of introducing you to Stephen and Adam St. James. Brothers, you know. Your neighbors, in fact. I just learned that you had never met."

Adam stepped forward before Stephen had a chance. "Mrs. Braxton. Adam St. James."

Belle's smile was friendly and welcoming as she offered her hand. "Mr. St. James. It is so nice to meet you."

"And this is his brother," Louisa offered, "Stephen."

Belle turned, and their eyes met once again. Stephen stared at her, his dark eyes penetrating. "Mrs. Braxton," he said simply, with a slight tilt of brow.

She stared back, her smile faltering, though only momentarily, until she extended her hand. "Mr. St. James. A pleasure to meet you."

As if they had never met before.

Stephen held her hand, longer than was appropriate, before she finally pulled away with a look and a quiet laugh that had nothing to do with vulnerability, rather amusement—as if she found the scene secretly amusing. Stephen set his jaw. She was laughing at him.

Louisa cleared her throat and giggled nervously, before she reached out and took Belle's hand in her own. "It's time we go in for dinner. Adam, why don't you escort Belle to the dining room? I've placed her between you and Stephen."

They were seated at ten round tables of eight instead of one long table as Belle had expected. And true enough, Belle found herself seated between her neighbors, with the remaining seats taken up by an older woman, the widow Roberta Hathaway; a Reverend and Mrs. Paul Fielding; and a Mr. and Mrs. William Smythe.

"So tell me, Mrs. Braxton . . ." Adam began.

"Call me Belle, please."

"Well then, Belle, tell me how you're finding Boston?"

Everyone at the table turned to her, clearly waiting for her response. Seven sets of eyes, staring. Sounds faded until all was quiet in her head, the scene looking more like a frozen daguerreotype than real life.

"Belle?"

She turned to Adam with a start. "Fine. I like it fine enough. Though it isn't at all what I expected."

"So very different from Wrenville?" Josephine Fielding asked.

Belle stiffened and tilted her head. "No secrets here, I see."

Everyone sat still. Adam looked on with a smile. Stephen simply looked on. No one said anything until the Widow Hathaway leaned forward on the other side of Stephen and peered at Belle. "Not a secret to be had, my dear. Not a one. People all living close together, everyone knowing everyone else's business. It's tiresome I tell you," she said, banging the table with her hand, making the silverware jump. "But such is life."

Belle liked her instantly. "And probably not so very different from Wrenville in that respect." She looked at Mrs. Fielding. "You simply surprised me. I haven't told a soul where I came from. To find that everyone knows anyway is disconcerting."

Josephine shifted in her seat and seemed to search through her mind trying to find something appropriate to say.

Belle didn't wait; she turned to Stephen. "So tell me, Mr. St. James, what happened to all your parties?"

Stephen rested casually against the chair back, the stark black sling holding his arm tight against his chest. "What parties?"

"You're teasing." She gave him a reprimanding look.

"No, I'm—"

"Stephen," Adam interjected, his voice low and embarrassed, "the *parties,*" he said with emphasis.

It took a moment, but eventually Stephen understood. "Oh yes, the parties, Adam's parties. I was out of town. And I assure you there will be no more such affairs in the future."

Belle laughed at this and glanced at Adam. "I should have known. I was having a difficult time reconciling your perfectly respectable brother with raucous parties."

"You know him?" Adam demanded. "I thought you just met."

The question surprised her. Her eyes met Stephen's. Yes, they had met. More than met. This dark, dangerous pirate-man had saved her from the cold.

After a moment, she looked away and forced a laugh just as several pigeon-breasted footmen placed steaming bowls of soup before them.

"This looks delicious," Belle answered instead.

"You've met?" Adam persisted, ignoring the soup.

Stephen still stared at Belle as if he too waited for her response.

"Briefly," she murmured, just before she sipped the soup. "What is this? It's delicious."

Everyone looked down at their bowls at the same time. "Well, I believe it is some sort of consommé," Mrs. Smythe offered hesitantly.

Mrs. Fielding took a sip. "Brunoise. Consommé Brunoise, I think."

"How do you know that?" Belle asked, leaning forward in her seat.

Mrs. Fielding sat back. "Well, I don't know, really. I guess it's the turnip and chervil that distinguishes it from other consommés."

"I wish I could cook like this," Belle said.

Josephine's eyes grew intense. "But surely you have a cook."

"Well, yes, and Maeve is wonderful. But still, I'd love to be able to cook something like this. Or at the very least, be able to recognize turnips and chervil and such." Belle went on with her soup as everyone at the table stared at her.

"Stephen, you never told me that you met our neighbor!" Adam ignored the soup as he looked back and forth between his brother and Belle.

Stephen reached over and picked up the rounded spoon to the right of the long row of knives. "At the time I was unaware of who she was."

Belle eyed him, her lips quirked up in a smile. "Would it have mattered if you had?"

Stephen's spoon halted midway to his mouth. After a frozen second he cleared his throat and consumed the soup.

"Ah," the Widow Hathaway interjected smoothly, "the next course."

The soup bowls had barely been taken away before thick cuts of roast beef with onion dressing, Duchess potatoes, and red cabbage were set before them. But with the fare came an almost palpable tension.

Belle felt it. She would have sworn Josephine Fielding cleared her throat nervously. Even Adam seemed uncertain.

Belle watched as Stephen stared at the meat on his plate—the meat that would undoubtedly take a knife, fork and two hands to cut.

How would he do it? she wondered. And she wondered as well why it mattered to him. She nearly said as much. But just then, she glanced back at his face and words caught in her throat when she saw it again, that look in his eye she recognized. Pain and frustration, all mixed up with pride—hating the inability to do for oneself, hating the weakness.

Her world began to buzz and spin. But unlike that night at the Bulfinch House, this time she wouldn't flee, indeed, couldn't flee short of staggering out of Mrs. Elden Abbot's dining room with some vague apology about having to leave. No, she wouldn't do that. Instead, she concentrated on cutting up her own meat into orderly, square, bite-sized little pieces, the precision of the action easing her. The others began to talk nervously all around her as if embarrased, clearly uncertain as to how to handle such an awkward situation with such a notoriously forbidding man.

Conversation grew more strained as Stephen sat silently, the tension from his body radiating in all directions. Belle was sure that Stephen sensed their unease. She felt his rage grow as if it were her own.

"So, Mrs. Braxton," Reverend Fielding said, clearly uncomfortable. "How do you like our Public Gardens? I'm sure you had nothing like it in Wrenville."

The voice came at her as if tumbling down a long hollow tunnel, echoing in her head. For a moment her hands stilled in their labor and she did nothing more than stare at him blankly.

"Mrs. Braxton?"

Her eyes focused and her mind cleared. Conversation had ceased and all but Stephen looked at her expectantly, hopefully, as if somehow she could save them from this awkward moment.

"A little too big for my tastes, Mr. Fielding," she said with surprising ease. "In fact, look at that painting over there. It reminds me of the Public Gardens." She nodded toward the opposite end of the room. Everyone turned, and with a sleight-of-hands that would have done a magician proud, Belle switched her plate with Stephen's.

A heartbeat passed, before she felt his tension increase, rolling over her like a wave of frigid cold water. Her world grew silent. Time held no meaning. She had insulted him, she thought with heart-wrenching certainty, when she had only been trying to help.

She told herself she didn't care, but she knew it wasn't true. She cared very much. And she hated that she cared.

Her body tensed much as Stephen's had. She wanted to go, flee out into the cold night. Why was it that she couldn't do anything right?

The question was painfully familiar. She had asked it of herself so many times she wondered why it wasn't emblazoned on her chest. She took a deep breath, then very softly—very, very softly—started to hum.

She didn't hear the others comment on the painting. She only heard the tune as it spun in her head, around and around, dipping and swaying, tangling with her thoughts.

"One of these days," Stephen began, his tone deep and low, "I'm going to put a name to that song."

His voice startled her. Her heart lurched, but when she glanced at him and their eyes met, it calmed. He had a look on his face that would have been deep and brooding to most, but Belle saw that his dark eyes flickered, however slightly, with gratitude. He wasn't angry, she realized, relief washing over her much as his tension had earlier. He was grateful and pleased, and she started to reach out to him.

"What song is that, Stephen?" Mr. Fielding wanted to know.

With a blush of color, Belle dropped her hand away.

Looking at Belle rather than the reverend, Stephen said, "Just a song I seem to hear everywhere I go these days."

"Really? Hum a few bars. Maybe I can help."

Everyone waited, all apparently eager to hear the tune. Stephen sensed that at any second Belle was going to flee, panicked, much as she had last night. Without regard for those who were around them, he started to place his hand over hers. But he never got much further than the thought when her distress magically evaporated like a tiny spill of water on a blistering hot day and she clasped her hands together.

"It could be like a game, really," she chimed. "A game where a person hums a tune and everyone else tries to guess the title. We could call it the Humming Game."

Stephen sat nonplussed as did everyone else, until Adam threw back his head and laughed.

"You are priceless, Belle Braxton," he said, taking her hand much as Stephen had wanted to do. "In fact, I think we should play right now. I'll go first."

The Fieldings and the Smythes shifted uncomfortably. But Roberta smiled. "No, dear boy, I'll go first." And indeed she did.

It seemed beyond belief. But there was no denying the fact that woven into the fabric of near silence at their table and the murmur of conversation at the tables around them, was the deep baritone of the Widow Roberta Hathaway's tune.

At first no one said anything, and Stephen thought for certain that they were going to lock Roberta away any second, with Belle close behind her, maybe even Adam for good measure. But he couldn't have been any more surprised when Josephine—Josephine Fielding, the president of the Women's League—leaned forward in her chair and called, "The Merry Wives of Windsor!"

"Just so!" Roberta exclaimed.

And before long the entire table was involved, with the exception of Stephen, who sat back and watched in amazement. The table became so lively, in fact, that they began to attract attention. But Stephen was hardly aware of the attention, he only watched Belle. He was alternately intrigued and bemused by someone so outrageous.

Belle had guessed Josephine's tune, then promptly launched into a song of her own, unrelated to the tune she had hummed earlier. She actually used her hands to conduct herself with delicate fingers dipping and swaying in the air, eyeing each person at the table with blue eyes sparkling excitedly. Her excitement was contagious, and when the tunes had ceased with the arrival of subsequent courses, and conversation spun off into a million different directions, Stephen watched as if studying a curious phenomenon.

Belle was direct, impulsive, original, and had a droll wit. She said unconventional things which others thought but dared not speak, and amazingly, she said them well. Suddenly, he wondered if that was why people said she was crazy. He wondered, too, if it wasn't perhaps true. But as he sat back in his chair, the meat she had cut for him gone, he found it difficult to remain indifferent. He felt some nameless something infiltrate his mind. It wasn't the lust or even sorrow he had felt the night before. It was something else, deeper, harder to grasp. And thoughts of craziness disappeared into the candlelit room.

Belle turned to Adam, her smile radiant. "I haven't had a chance to thank you for giving up your home, Adam. It is so lovely and I will cherish it always."

Adam shifted uncomfortably.

At the sight of Belle's smile, so gentle, directed at his brother, Stephen felt that nameless something shift inside of him, shift to something harsh and unforgiving. "About the house, Mrs. Braxton," Stephen said, his tone sharp.

Belle started in her seat, her blue eyes suddenly dark, her smile gone as if it had never been there. "What about the house, Mr. St. James?"

"There's a problem with the contract."

Adam groaned.

"Really? I can't imagine what it is. I can't imagine that there could be a problem, Mr. St. James," she continued, leaning closer, "unless you make one."

He looked at her for one long disconcerted moment without speaking, before he lowered his voice and leaned closer. "I am unsure if you are extremely naive, Mrs. Braxton, or quite good at manipulation."

He expected her to suck in her breath, to be outraged. Belle Braxton only smiled and touched his arm. "*I am unsure if you are truly as ill-tempered as you seem, Mr. St. James, or if you merely put on a very good show.*"

Thankfully the only person paying any attention to them was Adam, and he appeared to be torn between disbelief and the need to disappear.

Stephen stared at Belle's hand, which touched his arm, barely, just a hint of warmth coming through his coat sleeve. And he wanted more. Her fingers were long, though not too long, white and smooth, with short, well-kept nails, tiny crescent moons at the ends. "Careful, Mrs. Braxton." He practically whispered the words. "You really should be wary of me. Ask anyone. I don't like being toyed with." He glanced at her fingers on his arm once again, before returning her gaze. "Or at the very least, you should be concerned for your reputation."

This time Belle glanced down at her hand on his arm, though she didn't move it away. "A twenty-nine-year-old widow with more money than she knows what to do with has little need of a reputation, sir." Her smile became tight, somehow superior, before she lifted her hand away.

Yet again, Stephen was left with the impression that somehow this woman, this crazy woman, had bested him at some game for which he had yet to learn the rules. But before he could regain his balance, she nodded toward his sling, changing the subject with no apparent concern for continuity. "So tell me, Mr. St. James, what happened to your arm?"

Stephen was distinctly aware of the hiss of breath between Adam's teeth.

"A shooting accident," he said simply, shrugging his good shoulder. "In the country. Embarrassing, really." Stephen sat perfectly still, with a quick glance at Adam, daring him to contradict him.

"Tell me, Belle," Adam interrupted, "have you made any changes to my . . . rather, your house."

Belle ignored him. "Regardless of where you were shot, be it the country or . . . anywhere else, shouldn't you be using the arm by now? It's been weeks."

"Why do you say that?" He had only met her the night before.

Waving her hand in the air, Belle said, "Who cares why? You should be using your arm."

"Unfortunately, Mrs. Braxton, the doctor," Stephen said coldly, "thinks otherwise."

"Hogwash! Your doctor obviously doesn't know the first thing about anything." She reached over, took a hold of his bad wrist, and pulled slightly. Stephen grimaced. "See," she said, "it hurts."

It was all Stephen could do to keep from putting the woman in her place, but something stopped him. Was it hope—that same feeling he'd had when walking toward her while she had lain asleep in his bed—that same feeling he hadn't had since his parents hadn't come home?

"If it didn't hurt, if you didn't have any feeling in the arm, it would be one thing. But, good Lord, that arm has healed and now it's just stiff. It needs to be worked, and it can. It's your head that isn't working, along with that foolish doctor of yours."

If it had been hope Stephen had felt, it fled in the face of her insult. His stiff implacable form stiffened even further and Adam nearly dropped his head onto his folded arms on the table.

"Now I've offended you." She sighed. "Unintentionally, of course. And simply because I spoke the truth. Well, as I see it, that's your problem, not mine."

Just then the footman placed a dessert in front of Belle. Excitement sparkled in her eyes. "It looks wonderful. What is it?" she asked no one in particular.

Stephen shook his head in dismay. Would she never do anything he expected?

"It's a cherry tart," Adam said.

"Cherry tart. It looks delicious."

"You've never tasted a cherry tart?" Adam asked in disbelief.

"No, never." She cut a bite with her fork and put it in her mouth.

Stephen watched her curiously before, in spite of himself, he leaned close. "Where have you been all your life . . . Blue Belle?"

Belle looked up, startled, her fork held forgotten in her hand.

"Where have you been and what have you been doing that you haven't had a cherry tart?"

The light in her eyes dimmed. With apparent effort, she set her fork down, slowly, carefully, then started to rise. But before she could flee, Stephen reached out and grasped her hand. "Don't," he implored her without thinking, his normally fathomless eyes betraying emotion. "Don't disappear on me again."

She took a deep troubled breath, staring down at their hands, sun-bronzed against light. "Not twenty minutes ago you said I should be wary of you."

Her words caught him off guard, leaving him at a loss. But he didn't let go, couldn't seem to let go. "True," he said finally. "But first, eat your cherry tart, then be wary of me."

It seemed to Stephen that she sat there forever, staring at something very different and very far away from their hands which lay together on the linen cloth. And just when he expected her to lift her eyes to his and offer him one of her radiant smiles, she pulled her hand free and stood.

"Thank you, but no," she whispered. "I'd best go." And then she did just that, heading for the elegant doors which led to the stairs that would take her below.

Stephen nearly followed her. He pushed to his feet, the rest of the guests at their table turned to stare. But the image of her gaudy dress and her awkward gait mixing with the memory of her outrageous and irreverent behavior seared his mind. And in the end, he simply sat back down and watched her go. Not realizing he had begun to hum softly, quietly, he told himself he was relieved she was gone.

CHAPTER NINE

"What do you mean, Mrs. Braxton isn't available for letters just now?"

Wendell stood in the doorway of Stephen's study, a wax-sealed letter on a silver tray extended in his white-gloved hand. Stephen stood behind his desk, his good hand palm down on the top, his other holding a small leather-bound ball stuffed with horsehair.

"Well, sir, the maid took the missive, said 'Hold your horses,' I believe, then shut the door in my face, made me wait on the front steps for a good long while, before she returned, handed the letter back to me and said, 'My mistress is unavailable for letters just now.' With that the woman shut the door in my face yet again."

"Unavailable! How can anyone be unavailable for letters, I ask you?" Stephen pushed away and began to pace, his bad hand squeezing the ball rhythmically. "All I wanted to do was show her my progress," he muttered.

"Yes, and such good progress, if I could be so bold as to say so, sir."

Stephen glanced down at his hand, distracted. "Who does she think she is?"

"Pardon, sir?"

Stephen's gaze focused on the butler. "Nothing, nothing. Just talking to myself." He cringed at this. "Talking to myself. Before long I'll be as crazy as she is supposed to be just by trying to deal with her." He shook his head before tossing the ball on his desk, then picking the letter up off the tray. "All right, then, I'll just go over there myself," he said with grim purpose.

"To the Widow Braxton's?" Wendell asked, his normally unflappable demeanor flapping a bit. "As I said, she's not receiving."

Stephen didn't respond, but gave the man a look that said as clearly as words that he had stepped out of line. Then, without a hat or coat, Stephen stalked out his front door, then up the first set of stairs he came to. "She'll receive me, by damn," he muttered, taking up the brass ring with his good hand and bringing it down on the lion's head base with a crash.

His sharp, impatient knock was answered by a butler. "May I help you, sir?" the man inquired in droll tones, his chin jutting forward with importance.

Stephen held out the letter. "I've brought this for Mrs. Braxton."

"Very good, sir." Hastings took the letter, turned away and started to shut the door.

Stephen flattened the palm of his hand against the blue plank. "I expect a response."

Hastings raised an eyebrow, amazing Stephen. Even her staff didn't seem to know the first thing about propriety, not that his did, he suddenly thought as he remembered Wendell's uncharacteristic outburst. What had gotten into everyone lately? he wondered.

"I'll see if she is available," Hastings responded. But this time, before Stephen could think to stop him, the door was slammed shut.

More than a few minutes later, the man returned. "The lady of the house is presently unavailable for letters." Hastings extended the letter, the black seal still intact.

Stephen stood nonplussed in the frigid early afternoon air. "She didn't even read it! How can she be unavailable for letters?"

Hastings didn't respond, simply stood in the doorway, the letter extended in his white-gloved hand.

Stephen hesitated, staring at the man as if at any moment the butler would change his mind and let him in. Stephen was unable to fathom the fact that he was being turned away, but that was just what was happening.

"Well then, good day," he managed finally, taking the letter, his voice as stiff as his shoulder had been only the week before—before Belle had told him he needed to exercise his arm.

At first he had been angry that she would treat his wound so lightly. Who did she think she was? But the seed had been planted, and the day after the party he had taken up the ball and tried to squeeze it. The pain had been unbearable—nearly. But his fingers had actually gripped the ball for a tiny space of time, proving the doctor wrong.

After that, the pain no longer mattered. Over the course of the next week, the ball had never been far from Stephen's hand. He'd not experience another night of impotent anger, as he had when faced with that plate of meat which he'd had no ability to cut. He had Belle to thank for that. And that was all he wanted to do, nothing more. Just thank her. But she wouldn't bother herself to read his note and allow him to do so. The realization didn't sit well with Stephen, though he couldn't quite bring himself to admit it. He was used to getting what he wanted, and he wanted to say thank you.

He strode back into his own home with a bang, his bootheels resounding on the entry hall floor as he walked straight into his study.

"What's all the racket about?" Adam walked in and sprawled on the sofa, his blond good looks typically disheveled.

Stephen glanced at his brother. "Our neighbor is *unavailable* for letters."

"Belle?"

"Who else?"

"Unavailable for letters?" Adam asked, shaking his head. "I don't understand."

"Yes, unavailable. And neither do I. Who in the world is unavailable for letters?"

Adam laughed. "Belle Braxton, it would appear."

Stephen shot Adam an impatient scowl.

"Now, brother, if you want to see the widow so badly, maybe I can arrange something."

"You? How?" Stephen looked across the mahogany desk suspiciously.

"No guarantees, mind you, but come on, I'll give it a try."

After a slight hesitation and a look of great skepticism, Stephen followed his brother up the stairs to the second floor, wondering what in the world Adam had in mind, but more importantly, Stephen wondered why he was following, at all. But then he remembered the missive returned and the door shut in his face.

It didn't matter that deep down he knew he was acting like a spoiled child who hadn't gotten his way. Belle Braxton had an uncanny talent for making him act in ways he had no interest in acting.

Adam pushed through the huge double doors that led to the ballroom. The room was dark until he pulled open the heavy draperies, allowing the dim winter sun to fill the room with hazy light. With care, he moved the gramophone over to the wall which abutted the one next door.

"What are you doing?" Stephen asked, his brow furrowed, afraid he already knew.

Adam smiled, placed a record inside, then wound up the music box. "In the past, I've found that the best way to get the widow's attention is with music." He chuckled. "An orchestra would be better, certainly, but we'll see what we can manage."

It didn't go unnoticed by Stephen that not only was he acting like a child, but that he and his brother were acting a great deal like the boys they had been many years before tossing berries out of a tree. The furrows in his brow softened and he very nearly smiled.

"Do you think this will get her over here?" Stephen asked.

"Over here?" Adam shrugged his shoulders. "I don't know. I always stopped the music once she started to bang."

Pleasant childhood memories along with the sudden sound of Stephen's dismayed groan were washed away by the burst of music that flared in the room.

"My hope," Adam practically shouted, "is that if we don't stop once she starts to bang, perhaps she'll resort to coming over."

"That or she'll send for the authorities," Stephen yelled back.

"Maybe so." Adam grinned. "Though I have no doubt you'll do a marvelous job of dealing with that eventuality should it arise."

"There are some who would think that an admirable skill. No doubt you wouldn't agree."

"No doubt." Adam turned away, an amused smile on his lips, then put his hands over his ears.

After that, they waited. Minute by minute, both men standing like errant children in the middle of the ball-room. Until it happened—sudden pounding on the wall, which matched the sudden pounding of Stephen's heart. Adam only made the music louder.

The brothers stood, quietly amid the noise. Then as suddenly as it began, the banging stopped, though the sound still hammered in Stephen's mind. Without warning, reality washed over him in a hard rush like an unexpected wave with its unrelenting undertow, pulling, tugging, unforgiving. Instantly, Stephen felt ridiculous. He couldn't believe he was acting like a schoolboy—all over this woman, this odd duck whom he didn't even like, he told himself forcefully. If she had no interest in seeing him, why should he care? The only reason he was trying to get her attention anyway, was to thank her for her suggestion.

"Turn it down," he demanded, his words sharp.

"What?" Adam called.

"Turn it down!"

The music ceased as suddenly as it had begun. Abruptly, angrily, Stephen turned away, and when he did he found her.

She stood in the doorway, a look on her face that he hated to see. Wild. Furious. And he had caused it.

The reality which had come over him only moments before ceased as abruptly as the music had, though the buzzing memory of it still played on in Stephen's ears.

"What is going on here?" she demanded, her delicate, milk-white hands clenched at her sides.

Stephen and Belle stood face to face. Adam was forgotten.

"You were playing that thing loud enough to wake the dead!"

Stephen stood very still, calm in the face of the storm. "Yes, I guess that's true."

"You guess? That's all? That's all you have to say for yourself?"

"How about, I'm sorry. It's just that we thought—"

"I made it clear that I had no interest in being disturbed. Did it ever occur to you that your music, your obnoxiously loud music, would disturb me?"

"Well, actually—"

"Well, actually what?"

Even in anger she was beautiful—and fragile, so very breakable. He pulled his shoulders back. "I wanted to show you my progress."

"Progress! What are you talking about?"

"The progress with my wound." He held out his arm as proof, like a child presenting a special gift. "See, no sling."

Belle stared at his arm, her brow creased as if she was trying to comprehend.

"If you'll excuse me," Adam said, clearing his throat. "I'll just run downstairs and get us some tea."

He slipped out the door, but neither Belle nor Stephen watched him go.

Stephen offered her a disarming smile, one so very unexpected on this dark, forbidding man. "You were right. My arm *is* getting better. Slowly," he added with a grimace of pain when he tried to move it too far, "but surely."

But Belle was not so easily placated, neither by his smile nor his arm. Her porcelain features remained etched with aggravation. "You could have written that in your note."

"Then you read it!"

"Of course I read it."

"But the seal wasn't broken."

"Don't tell me you've never heard of popping the seal then reheating the wax and reattaching it."

Certainly he had heard of such practices, but he had never considered that she would do such a thing, never considered any woman doing such a thing. "Then why didn't you respond?"

"Because."

"Just because?"

"Yes, just because."

Stephen stared at her, uncertain about what he felt—many things, certainly, and as much as he hated to admit it, a grudging bit of respect. When was the last time he had met a person who wasn't intimidated by him, if not out and out afraid of him?

She turned away, making it clear she was no longer interested in him or his arm, to take in the dim elegance of the ballroom.

"I knew it would be beautiful." The words were very nearly an accusation.

She walked around the room, her hand extended, running her finger along the wainscotting on the wall. Tilting her head back, she gazed up at the huge chandelier, cocking her head from side to side to get a better look.

Stephen watched her, not knowing what to say. She did that to him, left him speechless. And other than that tiny bit of grudging respect, and even the gratitude which he acknowledged, he had no idea why.

Her limp was hardly noticeable today, or perhaps it was that when he usually saw her she was moving quickly, when she was upset, fleeing—when she was in a hurry to be gone. Today she walked slowly, and if he hadn't seen her limp before, if he hadn't seen her leg with his own eyes, he might not have guessed that she did.

"How long have you lived here?" She didn't look back at him, but continued along the wall, her fingers gliding along the edge between fine silk wallpaper and dark wood wainscotting.

"Since it was built in sixty-four."

"Really? Then you must have been one of the first to move to the Back Bay after they began filling in the bay with landfill. It's amazing really, to think this used to be part of the ocean."

"Part of the harbor, actually."

"Harbor, bay, ocean. All nothing more than salty seawater that flows endlessly around the world."

She seemed to consider, her milk-white features made whiter by the intensity of her deep blue eyes. Her dark hair curled softly in a loose chignon, tied up with a velvet ribbon. It was all Stephen could do to keep his hand at his side. He wanted to reach out and pull the ribbon free, to run his fingers along her cheek and jaw much as she was running her fingers along the wall.

"To think," she added, "the water in Boston Harbor might have touched the shores of England . . . maybe even France. Yes, all salty seawater, all the same thing in my book." She glanced at him with a grudging half smile. "But then you and I seem to read out of different books."

Stephen stood staring, having no idea how to respond.

"Did you buy the house from someone, like I did?" she asked.

"No, my father built it."

"And my house?"

"My father had the wall put up to make a separate house soon after we moved in. My mother used it for socials, and teas, and musicals. Father had plans for another wall, to divide the house into three."

"Really? Why?"

"Why?" Stephen shrugged. "I suspect he wanted Adam and me to occupy them once we were ready to move out and start families of our own."

"Ah, but you never did."

A quick flash of memory filled his mind. *They're never coming home.* "There was no need," he replied curtly.

"To move out, or to start your own family?" she asked with a teasing smile, unaware of the weight of his words.

"To move out. My parents died nine years after the houses were built."

"Really? I'm sorry."

"Yes, well . . ."

"Do you miss them?" she asked, studying him intensely.

His gaze was hard. Of course he did. "Missing people is a useless endeavor."

Belle considered his statement. "Soon my father will be arriving."

Her words startled him. He had expected her to say something about being embarrassed for having brought up his parents as most people did. He certainly hadn't expected this. "Your father is coming; he's coming here?"

"Yes."

"When?" he asked.

Silence. Then, "Soon."

"Where is he now?"

Her eyes clouded over, but only momentarily before she continued her journey about the ballroom, her long skirt swinging gracefully. "He's a famous explorer, you know. He travels all over the world, to England and even

France. Like salty seawater," she murmured. But then she breathed deeply. "He hunts, explores. You know, he makes discoveries and the like. He's busy. Very busy with his work."

"An explorer?" The groundskeeper? "What's his name?"

"Browning Holly."

Holly. Her maiden name. Truly she hadn't lied.

He had an urge to wrap her in his arms and dance her around the parquet floor. He stopped himself just in time.

"And your mother? Does she travel with him?"

She hesitated. "No, she doesn't travel with him."

"Where does she stay, then, while he's away?"

She glanced up at a portrait hanging above the mantel which stretched between two sets of massive French doors.

"Who is this in the portrait?" she asked, ignoring his question.

"The portrait?" Stephen glanced at the painting, then at Belle.

"Yes, who is it?"

"My father."

She squeezed her eyes shut. "That's what I thought. My house isn't perfect," she whispered. "No wonder he hasn't come."

He barely heard the words. In fact, he wasn't certain of what she had said. But he knew like he knew his own name that something was wrong. The same look on her face that he had seen before surfaced. Without thinking, without measuring the effect of every move, he came up beside her. "What is it?" he demanded softly. "What is it that you see?"

When she did nothing more than stand there, staring,

he determined she wouldn't answer. But then, at the very last second before Stephen would have let it go and gone on to something else, without ever looking away from the portrait, she began to speak.

"I see a beautiful ballroom where people dance and laugh, under a huge crystal chandelier, on a high-polished hardwood floor, with a portrait hanging over the mantel —a place of honor, a place of importance."

She pressed her eyes closed. "When does the pain stop?" she whispered. "When will those fragments of useless memories cease?"

The words had barely left her lips when she felt his touch. And suddenly, unexpectedly, the pieces of memory and the shadows of darkness were gone—gone with the simple touch of his hand, light upon her shoulder, strong and firm, his strength almost tangible.

"Belle," he said softly.

She turned abruptly, desperate to question him. How had he done it? But words and thoughts ceased when he ran his hand over her shoulder with an infinite slowness. Her breath caught in her throat as his fingers traced her neck before he cupped her cheek, searing her with sensation.

But then it stopped. He stopped. His fingers stilled. She watched, her breath rushing through her teeth, as he seemed to notice his hand on her for the first time and couldn't imagine how it had gotten there.

The change in him was lightning quick. Only seconds before he had been trying to get her to talk and laugh. Now, after seeing his hand touching her, it was he who seemed on the verge of fleeing.

Panic threatened. Without thinking, she grabbed his hand, refusing to let him go—or at least let the feeling go, whatever it was. After a moment, she forced a smile, and after a moment more, his hand held tightly in hers, the smile became real, the distress magically gone.

"You can't desert me now," she said, relief making her voice ring like chimes. "Not after you got me all the way over here."

"You hardly had far to travel."

Her blue eyes darkened. "Farther than you realize." But then she laughed and pulled him toward the center of the room.

"What are you doing?"

"Come on, quit worrying."

Stephen stiffened.

Belle looked him in the eye, never relinquishing her grip. She tilted her head and smiled at him.

"You look like an imp," he muttered.

"You look like a crotchety old man."

After one surprised moment, Stephen gave a short burst of dry laughter. "No one has ever called me a crotchety old man."

"Well, they should have long ago. Now come on." She tugged harder.

At the very center of the room, she stopped, looked around, then dropped his hand before she lowered herself to the floor. Stephen stood very still, watching, something close to shock written on his face as she laid down on the hardwood, her face turned to the ceiling.

"What in the world are you doing, Mrs. Braxton?"

"Belle, remember." Extending her hand to him, she said, "Come see."

Belle watched the emotions scud across his face. Yet again, she knew she had outraged him. She nearly laughed out loud, but held it back. It wouldn't do to insult him any more than she already had. "Come on. I'm sure you have the cleanest floor in all of Boston. You won't muss up your pretty clothes."

If possible, he stiffened even more. Good Lord, she grumbled to herself, she managed to insult him without even trying.

"I'm not concerned about my clothes, madam."

"Then what *are* you concerned about?" she asked, one delicate brow raised in question.

That seemed to get him. He stood there for a while longer, a debate to which Belle was not privy clearly going on in his head. At length, he lowered himself to the floor with an irritated sigh.

"Lie down on your back, just like me."

At the noise he made over this, Belle was certain he was going to leap to his feet and cast her out of his perfectly proper house. Instead, he surprised her by lying back.

They lay side by side on the hardwood floor, he in unrelieved black, she in her favorite blue velvet gown, his black hair perfectly combed, hers slightly askew. They stared up at the ceiling rather than at each other, and for a moment Belle forgot that he was there, until he spoke.

"What exactly is it that we are doing down here?"

"The chandelier. We're looking at the chandelier."

There was a pause. "We are on the floor to look at the chandelier?"

"Yes, the crystal chandelier. Like huge sparkling candle tears." The words were a whisper, barely heard, and she knew that Stephen had strained to hear, and she was surprised that she knew that he had. Rolling her head to the side, she looked at him. His profile was hard and chiseled, breathtaking really. "Sometimes it's as if I can read your mind, Stephen St. James."

He rolled his head to the side and met her gaze.

"It's as if we were of one mind," she continued. "I felt it the first time I saw you." She looked at him closely, intently. "What does it mean, Stephen?"

"What? What does what mean?"

Her blue eyes widened and she jerked her eyes back to the ceiling. What had she just said, to this man of all men? "Nothing."

She could feel him staring at her for a long time, and just when she thought he would question her further, Adam returned.

"Tea any—"

Belle heard the china rattle as he came to an abrupt halt.

"Good God! What has happened?" Adam demanded.

Stephen sprang to his feet and dusted his pants off with a few quick, stiff strokes.

Belle pushed up into a sitting position. "We were studying the chandelier."

Adam glanced between his brother and Belle, then up to the ceiling. After a moment, a smile sliced across his face. Putting the tray aside, he strode to the middle of the room and dropped down beside Belle. Belle watched Stephen, who watched his brother. What was it that she saw? What did Stephen feel? A mixture of resentment and love, she determined. And she wondered if it actually bothered him that his brother could so easily drop down on to the floor when he couldn't? She wondered as well what this dark, dangerous pirate-man felt for his brother, so light and amiable in contrast?

"It's beautiful," Adam said. "I've never really looked at it before. Especially not from here."

She wanted to reach out to Stephen as he turned away and headed for the door. She wanted to ask him to come back. When he had touched her, she remembered with a start, the memories had stopped and the murky darkness had been held at bay. With the simple touch of his hand. Gentle yet firm. The sensation penetrating down to her core.

She sucked in her breath. How easy. How simple. She should have suspected. She should have known that he could vanquish the darkness, just as the music had done before it had stopped. Yes, she should have suspected, especially after having seen the look in his eyes that evening when she had met him at the Bulfinch House.

But despite the look and despite the fact that she understood a great deal about him, Belle knew that Stephen didn't understand her and never would.

"Belle." Adam laughed. "Such a treasure you are. From here the chandelier looks like huge sparkling raindrops."

At length, she dragged her gaze away from Stephen, who hesitated in the doorway. "Huge sparkling candle tears," she corrected him quietly, as she laid back down.

"Yes! Of course! Huge tears, sparkling with prisms of multicolored light. Just think of the show we would have if the sun was bright."

She took a deep breath, forcing Stephen from her mind. "I would love to have a chandelier of my own," she said, the words barely audible.

"Then get one."

She jerked her head around to look at him. "What do you mean?"

"Go out and buy a chandelier, of course."

"Buy a chandelier? Where would I put it? I don't have a ballroom."

"Then build one," he pronounced.

Her breath caught in her throat. A ballroom. Of her own. "Do you think?" she breathed.

Adam glanced at her as if realizing for the first time that she might be serious. He stared at her for a moment before he shrugged his shoulders. "Why not?"

Why not, indeed? she thought. She came up on her elbows and glanced around the room, studying it. How perfect! To build such a room in her own home.

She could put it on the second floor, where she had her own suite of rooms now. She could manage to climb one more flight of stairs, maybe even two, and then she could put her room at the top of the house—where she could see all the world.

It was perfect. Excitement raced down her spine. "A ballroom."

"It would be marvelous!"

"Yes, I think you're right."

Adam's delighted laugh mingled with Belle's. A room where she could see the world by day and the heavens at night. And a ballroom of her own. How perfect.

But her delight vanished when she heard Stephen's heels resound against the floor as he suddenly turned, then quit the room.

She stared at the empty doorway, the chandelier forgotten. "Stephen," she whispered beneath her breath, "can you really vanquish the pieces of memory and darkness in my mind?"

CHAPTER
TEN

Three days later, Stephen nearly choked on his coffee at the deafening, reverberating sound that suddenly shook his house. Wendell stopped dead in his tracks, his white-gloved hand nearly losing its grip on the silver coffee pot. Janie, the parlor maid, screeched, then, unlike Wendell, lost her battle and dropped a silver tray of fine bone china on the floor.

Then silence. Only the slightly swaying chandelier over the dining room table and jagged pieces of dishware on the floor bore proof that something out of the ordinary had occurred.

Stephen and Wendell stared at the light fixture, transfixed. Janie, apparently unsure which she was most afraid of, the noise or the trouble she most undoubtedly would get into for having a tray of broken china at her feet, stared wide-eyed at her still extended hands. But then the reverberating sound crashed and echoed once again. Her fear of the noise won out.

"Oh, Lordy, the house is tumblin' down around our very ears, I tell you," Janie wailed, frozen to the spot.

Before Stephen could pull his thoughts together and react, Adam staggered into the dining room, his robe hastily pulled over his nightclothes, his blond hair askew.

"Good God, what's going on?" he demanded, an angry red crease from his pillow slashing across his jaw.

"It's all the sinnin', I tell you," Janie supplied, her

hands fisted in her skirts. "All the sinnin'. Too much sin-nin', and God has finally had enough. He's shakin' all the world in his fury, making us pay, every one of us. Just like the Reverend Barthalomew said would happen—"

The next bang sounded, cutting short her ramblings, causing her to leap a good foot into the air before she landed with a *humph,* then scrambled out of the dining room, no doubt to repent whatever sins she might have committed.

Stephen, Adam, and Wendell stared, mouths agape, at the maid's retreating back.

"The wrath of God?" Adam stated.

"Sinners?" Wendell added.

But then the pounding came once again, and all thoughts for the terrified maid fled.

"Good God, it's coming from my house!" Adam stated.

Stephen cast him a dry glance.

"All right, my old house, but still, I've never heard such banging." He glanced at Stephen suspiciously. "You haven't been trying to get her over here again, have you?"

"Hardly," he snapped.

"Then what in the world could she be doing over there?"

"That is what I am about to find out," Stephen said, before pushing up from his chair, tossing his napkin on the table, and heading for the door.

Despite the fact that Adam wore nothing more than nightclothes, with his slippers slapping against his feet, he followed.

They slammed out the front door, down the stairs, then around to the Widow Braxton's front door. Soon,

Stephen thought irritably, there would be a path worn in the pavement from all the trips he'd made recently.

Their knock went unanswered, and after a moment Stephen simply tried the knob. The door was unlocked.

"Hell, hasn't the woman ever heard of crime?"

Adam chuckled. "I doubt our Belle thinks twice about people doing her wrong."

Stephen stilled, the memory of her leg jarring through his mind. He doubted Adam was correct.

Once inside the foyer there wasn't a soul in sight, though there was enough noise echoing within the walls to deafen a mule. The noise led them up the stairs to the second floor.

And there, in what for Stephen was always a breathtaking experience, they found her, along with an assortment of large, burly men who were applying sledgehammers to an interior wall.

Furniture was gone. Curtains removed. Rugs nowhere in sight. The only things left in the room were chunks of plaster and splinters of wood lying here and there as if a tornado had set down, leaving a huge gaping hole that reached into the next room.

"What are you doing?" Stephen demanded, anger shimmering in his voice, bringing the workers to a halt.

Belle turned to him, surprise in her eyes. "Stephen! Adam!" But at the sight of Adam's attire, the surprise fled, replaced by concern. "Did I wake you?"

Adam opened his mouth to speak, but Stephen cut him off. "You could wake the dead with all the racket you're making. What the hell are you doing?"

The workers shifted their weight and glanced uncomfortably between Belle and Stephen. Belle looked confused. "I'm tearing down the wall," she stated simply, before she offered him a slight smile. "Or rather, *they* are tearing down the wall."

Stephen made a noise that sounded suspiciously like a growl. "I can see that, Mrs. Braxton, the question is *why* are they tearing down the wall?"

"So I can build a ballroom. Just like Adam and I discussed."

Adam had the good grace to grimace beneath Stephen's sudden, piercing glare. Belle didn't seem to notice. She turned away, almost a twirl, hugging herself.

"A ballroom, for God's sake," Stephen snapped at his brother. "You told her to build a ballroom?"

Adam shrugged his shoulders sheepishly. "I thought you heard."

"Yes, a ballroom," she whispered, the words emphatic, looking through the hole as if she expected to find dancers whirling across the floor on the other side. "It's going to be grand."

It was her tone that finally filtered through Stephen's anger and gained his attention. He had the fleeting thought that she was trying hard to believe what she said, but not actually succeeding.

She took a few awkward steps through the debris, dispelling his thoughts.

"With hardwood floors, fine wood wainscotting. And right here," she added, looking up at the ceiling, "I'll hang a huge crystal chandelier." She looked back at Stephen. "Just like yours. It's going to be perfect." She took a few more steps toward the mantel at the opposite end and pointed. "And right here—"

"You can't build a ballroom!" Stephen bellowed.

Belle stiffened, her arm dropping to her side, before she turned, slowly, and met his eye. Everyone else stared, too.

"Why ever not?" she asked, her porcelain features creased with concern.

Strangely, Stephen hated the look in her eyes. Only minutes before she had nearly twirled with delight over the ballroom she intended to build. Though why, he couldn't imagine. The woman could barely walk with any speed much less execute the intricate steps of a dance. A ballroom was the very last thing she needed. He needed it even less, and soon the house would revert to him. As he had told Adam, there wasn't a contract written that couldn't be undone.

But still, he hated that look in her eyes.

"Answer me, Mr. St. James."

Her tone was stiff and suddenly formal, forbidding. Stephen had the sudden, misplaced thought that this was the tone she had obviously used with Bertrand at the Bulfinch House. He nearly smiled.

"Why ever can't I build a ballroom? I've obtained permits and plans and competent men to do the work. What, pray tell, am I missing?"

They stood for some time, staring at one another, the others forgotten. He needed to tell her, get it out in the open, that soon he would have the house back and she would have another—a better one, he could promise. But the words wouldn't come.

"The paperwork is not quite in order," he equivocated. "It might be best if you waited . . ." His words trailed off and silence swirled around the room like a bitter winter wind.

"This is my house, Mr. St. James." The words rang obstinately. "And I will do with it as I please. Now, if you will excuse us, we have a ballroom to build."

Stephen felt his brother's as well as the workers' gazes resting on him, hard and questioning. But it was

Belle's blue eyes that held sway. He couldn't do it. He couldn't tell her that the house wouldn't be hers for long. The weakness stunned him, then infuriated him in turn. But still, with those haunting blue eyes staring at him, he couldn't do it. Muttering a curse, he turned on his heel and strode out of the room, then out of the house, into the cold winter morning, welcoming the hard bite against his skin.

Days passed. The pounding on the wall was the only sign that Belle Braxton still existed. Stephen had tried again and again to see her, but had been turned away each time with the excuse that she wasn't in. Of course he didn't believe the butler. She simply wasn't in for him. Just like before.

Strangely, he cared. And he hated that he cared. How many times did he have to tell himself that not only was she none of his business, but that she was the most inappropriate woman he could possibly find to gain his attention? She was too outrageous to be a wife, and something about her made it impossible for him to think of her as a possible mistress. And what else could there be? Nothing. And nothing it would be.

But still he found himself, day after day, at her blue painted door, only to have it slammed in his face. Resorting to Adam's method of turning up the music would do no good, as there was far more noise coming from her side of the wall these days than a sane person could possibly reproduce short of destroying a wall or two of his own. As a result, he was at a loss as to how to see her.

Even though he shouldn't.

And so it went, around and around in his head like a twirling top, making him dizzy, but never ceasing. He'd see her, he had determined, though the reasons why were beginning to cloud in his mind.

It was the end of the week, and this time when Stephen went over to Belle's house, he went armed with the pretense of making sure the workers didn't work over Saturday and Sunday. Noise ordinances or some such. But Hastings was unimpressed, simply stated that he would relay the message.

Frustrated, Stephen turned away—only to find Belle coming down the walk toward the house.

All thoughts of slammed doors, rude butlers, and ordinances evaporated into the gray skies. She was beautiful. Stunning, really. Whenever he saw her, she affected him that way, as if he had never seen her before, as if that time was the first.

In the muted winter sun, her hair was free of headwear, shining like lacquered enamel. A long cape of velvet swirled around her feet as she walked faster than usual, her limp more pronounced. At first he was worried. What had happened now? But then her lips parted with a smile and he found himself relieved.

And that made him angry.

"Where have you been?" he snapped.

Belle's step faltered and eyes widened before she laughed. "What in the world is wrong with you? Did you wake up on the wrong side of the bed? Or did someone write you a letter and fail to dot the 'i' or cross the 't'?"

Stephen grumbled. "I can't imagine how you expect anyone to get a good night's sleep with all the racket you've been making," he groused, though in truth the noise never started until well after he was up and stopped well before he went to bed. But the truth mattered little just then. "And as usual your sense of humor falls short of the mark."

He heard her *tsk* as he waited for her to come up next to him. But when she did she never stopped, only offered him one of her dazzling smiles as she walked past him up the few steps to her front door.

Before she could close the door in his face, he had the presence of mind to scramble up behind her and slip inside just as the door slammed shut.

Belle raised one delicate brow. "I don't believe I said you could come in."

Stephen raised a brow in return. "I don't believe I asked."

"No, I don't believe you did. Why am I surprised?" Her tone was sarcastic. "Do you ever ask for anything, Stephen?"

"Last week it was Mr. St. James."

"That was when you made me mad."

"And you're not mad now?"

She looked at him closely. "No, not now, or at least not yet." She smiled. "But the day is early yet. Besides, I'm much too happy to become angry."

She turned to Hastings and handed him her cape. "I found one."

"Splendid, madam. I knew you would."

She appeared to forget all about Stephen as she started up the stairs. Hastings gestured Stephen toward the front door.

"Not on your life, Hastings. I've gone to too much trouble to get this far."

In a few bold strides, he caught up to her on the staircase. But every streak of anger fled at the sight of her delicate hand clutching the bannister as she made her way up the stairs.

"I thought you were gone," she said without looking up at him, concentrating instead.

"You're not so lucky today," he replied, wanting to help her up the stairs, but knowing to offer would be an insult.

And then she laughed again. "But today *has* been my lucky day."

"Ah yes, you found something. And what might that be?" He was concentrating on her ascent.

She hesitated on the landing to catch her breath. Her blue eyes danced with excitement. "A man!"

Stephen froze. "What?"

"I've found one."

"One what?"

"One man."

A man? Stephen stood stock-still, dumbstruck.

"It's taken me days and most of my time. That's why I haven't been here when you've called."

She started up the second flight of stairs and had gotten up a few steps before Stephen snapped to and followed, uncertain of what to think, or how he felt. "You've been out?"

"Well, of course. I've been searching. Day after day. I nearly gave up. But my quest has finally borne fruit. I found one."

The elation he was trying not to feel over the fact that she had actually been out and not sending him away was dampened by the knowledge that she had been out searching—for a man. "You have found a man?" he repeated, incredulous.

"Yes!"

Stephen stopped in the middle of the staircase and stared at her back as she continued on up to the third then fourth floors. "You went out and found yourself a man?" When would this woman cease to say things that made him crazy?

"Yes. I went to the museum and watched all the men come and go." She hesitated and looked back at him. "You can tell a great deal about a person by simply watching him for a bit." She continued on. "The way he walks, the way he stands. How he looks at people when he thinks he isn't being watched. But of course, *I* was watching."

"Of course," he muttered. Stephen found his disbelief being replaced by a slow burning anger. She had gone out and found herself a man, for God's sake. She *was* crazy! Or at least that was easier to think than to consider what that very fact really made him feel.

Betrayed.

The word slithered through his mind.

"Day after day I waited and watched. I was on the verge of giving up actually. But then I saw him. He was perfect. And I knew he would do quite nicely."

"You can't just walk into a place and stalk a man, then decide to have him!" He hadn't moved another step.

She glanced down at him as if he were a silly child. "Well, of course not. Once I decided on him, I introduced myself and asked him some questions. I had to make certain my initial impressions were correct. Just because his fingers are paint-flecked doesn't mean he's perfect." She clasped her hands together. "But Marvin was. Perfect, that is."

"Marvin! Paint-flecked?"

"Yes, he's quite an artist, I assure you. Marvin Dubois, is his name. Studied at the Louvre."

Stephen pressed his eyes closed, trying to make sense of her words. By now, Belle had made it to the top floor and was heading down the hallway. With a spurt of energy, he raced up the remaining steps and practically leaped in front of her just before she stepped through a doorway. "You've gone out and gotten yourself an artist? This man is an artist?"

"Well, of course. What else would I need a man for?"

A great many ideas rushed through Stephen's head. And as if sensing this, she laughed. "I guess I could have needed a man for gardening or another construction project. No wonder you have such a look about you. But rest assured, I have no more construction plans in mind. The ballroom is it. This man is only going to paint, on canvas, not even on those precious walls that connect to yours. Not to worry."

He had the nearly irresistible urge to sweep her up in his arms and twirl her around the room much as he had after learning she hadn't lied. She had truly been out when he had called. She had gone out and found herself an artist, not simply a man. And he found suddenly that he didn't care that he was acting more the schoolboy than adult. "And what is this artist going to paint?"

She pursed her lips. "I knew there was something else missing in my house, but I couldn't determine what it was. Then I saw all the portraits at your house, especially the one over the mantel in your ballroom, and I realized what it was. A portrait. I need a portrait."

"Of you?"

Belle gasped. "Why, no! Of my father, of course." She stepped past him, into the room. "It's going to be wonderful. A fine painting of Papa over the mantel in the ballroom." She glanced back at Stephen, her eyes wide and worried. "What do you think? Have I done the right thing? Do you think it will be wonderful?"

Stephen didn't know what to think, though very little of his thoughts had anything to do with this father of hers, this world traveler who, if rumors were to be believed, had once been a groundskeeper.

When he didn't answer, her countenance fell, then she turned away from him, crossed the room, and went to the French doors that led to a balcony that ran along the side of the house. She sighed. "It's not perfect." The excitement fled, leaving her defeated.

"I'm sure it will be wonderful," he offered.

But it was too late. Belle clearly wasn't convinced. She leaned her head up against the glass door.

Stephen stepped inside what he found to be a sitting room. When he did, he could see through to the adjoining room. A corner of a bed. Her bed, no doubt, like a glimpse of stockinged ankle, with the promise of so much more so near. He looked at her as she looked out the window. Beautiful, like an angel.

He felt his body's response. How was it possible that this woman did this to him? And like every other time he had asked himself that very same question, he had no answer.

"I think," he began quietly, taking a step further into the room, drawn to her, "that you're going to drive me insane."

Her reaction was swift and genuine. She turned around and looked at him, her eyes imploring. "Don't say that. Don't ever say such a thing."

"Belle, I'm . . ." *I'm what?* he wondered as his words trailed off. His head spun with thoughts and feelings, none of which he liked. Her moods changed as quickly as lightning, and struck with the same unforgiving swiftness. Despite himself, he drew closer.

When he reached her, she sucked in her breath, then turned back to the window. They stood that way for some time, both looking out to the street, Belle's breath shallow, Stephen's thoughts raging.

He wanted to touch her.

It was late afternoon. The murky, overcast skies were brightened slightly by the sun, which lurked somewhere in the distance, unseen, casting the world in shades of silvery gray. Partly ethereal, partly eerie.

Yes, he wanted to touch her, but not to offer comfort. He wanted to hold her, feel her, press her close until he could feel the pounding of her heart. He wanted to touch her in much the same way he had wanted to touch her the night he had brought her in from the rain. Before seeing her leg.

Unease swept through him. That night. Her leg. Craziness.

He started to leave, to seek the respite of his home and a glass of brandy to calm his raging thoughts, but then she spoke.

"This must be the time of day when people decide to kill themselves."

At her words, his heart seemed to still in his chest. His mind raced. What did she mean? He searched for something to say. Something, anything. But nothing would come. He could think of nothing that would help him see into her mind—or to ease his. "Belle—"

"See over there." She pointed out through the French door.

He was a few inches behind her and a few more to the side. He looked not out the window but at her. He took in her hair, her cheekbones, and the delicate curve of her ear. So fragile, so easily broken.

"Over there," she persisted, as if knowing he wasn't looking, the tip of her finger pressing insistently against the glass. "That ledge across the way."

At length Stephen looked out and found the granite balustrade that surrounded the balcony of the home across the side street. "Yes, I see it."

"They say a woman tried to walk the ledge." Belle breathed the words in a delicate whisper. "But a gust of wind came out of the skies like the careless hand of an impatient God, sweeping her away, off into the wind, tossing her like an unimportant plaything to the earth." Belle cast her glance down to the street. "What do you think she thought about when she knew she was going over?"

Her voice wrapped around him like the delicate threads of a spider's web, seemingly fragile, though actually relentless, unwilling to let him go. "I've never heard that story in all the years I've lived in Boston or even in the years since I've lived on this street." His tone was overly sharp, indignant, and he wanted to step away, yet didn't.

Belle turned back. She looked up at him, her head tilted, the back of her head resting against a glass pane. They stood so close together he could feel the warmth of her. If he moved ever so slightly, they would touch. Thoughts of suicide and impatient gods vanished. He wanted to kiss her, wanted to taste the sweet promise of her full, red lips. He wanted to run his fingers up her arm to the curve of her breast. To feel the soft fullness pressed against his hand.

She watched him, and he had the strange feeling that she knew just exactly what he was thinking. But if that was the case, he couldn't tell if she returned the sentiments. Her face was more a mirror to his own feelings than a window to hers.

He leaned closer. "Belle," he murmured.

She met his gaze, her own intense. "Of course you haven't heard the story."

Her words dragged his mind back to places he didn't want to be. Frustration mixed with desire.

"If someone had tried to tell you," she continued, "you wouldn't have listened, or you would have put it from your mind as if it never existed. You don't like things that don't fit into your perfect, well-ordered world, Stephen."

His sharp intake of breath hissed through his teeth. His jaw clenched and his eyes narrowed.

But then, suddenly, she laughed, the lightning quick change threatening his balance. "Or perhaps I made the whole story up."

His mind stilled. She stood before him, watching him, one long sweeping curl having escaped her chignon to fall down her cheek, beckoning him, teasing him, before she slipped underneath his arm and quit the room, leaving him alone with unsettled feelings and the pounding desire that he so frequently felt whenever she was near.

CHAPTER
ELEVEN

She entered his house like the wind, through the front door, buffeting, disturbing, never unnoticed—breaking things, Stephen thought uncomfortably, though he doubted it was sofas or chairs or tables and such that were at risk. He had the unexpected notion that it would be something closer to his heart.

He cursed out loud. Belle Braxton, forever twisting his thoughts into unrecognizable musings.

He sat in his study, bracing himself against her impending onslaught. But he braced himself for naught. She didn't enter his haven. Only her voice wafted in from the foyer, making it clear that she wasn't there to see him. He cursed again for caring.

She hadn't been invited to his house this day, nor had she been expected. She never came when he invited her, nor when there was a real reason to come. He should have been annoyed. But he wasn't. He was thrilled she was there.

It was often that way, he realized. Again and again, Belle Braxton didn't have to do much to spin his mind off with contradictory thoughts—merely arrive at his door, or turn him away, or look at him with those little-girl-lost eyes that whispered of a dark stain on her heart. And whispered of pain. There was always the pain in her eyes, even when she laughed. Or perhaps it was there especially when she laughed, when there was no anger to keep the pain at bay.

He had avoided her each time she had come over. He snorted at the thought, for if truth be known, avoided was an exaggeration. Actually, whenever she arrived she provided him with no opportunity to avoid her—but, by God, if she had tried to walk into his study over the last few days, you can bet he would have sent her on her way, door slammed in her face just as she had done to him.

As it was, she had never bothered to come near enough to his study door for slamming it to have made an impression. She always came to see Adam or Cook. Even Wendell had spent time with her, though being the professional that he was, the butler had only nodded as Belle spoke, until she would give up and leave, or move on to someone more inclined toward conversation—though never Stephen.

He snorted at the thought as he sat back in his leather desk chair. Today, apparently, it would be the same, he determined, when he heard her enter the front parlor where Adam sat at a table, getting ready to play poker with an assortment of friends of which Stephen wanted no part. He would have told his brother as much if a tentative peace hadn't settled between the two of them recently. Stephen, despite the unruly men now seated in his front parlor, was disinclined to ruin that fragile truce.

But truces, just then, were the least of his concerns. Belle was. He set his pen aside, careful not to let the blue-black ink splatter his crisp clean files, and listened to Belle's deep throaty laughter and her fine silken voice sway toward him like a song on the breeze.

Her words always wrapped around him, just as their conversation about the woman who had supposedly been swept off the ledge wrapped around him—and hadn't let him go. Every time he started to think about the story he tried to push it from his mind, just as she had said he would. As a result, he would force himself for a few uncomfortable minutes to consider the possibility that the story was true. It usually happened at night, just when he was drifting off to sleep, filling his dreams with images of faceless women plunging to the earth. Always, just before the ground turned them into hopelessly broken toys, the indistinct features of the woman would sharpen until they were Belle's, who would laugh and fly away, up into the heavens.

Stephen seldom woke feeling rested. This day was no different. Though, oddly, the very voice that caused him so much turmoil at night drifted over him now like a soothing balm.

He nearly laughed aloud. From experience he had learned that it wouldn't last. She soothed from a distance, when he imagined her silky hair and stunning eyes, or heard her mellow laughter. Up close, she disturbed him in ways he wasn't interested in examining.

Abruptly he stood, as much to escape his thoughts as to find Blue Belle Holly. His determined stride took him out of the study and across the marble foyer to the parlor where he found the poker players. He nearly choked on the smoke that engulfed the room, making it appear more a tawdry saloon at midnight than a respectable parlor at noon. But even through the haze, he couldn't miss her.

His mind jarred as he tried to register the fact that her hair—pulled up in a loose design of curls at the back of her head, revealing the long, sensuous column of her neck—was lighter, seemingly gray, and her clothes, another velvet dress, though this one made up in deep

hunter-green, were covered in . . . dust. But that sight
was usurped by the sight of her hand resting softly on
Adam's shoulder, her hip resting casually against the arm
of his chair as she looked down at the cards he held in his
hand.

Heat churned in Stephen's gut, and he must have
made some sort of a noise, for without warning everyone
at the table including Belle turned to him.

"Stephen!" Belle called. "You're here!"

His brain registered the pleasure of her face, but another part of him, his heart, he thought fleetingly, was
still fixated on her delicate hand resting on his brother's
shoulder.

"So it would seem," he said, meeting her gaze, his
tone short. "As are you. Though why you're here this
time I can't begin to imagine."

Adam, along with the rest of the card players looked
decidedly uncomfortable. Belle only laughed. "For someone supposedly so intelligent and successful, you have the
imagination of a gnat, and that I'm afraid is being unkind
to the gnat."

The poker players gasped and choked as Belle and
Stephen stared at one another, deep pools of darkness
clashing with amused blue. Adam dropped his head down
onto his hands, unmindful of the cards.

"Surely," Stephen began, "a gnat is an exaggeration."

Belle tilted her head and seemed to consider. "Oh,
all right," she scoffed with a teasing smile. "A mayfly."

The room grew silent. Stephen's ominous stare would
have slain a lesser person, but Belle didn't even bat one
of her long silky eyelashes, yet again bringing a grudging
bit of respect for her to the surface. "Larger body, virtually the same size brain," he responded.

"So," she said, with an arch of brow, "you're smarter

than I thought. No wonder you're so successful. And there just might be a sense of humor in you somewhere after all."

"Don't count on it," he stated curtly.

Belle threw her head back and laughed out loud, up at the rafters, uninhibited. "I won't."

Stephen shook his head. Without conscious intention, his dark features hardened into disdain. "Didn't anyone ever teach you about little things like being polite to your host?"

"Of course. Though I was also taught that the host is supposed to be polite to the guest. But, alas, I'm not here to be hosted." She extended her hand in which she held a cup. "I've come to borrow, not to socialize. I need some sugar. I ran out, and I need some more to make my icing." She ran the back of her hand across her cheek, leaving a swipe of creamy skin exposed beneath the dusting of white on her cheeks.

"Sugar? You need sugar?" Stephen asked, perplexed. "And what is that all over you?"

She glanced down at her skirt. "Flour," she said proudly, as if she wore a badge of honor. "I'm cooking. Or at least I'm helping Maeve cook. Soon we'll be icing."

"Good Lord," Stephen muttered. "You look like you know as much about cooking as I know about imagination."

Adam groaned.

But Belle was delighted. "Touché, Stevie."

"Stevie?" Stephen repeated, with a look of disbelief stretched across his chiseled features.

Adam groaned even louder, while his friends muttered uncomfortably.

But Belle was no longer interested in the discussion.

She turned back to the table. "What is it you're playing, Adam?"

"Poker," Lewis supplied when no one else in the room seemed inclined to answer.

"Really?" She glanced at one vacant seat. "Who is going to sit there?"

"We had hoped Stephen would join us," Lewis offered.

"Stephen? Playing poker? I find that hard to believe. No wonder the seat is empty—just waiting for me," she added. "I'll play instead."

"You?" Adam asked.

"Yes me."

"But . . . we play for money."

Belle held her hands out palms up, the empty cup hanging from one finger, and shrugged. "I have money."

At this Adam laughed. "True. But we play for keeps, Belle. If you lose, you lose for good, or until you can win it back."

"What do you take me for?" she scoffed. "A dolt?"

Red crept up Adam's neck. "Well, of course not. It's just that . . ." He glanced up and met Stephen's hard stare.

"It's just that what?" she demanded.

"It's just that I would never want you to feel taken advantage of."

Belle waved his words away, set her cup on the table, and plopped down in the empty chair. "If I were you, I'd be worried that I might take advantage of you. Now, deal. I'm ready to play."

"No."

Everyone froze. Belle sat very still for one second before she turned very slowly around. "No?" she asked Stephen.

"Correct," he responded, never having moved from his place in the doorway. "No, you can't play."

"And why ever not, Mr. St. James?" Her tone was as formidable as Stephen's had been.

"I'll not be responsible for a woman . . . gambling in my home."

Belle narrowed her eyes. "Who made *you* my keeper?"

She was correct, he realized. Who, indeed, had made him her keeper? He wasn't, nor would he ever be. And he certainly didn't care one whit if she was fleeced out of every penny of her fortune.

"Looks like this game is going to be finished before it ever gets started," Lewis commented.

"On the contrary. My apologies," Stephen stated, his tone crisp, surprising them all. "Enjoy your game." And then he left.

The men around the table weren't certain what to make of the sudden departure, only Belle didn't seem to care.

"Pass those cards around, Adam," Belle said, excitement lacing her blue eyes. "It's time to play."

Adam stared at the empty doorway.

"Come on, Adam," Belle said. "Not to worry. He won't be back. He had that look about him that he gets when he's been offended and knows he shouldn't have been offended, or at least that he shouldn't care that he's been offended." She shook her head. "It's a wonder you're not more like him. But thank the Lord you aren't."

Adam cringed, giving Belle pause. She was about to say something when the clock struck the half hour. "Oh, my Lord, the cakes!"

The men started in their seats and stared at her.

"I forgot the cakes," she cried. "Adam, I need

sugar." She leaped out of her chair and snatched up the cup and thrust it at him. "Can you get me some sugar and bring it over to my house? I can't wait." She hurried to the door, then skidded to a precarious halt. She turned with a lopsided flourish. "All of you are invited over. We've made enough cakes for everyone." Then she dashed out of the room, only to stop short when she caught a glimpse of Stephen in his study. He stood at the window, looking out.

After a moment of just watching him she spoke. "I've made cakes," she said softly from the doorway.

Without turning back, he said, "So I've heard."

Red singed her cheeks. "Yes, hard not to when I'm hollering all over the place. I'm never quite the lady you think I should be."

He turned away from the window. Their eyes met and held. She saw the look—the one that said he was wondering if indeed the rumors were true, that she was crazy. Of course she had heard them—who hadn't? For a minute she cared. For a minute she wanted to turn back time and do things differently. But that, she knew with a sigh of defeat, was impossible.

With effort, she looked away, fading back to that place where censure and disdain couldn't touch her. "Nor will I ever be the lady you think I should be," she continued, her voice once again loud and laughing. "Nevertheless, you're still invited over for cake."

With that she gathered her long skirts and vanished; the only proof that she couldn't actually vanish like a magician was her voice rushing through the house when she hollered back, "Hurry with that sugar, Adam!" just before the door slammed shut.

* * *

Stephen was angry with himself when not thirty minutes later he stood on the steps at her front door. Adam and the others had already gone over. Stephen held his hand firmly at his side as he stared at the hard plank of deep blue. Without warning, a conversation of long ago sprang up in his mind.

"It has to be blue." His mother's words. Followed by his father's laughter.

"Blue, my darling? I've never heard of a blue front door."

Stephen remembered his mother had pressed her head against his father's broad chest—his heart, Stephen thought suddenly. *"We all need something blue in our lives, love."*

And sure enough, the next day, the door had been painted blue. His father, a man who had been strong and intimidating when he wanted to be, Stephen realized for the first time ever, had given in to a frivolous bit of nonsense.

The thought staggered Stephen and he nearly turned away.

Ever since he had returned from Europe to find a party going on in his house, his life had ceased to make sense. Between Adam and Belle, Stephen found himself questioning facets of his world that didn't need questioning, and doing things that didn't need doing, like coming over here. He knew he should return home. He knew he should seek out a woman who was even and dependable, a woman who would be a respectable addition to his proper home. Instead, he was drawn to a woman who only did what he least expected, not to mention was least appropriate at every turn. It was like being attracted to a hurricane, only to be tossed about and battered. But, he conceded in spite of himself, as with such a deadly storm, there were times when he was at the center of her attention that he felt a startling calm, a tiny piece of heaven.

With no help for it, he knocked.

"Afternoon, Hastings."

"Good afternoon, sir." Hastings didn't step aside.

"I was invited this time," Stephen muttered, wondering how he had gotten into such a position—with a butler, no less.

"Ah yes, for cake, that would be." Hastings gestured for Stephen to enter. "You will find Mrs. Braxton in the kitchen."

And sure enough he did, not in a parlor or dining room, but in the kitchen. Adam and his friends were laughing and talking, perfectly at ease sitting around a long wooden table in Belle Braxton's kitchen.

"Stephen! You came!" Belle held a small, dull spreading knife in her hand, her blue eyes dancing with pleasure. "I've made a cake especially for you."

Stephen didn't move, couldn't seem to move. Suddenly he saw his mother. In the kitchen, twirling around, laughing, a spreading knife in her hand.

The kitchen had been filled with gaiety, the aroma of cooking, coffee. And happiness. Much like this one was now.

He looked at Belle, who had crossed to the counter and was busy icing a cake. Her hair was wild, streaked gray by flour. He had the sudden thought that she would look every bit as lovely when she was old.

Trying to draw his mind back to safer regions, he took in her attire. Askew, was all he could think. He wondered if she even knew how to dress appropriately. The dress, which had not lost any of the flour that had covered it at his house, was properly enough cut for a change. But, as if in defiance, Belle had pinned a large, fake, bright yellow flower to her chest. A sunflower, he thought.

"Do you like it?"

Stephen started. When he met her eyes she had turned back to him and was extending a plate. "The cake?" he asked.

"No, the flower. My tiny piece of sunshine," she explained, "in the dead of winter."

"It's . . . interesting."

"We all know what that means," she said with a laugh. "You don't like it at all. No matter." She emphasized the cake. "Take it, it's for you."

He glanced down at the plate she held before him. His eyes widened at the sight. Quickly, he took in everyone else's. They all held plates with oddly shaped cakes. Birds, he finally realized, though by now birds with legs and tails missing as the pastries were devoured.

"In honor of our first meeting." Her smile dazzled him. "A bullfinch."

And sure enough, Stephen noted, the cake was indeed shaped like a finch, but instead of red, blue-gray, and black, the breast, cap, chin, tail, and wings were done up in pink, orange, and green spotted icing.

"Do you like *this?*"

Her question was tentative, as if the cake was much more important than her flower. He glanced between Belle and her cake, and felt his tension rise. Cakes shaped like birds, lying on floors, searching out men in museums. His head spun with all the craziness. Maybe she *was* crazy. Maybe *he* was crazy for being drawn to her.

And his mother. To have thought, even for a fleeting moment, that there was any comparison to this woman, covered in flour, with hair like Medusa's. So unlike his mother with her proper sweep of hair and pristine flow of gown. But then the image came again—his mother laughing and twirling. He had the sudden thought that either his mother was crazy or Belle wasn't crazy at all. His head spun. Sweet Jesus, Belle was driving him mad.

Without ever taking the plate, or without another word, his jaw tight, his throat oddly strained, Stephen turned on his heel and pushed out through the kitchen's swinging door.

Belle stared at the door as it swung to a halt, hating the way she felt. She had no time for diversions, especially with a man like Stephen St. James, who undoubtedly had the power to divert her from her plans. The bullfinch in her hand was proof enough of that.

She pushed the strange sense of loss aside. She had no room in her life for Stephen. Her father would be arriving anytime now. And after that he would take her with him traveling around the world. Surely he would want to show her all the places he had been. Africa and the Himalayas, Spain and France. Her heart began to ease. Soon she would be leaving with her father to travel. And when they came back, they would settle into this house on Arlington Street that would soon be as perfect as the one in her dreams—in her father's dreams.

"Sorry about that," Adam said, breaking into her thoughts just as the other men trailed out of the kitchen as if Stephen's departure announced that the impromptu party was at an end.

But Belle wasn't sad to see them go. She suddenly had no energy to make small talk or enjoy her cakes. She even wished Adam would follow his friends and leave.

"Are you all right?" Adam asked, his voice soft.

She turned abruptly to face him. "Of course I'm all right."

"You have feelings for Stephen, don't you?"

Her eyes widened. "What makes you think that?"

"Oh, I don't know. The way you look at him, perhaps."

"The look, undoubtedly, is indigestion. Besides, what makes you think I don't have feelings for you?"

Adam smiled fondly. "Then marry me."

"Good God, what a pair we would make. No doubt Boston would be set on its puritanical ear if we were to set about together."

"My darling Belle. You have a sense of humor that I love. No wonder we get along so well."

"Well, sense of humor or not, I have no interest in marrying you or anyone else."

"Then we are of like minds when it comes to matrimony." His smile dimmed. "Though in the end I wonder if either one of us will be able to avoid it."

"Speak for yourself. I've already been married." For a second, the blurted words caught her off guard. But having lived with the reality of those words for so long, she shook them off after only a moment more. "I don't have to marry again."

If Adam noticed the awkward moment, he didn't let on. He simply laughed. "Only because the old goat left you a pantload of money."

"True. And you should do the same. Marry, that is, someone with money. What about that Clarisse Webster I saw you with the other day?"

Adam grimaced. "Please, Belle, it's too early in the day for such talk."

"Don't you like her?"

"You're avoiding the subject."

"Which is?"

"Stephen."

Belle groaned.

"I'm certain you have feelings for him."

"The only feelings I have for your brother are impatience, then more impatience. An ornerier man I have never met. And bossy. Good Lord, he would try the patience of a saint, and I'm no saint."

Pursing his lips, Adam's eyes grew intense. "Don't be too hard on him. Though he would never talk about it, he's had more than his share of responsibility in his life."

"Because your parents died when the two of you were young?"

"He told you?"

"Yes. You seem surprised."

"Well, I am. Stephen rarely talks about our past, even to me."

"He didn't tell me much. And more than likely he was just plain angry and snapped at me."

"Then did he tell you that after our parents died he took over all of our father's responsibilities? I was only twelve, and some distant relative wanted me—for the money, I knew even then."

"No!"

"Yes. I was terrified. Not only had my parents simply never come home from what was supposed to be an afternoon outing, but people I didn't know wanted to take me away. But at only seventeen years of age, Stephen fought for me—and won. He's taken care of me ever since." Adam studied his fingernails. "He doesn't think I understand how hard it was for him over the years, but I do." Adam sighed. "No matter what else, he took care of me."

And suddenly she understood. With Adam's simple words, Belle understood the look she had seen in Stephen's eyes that night at the Bulfinch House. She had been correct. Stephen *had* experienced a moment of change—when his parents had died, leaving a seventeen-year-old with the full responsibilities of his father.

"And no matter how frustrated he makes me," Adam continued, breaking into her thoughts, "I'll always know that he is a fine man." He swallowed hard. "Much finer than I'll ever be."

She forced herself to concentrate on Adam. "Nonsense. You're a fine man, I know."

Adam sighed and she felt his sudden stab of pain.

"No, Belle, you just think you know me. You've been fooling yourself. Just don't keep fooling yourself about Stephen. For all his harsh and exacting ways, he's a very fine man, a man who would give his life for you if you would give him a chance."

Belle scoffed. "The last thing your brother wants from me is a chance."

Adam's smile was distant and sad as he headed for the kitchen door. "He wants a chance, Belle. He just doesn't know it yet."

The door swung shut behind him, but his words still hung awkwardly in the air.

Leaning back, Belle pressed against the counter. Plates with partially eaten cakes lay about, and she still held the bullfinch in her hand. Her precious bullfinch, which she had made for Stephen.

Stephen.

Her heart began to pound. Her pirate-man.

If only . . .

But "if onlys" meant nothing. If ever there were two people more ill-suited for one another, she didn't know of them. And she'd do well to remember that fact, just as she'd do well to steer clear of a man who she had sensed the first time she saw him could dissuade her from her path.

Disappointment surged.

But then the night in the park loomed in her mind. The night he had saved her. Yes, saved her. And that could mean only one thing.

She owed him!

A smile suddenly danced on her lips. He had helped her, had saved her that night. In return, she reasoned with a sudden burst of giddy excitement, she should help him, help him to be happy. But she quickly tamped down the excitement, telling herself she only wanted to help. Nothing more. She didn't want *him,* she told herself forcefully. This was not just an excuse to be near him. She only wanted to help him.

An unfamiliar lightness began to creep into her soul. She would spend time with him, starting the following morning. She would talk to him. Laugh with him.

Touch him.

She tried to quell the thought, but an odd sensation radiated through her body, filling her with a strange longing she didn't understand. Her head seemed to spin and her body pound. Suddenly, she wasn't certain if she was sick or delirious. Though she *was* certain, whether she was sick, delirious, or just plain stupid, that she couldn't wait for tomorrow to arrive.

CHAPTER TWELVE

At precisely nine o'clock the following morning, Belle stepped out the front door. She pulled her cape tightly around her slender form and headed for Stephen's house. Since she owed him for saving her life, she would spend some time with him just as she had promised herself.

Poor man. Saddled with such staggering responsibilities at such a young age. He needed some light in his otherwise dreary life. Or so she told herself, as it was easier to explain away her need to see him with that excuse than any other she was inclined to come up with—namely the fact that she wanted to see him because he had ceased the memories. Vanquished the dark places. With one simple touch.

Her mind filled with the memory of Stephen's hand, gentle on her shoulder. She had relived that sensation-charged moment again and again as the night had worn on. What would have happened had he not pulled away? Would he have kissed her? Or touched her breast? She inhaled sharply, embarrassed despite the emptiness of the street.

Fortunately, or perhaps unfortunately, in no more than a few steps she arrived at Stephen's front door. Otherwise she just might have turned around and gone home.

Turning the small knob in the center, she rang the bell inside. To her surprise, it was Adam who answered the door.

"What, no butler?" she inquired, her voice laced with humor.

"Did you ever consider, Belle love, with my ever-present need of money, that Stephen has given me employment?"

Belle gasped. "You're the butler?"

Adam's eyes twinkled with amusement. "No. But I'd make a good one, don't you think?" he said, displaying his dapper long coat, top hat, and gloves. "Actually, I'm on my way out, unless, of course, you've come to see me, giving me some divine excuse to stay."

"Believe it or not, I've come to see your brother."

"I'm crushed," he said, pressing his gloved hands to his breast. "But alas, he's not home." He bowed elegantly, making Belle laugh. "It's me or no one."

"What? Wendell isn't here?" she countered with an impish grin.

"Cute," he said, taking her arm and guiding her back down the front steps. "Come on, if it's Stephen you want, then it is Stephen you shall have. I'll walk you to his office building."

They walked south down Arlington Street to Boylston, then east until they came to Tremont, where up a few blocks they came to a towering eight-story building.

"Here we are," Adam announced.

"This is his office?"

"Yes. From here he directs his ships and supervises his investments."

"He must be terribly busy."

"He is. Though he has an army of people who work for him who are perfectly capable of taking care of many of the day-to-day concerns if he'd only let them."

"With so many people, he must fill the entire building."

"No, just most of it."

"It's so tall," she gasped as her head tilted back to take in the height of cut granite and smooth marble.

"Yes, and a marvel, really. With a view from the top floor of Cambridge to the north and the harbor to the south. Not to mention it has an electric elevator. No hydraulic motors for our Stephen."

Her delicate nose wrinkled in thought. "An elevator . . . ?"

"Yes, with a mural on the ceiling and marble on the floor."

"I would imagine, then," she began, sounding doomed, "if Stephen owns the building, his office is on the top floor?"

"Yes," Adam responded, suddenly distracted, transfixed by something in the distance.

"Adam?" She looked at him curiously, forgetting her unease about the elevator.

Adam only stared across the street, into the huge expanse of the Boston Common, which stretched out opposite them like a rolling carpet of winter-brown grass. "Tom," he murmured.

"What?"

With a start, Adam turned to Belle. "Got to go, love," he said with a forced smile.

And then he was gone, leaving Belle alone on the walkway as he vanished between the carriages and delivery wagons and horse-pulled trolleys that rolled past.

She stared at the place where Adam had disappeared. "Dear Adam," she whispered into the din of iron wheels on cobbled streets, "what is going on in your life?" But neither the carriages nor the passengers offered an answer. With pursed lips and a shake of her head, Belle turned back to the building.

She was greeted by a doorman, who led her to the elevator. Standing before the caged door, Belle debated taking the stairs. When she had stayed at the Hotel Vendome, her room had been on the second floor, making it possible for her to avoid using the elevator altogether.

Today, however, she had to concede she couldn't manage eight flights of stairs. For a second, she thought she would just go home and wait for Stephen there. But that was absurd. She would get in the blasted elevator and survive the experience, thank you very much.

A uniformed man closed the huge brass cage around Belle. He stood in the front corner, at the controls, seemingly oblivious to Belle as she stood, stock-still, a fine sheen of perspiration breaking out on her brow. Small rooms. Without windows. No way to see the heavens at night and the world by day. What if she screamed?

With determination, her pearl-white teeth biting her lower lip, she concentrated on the fine wood-paneled walls and the plush velvet seat. Up and up, further into the heights, farther from the ground.

Long, heart-lodged minutes later, she was deposited on the top floor. Safely. She wiped her brow and smiled, disproportionately pleased with her accomplishment.

"May I help you?"

Belle was startled out of her thoughts by the voice of a woman who sat at a desk just beyond the elevator.

"Yes, I'm here to see Stephen."

"Stephen?" The woman's eyebrow rose perceptibly. "Have you made an appointment with *Mister* St. James?"

"Oh, heavens no," Belle stated, the woman's tone escaping her, casting one quick glance back at the elevator. "I didn't even decide to come until just a little while ago. In fact, I didn't even know he was here until a little while ago."

The woman cleared her throat, then pushed up from behind her desk. "You can have a seat in the reception area while I see if he is in. He's a very busy man, however. What did you say your name was?"

"I didn't. Tell him Belle is here to see him."

Belle sat quietly, her gloved hands clutched demurely in her lap, before the receptionist finally returned.

"I told Mr. St. James's assistant that you're here. He'll be with you as soon as he can, unless you would like to make an appointment and come back later."

Belle glanced at the elevator. She might have survived the experience once, but again? "I'll wait."

"Fine." The woman walked back to her desk, leaving Belle alone in the waiting room.

And wait she did. Five, ten, fifteen minutes, until an intricately carved grandfather clock announced the half hour. At her best Belle was barely patient. After waiting thirty minutes without a word, she began to fume. She had a million things to do, and one of them wasn't sitting idly waiting to do a good deed for an ungracious neighbor. The least he could have done was tell her he couldn't see her, or that he would have to see her at another time. But no, not Stephen St. James. He couldn't bother himself to tell her anything, just let her sit out here by herself as if her time wasn't important. She harumphed out loud into the room. Good deed done, indeed.

Just when she would have made her way to the elevator, or perhaps the stairs, a tall, slender, middle-aged man walked into the reception room. "Ah . . . Belle, is it? I'm Nathan Banks, Mr. St. James's assistant." He glanced down at a large thin book he held in his hands. "I see no *Belle* among the appointments, and Mr. St. James is a busy man."

"So I've been told," she replied tightly.

"Is there something *I* can help you with?"

"Yes, you can help me see that busy Mr. St. James."

The man looked at Belle with disdainfully pursed lips. "If you will only tell me what you want, I'll see what I can do. Otherwise, I'll have to ask you to make an appointment, then come back at that time."

"Have you told him that I'm here?"

"No. As I said, he's a very—"

"Busy man," she finished for him. What could she say? She had no real reason for being there other than to be kind as she had told herself she would be. Stephen, as always, was making that very difficult to do.

"Never mind. I'll see him another time."

With that she left, leaving Stephen's assistant standing in the entryway shaking his head.

Stephen was glancing over some papers when his assistant entered the office. "Nathan," Stephen called, tossing the sheet aside and smiling. He was feeling good this day—good and quite pleased with himself. Last night had been the first good night's sleep he'd had in weeks. He had gone to bed vowing to put Belle Braxton from his mind, and he had. The average man might have difficulty forgetting the woman, but he had proved last night that he was no average man. The steely St. James resolve was still in place. He wasn't addlepated, as he had begun to fear.

"Here are the files you requested," Nathan said. "The construction project taking place in young Adam's house is being worked on by a man named Wilson. He's done quite a bit of work for Elden Abbot. It should be easy enough to get him to stop working on the house. A ballroom, you say?"

Stephen shook his head. "Yes, a ballroom. What about the contract of sale Adam signed?"

"I don't have it yet. But I've sent word to Peter Maybry. I should have a copy of the contract within a few days. I'll see what can be done."

Nathan set the stack of files down on the desk in front of Stephen, then turned to go. "Oh, I almost forgot. Some woman calling herself Belle was here to see you."

Stephen's hand froze in midair as he leaned forward to pick up his pen. "What? Belle was here?"

Nathan was clearly taken aback by the reaction. "Well, yes."

"Belle? Came here?"

"Yes, sir."

"When?"

"Just a few minutes ago."

Stephen leaped up from his chair, all concerns about being average, maintaining resolve, or becoming addle-pated disintegrating—all thoughts of forgetting her forgotten. "Where is she?" he demanded.

Nathan cleared his throat uncomfortably. "She's gone."

"Gone?"

"Yes. You see, sir, she didn't have an appointment."

"And you let her leave?!"

"Well, yes. I didn't realize—"

"Where did she go?" Stephen inquired as he came around the desk, pulling his greatcoat out of a discreet cabinet in the wall.

"I'm not certain, sir. She didn't say."

Stephen dashed out of his office. The elevator, always slow, seemed to take forever. But eventually it arrived, then sank down with the ease and swiftness of an ancient

queen. By the time Stephen hit the street, Belle was nowhere in sight.

Why had she come? he wondered, his mind racing, as
he scanned the crowds of people and rolling carriages.
This was the first time she had ever sought him out, and
she had traveled to his office to do so. He could no more
imagine her seeking him out than he could imagine all
the water in Boston Harbor rushing out to sea. No telling
why she had come. His heart raced as much as his mind
did. She *had* come, however, and just then that was all
that mattered.

But then he stopped and cursed. He reined in his
careening mind. What was he doing? Racing out of his
office like a fool. More than likely, she had sought him
out because of some problem at her house. One too many
walls razed by her laborers. Plaster plastered in the wrong
place. Wallpaper papered on a floor.

Disappointment flooded him. And that made him angry.

He started to turn away, return to his office where he
belonged, but through his circling thoughts and the thick
bustle of people, he caught sight of black enamel hair
wild and uncovered. "Belle," he breathed involuntarily.

At the sight of Stephen, Belle wished with all her
might that she could disappear into the pavement, melt
like ice on a blistering hot, bright summer day. But no,
she wasn't going anywhere, she was stuck—literally. Her
back was to the fence and her black-booted foot was bent
behind her, wedged in between two unrelenting wrought
iron slats. The last person in the world she wanted to see
was Stephen St. James.

He stared at her from across the busy street for what
seemed like ages, and just when she started to breath a

sigh of relief, certain that he was going to return to his office, he shoved his hands deep into his pockets and started toward her.

"Hello," he said simply, reluctantly, she thought.

"Hello, to you, too." Belle offered him a wry smile from her place in front of the fence, her long skirt covering her shoes.

"I understand you were looking for me."

"Yes."

Then silence.

"What for?" he prompted.

"Oh, that. It was nothing. You're a busy man. You really should get back to your office. Papers to sign. Appointments to keep. You know the sort of thing. I'll just see you later."

Stephen eyed her curiously. "Why do I get the feeling something is going on here that I'm unaware of?"

Belle rolled her eyes and snorted in a way that she hoped implied he must be imagining things.

"Belle, why are you standing there?" he persisted.

She searched her mind for an answer. "I'm admiring the scenery," she offered at length. She straightened and smiled, then gazed off into the bustling street with purpose.

"Admiring the scenery? The scenery is behind you in the Common, not in the street."

"Go figure," she offered with a shrug of shoulders, though she didn't dare try to turn around.

"This is ridiculous, Belle. Either come inside with me or let me see you home. You can't just stand here."

It was all she could do not to say, "Try me." But she managed to hold back and said instead, "I'm fine, really. You go on without me."

"Belle," he said, his voice a warning, "what is going on here?"

Belle cringed not only at his tone, but at the sight of him, as well. He stood before her, more handsome than any man had a right to be, so tall and elegant, regal really, making her feel more awkward and clumsy than usual. He was a swan. She was an ugly duckling, waddling through life, mucking things up at every opportunity. Her embarrassment grew tenfold.

She started to look away.

"Belle," he demanded softly. "What is going on?" He hesitated, reaching out and gently taking hold of her chin. "Why did you come for me?"

Her heart leaped. Her mind stilled with the simple touch of his hand. So soft. So gentle. Yet so secure, making her feel as if she could never get lost. "I love it when you touch me," she breathed.

She felt his gentle grip stiffen against her skin. After a moment, he dropped his hand away.

She could have died a thousand deaths. "God," she groaned. "I try to say the right things, really I do. But somehow, other things, not-so-right things, come out instead." She glanced up at him. "I'm sorry," she offered, then sighed. "That seems to be the way with us. Too many sorrys."

"Oh, Belle . . ." he said, though that was all. Just an "Oh, Belle," hanging in the air, a thousand possible meanings rushing through her mind. Without thinking, she started to turn away, forgetting her foot.

"Aggh!"

"What is it?"

The look in his eyes was her undoing. Her pride be damned. For all she made him angry, she knew he would help her. "Before you go," she said with a self-deprecating laugh, "could you help me? I seem to have gotten myself in a bit of a bind."

A look of confusion passed over his features. She gestured toward her feet. After a curious look, he leaned over and peered behind her. "Belle, your foot is in the fence!"

"Really," she snapped sarcastically, mortification making her response overly sharp.

His all too familiar scowl darkened perceptibly. "How in the world did you manage this?"

"Well, you see, I was standing here, minding my own business, of course—"

"Of course," he interjected dryly.

"Your sarcasm isn't appreciated."

"Neither was yours. Furthermore, I wasn't being sarcastic."

"As I was trying to say," she said in exaggerated tones, "a huge clanging red wagon with brass wheels raced through the street."

"A fire engine," Stephen explained automatically as he hunched before her foot.

"Really?" she asked, intrigued. "How does it work?"

"Your foot, Belle."

"Ah, yes. My silly old foot." She grimaced involuntarily when Stephen tried to free her.

He stopped immediately at the sound. "Have you hurt yourself?"

"No, no." she equivocated. "Just sore." She wasn't about to explain that it was the pressure on her bad leg when he tried to free the good one that made her grimace. In fact, she hadn't let out a peep to anyone, because she had hated to admit that she couldn't get her leg out of this idiotic predicament. It was her good leg that was caught, and every time she tried to put her full weight on her bad leg to pull her good one out, pain seared up her body. *This is ridiculous,* she thought. At the rate she was going, she would have been there for days due to foolish old pride. But pride, she had learned, could be a lifeline. Not so unlike Stephen that night at the Abbots' as he had stared at that thick cut of beef.

She started to comment, but then thought better of it. She knew without a doubt that the last thing Stephen St. James would want to be compared to was her.

"You still haven't told me what you were doing," he said as he studied the situation.

"Oh, yes, the fire engine." She looked down the street to where the huge flatbed wagon had disappeared. "Everyone on the walkway just stopped. Lots of men."

Stephen tensed.

"And I couldn't see over them." She shrugged her shoulders. "So I stepped up on the rung here in hopes of seeing what all the commotion was about. Alas, my foot slipped, unfortunately backwards. And here I am. But I did manage to get a glimpse of that fire engine."

Stephen cursed under his breath.

"I heard that."

"You're lucky you didn't hear something a whole lot worse."

"You must be the testiest man in Boston."

His only response was an ominous look, before he said, "Look," while pointing down the street.

Belle swung her head around to do as he said, and when she did, Stephen forced her foot through the fencing. When she found herself free, she stared for a moment before she launched herself into Stephen's arms. "You did it! I thought I'd be there all night," she replied, laughing her relief up to the skies.

Stephen looked down at her, the bright winter sun

highlighting her cheekbones, and couldn't keep his smile away. Unexpectedly, despite his better intentions, he wanted to kiss her. He wanted to feel her lips beneath his. He wanted to touch her and hold her with an intensity that amazed him, then left his body throbbing with desire.

And there, in the streets of a town whose history included a husband who was sent to the pillory for doing nothing more than kissing his wife at his own front door, they stood, silently, unmindful of the people all around. Stephen reached out very slowly and touched her cheek. He didn't care about propriety. He didn't care that friends and acquaintances alike undoubtedly passed by on the street. The touch was like fire, burning him to the quick.

"There is an outside possibility," she said, her glance drifting to his lips, "that I am actually growing to like you."

His hand froze, and he forced her to meet his gaze. "Would that be so terrible?"

"Yes," she whispered.

"Why?"

Taking a deep breath, she answered. "Because I like people who aren't like you."

Her words, as well as a wagonmaster who rolled by shouting obscenities at a pedestrian who had obviously gotten in his way, broke the spell. Stephen dropped his hand back to his side. "Which is?"

Red flooded her cheeks. She shook her head as if shaking cobwebs out of her mind. After a moment, with a jerk, though without another word, she turned away and headed down the walkway toward home.

With a start, Stephen fell in step beside her. "Which is?" he demanded once again, his voice unrelenting.

"Forget it, Stephen."

"I will not forget it." He knew he should flee. He knew he shouldn't care, but he desperately wanted to know—needed to know. "What kind of a person do you think I am?"

"You," she began with a sigh, "are stiff and inflexible, and undoubtedly have your entire life planned out from now until you die."

Stephen's stride became rigid.

"See," she said, glancing over at him as they walked side by side. "Getting all stiff and insulted on me."

"I am not stiff and insulted," he replied, his voice like steel.

Belle snorted in a most unladylike fashion. "And I'm not female or wearing a dress."

Despite thirty-seven years of having seen a great many things in his life both here and abroad, Stephen's eyes opened wide with surprise before he groaned and shook his head. "The things you say, Mrs. Braxton. Not wearing a dress. I can't begin to understand you."

"I was simply making a point. And you don't understand me because you are narrow-minded and would never dream of doing or saying something not altogether proper."

He remembered having nearly kissed her right there in the busy streets. "That's not true."

Belle took a deep breath and stopped abruptly, wheeling around to face Stephen, who nearly tripped over himself when she stopped. She shook her head as she looked up at him. "Face it, Stevie, you're stodgy, dull as dishwater."

Stephen's lips pressed into a hard line as he stared down at her. "My name is not Stevie," he could only manage.

"Proof in point."

"No, Mrs. Braxton. That is beside the point. Stevie or Stephen, I am not stodgy."

Just then the bells from Arlington Street Church began to toll loud and clear, crisp. The sound seemed to startle her. She snapped her mouth shut on whatever she had been about to say, before lifting her face toward the sound.

For the moment, she appeared to forget Stephen altogether as she closed her eyes and simply listened, taking in the distant clangs like a connoisseur savoring a fine wine. Stephen watched as a kind of peace settled over her —the sound, like a wine, filling her with a temporary ease. Not until the bells quieted did she take a long deep breath before letting it out slowly. "If you're not stodgy," she said, her eyes still closed, "then prove it . . . by climbing the belfry of Arlington Street Church and ringing the bells."

Stephen stood nonplussed. "Ring the bells?" he finally said, his voice tight.

"Yes, but you'd have to do it at an odd time, like . . . eighteen minutes after three for it to mean anything."

"Ring the bells?" he repeated. "At eighteen minutes after three! Such an act would only prove that I am capable of being irresponsible."

Belle opened her eyes. She stared at him, her blue eyes imploring him to something—something he couldn't fathom.

When he failed to respond, she sighed and nodded her head as if his silence was answer enough, then she gathered her long skirts then headed off into the park. "See?" she called back to him with husky satisfaction. "You are a stodgy old thing."

CHAPTER
THIRTEEN

The next morning, Belle sat on the front steps of Stephen's home, her elbows planted on her knees, her breath billowing in white puffs in the early morning air. She had been reluctant to knock on the door or ring the bell for fear of either being sent on her way or infuriating Stephen even further by her continually unladylike behavior. Even she knew a lady never called on a gentleman, though before today she hadn't cared.

But today she needed to care. How else would she finally be able to be kind to him and repay her debt?

Belle kicked herself for yesterday. She had tried to be pleasant to the man, but had ended by calling him stodgy. Good Lord, she had mucked her good deed up quite nicely. But today she would make amends. She was going to be kind, by God, if it was the last thing she did.

Upon waking that morning, she had developed a plan to accidentally bump into Stephen on his way to the office. But after walking up and down the street for a good thirty minutes without a single glimpse of him, Belle had plopped herself down on his front steps with an impatient sigh. Stephen St. James wasn't making it easy to be nice.

The cold from the hard granite was beginning to seep through her thick coat, skirt, and petticoats, making her bones ache. But sooner or later, he had to come out of that house. Hopefully, it would be sooner rather than later.

Just then, the front door opened. Before she could turn around, she heard the hard step of boot on granite come to an abrupt halt. Only a heartbeat later, the door slammed shut.

Slowly, almost reluctantly, she turned around to find him standing at the top of the steps, his back to the closed front door.

Stephen, so darkly handsome that he took her breath away.

"Mrs. Braxton," he said simply, with a curt nod.

She smiled, almost shyly. "Good morning."

"Is it?" He looked out into the overcast skies, his countenance just as dark.

Her heart sank. For a moment she concentrated on his wool coat, before she slowly closed her eyes. Unwelcome feelings, dangerously close to disappointment, stung at her lids. He was angrier than she had suspected he would be. "I see you're in a worse mood than usual," she said before she could stop herself.

He turned back to her with an arctic stare. "I suppose I would have been disappointed had I met with anything other than that sharp tongue of yours."

"I was trying to be nice. You're the one who started it."

"Me?"

"Yes, you with your caustically thrown out, 'Is it?'"

"Of course. How foolish of me. Somehow everything always ends up as my fault."

Her shoulders slumped. "What's wrong, Stephen?" she asked with a defeated sigh.

He almost said that she was what was wrong, but stopped himself just in time. He came down the steps with an arrogant swagger until he was standing below her.

"What can I do for you, Mrs. Braxton? You obviously

aren't here to admire the scenery." He seemed to consider. "Though with you, one never knows."

"No need to get nasty, Mr. St. James. Especially when I came over to apologize."

"Apologize?" His dark eyes narrowed with suspicion. "What for?"

Belle glanced down at her gloved hands. "For calling you stodgy."

Stephen grimaced. "Ah, yes, your blithely tendered assessment of my personality. Well, not to worry, it didn't cause me to lose any sleep."

She met his eyes. "No," she said quietly. "But *I* lost sleep over it. It wasn't a nice thing to say."

"When did you start caring about what you said?"

Her throat constricted. "I don't know where people get the idea that I don't care about anything." She clasped her hands and her voice became strained. "I *do* care, about a lot of things. More than you'd think. And I hope you'll accept my sincere apology."

Stephen stared down at her, so sad and clearly contrite, and while he was amazed that she truly seemed to regret what she had said to him, he wasn't really surprised to hear that she cared. Stephen felt a stab of sorrow for her, and before he could think, he said, "Apology accepted."

A silent moment passed as his words appeared to register in her mind, before the sadness disappeared as quickly as it had appeared, making him suspect he had imagined it, maybe even willed it.

"Really?" she asked, clearly hopeful. "I'm forgiven?"

Stephen looked at her, wondering if her words held greater meaning than what was on the surface. "Of course you're forgiven," he said softly, uncertain what he felt, finding all of a sudden that he had to forcefully hold his hand at his side to keep from reaching out to gently stroke the creamy white curve of her face. "Of course you're forgiven," he said again, taking a deep breath, then offering her a stiff, formal smile. "Now up with you and I'll walk you home."

"But I don't want to go home! I was hoping we could do something."

"Do something?"

"Yes, you know, make a day of doing something, going somewhere."

One slash of dark brow rose. "What did you have in mind?"

She shrugged her shoulders. "I don't know. We could walk through the Public Garden, or go to a museum."

He stared at her without responding.

"I'll be on my best behavior," she offered quickly. "I won't embarrass you, or I won't do anything to make you angry, I promise."

As soon as the words were out of her mouth, her eyes widened. She was worried, he thought. And that made him laugh out loud into the early morning winter cold. "Sweet Belle, you shouldn't make promises you will no doubt be unable to keep."

"True," she conceded. "But I'll try," she said fervently. "Really, I'll try."

With a shake of his head, he laughed again. How could he deny her? "All right, Mrs. Braxton. I'm at your disposal. Take me where you'd like."

He offered her his hand and pulled her up from the steps, then headed for his carriage, which had just pulled up in front of the house.

When she saw where they were headed, she tugged free of his grip with a sharp yank.

"What is it?" he asked, turning back to her.

"Not in that."

"Not in what?"

"Not in that carriage. I rode in the elevator, but I *won't* ride in a carriage." Her tone was emphatic, leaving little doubt that she meant her words.

"You won't ride in a carriage?"

"No," she stated simply, staring at the black enamel landau.

He looked at her quizzically, and when he realized she wasn't going to elaborate, he asked, "Could you expand on that?"

At length, she returned his gaze. "Well," she said as if speaking to a child, "when carriages are driving along, I'm not in them."

His scowl returned.

"You can't scare me with that look," she stated. "I'm not getting in that thing."

"I don't understand. I've never heard of anyone who won't ride in a carriage."

"You also haven't heard of anyone who makes cakes that look like birds or women who get their feet stuck in fences," she added.

Suddenly, she looked as old as the hills, shining with a sad luminescence that made his chest ache. But before he could say something, anything, she shook her head as if shaking melancholy feelings away, then passed him on the steps and headed for the Public Garden.

"Are you coming?" she called back to him when he did nothing more than stare after her in uncertain dismay.

At length he sighed, dismissed his driver, pulled his coat closed, then took the few strides necessary to catch up to her.

*   *   *

Belle guided Stephen through the streets of Boston as if she had lived there her whole life. They ate scones on Boylston Street, peanuts on Park Street, and listened to a hurdy-gurdy man at Scollay Square. After Belle insisted on buying flowers from a street vendor for Stephen, he returned the favor by buying her a hat from a milliner's shop on Summer Street.

When they returned to her house, the day was nearly spent and her leg was sore from all the walking. But Belle didn't care that her leg hurt; she was ecstatic. She felt wonderful and alive, better even than she had hoped. She had been nice. Nearly the whole day long.

"Thank you for a marvelous day," she said on the top step, he on the one below.

"It *was* marvelous." He smiled. "I can't begin to imagine how we accomplished it."

"It goes to show you that if we try, we can be good friends and good neighbors, just like Adam and I are."

He looked at her lips. "Is that all you and Adam are?"

"Of course that's all we are." She tilted her head. "Did you think otherwise?"

"It crossed my mind."

"Ah, Stevie, were you jealous?" she teased.

"Should I have been?"

A dog barked in the distance. "No," she said quietly.

Her arms hung at her side. Very slowly, he reached out, taking her hands, pulling her close.

Her heart seemed to still. Her world moved in slow motion. Stephen coming closer as he pulled her near. His lips slightly parted. "Are you going to kiss me?" she asked with breathless anticipation.

His reaction was swift and startled. One minute he was leaning toward her, the next he had stiffened and jerked back. Carriages rolled unnoticed through the street. "No," he replied curtly. "I would never be so forward."

She cursed herself silently. Ladies didn't ask if they were going to be kissed. Inadequacy overwhelmed her. "I'm sorry. I never should have asked such a thing."

His sigh whispered through the air. "Ah, Belle. Don't get that look."

"What look?"

"The one that makes me wonder . . . who you are. The look that makes me feel things I have no interest in feeling."

Her breath came out in a rush. "I'm no more or less than you see."

"My guess is that you are a great deal more than what I see," he said, coming closer still.

She was mesmerized by his intense, unreadable gaze as he slowly leaned forward. This time there were no questions, nothing to get in the way.

And then he kissed her. No embrace. No nuzzling of cheeks. Just lip to lip, his slightly parted as he drew a breath, seeming to breath her in, out of herself, until she was lost.

Her eyes closed at the feeling. Heaven. More than she had ever dreamed it would be. Enough that she could lose herself forever. And for that moment, she did. She lost herself to the feeling as he brushed his lips gently over hers, from side to side, slowly, maddeningly, making her want more.

His fingers entwined with hers, held tightly at their sides. With Stephen on the step below they were of a like height, so close together, their bodies nearly touching but not, except for their lips and hands.

"Belle," he said in a whisper filled with longing.

With exquisite patience, he trailed his kiss down her jaw to the delicate curve of her throat, barely revealed beneath layers of heavy velvet and wool. He sucked gently at the heartbeat in her neck. But with the unexpected and unfamiliar intensity of feeling came reality. Sharp and harsh. She pulled herself away.

"Don't," she implored, a murmur of distress.

Sudden, unexpected desperation flashed through his eyes, as if he needed her in ways she didn't understand. Couldn't understand. Wouldn't understand—despite her ability to interpret the look in his eyes—despite his ability to vanquish the darkness.

She owed him, and she would return the favor, but that was all. She couldn't afford anything else.

She turned away sharply and would have pushed through the front door without a word if he hadn't reached out and caught her hand. She looked back, but whatever he would have said died on his lips. They stared at each other for long drawn out moments, until he dropped her hand, his gaze once again dark and unreadable.

"My apologies," he said gruffly, then descended the stairs, never looking back as Belle watched him go.

Stephen was sitting at his dining table, plates of food covering the expanse, when the front bell rang the following morning. Steps sounded down the hallway.

"Stevie!" Belle called as she entered the room.

The cup of coffee he held halted halfway to his mouth. He stared at her over the rim for a moment before he brought the cup to his lips, took a sip, then set it back down. "So we're back to Stevie, are we?"

He studied her curiously. He hadn't expected to see her again for days, if ever, after what had transpired on her front steps. And rightly so. No decent woman would allow such a thing to occur, then waltz through his door as if nothing had happened—as if it had meant nothing at all. The thought brought a surge of bitter anger close to the surface.

He didn't like thinking about what *he* had felt when he had kissed her. Desire, intense and raging. Like nothing he had ever experienced before. He'd done nothing more than kiss her, though he felt as if he had caressed her naked in the privacy of his own bedroom. His body responded at the memory. He cursed beneath his breath.

"Do you always wake up in such a terrible mood?" she asked, picking up a slice of ham with her fingertips.

Only since she had moved in, he wanted to answer, but refrained, though just barely. "Would you care for a plate?" he asked dryly.

"No," she said, taking a bite. "I've already eaten." She finished the ham, then took a biscuit. "I thought we could go to the Old Corner Bookstore. Based on all the books you have in your study, it's easy to see you like to read. Not only do *I* like to read, too, but I'd love to see the place where so many famous people go. A perfect place, it would seem, for the two of us to go today."

It took a moment before he could gather his wits as he tried to make sense of what to him was a nonsensical situation. Clearly she wasn't there to slap his face or demand marriage—or, in her case, he thought unkindly, she would be more inclined to call him out! A good, old-fashioned duel, he could hear her say. A grudging smile sprang to his lips at the thought. A duel, indeed. Never had he met someone so outrageous . . . and so beautiful . . . someone he so urgently wanted to kiss.

Without warning, right there at the table laden with breakfast fare, it was all Stephen could do to keep himself from leaning over and kissing her. Damn her hide for affecting him so, he cursed beneath his breath when he realized what he was thinking.

"I'm a busy man, Mrs. Braxton," he growled.

Belle rolled her eyes. "You sound just like that little prig of an assistant you have," she said, taking a bite of biscuit. "Could you hand me some of that jam?"

Stephen glanced back and forth between Belle and the preserves in question. Not knowing what else to do, he passed her the dish.

"Hmmm, apricot," she announced. "Delicious. I'll have to ask Cook for the recipe. Maeve is wonderful in the kitchen, but not quite as good as your cook." She licked her fingers delicately. "So how about the bookstore?"

"I must not have made myself clear. I have a business to run, Mrs. Braxton."

Belle scoffed at this. "How hard could it be to direct a few ships, manage a little money, and whatever else it is you do? Besides, an outing will do you good."

She looked like a little sprite as she sat a few chairs down from him, and he knew from the look on her face that she was teasing. How strange. He couldn't remember the last person who had teased him. "I don't think my legs can take another day of traipsing around town."

"It's not far. And don't tell me that I can walk farther than you, the big strong man that you are?"

How could he respond to that? It certainly had seemed that despite her leg she could walk far greater distances than he. "It's winter, for God's sake. It's cold outside."

"Hardly," she chided. "The sun is out, bright and beautiful, as close to a winter thaw as we're likely to get.

But if you're so weak-kneed and thin-blooded . . ." Her words trailed off.

With a growl in response, he pushed back his chair, tossed down his napkin, and said, "I'll show you weak-kneed and thin-blooded, Mrs. Braxton."

And so he did. They spent a good part of the day at the Old Corner Bookstore where the likes of Ralph Waldo Emerson and Henry Wadsworth Longfellow used to meet and discuss the issues of the times. The next day it was an evening at the Boston Museum, where adding the word museum to the name made it possible for Boston habitues to rationalize attending what otherwise would have been considered vulgar plays. And the next day after that, after she had shown up unexpectedly at his office late in the afternoon, it was a walk down Newspaper Row, where proper Bostonians and new immigrant Bostonians alike once brought traffic to a standstill while waiting for news of the outcome of the John L. Sullivan-Jake Kilrain boxing match. Regardless of where they went, however, each day Belle failed to fulfill her quest to repay her debt. Every outing ended with Belle and Stephen exchanging words, if not exactly harsh, then unpleasant. And to think, she was trying to be kind to him!

It was Thursday when Belle spread a blanket out on the brown grass in the Public Gardens. As Stephen stood over her, slightly out of breath, his arms akimbo, his feet spread wide, she knew he was put out with her.

"Your note said there was an emergency!" His tone was short, clipped. "It doesn't look to me like there is an emergency, Mrs. Braxton."

"How else was I supposed to get you to come to my picnic?" she asked, as she smoothed nonexistent wrinkles out of the blanket.

He took a deep breath as if trying to calm himself

before he glanced around. "A picnic, in the Public Gardens? It's not allowed."

"Who will know? Nobody's around."

"Nobody's around because it's too damn cold."

"Good heavens, I've never heard anyone complain so much in all my life. Too much walking, the play too loud, the day too cold. Does anything make you happy, Stevie?"

Stephen grumbled. "When you bother yourself to call me by my given name."

"How is it possible for such a seemingly intelligent man to be so priggish?" As soon as the words were out, Belle wished them back. Not because she didn't think they were true, but because she had promised herself this day, yes this day, she was going to be nice all day long. And the fact that no more than five minutes into their encounter she was already failing made her mad, mad at him. "You are the most exasperating man I have ever had the misfortune to meet."

"You're one to talk," he snapped, dropping to his knees and rummaging through the basket she had brought along. "You'd try the patience of a saint." He pulled something from the basket. "What's this?"

With pursed lips, Belle looked down at the item in question. "Custard pie."

"Did you make it?"

"No. Maeve did."

"Humh."

"And what does 'humh' mean?"

He met her gaze and smiled devilishly. "Humh means . . . humh."

Belle didn't know what to make of this change. One minute he was all but overtly disdainful, then the next, he was smiling and just possibly teasing her.

"Well, are you just going to sit there," he said, pulling his coat tightly closed, stretching his long, booted legs out, and leaning back against the craggy trunk of a willow tree, "or are you going to serve up this picnic that you have dragged me to?"

With a burst of delighted laughter, Belle piled food onto a plate with pale yellow and blue flowers along the rim.

"That looks like fine china," he said as he took the fare.

She considered the plate. "You could be right," she said, then dropped a generous dollop of potato salad right in the middle.

Stephen shook his head then retrieved a chicken leg.

They ate their meal, both quiet, neither knowing what to say when they weren't at odds.

Belle finished first and set her plate aside. Lying back on the stiff blades of winter-browned grass, the muffler around her neck coming up to cover her lips, she stared up into the sky.

Stephen watched her as he leaned back against the willow tree, the chicken leg held in his ungloved hand.

After a moment, she glanced over at him. "Do you always eat and stare?"

His eyes widened, then narrowed mischievously. "Only when I have such a sight in front of me."

"Is that supposed to be a compliment?"

He looked at her for a second without answering. "I don't know."

She rolled her head back and scoffed. "Typical Stephen." Moments later, she pointed into the sky. "A bull."

"What?"

"A bull. That cloud. It looks like a bull."

Stephen leaned forward and squinted up into the sky.

"Looks like a cloud to me. Cumulonimbus, to be specific."

"Cummulo what?"

"Cumulonimbus. One of the three types of clouds. A new classification system."

Her snort of disdain was whisked off in the breeze. "Leave it to you, Stevie, to have no imagination at all."

"Seems like we've been over the imagination issue already. Perhaps we could move on to new territory."

"Then find a cloud and tell me what it looks like—other than cummubus."

"Cumulonimbus."

"Yeah, yeah. Just play along."

"You sound like Adam."

"Thank you."

"That definitely wasn't a compliment."

"It should have been. I think Adam's a grand sort."

"Yes, you've made that clear."

"Don't tell me we're back to being jealous again."

"I'm not jealous."

"Good, because as I told you, we're just friends."

"Yes, as he is with just about everyone around. Men, women, everyone likes Adam. I just wish he would stop acting like a boy."

"Then stop treating him like one."

"I treat him as he deserves to be treated."

"Open your eyes, Stephen. Adam is a man, not a boy. Give him the opportunity to prove it. Stop trying to run his life. Give him a chance."

"I've given him a chance! Hundreds of chances."

"And no doubt you've always expected him to fail."

"I never told him that."

"You didn't need to. It's clear that's how you feel, even to me, and I've only known you for a matter of weeks." She hesitated while she pushed up into a sitting position on the blanket. "He thinks the world of you, Stephen. He thinks you can do no wrong and no matter what he does he can do no right. Don't hurt him any more. Help him."

They sat scant inches apart, neither speaking, eyes locked, breaths mingling.

His gaze dropped to her lips. "I think I'm the one who's in need of help."

She inhaled sharply.

He only leaned closer. "Aren't you going to ask if I'm going to kiss you?" he asked, his voice deep and low.

"No," she whispered, repeating the words he had said to her. "I'd never be so forward."

A shadow of a smile flitted across his face, then it was gone and he leaned forward to kiss her.

She realized with a start through the myriad emotions she was feeling, that she had been waiting for this, waiting for him to touch her, waiting yet again for him to push the darkness away. The pie and the chicken had merely been an excuse. The realization filled her with fear. But then he pressed his lips to the tender spot beneath her ear and the realization along with the fear dissipated into the beautiful winter sky.

"Stephen," she murmured.

Gently, he pressed her back against the ground, her cape falling open. He stared at her. The same desperation that had flashed through his eyes only days before returned. And like a drowning man reaching out for a lifeline, he reached down and grasped her wrist lightly, the tips of his fingers pressed to her pulse. With breathtaking slowness he trailed his fingers up her arm until he grasped her shoulder.

And then he kissed her again, finally, desperately.

She inhaled deeply, and when she did she felt his tongue, fleetingly, against her lips. The intimacy amazed her, as did the strange feeling that coursed through her body, making her want to press closer.

With infinite care, he moved over her. She could feel the steely ripple of muscle beneath the thick wool. As if sensing her frustration, he opened his coat and pulled her inside, until she could feel his heat, feel his heart beat heavily against hers—strong and steady, melding into hers, joined as if one. He cupped her breast, then caught her moan of pleasure deep in his mouth, sucking it in, then grasping her tongue with his own, as if he couldn't get enough.

"Belle," he groaned into her mouth, before lowering his head to nuzzle the taut bud of her breast beneath the velvet.

She gasped at the unfamiliar touch. "Stephen," she whispered again. "I don't know. I don't understand. I don't understand what I feel."

"When, love?" he asked, the words a murmur as he pushed the velvet aside.

She cried out when his tongue found her nipple, her back arching to his touch.

"When you kiss me. It feels so . . . so wonderful. I've never felt such a feeling." She took a deep breath and smiled, tilting her head back. "Though I've also never been kissed before," she added with a tiny self-conscious laugh.

Stephen froze, then pulled back. He looked down at her, confusion warring with the desire in his eyes. She realized her mistake instantly.

"I mean, I've never been kissed like *that* before."

She rolled away and hated that she cared when he let her go.

"You've never discussed your marriage," he stated flatly, pushing up into a sitting position.

"Surely I have. He was such a fine man," she said quickly, searching for the pleasant expression she had perfected in the mirror long ago. "He loved me a great deal," she added as she worked the fastenings of her gown. "Practically worshipped the ground I walked on."

She could feel him studying her. She wished he would look away.

"Then you must have been heartbroken when he died."

Her fingers stilled in their task and she stared at him, wide-eyed like a startled doe. Heartbroken? Her nostrils flared.

Suddenly, words tumbled toward her from years before. *"You're my wife!"*

Her heart began to pound. But then the bells in the distance began to toll, deep and low, filling the skies. "Oh, heavens," she said, pushing up with effort. "The time. Got to go." And without bothering to gather the basket or the blanket or any of the picnic items, food and china alike, Belle hurried away, her gait awkward as she made her way along the path toward home.

Stephen was too stunned to follow. He simply watched her go, unable to make sense of his thoughts. Based on her clumsy attempts during their first kiss, and on the innocent delight she had shown today, he was inclined to believe she *hadn't* ever been kissed before. But that was impossible. She had been married, for God's sake. No one seemed to doubt that fact. Not Louisa or Adam or anyone else who gossiped about Belle. But still . . .

The thought trailed off, toppling into another. It didn't matter if she had been married or not. He had no business kissing her, or even having a picnic with her in the cold winter landscape. She had nothing to do with the kind of life that he was building for himself—had spent years building for himself. The kind of life of which his father would have been proud.

Unexpectedly, the image of his mother loomed in his mind. Laughing, caressing his cheek, her kind maternal eyes looking down into his. Eyes so very similar to Belle's, if not in looks, then in the emotions that danced so clearly in them.

He turned away from the image, not knowing what to make of it. He realized the memories of his mother were no longer so clear. And it was all Belle's doing, he realized. That combined with the memories Adam had of their mother which were so different from his own.

"Damn Adam, and damn Belle Braxton," he muttered to himself.

He glanced down at the blanket spread with half-eaten food and perfectly good china, and shook his head. Only Belle Braxton would leave such things behind. He started to smile, but stifled it with the iron-clad willpower that had been sorely lacking of late. Belle Braxton had nothing to do with the kind of life he wanted, he reiterated, though the inevitable *but* lurked in his mind. And that was the problem. Ever since he had met her, there were too many *buts* in his normally ordered life. He didn't like it now any more than he had that first evening he encountered her.

Grumbling, he pushed himself up from the ground. Damn her for too many *buts*. Damn her for making him lose control.

Damn her for making him feel like he had never felt before.

But his curses began to lose their force. He fought to

maintain his anger, searched for steely resolve. Found instead the image of Belle.

Belle. Sweet Belle. Bursting with life. Bursting with passion.

And suddenly he wondered which would be worse—a life *with* Belle Braxton, or one without her.

CHAPTER
FOURTEEN

The missive arrived first thing the next morning. Handwritten. Delivered by Belle's maid.

Stephen stared at the invitation to a party that very day, before he crumpled it up angrily, then tossed it into the fireplace in his study. Sure enough, the woman was going to drive him mad.

"Why is she doing this?" he murmured aloud to the flickering flames. "Why has she set out to see me every day of the week, even though she insults me at every turn and barely seems to like me."

His words were instantly disproved when he remembered the intimacy they had shared. No, she didn't entirely dislike him. She liked his embrace well enough, though he couldn't imagine any woman spurning him one minute then desiring kisses the next. Which brought him right back to the plaguing question. Why was she continually seeking him out? And still he could provide no answer.

Though Belle Braxton could.

Before he could think better of it, Stephen pushed up from the leather chair. Prior to meeting Belle, he had always been a man of action. Sitting back and letting the vagaries of life toss him about at their whim had never been his way. He never would have survived had he done so. But since their first encounter, he had begun each day telling himself to avoid Belle Braxton, then falling in behind her like she was the Pied Piper, luring him into a world that he hadn't known existed.

An uneasy tremor raced down his spine. He didn't like being the moth to someone else's flame, and that was just what he had become since the night at the Bulfinch House when she had turned around and asked to share his bread.

His mind reeled at the memory. Her beauty had stunned him. He remembered that night as if it was only yesterday. And then she had fled. *Oh, Belle,* he thought without warning, *what are you running from?*

His hand fisted at his side. He didn't care what Belle Braxton was running from. He would not be lured into her crazy world.

He called for Wendell, who appeared in the doorway with a swiftness that said he had expected the summons.

"I'm going out," Stephen said.

"To the party, sir?" he asked, his normally unreadable expression hopeful.

Stephen shot him a withering glare for daring to question him. "My guess is you've been spending too much time around the Widow Braxton and her inappropriate ways."

Wendell looked abashed, but a tiny bit defensive, as well, Stephen thought. Obviously Belle had wrapped his ever-faithful servant around her tiny little finger along with the rest of his staff. Whether he was breaking his fast or reading the newspaper, one of his servants happened along and none too subtly sang his neighbor's praise. They, apparently, had not felt the sharp edge of her tongue. He had.

"We all know about the party, sir. Belle, I mean Mrs. Braxton, was over prying recipes out of Cook late yesterday afternoon."

"Why wasn't I informed that she was here?"

"You had said you were not to be disturbed—for any reason."

So he had.

"Anyhow," Wendell continued, "she wanted it to be a surprise for you. Though she invited me."

"You're invited?" Stephen asked incredulously.

"And Cook, too. But of course we declined," he hurriedly added. "Not proper and all."

Stephen shook his head. Propriety was becoming a distant memory in his life. With that, he slammed out the door, determined finally to confront the very woman who had turned his life upside down.

Belle hurried past Hastings when the bell rang. With a huge smile, she threw open the door. "Stephen!"

Stephen hadn't bothered with gloves and hat, or even a coat. He entered with a panther's luxury. Smooth and sleek. Predatory. Belle stumbled at the sight, then laughed. "You came!"

"You sound surprised."

"I'm always surprised when you do anything I ask." She reached out and took his hand.

If possible, his countenance grew more fierce and he pulled free. "I'm not here to attend your party, Mrs. Braxton."

A dark cloud flitted across her face. But then she smiled and clasped her hands at her waist.

"See. I did have reason to be surprised. You aren't doing what I asked."

"That, exactly, is why I'm here. Why *have* you asked me to do all the things you have this week? Why are you doing this?"

She had been asking herself the same question since

the day she had gone to his office to be kind to him. Even she had to admit that her reasoning wasn't so sound. But it was impossible to accept that she, Belle Braxton, would use owing him for saving her as an excuse to feel his embrace.

Just then she wished that the servants weren't busy in the kitchen. She didn't feel safe standing alone with Stephen, and not because of what she thought *he* would do, but because of what *she* might do—throw herself in his arms and beg that he hold her.

Belle held her breath before she turned away, intent on forgetting a party that suddenly seemed silly. She wanted to flee to safer regions. And she would have fled, but he reached out and took hold of her shoulder, his grasp gentle though firm.

"Don't run away again, Belle. Just tell me why? Why are you doing this?"

Her breath came out in a rush, but she didn't answer.

"Belle, tell me. Please," he urged gently.

His eyes beseeched her, and while he had entered angry and demanding, now the anger had evaporated, leaving behind an intense desire burning in his eyes. She knew it because she could see it. He wanted her. But he hated that wanting.

"Because you saved me," she answered finally.

The words startled him. "Saved you?"

"The night in the park."

He flinched as if struck as he remembered the sheets falling away, revealing her naked body. God, how was it possible that he hadn't left the room? "I didn't think you remembered."

Her burst of laughter was harsh, and his blood ran cold. *Please, no,* he implored silently to a God he had not thought of since his parent's death.

"How could I forget," she explained, "that pirate-man, so dark but beautiful, who hovered over me, the cold all around, as he saved me?"

She remembered, he realized. But how much? The answer was important, because if she remembered everything, she should slap his face and damn him to eternity. In fact, he deserved much worse. "How much do you remember?" he had to ask.

She shrugged her shoulders and actually looked apologetic. "Not much, I'm afraid," she said dismally. "But enough to know that had you not come along, I most certainly would have perished in the cold."

His breath hissed through his teeth.

"And then, of course," she continued, "there was that unfortunate little incident with my foot and the fence." She smiled at him, a soft smile. "Every time I turn around, you seem to be saving me. Now I'm saving you . . . from stodginess, I suppose . . . because I owe you."

Her words were caught in the tumble of his mind. All he could think about, with a selfish sigh of relief, was that she didn't remember everything. But on the heels of that thought came shame—harsh, damning shame, quelling the relief.

His eyes darkened and his grip loosened, and before he could think better of stepping onto such a dangerous path, he spoke. "Why do I feel that both of us need a good deal more saving than warming hot fires and freezing cold picnics can provide?"

The words pierced her soul, cutting to a truth she had long kept away. She took a deep breath, searching for peace and solitude, hoping for sanity. "I'm afraid you might be right." Her thick lashes fluttered when she looked back at Stephen. Dark hair, chiseled jaw, eyes with depths a person could drown in—the kind of looks that could drive a woman mad. At this she suddenly smiled. If rumors were to be believed, she already was crazy; she needn't worry about Stephen driving her over the edge.

Relief rushed into her mind. "So it's settled," she announced. The precarious edge was safely distant once again. "You'll stay."

She turned to go, though this time she wasn't trying to flee.

He stiffened. "I never said I'd do any such thing."

"Oh, come on, Stevie. Quit being a stick in the mud. Stay, you'll have fun."

"That's what you've been telling me for days now."

She glanced at him from beneath raised eyebrows. "And haven't you had fun?"

His lips tilted in what looked like a cross between a smile and a grimace.

"There," she said triumphantly, "you did have fun."

"And how, pray tell, did you come to that conclusion?" he demanded, but his lips were tilting precariously by now.

"Because you're smiling."

This time, when she took his hand and pulled him along, he didn't resist.

Inside the parlor, the furniture had been pushed to the sides, and a blanket had been spread across the thick Oriental rug.

"We're eating on the floor?" he asked.

"My invitation said it was a picnic—since our other one didn't turn out so well."

Their glances caught. She looked at his lips, remembering, before she turned away sharply.

"Stephen." Adam strolled in with a plate of food and

a glass of lemonade made from imported lemons. "Didn't expect to see you here."

Stephen could have said the same to his brother, but refrained. He was not going to let irrational jealousy flare up once again. He was not a jealous man. "I didn't expect to be here myself."

Maeve bustled in with Rose right behind her, each carrying trays laden with food.

"Ah, Mr. St. James," the cook said, "so good it is that ye came. Mistress Belle was up all night planning this party, she was."

Stephen didn't know how to respond. Adam, as usual, had no such problems. "Come sit down, Stephen. Have something to eat," he said as he plopped down on the floor.

"The mistress here made everything herself," Rose added proudly.

Belle blushed as she guided Stephen further into the room and gestured to a spot on the floor where she obviously expected him to sit. Amazingly, he did.

Stephen was stunned by the sheer quantity of food. If they had not been sitting on a blanket in the middle of the floor, the affair would in no way resemble a picnic. Each place was set with leaded crystal and fine bone china. A large array of dried flowers graced the center, and Stephen wondered what kind of a party she could put on if she were actually entertaining at a table. In spite of himself, he was impressed.

Though not for long.

The first bite he took nearly broke his jaw. He was remotely aware of Adam's sudden grunt of surprise when he, too, took a bite. But Stephen's attention was focused on his all-consuming effort to chew the meat without dislodging a tooth.

"Do you like it?" Belle asked, her eyes wide with what Stephen could only call a mixture of hope and resignation.

Adam guzzled first one glass of lemonade then another. Stephen managed to swallow without choking, though his jaws throbbed from the effort. Belle waited expectantly. Maeve and Rose and even Hastings waited for his answer, as well. Oddly, he hated to disappoint any of them.

"After the 'humh' you gave me when I told you I hadn't prepared the food for our other picnic," Belle stated shyly, "I wanted to show you that I *can* cook."

Well, she had showed him all right, he thought grimly, though she hadn't shown him that she *could* cook. Good Lord, a starving man would be hard-pressed to eat the fare set before him. He rubbed his jaw in thought. "Indeed, Belle, you have certainly shown me," he hedged, at which Adam choked on his third glass of lemonade.

"You're pleased, then?" she persisted.

The sight nearly broke Stephen's heart. God, how had he ever thought that she didn't care what people thought about her? Plainly, she wanted desperately to please despite the antics that again and again appeared to prove otherwise. The sight almost made him have another go at the meat. Almost. Reason, however, told him neither his teeth nor his stomach could take any more.

With a dignity and politeness that had served him well over the years, he offered, "Of course I'm pleased. I'm pleased that you would make such an effort on my behalf."

"You hate it!" she cried in a burst of emotion that made Stephen jump.

"What are you talking about? I never said that."

"You might as well have. 'Pleased about the effort.' It's the same as saying a woman has a nice personality and makes her own clothes. Everyone knows what that means! That she's as ugly as a dog! Oh, God, I'm a failure!"

"That's not true!" he blurted out, his mind searching for a way to soothe her. He was on the verge of out and out lying when it came to him. "You are not a failure. There are days when the Bulfinch House couldn't prepare a meal as fine as this." This wasn't a lie. There *were* days, when the chef was laid up with a raging fever and Bertrand was forced to let the washboy cook, that the food was deplorable. But Belle didn't have to know that.

She eyed him suspiciously. "Really?"

A smile tugged at his lips. "Really."

Her burst of joy brought audible sighs of relief from Maeve, Rose, Adam, and even Hastings. Stephen glanced over at the butler, and was oddly pleased when the old retainer offered him a nod of approval.

Just then, the bang of the brass knocker sounded through the house. Hastings went to the door and returned a few moments later, announcing the arrival of a Mr. Dubois.

"Mr. Dubois!" Belle exclaimed, pushing herself up off the floor.

Both Stephen and Adam stood automatically.

"He's here?" she demanded of Hastings.

"Yes, madam."

"So soon?"

Hastings seemed at a loss. "Yes, madam. So soon."

"Oh, my stars! He's here!" Belle hurried through the doorway to the foyer.

Stephen glanced at Adam in question, who only shrugged his shoulders.

Seconds later, Belle pulled a stranger into the room. "Stephen, Adam, please meet Mr. Dubois, my artist!"

When Stephen looked uncertain, Belle added, "You know, Marvin!" She turned to the painter. "Mr. Dubois, my neighbors, Stephen and Adam St. James."

Stephen looked the length of the man who held what must be a canvas underneath a white sheet of muslin. *This* was the man she had found in the museum? He was short and fat and balding, and Stephen felt an irrational need to smile.

Belle twirled back to the artist. "Let me see it! I've been waiting so patiently, but now I don't think I can wait a second longer."

"Madame will be pleased," Mr. Dubois said with an arrogant smile and a suspiciously thick French accent. "Marvin Dubois's work is always worth waiting for."

Stephen thought the man looked more the butcher than the painter, and he couldn't imagine that anything underneath the white drape could resemble art. Besides, his accent sounded fraudulent, and moreover, what true Frenchman was named Marvin?

The supposed artist studied the room, looking toward the windows. At length, he said, "Over here." He bustled over to the window, pushed the draperies wide, then turned back toward the room like an actor expecting applause. When he had determined he had everyone's attention, he removed the white cover with a flourish.

Muted sunlight streamed into the silent room. Everyone stared, first at the painter, then at his painting. Stephen nearly shook his head. He had obviously been correct. This man was no artist.

Stephen turned back to Belle to say just that. But the sight that met his eyes stole his breath away. Belle stared at the painting, the excitement frozen on her features, before slowly, gradually, her eyes darkened, her smile hardened, and her flushed cheeks blanched. "What is this?" she demanded, her voice strained.

Marvin's eyes widened. "Why, your father, of course."

"Of course, nothing!" She strode forward, her limp pronounced, until she was mere inches from the painting. "This is not my father!"

"Of course it is," the painter stammered, glancing down at the picture as if perhaps he had mistakenly brought the wrong canvas. "No, see, it *is* your father. Just as you described."

"This is nothing like I described!" Her voice grew shrill.

Stephen and Adam watched. Hastings stood in the doorway. Rose and Maeve peered from behind him.

"This doesn't look anything like him!" Belle said, taking a step back. "It can't!"

"But madame—"

"You told me you could paint!" she cried angrily. "And I believed you!"

She threw her head back and laughed, but Stephen could see the laughter didn't reach her eyes.

"Madame, please," Marvin begged her. "This is exactly as you described."

"My father's forehead is high. Regal! Like a king's! His nose is patrician, his shoulders are broad. This," she sneered, waving her hand at the painting, "is rubbish! Do you hear me, rubbish!"

Stephen looked on. She was dazzling and repulsive, alluring and repellent. She was dressed bizarrely, but looked more beautiful to him than any of the perfectly dressed women he had seen around the world. One minute she was laughing, the next she was raging mad. More proof that the rumors about her were true. But oddly, that didn't seem to matter. He wanted to go to her, to comfort her, and he found that he didn't particularly care why.

"Belle," he said softly.

Everyone looked at him, including Belle, who swung around to face him. When their eyes met, he saw her surprise. Then he saw the red creep back into her cheeks, but this time, he knew the red was caused not by excitement but embarrassment.

"It's all right," he said to her as if no one else was in the room. "We'll get another painter. In fact, I know of one who could do it. I'll contact him immediately."

"No, it's not all right," she cried, raising her hands to her cheeks and pressing hard. "It's not all right at all."

Belle glanced from Stephen to Adam, then to the servants in the doorway. She took in the painting one last time, pressing her eyes closed, before she rushed awkwardly from the room without another word, the picnic she had so painstakingly planned forgotten.

"I did exactly what she told me," Marvin lamented with an exaggerated sigh. "I swear to you, *monsieurs,* exactly what she told me."

But the others ignored him.

Stephen started to follow Belle, but was stopped at the door when Hastings placed a restraining hand on his arm. Stephen gave the man a look of hard resolve meant to put him in his place. Hastings only pulled his shoulders back and said, "Leave her be, sir, please."

"Maybe he's right, Stephen," Adam said from across the room. "I don't know how much more she can take."

Stephen's jaw clenched as he glanced back and forth between the men who tried to keep him from Belle. What did they think he intended to do? Hurt her? He only wanted to help her. But was that truly all he wanted from her?

"Despite what you think," he said tightly as he turned to go to her, "I have no intention of hurting Belle."

Adam took a step forward. "I know you'd never do it intentionally."

Adam's words stopped Stephen cold, piercing him in a way that he didn't understand. He didn't turn back. "Is that what happened to you, Adam?"

His brother's lack of response was answer enough. A great heaviness pushed at Stephen's shoulders.

"Well, now," Maeve said, breaking into the silence. "Best be gettin' about cleanin' up."

Reality washed over Stephen. Here he stood, saying things that he normally wouldn't say even in the privacy of his own home, much less in someone else's. What was happening to him? He should leave this house, leave Belle Braxton alone just as his brother had said. But then he caught sight of the painting, and saw not the portrait of a man captured ineptly on canvas, but the image of Belle, her pain etched in his mind.

With that he slipped by Hastings and headed up the long stairway that led to the upper regions.

He found her upstairs, on the top floor, sketching furiously on a large pad of paper. He stood quietly for some time, uncertain what to do. The sight tore at him. He wanted to wrap her in his arms, to protect her from a world she was not quite at home in. He wanted to make things right, still her upset. But how? he wondered.

"Belle," he whispered at length.

She looked up with a start, her blue eyes wild, tears streaking her cheeks. Her fingers stilled in their task. "I can't remember what he looks like," she said, her voice tortured.

Stephen's brow knitted as he sank down onto the floor beside her. "Who, Belle? Your father?" he asked gently.

"Yes," she groaned. "My papa. I don't remember what he looks like."

Her tears came again. But this time Stephen didn't wait. He pulled her into his arms, and after only a slight hesitation, she pressed her head against his chest and cried.

"There, there," he soothed, his hand stroking her head as if he had done it a million times. "What do you mean you don't remember what he looks like?"

"I just don't, is all. I can't see him clearly anymore."

"You can hardly gauge your recollection on that canvas downstairs. Your Mr. Dubois is no artist, love."

"Oh," she groaned, "that doesn't matter. I can't remember. Truly can't. When I was describing him to Mr. Dubois, I knew I was having trouble remembering, but I denied it. I had hoped that once I saw the portrait it would prove that I hadn't forgotten." Her hands fisted against his chest. "It only proved that I have."

He pulled Belle close, unexpected emotion sweeping through him as he suddenly recalled a time so long ago. "It was about a year after my parents died," he began, his voice barely a whisper, "when I realized that I couldn't remember the sound of my mother's laughter."

The muted winter light seeped through the windows, wrapping around them like the silken threads of a spider's web. "A year after the accident," he continued, "it hit me. I couldn't hear her laughter any longer, couldn't remember what it sounded like. I searched my mind frantically, day after day, trying to find the memory buried away somewhere, the memory of the sound."

"Oh, Stephen."

He took a sharp deep breath. "But no matter how hard I tried, I couldn't remember. Her face was still vivid, but only because a painting had been done of her just before she died. Her laughter, however, was gone. But I loved her," he said fiercely. "Truly I did."

He looked down into Belle's eyes, his own dark and intense. "You may have forgotten what your father looks like, but he will always be in your heart."

After a moment, a wry smile crossed his lips as he touched the tears on her cheek. "I know that for certain. Every time I turn around, you're telling me something about that father of yours. If I were an insecure man, I might be jealous."

He looked at her with a caring softness. "What matters is that you obviously love him very much."

His intention was to ease her, to help her. His heart clenched when she only pressed her eyes closed, tears cascading down her cheeks.

"Not enough," she whispered. "Oh, dear Lord, not enough."

CHAPTER
FIFTEEN

The day was cold, the earth hard. It had taken six grown men to dig the grave.

Browning Holly stood beside the casket, staring, tears freezing on his cheeks. Young, sweet Belle stood beside him, frozen with grief, but with uncertainty as well. Her father hadn't uttered a word to her since Doctor Williams had pressed her mother's eyelids closed two days before and said she had gone to heaven.

Her father had seemed confused, unable to grasp the truth of the doctor's words. But Belle had understood. Even at twelve years of age she had known her mother was dead.

Scarlet fever had come to their valley, wiping out friends and neighbors, sometimes whole families. But Browning and Belle had survived. Though with the way her father didn't speak now, Belle was afraid that he was getting sick, too.

The same men who had dug the grave lowered the casket into the earth. Grief threatened to overwhelm Belle. Her mother, gone, forever, buried.

What if she wasn't really dead? Belle suddenly wondered, her mind swirling with panic. What if she was just asleep, tired? What if she woke up in the box, blackness all around, screaming? Would anyone hear her?

Belle's heart hammered in her chest and she started

to ask her father, ask him to make sure she wasn't awake in the box, trying to get out. Her father's large calloused, ungloved hand hung at his side. Carefully, she reached over and tried to take his hand.

He glanced down at her with a start. "Madeline," he breathed.

The word pierced Belle's heart. She knew she looked just like her mother, her father had told her often enough. But just then, she didn't want to look like anyone else; she wanted to look like Belle, his Blue Belle. "No, Papa. It's me, Belle."

She watched as his eyes widened, then filled with pain. She tried to wrap her fingers around his, expecting him to return her grasp. But his hand only stiffened as he turned back to the grave. For a second she held on anyway, her tiny gloved hand holding on. She started to speak, but stopped herself. The thought of that awful, glacial stare turned on her again made her drop her hand away.

Out of the corner of her eye she caught sight of the old farmer her father worked for. The man stared not at the casket but at Belle. With a shudder, she felt the need to press close to her father, but didn't.

No one, she suddenly realized with wisdom beyond her years, was going to help her determine if her mother was truly dead or help her deal with the old farmer. She would have to do things on her own now.

So she took a deep breath and forced herself to think of every detail of her mother's death. Eyes closed. Chest still. Skin unnaturally white. Lips stiff and blue. Yes, her mother was dead, Belle reasoned, her twelve-year-old mind sorting through the events. Her mother wasn't lying in the box trying to get out.

But the farmer? He was alive. Very much so, and staring at her in a way that made her blood run cold.

And on that day, standing next to her father, reasoning out such things, Belle Holly began to change.

In the days that followed the funeral, Belle made every effort to keep the house clean, cook the meals, wash the clothes, make the beds. Having helped her mother for years, she was fairly accomplished at most tasks, though cooking a decent meal and washing clothes in the cold winter proved nearly beyond her capabilities. For several days her father did nothing more than sit in a chair by the fireplace. He wouldn't eat the meals Belle offered. He wouldn't speak when she spoke to him. Frequently, he confused Belle with her mother. And when his mind was clear, he did nothing more than mutter and mumble about how he had failed to fulfill his promises.

Then, on the third night, the old farmer came and told him that if he didn't show up at work the next morning he would be replaced. Browning had stared at the man, but said nothing. And that was when Belle watched her father's stony grief begin to turn to anger—slow, hot, molten anger.

Belle looked on helplessly. In a matter of days, her once bright, vibrant, and wonderful father had turned first despondent with grief then riddled with anger. The father she had known disappeared, replaced by someone who scared her. At night she prayed that her mother wouldn't be dead, and that her old father would return. But in the morning, her mother was still gone, and her old father hadn't returned. The new father, however, went back to work.

Days turned into weeks and Belle continually tried to fill her mother's shoes. Her father began to speak to her.

"The meat is tough."

"The clothes have soap in them."

"The house is a mess."

Never enough. Nothing she did was ever enough. Never enough to make him love her again.

The following evening he didn't touch his meal.

"You should eat, Papa. It's not good to go without food."

His fist hit the rough hewn table making the dishware dance. "Don't you be telling me what I should and shouldn't do, girl! Just leave me alone!"

His anger sizzled through the room, scorching Belle. Never had her father spoken to her in such a way, crazed as much as angry.

And then he began to look at her strangely. "How old are you?" he demanded one night, surprising her.

"Twelve, Papa. Soon I'll be thirteen." He knew that, she was sure of it. Why had he asked?

"February fourteenth, isn't it?"

"Yes, St. Valentine's Day! You remembered!"

He seemed to consider her before he nodded his head, then turned away and didn't speak to her for the rest of the evening.

But he didn't have to. Her young, hungry heart burgeoned with joy. He had remembered. St. Valentine's Day. Her birthday. It was all the sign she needed to make her believe that everything was going to be all right. They would dance, if not in the grandest of ballrooms, then at home, just as they always did, on her birthday. The would share a fine meal, then dance in twirling circles. They would remember Mama. They would miss her dearly. But the love she and her father had shared would bloom once again. His anger would flee. And they would dance.

From then on Belle began to count the days until her birthday. She made plans. The meal. A cake. On her hands and knees, she polished the floor. She lived for February the fourteenth, the anticipation like food for a starving man. In only a matter of days her birthday would arrive, she repeated to herself every day upon waking, then again just before drifting off to sleep.

Just days until everything would finally be all right.

CHAPTER SIXTEEN

December fourteenth. St. Valentine's Day was only two months away.

Belle woke early in the morning, rain washing the windows blurry, and despite her sore leg, she leaped out of bed and hurried her ablutions. She wanted to get downstairs and check the progress of the ballroom. The construction had been going so well. Soon the men were bound to be done, and then everything would be all right. Her confidence wavered, but she pushed doubt aside with an ease gained from long years of practice. She took a deep, calming breath before she smiled and hurried out of the room.

Once downstairs, however, her smile faltered when she found the workmen packing up their tools, walls unfinished, chandeliers unhung, and the day just begun.

"What are you doing?" she cried, coming to a halt in the gaping hole which had yet to become a beautiful French doorway.

Several of the men grumbled, but didn't meet her eye, simply nodded toward the foreman.

"Mr. Wilson," she said to the man in charge. "Why are the men packing up? They've only been here a few minutes."

Mr. Wilson looked decidedly uncomfortable. "Another project," he mumbled.

"Another project! You can't take on another project when you haven't finished mine!"

When his work crew hesitated in their packing, he waved his hand to hurry them along. "Sorry," he muttered with his head down.

"Sorry? You can't do this!"

"Sorry," he repeated. "Nothing I can do. Like I said, we got another project."

Belle blinked in disbelief. "This makes no sense. When will you be back?"

Mr. Wilson grimaced. "Don't know."

"You don't know?" She stared at the man in shocked confusion, but slowly it was sinking in that for reasons unknown he was going to leave, and from the sounds of it he might very well never return. "Don't leave," she suddenly commanded. "I'll be right back." They might not listen to her, but they would certainly listen to Stephen.

The knowledge that she would have to rely on him infuriated her, but just then her ballroom was more important than her pride.

With that she hurried as best she could out of the room, down the stairs, through the front door, and over to Stephen's house. Wendell answered the door.

"Good morning, madam," he said kindly.

"Hello, Wendell. I need to see Stephen."

"Let me see if he's in."

After shutting the door behind her, Wendell headed for the breakfast room. Without waiting, Belle followed.

"Mr. St. James—"

"Stephen!" Belle burst in, cutting Hastings off.

Stephen and Adam snapped to attention. They sat at the long dining table, each with a copy of the *Boston Globe* before them.

"No," Stephen grumbled without preamble, returning his attention to the paper with determination.

"No? No what?" she wanted to know, her hands planted firmly on her hips, raindrops glistening in her hair.

"Just 'no' to whatever you were going to ask me." He turned the page.

Belle puffed up like a blowfish. "You can't say no before I ever ask you my question."

"Of course I can, and I have. See? No." He glanced at her and smiled.

Wendell shifted uncomfortably. "Mrs. Braxton here to see you, sir."

Stephen's smile flattened before he provided the retainer with a scathing glance, while Adam pressed his napkin to his lips to stifle a short burst of laughter.

"Stephen!" Belle's tone was incredulous. "You're being unfair!"

He took a sip of coffee. "Regardless," he said, setting the cup in its saucer, "the answer is still no."

His feelings for Belle had begun to shift in a direction that wasn't to his liking. But shift they had, whether he liked it or not, filling him with a perverse need to redouble his efforts to resist her.

"Stephen," she demanded. "You have to do something!"

Stephen, however, turned his attention to Adam. "I understand you have invited Clarisse Webster to join you at the Music Hall."

"Well, yes," Adam stated with a grin.

"What's playing? I haven't had time to—"

"Stephen! You're not listening to me!"

He paused, then hung his head with a groan. "Self-defense," he muttered ungraciously, conceding that ignoring her wasn't going to work.

"Stephen! Please! You have to do something!"

"So you've said," he replied with a sigh of resignation. "But what is it I have to do?"

"The workers! You have to make them go back to work."

Adam dropped his fork with a clatter to his plate. Stephen stiffened.

"They've stopped working," she explained. "Those arrogant men. I'd bet money, if I were a man they would do as I ask. But alas, I'm not, so you go tell them to get back to work. They say they have another project, but they haven't finished mine. They can't do that!" She took a deep breath and visibly tried to calm herself before she added, "Please, talk to them, Stephen. They'll listen to you."

He stared at her without speaking. She stood before him, a contrast of raging anger and budding hope, but beautiful beyond dreams. And her words, he thought with a bemused smile, were so simple yet so sincere that they made him feel like no one else made him feel—wanted, needed, alive.

How amazing, he thought, that this woman, so different from any woman he knew, so different from any woman he had ever wanted to know, could captivate him so. She was an astonishing combination of startling contradictions—of weakness and strength, uncertainty and courage, stunning beauty and astounding outrageousness. How amazing that this woman who clearly had a dark past, as evidenced by her crippled leg and the haunted look that frequently came into her eyes, could bring such unexpected light into his life.

And it hit him then, hard. He knew suddenly, with

blinding clarity, that he could redouble his efforts to resist her, even triple or quadruple them, all to no avail.

Because he wanted her.

That was nothing new, certainly. But he realized then that he wanted more. He wanted her forever. He didn't want to wear a path in the walkway between their houses. He didn't want to play music loudly in order to see her. He wanted to wake up in the morning and find her in his arms. He wanted marriage. To this woman. Man and wife. To have and to hold. Yes, forever.

His head spun at the realization. He wasn't sure if he should laugh or cry. Marriage, to Belle Braxton, to the Widow Belle Braxton, to the Crazy Widow Belle Braxton.

He shook his head in wonder, because none of that mattered. Truly he wanted to marry her, he realized with a certainty that made him believe he must have wanted her for a very long time, perhaps since that evening she asked to share his bread. Yes, he would share his bread with her, and his life as well.

"Stephen!" Belle demanded once again. "Listen to me!"

Adam cleared his throat, angry lines creasing his forehead. "This farce has gone on long enough," he snapped, pushing out of his seat and tossing his napkin down on the table. "If you won't tell her, then I will. Belle, the men aren't working—"

"But they will," Stephen interjected with a pointed glare at his brother that said as loudly as words to keep his mouth shut, "just as soon as I go over there and have a word with them."

"Have a word with them?" Adam's mouth dropped open and his eyes widened.

"Yes, I'll have a word with them."

"This . . . this . . . is outrageous!" Adam stammered. "What do you plan to tell them? That you have changed your—"

"Adam!" Stephen's voice rang through the suddenly silent room. "Enough," he finished more quietly. "I will go over and straighten this mess out."

Adam muttered under his breath. But Stephen ignored him, then guided Belle from the room.

Adam followed, glowering the whole way.

Once at Belle's house, Stephen confronted the foreman.

"But, sir—"

"No, buts, Wilson. I want this ballroom finished up as soon as possible."

"By St. Valentine's Day," Belle interjected. "For my birthday."

Stephen looked at her curiously before he nodded his head and added, "By St. Valentine's Day."

After a confused look, Wilson shrugged his shoulders and agreed.

"I knew you could do it!" Belle threw her arms around Stephen, hugging him tight, then pushed away to arm's length. "You really can be the grandest of men when you want to be."

Before he could respond, she turned and walked over to Wilson and his men to give additional instructions.

Stephen and Adam stood back and watched.

"Do you mind explaining this turn of events to me?" Adam asked finally, his tone scathing.

"What do you mean?" he asked. But of course he knew.

"You know damn well what I mean. You're the one who had Wilson stop the work. You were going to tell her today that the house is reverting to you. Instead, you act as if you're saving the day. What kind of game are you playing, brother?"

"Game? I'm not playing any games," Stephen said, still awash with the wonder of his realization, hardly affording his brother a thought.

"Then why are you letting them continue with the ballroom when you know you're getting the house back?"

"Because it will be easy enough to tear down the wall between this ballroom and mine to make one big ballroom once we are married."

A heartbeat passed. "Married?"

"Yes, married," Stephen replied simply.

"When did all this come about?"

"This morning, actually."

"This morning?" Adam eyed his brother speculatively and with not a little disbelief. "You decided this morning? What about Belle? When did she decide?" His blond brows drew together. "Or has she?"

A schoolboy's smile crossed Stephen's lips; a lock of dark brown hair even fell forward on his forehead to make the picture complete. "No, but she will. She's not as indifferent to me as she likes to pretend. She'll come around. In fact, since you are so fond of parties, why don't you plan one? A huge ball on St. Valentine's Day, right here, to celebrate both our engagement and Belle's birthday. Keep it quiet, though. I'd like it to be a surprise."

"Don't you think you're jumping ahead of the game?" Adam's face was etched with concern.

Stephen only smiled. "No."

"Then when do you expect to tell Belle of your plans?"

Stephen ignored the sarcasm in Adam's voice. "Soon. But not yet. I'm only just becoming accustomed to the idea myself." His boyish grin widened. "And I'd like a chance to woo her. We've done nothing but argue for the most part since we met. I'd like a chance to change that before I tell her of my plans."

"Just like that," Adam scoffed. He ran his hand through his hair and followed Stephen's glance toward Belle, who was just leaving the room.

When she didn't bother to usher the brothers out or at the very least say good-bye, Stephen only chuckled at what he was rapidly beginning to think of as typical Belle. But when Adam spoke again, any humor he had felt fled.

"She's a wounded bird, Stephen."

Stephen tensed, but Adam continued. "If you insist on pursuing her, tread carefully, please."

Turning abruptly to face Adam, Stephen searched for words through the churning of his thoughts. He was angry, angry with Adam, or so he told himself. But deep down inside he was ignoring the glimmer of truth with which his brother's words rang. He did have to be careful, because if he wasn't, he might end up hurting her. But that wouldn't happen, he reassured himself with an arrogant nod. He was doing what was best for Belle, not what would hurt her.

After a moment, he held out his arm. "Do you see this arm?"

Adam's eyes narrowed in question. "Of course I see your arm."

"Good as new. With the exception of rainy days, I don't even know I was shot."

"Well, yes." Adam grimaced. "I can't tell you how relieved I am—"

"Against all odds," Stephen said, cutting off his brother, stepping closer, intent. "When the doctor told

me it was useless, Belle said the man was a fool. Against
all odds, I have regained the use of my arm."

"Yes." Adam took a step back. "I'm pleased, but—"

"Just as against all odds I will make Belle Braxton my
wife."

Adam left. Stephen stood among the workmen in the
space that was rapidly becoming a ballroom, a mirror image of his own. Feelings that he could hardly fathom
surged through him. Trepidation, yes, but mostly happiness and intense excitement.

He tempered his feelings with caution. No matter
how confident he had sounded to Adam, he wasn't nearly
as certain of his abilities to convince Belle to marry him
as he had led on. But what woman didn't want to marry?
Over the years, more than his share of women had
wanted to marry him. After all, he had what most women
wanted. Reasonable looks. Good reputation. Fine family
line. Money. But therein lay his concerns. His experience
was with other women, not Blue Belle Holly. She seemed
to have little interest in what most other women wanted
from a man.

But he would convince her. He would find a way to
make her see how right it was for them to marry. A smile
spread on his lips. Yes, he would find a way.

When he didn't locate her in the parlor or kitchen or
any other room on the first and second floors or even the
third, he took the stairs to the top. The fourth floor was
quiet. The sounds of the workmen were distant, dis-
jointed. Making him feel alone.

"Belle," he called.

No answer. Silence save for the rain tapping its relentless staccato against the roof.

He made his way down the dim hallway to the room

he had found her in once before. Her bedroom. Her sanctuary, he thought uncomfortably.

She stood with her forehead pressed against the windowpane. He could see her gossamer reflection in the glass, distorted by the rain. He watched her without moving. The sight of her brought that surge of emotion he wasn't sure he would ever get used to. She struck him with a mixture of fierce desire and a fierce need to protect her. His desire to flee had been washed away like soot beneath the rain.

He took her in, silently, not alerting her to his presence. He could have looked at her for hours.

"Thank you."

Her voice startled him. "Pardon?"

"Thank you." She didn't turn from the window, though she pushed away slightly, until only her shoulder pressed against the hardwood window casing.

"Thank you for what?" he asked, stepping into the room.

Her unladylike snort echoed in the room, making him laugh. Even her snorts were filling him with joy today.

He took the few remaining steps that separated them until he stood just behind her. But his smile faltered when he saw the trace of tears on her cheeks glistening in the gray winter sunlight, checking his joy. "What's wrong? The men are back at work. Your ballroom will be completed by Valentine's Day."

When she didn't respond, he gently took hold of her shoulder and turned her back to face him. "What's wrong, Belle?" he persisted.

"Nothing," she said with a forced smile.

He ran the tip of his finger along the glistening path of her tears. "Are you telling me this is nothing?"

With a sad laugh she turned back to the window. "It's the rain. It makes me . . . cry," she said, her voice barely a whisper.

"Why does it make you cry?"

She stood there as if thinking. At length she shrugged her shoulders. "It makes me want to escape. To sunnier places, so I can run my toes through the sand, with the sun burning a kiss on my skin. To watch that huge heated orb fade from yellow to red then purple as it lowers on the horizon. To taste water and wine. To dance with destiny under the stars." She took a deep sighing breath. "And to still my mind—most of all, to still my mind."

He felt the tremor of emotions course through her body, and he knew if he turned her around, once again he would see that look in her eyes which spoke of the deep sorrow he was afraid he would never fully understand. "What is it in your mind that you want to still, Belle? Tell me, please."

She turned to him abruptly, her long hair swinging out, and looked up into his eyes. Her own were intense as if she sought something from him. He had the feeling that she expected him to know what it was, to understand her simply by looking into her eyes, just as she had that day outside his office. But this day he refused to let it pass. "Truly, I don't know, Belle. Tell me."

He would have sworn a flash of disappointment flared in her eyes. But then, very carefully, she reached up and touched his forehead, making him forget.

He didn't move as she ran her fingers along his brow, then down his temple and cheek until she came to his lips. When she pressed her fingers to them like a delicate kiss, he opened his mouth and very carefully took one finger in.

She sucked in her breath when he wrapped his fingers around her wrist, pulling her arm down to his side. Slowly, he ran his hands up to her shoulders. When he bent his head to kiss her, she didn't turn away, but accepted him, almost desperately, he thought.

He felt her intake of breath against his lips and his body surged with desire. With one hand he cupped her jaw while the other tangled itself in her hair. He forgot about unfinished ballrooms and unanswered questions. His mind and body were filled with nothing more than desire.

"Belle," he murmured against her temple.

He kissed her again, slowly, nipping at her lips. When he flicked her lips with his tongue, she opened to him. He felt as much as heard her groan of pleasure when he touched his tongue to hers.

Their kiss grew intense. Belle locked her arms around his neck as his hands slid down her back, pressing her close. When he felt the sweet curve of her hips, he groaned his desire. He had known she had the body of an angel, but the feel of her beneath his hands was nearly his undoing. She nestled against his body, part woman-child, part wanton, so unlike anything he had ever experienced in the past.

How had he ever thought he could live without her once he had looked into those deep blue eyes and she had looked back at him as if she could see into his soul? Because he knew now that he couldn't. He wanted her, desperately, as if he were the wounded one, and she the savior.

He held her tightly, afraid to let go. He could feel the beat of her heart, the curve of her body. She smelled of fragrant, wild prairies. The aroma was heady.

She sighed and looked up into his eyes before a tentative smile trembled on her lips. "You have a knack for wheedling your way into a person's life, Mr. St. James—little by little, until that person comes to the realization that if you were suddenly to disappear she might just miss you."

"Might?" he breathed.

She laughed outright. "Greedy, aren't we?"

"No," he whispered, his eyes intent, almost vulnerable. "Just strangely hopeful that it would be more than might."

The words stilled her heart. She had expected him to say something flip or disgruntled. Something she could deal with. But not that. Of course it was more than might. If he was to disappear from her life, she would definitely miss him—a great deal, she was afraid. And that was unacceptable.

She pushed free, then looked into his eyes. The desire she had grown used to, but the caring that she saw there now left her panicked and scared. He couldn't care. She didn't want him to care. She preferred his disdain.

When had his feelings for her changed? she wondered. Why had they changed? But this time when she looked into his eyes, looking for answers, she saw only the caring mixed with desire—the disdain utterly gone.

As much as she had cursed herself for making him angry, deep down inside she knew she did it on purpose. Stephen St. James was too strong. He was like a magnet that pulled her to him. The only thing that had saved her in the past was the fact that he had wanted nothing to do with her, had crushed his desire, had looked at her with disdain—until now. She could see it in his eyes.

"You should go," she stated, her tone short.

She watched his eyes begin to clear as he tried to make sense of her words.

"What?" he asked.

When he tried to take her arm and pull her back, she stiffened until he let go. "I want you to leave."

"Belle, talk to me. What has happened?"

"No, Stephen, there is nothing to talk about."

He looked at her for a long time, and she steeled herself against the intense need she felt to damn all else and lose herself in his arms. But she couldn't. Even if she weren't waiting for her father, she couldn't give in to Stephen. He might want her now, but not for long. No, not for long. She had learned that lesson ages ago.

CHAPTER
SEVENTEEN

"I'm worried about our Belle." Hastings stood in the kitchen slicing onions, a starched white apron tied around his waist, while Maeve stirred a pot of stew on the stove.

Maeve's hand stilled in its task. "Me, too, Mr. Hastings." She looked at the wall before her, then sighed and went back to stirring. "Her behavior is more erratic now than ever. At first I thought it was because of the holiday season. Christmas, ye know. It's not healthy for a young woman like our Belle to spend such a time alone. But now we are well into January, that blasted ballroom nearly finished, and still she is worse than ever. One minute she is laughing and gay, then the next . . ." Maeve shrugged her plump shoulders.

"The next, pardon me for saying, she is raving mad," Hastings finished for her. "And it's all because of that Stephen St. James, I tell you."

"Posh, he's not her problem."

"How can you say that? She might have been odd when first we arrived here, but as you said yourself, she has become downright erratic since she met that man. I tell you he's no good for her."

"Well, I disagree." Maeve sighed. "He *is* good for her. And if I may say, everyone needs someone to love them."

"Love her? My word, he doesn't even like her."

Maeve scoffed at this. "Just like a man, I tell you, not

seein' beyond the surface. Why else would a gentleman of Stephen St. James's standin' be actin' like such an idiot if he wasn't in love?"

Hastings stiffened. "Not all men in love act like idiots, Mistress Maeve."

Maeve continued to stir, laughing as if Hastings had told a joke, missing the sudden intensity that had crept into his voice. "Show me one, Mr. Hastings."

"Me," he said very quietly, though clearly.

At first the words didn't register in Maeve's mind, but when they did she twirled around like a schoolgirl, thick succulent sauce flying off the spoon as she turned. "You?" she asked amazed.

"Yes, Maeve, me."

They stood silently, staring at each other. When Hastings didn't elaborate, Maeve began to fidget. "Well, old man, are ye goin' to tell me who it is yer in love with or are ye just goin' to stand there and make me wonder?"

Hastings's features washed red. His stiff form stiffened even further. "With you, of course."

Maeve's face crumpled in joyous disbelief. And then she was in his arms, barreling into him with a force that nearly knocked him to the ground. "It's aboot bloody time," she murmured in a tiny voice that belied her sharp words.

"Ah, Maeve," he said, awkwardly stroking her hair.

Despite long years of training, it took a moment for Hastings to realize someone was knocking on the front door. When he did, he kissed Maeve on the forehead, stripped off his apron, then hurried up the stairs to the door.

"Mr. St. James."

"Is Belle in?" Adam asked.

Hastings took in the younger man's disheveled appearance. "One moment, sir, while I see."

Wrapping a woolen shawl tightly around her shoulders, Belle pushed out of her favorite overstuffed chair. Moving toward the window, she caught a glimpse of her reflection in the full-length mirror. She studied herself in the silvered frame for a long while, the sounds of her house fading into the recesses of her mind.

Though she couldn't put her finger on it, somehow she felt different. Her long dark hair, which was pulled up and away from her face, was the same. The color hadn't changed. Even the maddening tendrils that frequently escaped to curl softly about her face were doing just that. Her eyes were the same deep blue, and she was still the same size. Certainly, she looked no different today than yesterday or the day before.

Still, she felt she had changed.

But how? she wondered. Was it this house and the life she was finally carving out for herself and her father? Was it that her birthday was rapidly approaching and she was certain she would be reunited with her father? She stared hard at her reflection. Or did she feel different because Stephen had come into her life?

After several minutes passed, she sighed. Frustration grew. She didn't know.

She glanced around the room on the top floor that since she'd begun to build the ballroom had become her sitting and bedroom. Her sketch pad lay open on the table. The hat Stephen had bought for her hung on the back of a wood-slatted chair. This room, as no other in the house, was hers and hers alone. Nothing here for her father. And she loved it, more than all the others.

She closed her eyes against the sudden, nearly painful insight. That's what was different. In the days since she had tried to be kind to Stephen, she had spent more time thinking of that man than anything else. When she should have been searching out the musicians to play in her ballroom for her father, she had been dragging Stephen through the streets of Boston. When she should have been readying a bedroom for her father's arrival, she was preparing a picnic for the very man she had no business being with. There had been too many diversions taking her away from what she had come here to do, all adding up to the same persistent idea that had been simmering in the recesses of her mind with growing alarm each day.

Perhaps she wanted more from Stephen than she was willing to admit.

The thought took her breath away. She staggered back a step until she caught herself by grasping the windowframe. Her reflection washed pale in the mirror. It was not true, she immediately chastised herself. She wanted nothing more from Stephen St. James than friendship. *And his touch,* some deep voice said.

But in spite of her words, thoughts of trading stories in the winter by the fireplace, or watching butterflies in the gardens in the spring, or sharing a gentle kiss on a swing swirled traitorously through her mind. She longed to give parties, to attend the symphony, to work on charity auctions. She longed for a normal life, not a life of waiting for her father's arrival.

Because, perhaps, she thought suddenly, he wouldn't arrive.

She sucked in her breath. Her delicate hands pressed hard over her ears as if in doing so she could block the words out.

He was coming! He *was!*

"Mrs. Braxton." Hastings stood in the open doorway.

She whirled around, causing him to take a step back. "Is everything all right, madam?" he asked, his stern features creased with concern.

"Yes, Hastings," she said in a tone that was anything but fine. "What do you want?"

"Mr. St. James is here."

Her blue eyes lit with excitement. "Stephen's here? Downstairs!"

"No, Mr. Adam St. James," he quickly explained.

The light in her eyes dimmed. "Of course, Hastings. Send him up."

"Adam," she gasped a few moments later, forgetting her own concerns as she took in his disheveled appearance. "What happened to you?"

A wry smile crossed his lips. He walked across the rug and dropped down onto a small sofa that faced the fireplace. All traces of the smile disappeared. "Oh, Belle, what am I to do?" he moaned, dropping his head into his hands.

Without compunction, she went to his side. As a mother would a child, Belle pulled Adam into her arms and stroked his blond hair. "What is it, dear? Tell me what has happened."

After a moment he began to speak, slowly at first, then faster, until all that had been bottled up inside him spilled out in an angry, desperate rush.

Stephen stood in his study, rather pleased with himself this morning. He felt certain he was making progress in his pursuit of Belle. Someone might argue, he conceded, that many of their encounters did not end so well. But on the other hand, she had made it more than clear that she was greatly attracted to him. She wanted him, whether she was willing to admit it or not.

Things were definitely falling into place. Marriage was a perfectly logical arrangement. He needed a wife. She needed a husband. And since she was going to be *his* wife, he had gone out that morning and found a seamstress to make her a new wardrobe. While he was at it, he had hired a renowned French chef to teach her how to cook, and a leading authority on manners to teach his dear Belle the finer points of etiquette.

He pulled his coat on. He couldn't wait to see the look on her face when he told her.

"Oh, Adam, everything will work out," Belle said, trying to believe the words herself. But it was difficult. Anxiety crept back into her soul.

Adam was hurt, but she didn't know how to help.

Anxiety grew into panic, wrapping around her, making it difficult to breathe.

We will dance, Blue Belle.

The words hit her hard. "Not now," she whispered into the room. She pushed away.

Tears streaked Adam's stubbled cheeks.

"Adam, dear, why don't you go splash some water on your face? There's a basin in my room."

She needed a moment alone, to gather herself.

She breathed a sigh of relief when Adam disappeared through the doorway that led to her bedroom.

In the grandest of ballrooms.

With wild eyes, she searched the room. She searched for something to command her attention, something to wash her mind clean. But the music was gone, and she still had found nothing else to take its place.

Except for Stephen.

"Has anyone told you today how beautiful you are?"

Belle twirled around at the sound of the voice. His voice. As if her thoughts had made him appear.

"Stephen," she breathed, afraid that her imagination was playing tricks on her.

Her heart pounded. Adam and painful memories were pushed aside, at least for the moment, as Stephen stood no more than a few feet from her, so handsome that he took her breath away. He wore a loose-fitting white shirt and thigh-hugging black pants, so unlike the stiff black coat and trousers he normally wore. His black hair was tousled, as if he had been out in the wind, and she had the sudden need to run her fingers through the mass, smoothing it back, relishing the feel.

Tears stung her eyes. God, he made her feel things she didn't understand—more than simply quieting her mind. Her eyes nearly fluttered closed as those unfamiliar feelings washed over her.

"Good thing I'm younger than Hastings. He's right behind me, as usual, attempting to throw me out on my ear."

Relief swept through her. His words were real. He was truly there. Once again, he had saved her. "Oh, Stephen," she practically sang. "How lovely it is to see you."

He chuckled and stepped forward into the room. "This is a change. I'm not used to receiving such a welcome." His smile turned devilish. "There must be a reason," he teased. "You must want me to engage in some outrageous act and I have fallen into your hands by arriving on my own."

His smile was lopsided and she yearned to reach out and touch his lips. Perhaps he was correct. She did want to coerce him into an outrageous act. She wanted him to kiss her and hold her . . . and vanquish the darkness.

"Miss Belle!"

Hastings stopped in the doorway and slumped against the frame, his normally perfectly combed gray hair falling across his forehead, his breathing labored as if he had run the whole way.

"Sorry, Hastings," Stephen said. "Had to do it. If it were up to you, I'd never get to see Mrs. Braxton." He walked back and actually wrapped his long, strong arm around the servant's shoulders. "Rest assured, I'm pleased that you feel so protective of her."

Hastings was as shocked as Belle at the change in the notoriously proper Stephen St. James. Putting an arm around a servant? Belle had the unexpected thought that perhaps there was something in the weather that was making people act strangely.

Stephen slapped the man on the back good-naturedly, then turned him back toward the stairs. "She's safe with me, not to worry."

"But . . ." Hastings looked at Belle.

"It's all right, Hastings." She met Stephen's gaze. "He can stay."

After a moment of clear indecision, Hastings said, "As you wish," before disappearing down the hall.

"He's a good man," she said softly.

"I agree with you now, though just a few weeks ago I was ready to wring his neck."

Belle turned away, her gown swirling a bit around her ankles. "I think he still wants to wring yours."

"Probably," he responded, his smile boyish as he stepped further into the room.

His good cheer, however, was lost on Belle when she suddenly remembered Adam. What could she do? What should she do? Panic threatened once again. But then Stephen came up beside her, and when he did, their shoulders collided softly. The touch was electric. She felt it. She was certain he felt it, too.

But the moment collapsed, Stephen's chiseled features hardening, when Adam stepped through the doorway, out of her bedroom.

Adam stopped at the sight of his brother. "Stephen," he said, his tone self-conscious.

Belle's relief died an unmerciful death at the look that came into Stephen's eyes.

"What are you doing here?" Adam asked.

Stephen stared at his brother. "A better question might be, what are you doing here?" His dark eyes ran the length of him. "Or need I ask?" His question hung in the air, his meaning clear.

Belle went to Adam, wrapping her arm around him. "You *should* ask. And the two of you should talk."

Stephen looked on, the sight making his throat tighten. Belle stood next to Adam, caring and concerned, protective. His jealousy grew.

Suddenly, he was years younger. He saw his mother comforting Adam, whispering words of love. Stephen felt the stinging bite of regret. He had always been jealous of Adam's easy relationship with their mother. So often as a child Stephen had longed to throw himself in her arms and cry. But that wouldn't do. His father wouldn't have approved. Even Stephen, at such a young age, had known that there was a different set of rules for him than for his younger brother. Sometimes he hated the fact, though at other times it made him proud. He had made his father proud. Growing up, that had been all-important to him. As a result, he had chosen to have a solid relationship with his father over an easy relationship with his mother. And as he stood silently, his throat tight and aching as Belle wrapped her arms protectively around Adam, Ste-

phen realized with a sharp pang of regret that his mother
had known he had made a choice.

Would he lose Belle, too? Would Adam's easy way
gain Belle's love?

With his heart clenched and cold, he started back
toward the door.

"Stephen!" Belle said. "Please don't go."

"Don't leave because of me," Adam added. "It's not
what you think."

Was it? Wasn't it? Stephen didn't know.

He looked back. They stood together, Adam and
Belle, as motes of dust, caught in a long ray of sun,
drifted through the room. He knew they shared some sort
of affinity that he neither understood nor could duplicate.
And like so many times in his past he felt alone, discon-
nected.

Belle came forward and touched his arm. "Stephen.
Please don't leave."

Stephen cleared his throat uncomfortably, then
started to step away.

"Don't go," she whispered, the words like a caress.

His heart tightened in his chest. He didn't want to go.
When he turned back, Stephen saw something different
in her eyes. With a start, it occurred to him that her
words hadn't been a caress. They had been a plea. Her
eyes were desperate, filled with that haunted desperation
he hated to see. He realized then that regardless of whatever it was that she shared with Adam, his brother
couldn't extinguish the darkness in her eyes. But somehow, he could. The thought gave him hope.

As if sensing this truth, Adam headed for the door.
"I've got to go," he said with a smile that didn't quite
meet his eyes.

"Please stay, Adam," she said. "The two of you need to talk."

"No. Not now, at least," he equivocated. "I have an appointment."

And then he was gone, the sound of his footsteps receding down the stairs.

Belle and Stephen stared at the empty doorway.

"Talk to him, Stephen. He needs you." She turned to face him. "Just as I need you . . ."

Surprise snaked down his body.

". . . to kiss me," she added almost desperately.

He stood speechless. And when he finally spoke, his voice was strained. "I don't think that is wise," he finally managed.

It wasn't embarrassment that he saw fill her eyes, but hurt, as if he had rejected her. "Oh, Belle, don't look at me like that."

"You think I'm horrible. First, I'm never quite the lady you think I should be; now, I'm throwing myself at you, proof that I'm no lady at all."

He knew he should make rational explanations. He knew he should tell her that he wanted to hold her and to kiss her, but that he respected her, and therefore would wait. The words, however, stuck in his throat. As always, he wanted her, propriety and better intentions be damned. "You have proved nothing but that you care for me as much as I care for you."

A sudden wariness sprang to life in her eyes. But then it was gone, as if imagined, when he took her into his arms. She tensed only for a moment before she melted against the hard strength of his chest.

He kissed her hair, then her forehead, his lips trailing lower until he kissed her cheek. And then, amazing him, she turned her head ever so slightly until her lips met his.

He groaned at the touch, savoring the contact, running his hands up her arms to the slim column of her neck. Their kiss became heated. He nibbled at her lips, his tongue flicking, feeling. At his insistence, she hesitantly opened her mouth, her body melting into his when their tongues intertwined. She pressed closer, as if seeking the fire his fingers ignited as they danced over her body.

"Stephen," she murmured, her eyes closed.

He pulled back to look into her eyes. He held still until her eyes fluttered open, vivid blue colored with desire.

"How is it, Belle, that you make me lose control?"

Before she could speak, he pulled her back with a groan, his lips capturing hers in a savage embrace.

His mouth slanted over hers, almost desperately. "Oh, God," he murmured against her lips, growing hard and long against her belly.

His hand trailed down her back, pressing their bodies together.

She felt his heart pounding against his ribs, though they were pressed together so tightly, Belle was uncertain where his heartbeat ended and hers began. Unwanted memories were gone as her fingers found their way into the thick strands of his glossy dark hair. Her senses reeled when his tongue demanded entry to the hidden recesses of her mouth once again to explore and taste, leaving her shaking with longing.

"Belle," he murmured. "Sweet, sweet Belle."

Her body was flushed with desire, awash with waves of a new and overwhelming need. With trembling limbs she clung to him, lost in the swirl of mounting passion that centered at the core of her being. Her body throbbed with sensation, and she wanted more.

His hands trailed up over her hips and along her sides until the heels of his palms pressed intimately against the full swell of her breasts. The contact made her heart pound even harder, with both fear and anticipation. When she felt his long, strong fingers move to the row of tiny buttons down the front of her dress, she thought of stopping him for no more than one sanity-filled moment. She wanted to feel his hands caress her bare skin. She wanted his touch. Finally, she thought. Finally she would know.

The buttons on her gown gave way, and her chemise fell free with surprising ease under his deft manipulations. She nearly commented on the fact but was stopped when his fingertips touched her skin.

She sucked in her breath when he breathed her name. Her head fell back and her body trembled when he opened his hot mouth on the pulse in her neck.

He swept her up in his arms and carried her out of the sitting room and into her bedroom. With great care, he lowered her onto the thick feather bed, until she lay on her back, his hard chest pressed against hers.

"You are so beautiful," he said, his gaze worshipful.

"So are you," she whispered, making him smile.

But his smile disappeared when he looked down and took in the rosy peaks of her breasts. Without another word, he lowered his head and pulled one nipple deep into his mouth.

She arched her back against the bed and moaned. Never had she felt such a sensation. Her hands came up and tangled in his hair, pressing him closer. He laved one nipple, then the next, while his hand reached down and gathered the long folds of her skirt, until he touched the sweet curve of her hip. He moved slightly to the side until only one strong leg covered hers.

His hand trailed over her body beneath her velvet gown and she whimpered with the intensity of her response. She wasn't sure which would be worse—for Stephen to stop, or to continue. She felt as if she were burning up, hot, molten, wanting more, but what exactly she was yearning for, she had no idea.

She gasped when his fingers slipped beneath her pantaloons and brushed against the triangle of hair between her legs. "Stephen!"

"Shhh," he whispered. "Let me love you."

And then with maddening attention he teased the lips of her sex. She held on to him, afraid to let go. When his fingers stopped, she was nearly overcome with embarrassment when of their own volition her hips moved against his hand.

"Sweet Jesus," he groaned, his manhood burgeoning almost painfully. "You are filled with so much passion." And then he was lost.

He slipped his fingers inside her body, slowly, again and again. Belle cried out her pleasure, and she was hardly aware when he nudged her legs further apart with his knees.

His fingers went deeper, brushing against a terribly sensitive spot that she thought would make her go mad. Her body started to move again of its own volition. Her hips immodestly sought his touch.

"Yes, Belle," he whispered, the words a caress against her ear, before he plundered her mouth once again.

With a clearly knowledgeable touch, his fingers continued to move, sliding against the slick walls of her womanhood. The intensity of feeling rose quickly this time, not building slowly, but starting at a level that left her breathless. She lost herself to the feeling, her hips moving to a rhythm he prescribed, until wave after wave of soul-shattering intensity washed over her and she cried out.

"Stephen," she breathed, wondrous, her body tingling as they lay together, bodies entwined.

She felt him tense, and after a moment he grasped her arms and gently forced their bodies apart. He took in the sight of her creamy breasts, revealed from beneath the bodice of her gown, and her hips, glowing white above thick black stockings. She didn't bother about her leg—didn't think about her leg. She only knew that she had just experienced something that she didn't know was possible.

She saw the awe return to his eyes along with the desire, and just when she thought he would pull her close again, she watched, helplessly, as he drew a deep, ragged breath, the muscles in his jaw working.

It seemed that his hands were trembling when he reached down and lowered her skirt, then slowly pulled her gown together and began to button the long line of fastenings. "I'm sorry, Belle," he said, the words strained. "I don't usually have so little control."

"Don't be sorry, Stephen." She halted the progress of his hands with her own. "I don't want you to stop."

His head came up and their eyes met.

"Yes, I want you to hold me, I want you to kiss me."

"Belle," he said, his tone warning.

The shadow of a smile lurked on her lips. If possible, Stephen's dark countenance grew even darker.

"Just once more," she said.

"Belle, no. Not yet."

Her head tilted to the side and her smile grew more bold. "When? Do I have to put on another picnic or tear down another wall?"

He looked at her for a long moment. "No, Belle. When we're married."

If he had said she should run for President, she couldn't have been more shocked.

"Damn," he muttered. "This was not how this was supposed to be."

"How what was supposed to be?"

"My proposal." Stephen took a deep breath. "I want you to be my wife, Belle."

With mouth agape, Belle stared at him, having no idea what to say. Marriage. Good God, no. Never again.

She moved away with a jerk and walked to the bureau, her hands smoothing a doily though her mind was not aware, her gaze distant.

Stephen followed. "Belle, look at me, please."

When she didn't, he gently turned her to face him. "Belle, don't you see? I want to marry you. I want to spend the rest of my life with you."

She could see he was serious. He truly did want her to be his wife. Though why, she couldn't fathom. Good heavens, they hardly got on together. They could conceivable kill one another within a year of marriage with the way they got along. But then the all too recent memory of their kiss and the soul-shattering event she had just experienced came to mind. Her body still trembled and was weak in the aftermath. And that made her smile. If they could just kiss and not talk, they might have a chance; she nearly said so out loud, but kept the words to herself, since she doubted Stephen would appreciate her humor.

With a sigh, she reached out and took one of his strong hands between her own. "Dear, dear Stephen. How kind you are."

Stephen's brow furrowed.

"I can't tell you how flattered I am by your proposal

of marriage. It is so sweet, but totally unnecessary. As I've said, I've already been married and have no interest in marrying again."

Stephen could hardly believe he had heard her correctly. *Sweet.* She had called his offer sweet?! he thought, his mind circling with disbelief. But more than having his pride wounded over having his offer of marriage tossed back in his face, he felt a pang in his chest over the fact that he was afraid that she was serious. And that was unacceptable.

His mind shifted through his thoughts, trying to make sense of the situation, trying to determine why she wouldn't marry him. Clearly, she was a complicated woman, but she enjoyed his company, sought him out, in fact. Something, however, made her hold back. But what? he wondered. Though of course he knew, or at least suspected. In some measure it had to be due to whatever had happened to her leg. And that was just it. What *had* happened to her leg? Would he ever be able to find out in order to help her deal with it, allowing her to move forward with her life and into his?

A stab of conscience halted his thoughts. Suddenly he felt selfish. He wanted Belle, and he was thinking only of himself. But then, he rationalized, he was also thinking of her. She needed him, he thought with an arrogance typical of a man who had gone through life having to force his way to success. He knew no other way. He could help her, and he would. If only he could convince her to marry him. But how?

He strode to the window. As he passed a small table, his eyes lighted upon a sketch pad which laid open. Amazingly, the drawing was good—very good, in fact. For a moment he wondered if she had found another artist. But then he saw the drawing pencils to the side and he realized with a start that Belle must have done the work herself.

"What's this?" he asked, all thoughts of marriage put aside as he stared at the drawing.

Drawn on the single sheet of heavy white paper was a man. He was big and burly. Rugged.

When Belle looked back and found the drawing, Stephen saw the surprise that sprang to life in her face as if she had never seen the picture before. She sucked in her breath, and red stained her milk-white cheeks. For a moment he wondered if he had been wrong, if someone else had made the sketch.

"What is it, Belle?" he asked, his words laced with concern.

"It's him," she breathed.

"Who?" By now he was truly confused.

She seemed oblivious to Stephen, only stared at the drawing. "I did it," she whispered, sounding amazed. "I can't believe I did it."

"Did what, Belle?" Stephen glanced back and forth between Belle and the drawing, unease beginning to filter through his mind.

"The sketch. It's him." She took a step closer. "When I was drawing, I just kept drawing and drawing, thinking I had failed until I couldn't stand it anymore. Late last night I tossed it aside." She brought her hands up to her cheeks. "I nearly threw it in the fire."

"What are you talking about Belle? Who is this in the drawing?" he demanded.

She looked back at him like a startled doe. Minutes ticked by, then she lowered her hands and a slow smile began to spread across her face. "It's my father."

He should have known. This father, who overshadowed everything Belle seemed to do, was the man staring back at him with harsh charcoal eyes.

"This is wonderful!" she chimed. "Such a good sign that I remembered."

"What did you remember, Belle?"

"I told you I couldn't remember what he looked like. And last night when I was drawing I was so intent that I couldn't see clearly. But now, looking at it unexpectedly, I see that it's him. I remembered what he looked like!"

She came over and picked up the drawing and held it at arm's length. After a while, she dropped her hands, the sketch held in one. "You didn't understand why I wouldn't marry you. And up until this second I thought that perhaps I had been wrong. But now I know I was right. He will come. And I can't marry you because my father is coming for me." She flung her head back and tried to twirl. "First we'll go to London, then Paris, and Geneva, Vienna. He's coming. I can feel it."

The muscles in Stephen's jaw tightened. "You've been saying that practically since the day I met you. And up until this drawing, I haven't seen hide nor hair of the man. What makes you think that just because you drew a picture of him means that he will return?"

Her head snapped forward, her porcelain features growing harsh with anger.

Stephen, however, couldn't let it go. "I don't know what your life was like before you came to Boston, but I do know that since you arrived, you have been telling me that your father is coming." He hesitated at the look that was rapidly filling her eyes. But he had come too far to turn back. "What if he doesn't arrive?"

Her reaction was swift and furious. "Don't say that! It's not true!" She threw the sketch aside, the sheaf of paper tumbling in the air before it settled among the motes of dust and seesawed back and forth until it fell to the floor. "You are a hateful man, Stephen St. James! You are hateful and jealous. You are jealous of my father just as you are jealous of Adam. But you're wrong about both of them. Adam is my friend, only my friend . . ." She looked at him with scathing eyes. "And my father will come for me."

She turned away abruptly, uncertainly, Stephen thought, making him feel that even she didn't quite believe her words. He started to go to her, but the sound of her voice, now void of anger, only soft and yearning, stopped him.

"He has to come. For our dance. In the grandest of ballrooms."

Though her back was to him, he could see that she had covered her eyes with her fingers. He felt as if his heart would breaking into a million tiny pieces. But still he didn't know what to say, or how to help.

"He *will* come for me," she stated emphatically, though her shoulders were rounded, seemingly with defeat.

CHAPTER EIGHTEEN

"If he's alive, get him here. If he's dead, get me proof."

"Yes, Mr. St. James," Nathan said, scribbling quickly on a pad of paper. "What did you say his name was?"

"Holly, from Wrenville. Browning Holly, I believe she told me once. Surely there can't be too many."

"Yes, sir."

Stephen stood before his office window, his hands thrust into his pockets, his brow furrowed in concentration. "And her husband. Find out everything you can about the man she was married to. Someone named Braxton in Wrenville, as well."

"Yes, sir. Is there anyone else you want me to inquire after?"

"No," Stephen replied after a moment. "There's no one else."

"Very good, sir. I'll get on it right away."

Nathan quit the room, leaving Stephen alone with his thoughts. In the distant harbor, visible from his office, boats pulled against their moorings, just as Stephen's mind pulled against the possibility that he couldn't make Belle his own. He had never failed at anything in his life. He found it unacceptable that he would fail at this.

What had transpired between them yesterday had done two things. It had made him want her more than ever after having experienced the full force of the passion that lay dormant, waiting to be awakened. Which in turn made him wonder why a widowed woman didn't know the first thing about making love.

When she had said she had never been kissed, then explained she hadn't been kissed like that, at first he had doubted, then grown into acceptance. He had no reason not to believe she had been married. But now? He had to wonder.

He sat down in his chair and rubbed his temples. He had known Belle for nearly three months now, had known he wanted to marry her for a month. Closing his eyes, he pressed back against the chair.

As much as he hated to admit it, as much as he hated to admit defeat, there was nothing in any of his dealings with Belle that could possibly lead a rational man to believe she would marry him. Hell, he sighed silently, she had told him so herself. And if there was one thing Stephen knew about himself, it was that he was a rational man. Or at least he had been until he met Belle Braxton.

Belle.

The word wrapped around him, soothing at first, until the hold tightened, squeezing him until he couldn't breathe. He felt as if he were on one of the roller coasters that had become so popular in the last few years. One minute up, the next plunging to the earth, his heart lodged in his throat.

As hard as he tried, he could determine no way to break through the barriers that she had erected around herself. And all because of this father of hers, perhaps even this husband who she said had worshipped the ground she walked on. How was he supposed to compete with a father, who was more than likely dead, and a husband, who by all accounts was? Yes, her husband. More questions. Always more questions than answers.

What kind of a man had she been married to that she

had never experienced passion? One who loved her dearly? He doubted that.

Soon, however, Nathan would find the answers. But what then? Stephen wondered. Would he confront Belle? Force her to admit the truth? That her father didn't exist and her husband hadn't loved her?

He closed his eyes and sighed. Of course he wouldn't. And as the sun drifted through the sky, then began to sink on the horizon, Stephen realized he was foolish to think that he would ever be able to convince Belle to marry him. He should simply sign the house back over to her. He should leave her alone, and then maybe, with time, he could get her out of his mind.

The thought left him empty with loss. Cold and bereft. But it was for the best, he reasoned. This relationship they shared was obviously no good for either one of them. Perhaps the sooner he accepted that fact, the better. For both of their sakes.

Tired beyond his years, Stephen pushed out of the chair, his body stiff from sitting for so long. Without straightening his desk or looking at his schedule for the next day, he strode from his office and made his way toward home.

His house was quiet when he pushed through the front door. Dinner would be waiting for him, but Stephen had no interest in food. He just wanted to go upstairs to bed and sleep. He had never been so exhausted.

Shrugging out of his coat, he tossed it on a chair before taking the stairs up to his room. The portraits along the walls mocked him, teased him with their cold, frozen stares. He turned away, into his room, seeking solitude.

But found Belle instead.

His mind reeled. His heart stilled. She sat by the window, staring out into the night, curled up in a wing chair.

She looked so sad and forlorn, like a child in need of comfort. He watched her as she watched something unknown in the distance. She didn't acknowledge him, but he knew she had to know he stood there. So he waited, his heart hammering, wondering why she had come.

"My favorite chair was ruined today," Belle said without looking back at him.

Her voice was soft and tiny, whispering through the room like a hesitant breeze. He stood very still, bracing himself against the sound.

"Your chair?" he asked, confusion lacing his voice.

"Poor Rose. She spilled lye soap on it. A huge spot. Right in the middle." She heaved her distress. "She's beside herself."

"You've come here to tell me about a chair?"

"It's an old chair." She pursed her lips, then said, "But I love it."

"What are you talking about, Belle?"

"My chair. My favorite chair. Rose tripped. But she's okay. Though my chair isn't. It's ruined."

"Then go out and buy a new one," he snapped. He saw her stiffen and hated the stab of pain he felt in his heart.

"I don't want a new one," she stated obstinately, with a strength that shimmered through the room. Then suddenly, unexpectedly, she jerked her head away, tears catching in a length of moonbeam.

"Ah, Belle," he said softly, his defenses crumbling like a decrepit buttress under a battering sea.

"You hate me, don't you, after everything I said to you at my house?"

He took a step closer, wanting to stay back, but unable to do so.

"I didn't mean it," she said. "I don't really hate you." She turned to him then. "Do you hate me?" she asked hesitantly.

"Sweet Belle," he whispered, the words nearly a groan of despair, before he dropped down beside her and took her into his arms.

He swept her up as if she weighed no more than a feather and buried his face in her hair. "I don't hate you, sweetheart. I could never hate you."

She pressed her cheek against his chest as he carried her toward his bed. With infinite care, he lowered her, his body following in her wake to lie down beside her.

"Thank you," she whispered.

"For what?"

"For not hating me."

His chuckle was haunted, but he didn't respond, only pulled her closer.

They lay together, each silent until Belle sighed and turned her face into his shoulder. He felt her silent sobs.

"What is it, Belle? Why are you crying? Is it because of your chair?" He asked the question in disbelief.

"Yes, it's the chair. I love that chair. And now it's ruined."

Dear Lord, what kind of person became so upset over a chair? he wondered, not liking the answer that tried to push into his mind.

"I know you think it's crazy to be so attached to a piece of furniture. Rose and Hastings and even Maeve had the same reaction."

Long minutes passed without another word from her. He felt as much as heard her sigh.

"I've had that chair for years. Since I was a child, then when I was married, and finally here when I moved to Boston." Her words were tight in her throat. "I can't remember a time when I didn't sit in that chair. Always so big, and warm . . . and comforting."

It was as if he could feel the blood singe her cheeks, and she quickly added, "It was silly, really. And I haven't thought of it as anything but a chair in years." She sighed. "But it was the only thing I had left from my past, left from the days when I was a child."

When life was better, he found himself surprised to think. "Lye soap or not, I'm sure I can have it repaired for you."

She sprang away from him, up on one elbow. "Really? You can fix it?"

As always, her beauty hit him hard. He realized then, with a start, as she looked at him with painfully blue eyes expectant, that he loved her. He didn't just want her because she made him feel alive. He wanted her because he loved her as he had never loved anyone in his life. This strange woman-child, with a past that undoubtedly held events which were better left buried, had woven her way into his life until he felt that if she were to disappear, he might unravel at the seams.

How had it happened? he wondered. How had someone he had no interest in, become such an important part of his life? But just then it hardly mattered. What mattered was that she was here with him, in his arms.

With his realization, he was forced to concede that in his proposal of marriage, he had failed to mention love. He had stated it as if it was a business proposition which she should be flattered to accept.

He wanted to tell her of his love, to wrap the words around her until she admitted that she loved him, too. He

sucked in his breath. Did she love him in return? he wondered. She had come here tonight not to ask him if he
still loved her, but because of some chair. The thought
that she might not love him was devastating. So he held
his words back. He had made a mess of his courting. He
had made a mess of showing her that he cared. He would
bide his time. He would *show* her that he loved her, then
tell her of his feelings when he asked her once again to be
his wife.

"Stephen," she said, shaking him, "you're not listening to me."

His smile grew luminous in the murky night. "I'm
listening, love. And first thing tomorrow morning, I'm
going to take your chair and have it repaired."

"You will?"

"Yes, of course I will." And he would, even if he had
to find the material and stuffing and repair the chair himself.

He looked up at her, his smile filled with all the happiness he felt. She was here, next to him, and he had
never felt so right.

She reached out, very slowly, and touched her finger
to his lips. The simple gesture sent tremors of longing
down his body.

"It's late, Belle. Let me take you home."

Her blue eyes darkened, then in turn seemed to consider. "I don't suppose you'd be interested in kissing me
again, instead?"

Interested? Dear Lord, he was more than interested.
He was desperate to kiss her. His body yearned to impale
her delicate womanhood again and again. But he
wouldn't. Not yet. This time he wouldn't lose control.

Her sigh drew his attention. "I know," she grumbled,

"I'm being much too forward. You don't have to kiss me." Her brow creased. "But please don't send me home."

He stared at her forever, knowing he should do the proper thing, but hating the look in her eyes. At length, he merely pulled her down beside him.

He pulled her close as she curled up in his embrace. Then with exhaustion battling an unbelievable happiness, he drifted off to sleep.

Belle lay in his arms. Waiting. At any moment he was going to kiss her. She knew it. He would make her feel all the wondrous feelings he had made her feel earlier. Her body tingled at the memory. But it wasn't the tickle of fingers drifting across her neck that she finally felt, but the whisper of breath making it clear that there would be no kissing tonight.

Disappointment licked at her mind, bringing with it a tremor of foreboding. She had slipped unnoticed into his house earlier despite better judgment. But when had she ever listened to better judgment? Tonight, however, she wished she had.

She should have simply left things with Stephen as they had been the day before—him ready to be done with her. She needed to break the tie, couldn't afford the tie. But today, as the hours had drifted by, she hadn't been able to leave it alone. She hated the thought of how she had acted. The thought of never seeing him again, the thought of never again feeling the things he had made her feel, left her scared and alone.

Despite that, or perhaps because of that, she shouldn't have come. She pushed from her mind the thought that the only reason she was feeling strong just then was because Stephen's arms were around her, holding her secure. She had relied on herself since she was twelve, almost thirteen. She would not become dependent on this man now. But as she lay there, she knew she was wrong. She had easily come to depend on him, to fix her house, to fix her chair. But he could never fix her life.

Belle shook the drowsiness from her mind and pushed herself up to look on the sleeping man. She ran her hand delicately over his high cheekbones, and across the half-moon scar, no less formidable even in sleep. Tears glistened in her eyes.

"I wish I could tell you that I love you," she whispered to this dark pirate-man who had become such an unexpected part of her life. But she couldn't tell him, and she wouldn't. She carefully pulled free, then quietly slipped away.

He woke in the morning. The room was dusted with pale gray light, announcing the sun's impending arrival. He felt peaceful as a wholeness settled over him.

Everything was going to be all right.

He stretched and rolled over to pull Belle back into his arms.

But Belle wasn't there.

Like a bad play that was running for a second time, Stephen swung his legs over the side of the bed as he scanned the room, looking for her, just as he had that morning those months before, after he had retrieved her from the cold.

Yet again, he expected to find her looking out over the park, or curled up in a chair waiting for him to wake. But as before, the park below remained unwatched and the chair across the room sat empty. She wasn't there. She was gone.

Frustration nearly overwhelmed him. His throat

tightened. He remembered Adam's words that he was afraid Belle was going to be hurt. Standing there, alone and abandoned, Stephen was afraid it wasn't Belle who was in danger.

CHAPTER
NINETEEN

Stephen paced the confines of his study like a caged panther. He had been there for hours, thinking, ever since he had awakened early that morning to find Belle gone. And now, as the minutes turned into hours, he could no longer deny that she had truly slipped from his bed.

His pain crystallized into fury. He hated to think about why. Instead, he concentrated on other issues. How was it possible that such a woman-child could be his undoing? Not one of the powerful men Stephen had gone up against since he had taken control of his father's estate had been able to achieve what a mere slip of a woman had managed to do in a matter of months.

And that infuriated him as nothing else could. He had spent too many years gaining power, overcoming his fears and anxieties after his parents' deaths, to let any woman prove his downfall.

But no matter how he tried to banish her from his mind, she stayed, obstinately, the memory of her joyous laughter swirling around in his head like a violent spring storm.

In the last hour, Nathan had stopped by the house to drop off a preliminary report on the husband.

"Haven't found the father yet," Nathan had stated. "In fact, are you sure his name is Holly?" He hesitated. "Are you certain he exists?"

Stephen had only looked back. How could he respond? He *wasn't* certain the man existed. "Just keep looking."

"Good enough. Fortunately, I've found something on Braxton," Nathan had said, placing the folder on the desk before departing, leaving Stephen alone with the information he sought. But Stephen had only stared at the folder for an eternity, uncertain if he wanted to know the contents after all. In the end, he'd had to know.

The facts were simple. Hershal Braxton, a strict Quaker who was zealous about his religion, had been a farmer in Wrenville, the wealthiest farmer, who owned almost everything around the area. Later, Belle had lived in the man's house, though from when to when was unclear.

But most interesting of all was that in Nathan's search, though certainly only a quick search, he had been unable to find any record of a marriage between Hershal Braxton and Belle Holly.

Stephen thought about Belle's obvious innocence when it came to matters of intimacy. Was it possible that she had never been intimate with a man? Was it possible that she had never been married? But then why had she lived with him? And why did she bear his name? And why did she apparently have his money if she had never been married to the man?

Too many questions and not enough answers.

The front bell rang, and with the sound, hope rushed through him. Foolish hope, he admonished himself, when he heard the door being opened and no throaty laughter or joyous "hello" echoed in the foyer.

Belle had not returned.

Nor would she, he reminded himself harshly. He ran his fingers through his hair, leaving ridges in the dark strands.

"Damn!" he muttered irrationally when a slice of sun peeked through the window and caught him in the eye.

"Sir, a package for you," Wendell announced from the doorway.

Stephen eyed the paper-wrapped parcel speculatively. "Set it on my desk."

"Very good, sir," the servant said as he set the package down, then quit the room.

Since Nathan had alrady been there that morning, Stephen doubted the package would be from him. He wasn't expecting anything else. Besides, even if he were, who would send him a plain paper package with a drawing of a big bright bullfinch on the cover.

Belle Braxton.

And he doubted this was a package that contained glad tidings.

With great reluctance, Stephen untied the string until the paper fell open. A note was attached to another paper-wrapped package.

> *My dearest pirate-man,*
> *I have no desire for marriage, and you have no*
> *desire for anything else. It's best we stay*
> *apart.*
>
> *Belle*

His fist smashed against his desk, blue-black ink from the inkwell spattering the crisp clean surface. He took a deep breath, then opened the second package. He found a sketch, of him, his dark eyes staring back, mocking his inability to make her his.

It was all he could do not to crumble the note along with the sketch and throw them both in the flickering fire that roared on the hearth.

Stephen resumed pacing, his anger and frustration growing with each agitated step he took, the sketch staring at him, watching him.

"Am I bothering you?"

Stephen turned with a start, only to find Adam in the doorway. "Does it look like you're bothering me?" he snapped.

Adam cringed and hesitated. At length he came forward.

If Stephen had not been so tied up with his own thoughts and worries, he would have noticed that Adam looked as if he hadn't slept in days. His eyes were red and his hair appeared to have been combed with his hands. But Stephen *was* tied up with his own problems and didn't notice Adam's state. Instead, Stephen simply started talking as he continued to pace across the room.

"I ask a woman to marry me for the first time in my life," he muttered, "and she only wants to have an affair."

A rueful smile momentarily crossed Adam's lips. "That's our Belle."

"I must be the first man in history to have the roles reversed on him. Every woman wants marriage! No woman wants to be nothing more than a paramour!" Stephen shook his head. "Every woman but Belle Braxton, obviously. She's clearly as crazy as the rumors would have her."

"I doubt that," Adam responded despondently.

Stephen stopped and stared at the flames.

"Stephen," Adam said, hesitantly, a few moments later.

Stephen turned back with a start, having forgotten Adam was there. "What?"

"I was wondering . . . well, I wanted . . ."

"Spit it out, man," he said, his tone impatient.

"I wanted to talk to you."

"Talk to me? About what?"

Adam thrust his hands in his pockets. He didn't know what to say. While he was walking aimlessly through the slush and snow in the Public Gardens, the thought to come here and talk to his reasonable brother had seemed the right thing to do. He had wanted to for weeks, but had never been able to gather up the courage to do so. Standing here now, with that sardonic look creasing his brother's face, what little courage he had mustered together was rapidly deserting him.

"What is it, Adam?" Stephen snapped. "Are you in trouble again? Drinking, gambling? Have you gotten some woman with child? Or is someone else trying to kill you?" The chiseled lines of Stephen's face curved with sarcasm. "If so, let me know so I can keep out of the way."

And with that, what little control Adam had collapsed. "Quit acting as if I were a child! I'm an adult. I'm no longer a twelve-year-old boy who you can boss around!"

Stephen's countenance grew incredulous. "Do you think I wanted that responsibility? Do you think I wanted to have my life come to a halt so I could take care of you? Did it ever occur to you that I wanted someone to take care of me?" He turned away sharply. "I wanted someone to tell *me* that everything was going to be all right. But that didn't happen. I had to learn how to be strong. And I did, damn it! And all you've learned to do is drink and gamble and get yourself in trouble!"

Adam gritted his teeth against the biting sorrow that stung at his eyes. "Whether you admit it or not, I am an adult. And you are no longer my keeper."

"Fine, keep yourself," Stephen snapped, before, with

stiff, angry movements, he turned on his heel and slammed out of the study.

Adam watched him go, all feelings of hope following his brother out the thick mahogany double doors, leaving Adam in despair.

How had his life come to this point? Adam wondered, sinking down into a leather wingback chair. He was an utter failure, just as he knew Stephen had always believed.

A crystal decanter of brandy sat next to the chair. Rolling his head to the side, he studied the intricate designs, colored amber by the liquor. Reaching over, he poured himself a glass—then another after that.

He had just poured another when the bell rang, announcing someone was at the door. Adam hardly noticed. He sat back, swirling the brandy, fascinated by the long liquid legs that ran down the sides.

"Sir," Wendell intoned from the doorway, breaking into Adam's reverie. "Someone is here to see you."

"I'm not here," he drawled.

"Yes, sir."

The butler grasped the brass knobs, to pull the doors shut, when a man pushed in behind him. "You can't just walk in here," Wendell stated, outraged.

"I've come to see Adam," the man stated calmly, "and I'll not be turned away."

Adam came up in his seat, sloshing the drink. "Tom."

"Hello, Adam."

The two men, of equal age, stared at each other, their gazes hard.

"Sir," Wendell interjected, "should I call the authorities?"

Adam eyed the man who had pushed his way into the house once before. This night, however, the man's blue eyes were clear, his dark hair was combed back from his forehead, and his coat and trousers were perfectly pressed.

"No, Wendell," Adam said. "I'll take care of this."

Reluctantly, the butler quit the room.

"Nice place you have here," Tom said with a casualness that was belied by the slight shake of his hand.

He's nervous, Adam thought, sinking back in the chair. "No surprise you didn't notice the furnishings the last time you . . . stopped by."

Tom visibly cringed as blood colored his neck. "I guess things got a little out of hand."

"A little?" Adam asked, his brow rising in a surprisingly good imitation of his brother.

"I hear Stephen regained the use of his arm."

"Luckily," Adam responded, the words as dry as kindling in a drought.

"Yes, luckily," Tom said, before striding boldly into the room. He walked from window to window, bookshelf to desk, until he turned back, looking as if he wished he were anyplace else in the world but there.

"I shouldn't have come," he said finally.

"Then why did you?"

Tom sighed. "Because I wanted to apologize. And since you have avoided me since . . . that night, not to mention that I needed to lay low until I knew what your brother was going to do—"

"Yes, not to mention," Adam interjected sarcastically.

"All right, damn it!" Tom exclaimed, his eyes blazing. "What do you want from me? I was wrong. I was stupid. Just because you were trying to buy me off to keep me quiet was no reason to come here that night brandishing a gun. I made a mistake. You have to believe me when I say that I didn't mean to shoot him—or anyone. I was upset." The fire in his eyes died. "What can I do to make things right?"

Adam dropped his head into his hands. "I don't know, Tom. I don't know if there is anything to make things right again."

Tom stepped forward. "There is always hope."

"Where?" Adam scoffed. "What hope do I have of ever making a life for myself?"

Tom stepped closer, until he stood next to the chair. A moment passed, before Tom reached out and pressed his hand to Adam's shoulder. "You can make a life with me."

CHAPTER
TWENTY

No sooner had Stephen stalked out of the house than he cursed. He pressed his eyes closed and rubbed his temples. Where had he gone wrong? he wondered. And suddenly he knew. He had gone wrong the day he had decided to try to fill his father's shoes.

He laughed, the sound harsh and bitter. He had proved he was not the man his father was. But then, just as suddenly, Stephen wondered if he could just be himself. But who was that? Who was he if he wasn't running his father's business, or trying to raise his father's son? The questions left him uneasy, for he had no idea. He had spent years trying to *be* his father; he had never tried to be himself.

He crossed the street and slipped through the wrought iron fencing and into the gardens. He needed to clear his head so he could think straight. He walked quickly along whatever path he came to, his mind swirling with thoughts. With each step he took, his anger with Adam dissipated until guilt was all that remained. His brother had needed him and he had selfishly taken out his own frustrations on Adam. Shame mixed with the guilt. His brother needed him, and he had failed. Yet again. ·

With that thought, Stephen turned back to head home. He might not have been there right when his brother had needed him, but hopefully it wasn't too late.

But just as he came over a small rise he saw a bundled figure in the distance, stepping out onto the ice that covered the lagoon where swan boats glided in the summer. The winter had provided a mix of slush and snow with several unseasonably warm days. Stephen knew that despite the freezing cold today, the ice wouldn't be solid. He felt a stab of concern that the ice couldn't possibly hold.

He broke into a run when the person took another step forward. Despite the heavy coat and knitted cap, he could tell even from this distance that it was a woman.

"Stop!" he hollered as he ran forward. "Don't move."

The woman stopped, her arms extended on either side, trying to gain her balance. She turned her head back to look at him. The sight of her luminous blue eyes nearly stopped him dead in his tracks.

"Belle," he breathed, his concern crystallizing into fear.

When she saw him, she lifted her hand to wave, but at the sudden movement a long snaking crack groaned into being. She froze at the sound. His heart froze at the sight. Belle looked down at her feet, as if unable to comprehend what was happening. She tried to take another step back toward Stephen.

"Don't move, Belle," he yelled, coming up to the edge of the lake.

She didn't. She stood quietly, without looking at Stephen. In fact, he thought, she didn't even look scared. As if in proof, very slowly she tilted her head back until she gazed up at the cold, clear sky.

"It's the first nice day we've had in weeks," she said. She moved slightly and the ice groaned again.

"If you don't keep still, it will be the last day you'll

ever have," he stated, his voice stern, though his mind churned with concern.

Her strange, haunting laughter was his only answer.

After determining that the ice was indeed too thin to support him, he tore off his coat and laid it on the ice like a bridge between Belle and safety.

"Did you get my present?" she asked.

"Take a step toward me, Belle, carefully."

"Did you get my present?" she persisted.

"Yes, I did. Now will you please very carefully step forward?"

"Did you like it?"

Stephen groaned. "Belle, this is neither the time nor the place to be discussing your artwork."

"Then you knew I did it?"

"Of course, I knew."

"How?"

"Belle," he warned.

"Tell me how you knew?"

"Your style, all right," he said impatiently, concentrating on the ice. "It was the same style I saw in the other sketch you had done."

"You're very good."

"I try," he said dryly. "Now, can we please get you off the ice?"

"But I haven't gotten my scarf."

"Your scarf?"

"Yes, why else do you think I would be out here like a fool? It caught on the breeze, and the next thing I knew it was gliding across the ice like a skater."

"Just come on, Belle. Forget the scarf."

"But I just bought it."

"I'll buy you another one."

"That's not the point." The ice groaned again. "But

maybe it is," she added, then hurried across his coat just as the ice separated into a series of broken pieces.

"Whew!" she cried, excitement lacing her blue eyes. "That was close."

"Too close. You should be smart enough to know better than to do something so foolish."

"True, I *should* know better." She laughed up into the skies. "But I don't."

Now that she was safely on solid ground, his coat but a memory beneath the patches of water and ice, the situation wrapped him in a blanket of unease. Standing there, laughing, her hair wild from having ripped her knitted cap free, Belle looked every inch the crazy woman people called her.

He was drawn to her in ways he didn't understand—and repelled by her in ways that he did. The combination left him feeling adrift in a raging sea. No port for safety. No manageable breeze to set him free.

"Why do you do things like this?" he asked quietly. "You told me once that you care what people think of you. I'm finding that harder and harder to believe." He hesitated. "Or is it that you don't understand what people are saying about you?"

Her laughter stopped with haunting finality. Her sunny countenance hardened into a stormy mask. "Of course, I understand! What do you think I am, an idiot?"

He looked into her eyes. "No, Belle, never an idiot. But there are those who say you're . . ." His words trailed off.

"Crazy?" A hint of a smile reappeared.

Stephen grew uncomfortable, but wouldn't turn back. "Well, yes. Crazy."

Her smile broadened and she stepped closer. "They're right, you know. I *am* crazy. Crazier than a loon.

But as rich as Croesus, so people put up with me. Do you think I don't know that?" Her smile vanished. "But who wouldn't be crazy in this world gone mad where money and manhood means more than family and friends. God forbid you be born a woman at the mercy of men, especially a woman with thoughts about anything other than her social calendar or opinions on anything other than the latest fashions."

"I find that hard to believe."

"Really?" She eyed him speculatively. "What if your wife had tried to found the National American Women's Suffrage Association?"

Stephen's brow furrowed.

"Or what if you had been married to one of the many women who were part of the Underground Railroad that helped free slaves?"

"That's different," he stated firmly.

"Why?" she challenged.

"We aren't talking about other women," he said, avoiding her question. "We are talking about you. And I find it hard to believe that the people around here are basing *their* opinions solely on you *having* opinions."

She tilted her head and looked at him through lowered lashes. "Really?" she said, her tone challenging. "Then do you think I'm crazy?" She stepped even closer and ran her fingers down his chest.

He grabbed her wrist. His grip was tight and painful. "Stop it. Stop this game. Yes, damn it, I have wondered if you were crazy, too many times to count."

She sucked in her breath and her eyes suddenly glistened. She tried to pull free.

"Belle." He spoke her name like a tired caress, the anger magically gone. "Why? Why do you do things to make me think the worst of you?"

"You'll believe what you want, regardless of what I do."

"What do you expect me to think when you run your fingers down my chest in the middle of a public park, or you traipse into dining establishments unescorted?"

"It's archaic that women aren't allowed to go out to dine alone. You were there alone."

"I'm a man."

"My point exactly. We wouldn't be having this discussion if I were a man."

Stephen grumbled under his breath but persevered. "You have parties and invite gentlemen and servants alike."

Belle eyed him closely. "Who are you calling the gentlemen? Wendell and Hastings, or you?"

"You know what I mean."

"Are you telling me it's wrong to be kind to the staff?"

Stephen hung his head at this. Even in his own ears his words were beginning to sound absurd. "Right or wrong, it's just not done."

"Maybe in your house, or in any other house in Boston, but in my house I'll have whoever I want at my parties, Wendell and Hastings included! What else have I done that's crazy?"

Frustration was mounting. "You show up at dinners in outdated gowns."

He didn't notice the color that streaked through her cheeks.

"You say whatever is on your mind, whether it is appropriate or not. The humming game, for Christ's sake!"

Belle turned away so that Stephen couldn't see her face. "What would you have me do?" she asked. "Sip tea with Louisa Abbot, or crochet altar cloths with the Widow Hathaway?"

"For starters."

She pressed her eyes closed. "I might as well be locked away in a wooden house in the country."

"You don't mean that!"

She turned back to him, slowly, and looked him in the eye. "I'm not certain that it would be any worse."

"What are you talking about, Belle?" His heart suddenly pounded. "You've been talking in riddles for so long that I have more questions about you than answers. Tell me about the past. Please. You sound as if you've already been locked away in a house in the country."

She stood for an eternity, staring. When he thought she would finally speak, she only reached up and pressed her hand against his chest. He tensed against his body's unbridled response. His mind demanded answers, but his body remembered only the jagged shards of passion they had already shared, and wanted more.

"Belle," he said, his tone a warning.

But his warnings went unheeded when she whispered, "Hold me, Stephen," and he was lost.

He pulled her close, almost frantically. He opened his mouth on her neck, feeling her warmth. Belle cried out. Her head fell back, revealing more of the creamy skin, which hid beneath the layers of velvet and wool. His hands slid down her back to cup her hips, pressing himself closer to the heat that burned between her thighs, only to let up then press again harder, a demand.

Her hands trailed across the hard planes of his back, setting him on fire, urging him on. And that was just it.

The groan that rumbled in his chest was feral when he set her at arm's length. "No," he ground out painfully. "I will not do this. I have no interest in being little more than an usher along your path to carnal oblivion, or a navigator for your flight from whatever it is you're trying to escape."

He watched as she sucked in her breath.

"What? Did you think I didn't know that whenever things start making you crazy, you turn to me? Whenever the questions get too pointed, or perhaps too close to the truth, I find you in my arms. For reasons I don't understand, I help you forget the darkness that I see so frequently racing through your eyes. Well, no longer, Belle. *No longer.* I want to help you remember. I want you to face whatever it is that haunts you."

She tried to pull free from his grasp, but he held her firmly. He wanted to possess her, mind and soul, to love her, and for her to return his sentiments. But that would never happen if they couldn't get beyond her past.

"I've been looking into this husband of yours," he said.

He felt her shoulders tense.

"And I've been looking into this supposedly world-famous father of yours, too. Admit it, Belle. They don't exist." She tried to jerk away, but his grip was like a shackle. "Accept that your life is here, now . . . with me."

The look in her eye was wild and frantic. But yet again he had come too far to turn back. "You must face reality, Belle. There is no father who is coming for you."

She wheeled free, anger streaking her features. "You're lying!" she hissed.

"I'm sorry, but—"

"I hate you, Stephen St. James. I hate you with every fiber of my being." Her immense eyes flashed vehement, overwhelming contempt for him as she took a deep, fortifying breath. "My father does exist. He does. And he is coming for me, just as I said."

He caught ahold of her arm when she tried to flee. "Belle," he said softly.

The anger in her eyes flickered as if trying to burn out. Tears surfaced. But then she visibly shored herself up. "Let go of me, Stephen."

"Belle, please listen—"

Furious, she jerked free of his hold. "My father will come for me, and then you'll see. But until that time, do not touch or talk to me ever again!"

Her hands trembled with rage, as she turned and hurried along the path toward her home.

The cold, bitter breeze ruffled Stephen's hair. But he didn't feel the cold; it felt no different from the state he was already in. Frozen. A block of ice forming around his heart.

How had his life gone so awry? he wondered. First Adam, now Belle. His life was unraveling. And as he stood there, watching the place in the gardens through which Belle had disappeared, his anger began to grow once again. Anger he understood and could manage. Hollow despair he could not.

Stephen returned to the house, and with every step he took, his anger mounted. He only wanted to help Belle, to provide her with the safety of his name and security of his home. A voice in his head, which he did his best to mute, whispered that he wanted to cast her into a mold society deemed acceptable—which he deemed acceptable. But he pushed the words aside. He only wanted what was best for Belle; it had nothing to do with what he wanted, he told himself firmly, his angry steps pounding against the pavement.

When he reached his house, Wendell was just coming out.

"Good afternoon, sir," Wendell said.

Stephen didn't respond, simply stalked through the open door and headed for his study.

His mind was filled with Belle and Adam, and more importantly, his mind was filled with anger as he pushed through the double doors to his study. Then he saw them.

The world grew quiet. Time lost all meaning as Stephen tried to make sense of the sight before him.

Adam and Tom jerked apart, leaping up from the sofa to stand, staring wide-eyed at Stephen. Stephen's mind worked as if swimming through dark murky waters. Adam, embracing another man—a man who looked familiar. Then he remembered.

The man who had shot him.

Stephen's mind reeled at the double, soul-shattering shock.

"Stephen," Adam breathed, but said nothing else.

"I seem to have a way of arriving when you least expect me." Stephen's voice was calm, too calm.

"It's not how it looks," Adam blurted out.

"Really?" Stephen replied, his face a mask of stone. "And what is it supposed to look like?"

Adam cringed. "Well, uh—"

The unnatural calm evaporated, and Stephen lashed out in fury, his fist catching a lamp that stood on a table next to him. The shade crumpled and the porcelain base crashed to the hardwood floor, shattering into pieces. "Did your friend have something in his eye and you were trying to get it out? Was your friend ill, and you were trying to soothe him?" His voice boomed through the study. He took a step forward. "Were *you* ill, Adam? Was your friend, your gunman friend, soothing you?"

Adam blanched, as did Tom.

Slowly, Stephen's mind began to work, to fathom what was happening. He grabbed Adam by the lapels, virtually lifting him off the ground, leaning him back against the desk like a bow without an arrow. "What the hell is going on here?"

"Surely you can figure that on your own," Tom said sarcastically from behind him.

Stephen turned on him in a feral rage. The bravado slipped from Tom's face, replaced by panic. But he had no time to move. Stephen was on him in a second, shoving him backward. The crash of table and glass on the floor when Tom stumbled into them gave Stephen no thought. He only pushed him again, harder, toppling him over a small table which held a brass and glass dome clock. The timepiece tolled crazily when it hit the floor.

Belle stood in the foyer of her home. Hastings stood with her, as did a man who said he was there to see the ballroom. He needed to measure for flowers.

"Flowers?" Belle inquired, confused. "I don't understand."

The man glanced down at his work instructions. After rereading them, he shrugged his shoulders. "That's all it says. I'm supposed to measure a ballroom for flowers."

"The ballroom? On whose orders?"

"Well, let's see." He read once again. "James, maybe. S. James."

"St. James. Stephen," Belle determined, her jaw set. "What could Stephen be doing that he is having my ballroom measured for flowers?"

Neither man answered. Her blood began to boil. What was he up to now? Everytime she turned around, he was trying to run her life, and that made her furious.

Though in truth, the fury was born more of fear that she would give in to his demanding ways, as she longed to do, than pure anger at the man. But of course she wouldn't give in! She was an independent woman. She had painstakingly recreated the very house her father had dreamed of. Now all her hard work was about to pay off. St. Valentine's Day was only two weeks away.

Stephen's admonitions that her father wasn't coming commandeered her mind. She looked around at the surroundings that were supposed to provide her with hope. Cold seeped into her, cold that had nothing to do with the winter breeze just beyond the door. Instead of the hope she had traveled here to resurrect, she felt surrounded by nothing more than despair.

Who was she fooling? her mind screamed. Stephen was right. How in the world could she possibly believe that her father would truly come for her?

She closed her eyes against cold, biting reality, unmindful of the two men who stood in the foyer, watching her, concern creasing their faces. The foundation of her life began to crumble. All that she believed in, all that had kept her together for so many years, began to disintegrate, leaving her adrift in a raging sea.

"Madam?" Hastings said.

Her eyes flashed opened.

"The flowers?" the flower man inquired.

The flowers that Stephen wanted in her house for reasons unknown—Stephen, who would dash her dreams against unyielding rocks, then move in and take over her life.

The fury returned, and she welcomed it.

It was all Stephen's fault, she thought unreasonably. He had stripped her clean of hope, and she hated him. Without a word, she turned and slammed out the door and stalked over to Stephen's. She didn't bother with the bell, didn't think of the bell. Throwing the door wide, her raging thoughts were checked by the crash that echoed through the hall. The next crash and the sound of Adam's desperate pleadings pierced her own despair, and she hurried into Stephen's study.

The sight that met her eyes stunned her. She had always thought that Stephen was feral, moved like a panther. But now it was more than a simple thought. He stood before her, a tower of animal rage, tossing a man she had never seen before around the room like a rag doll. Adam was trying to pry Stephen away unsuccessfully.

"What is going on here?" she demanded.

Like the tide rushing back to sea, the raging fury seemed to be sucked from the room. Stephen froze. Like nothing else could have, Belle's voice pierced the cloud in his mind.

With something close to shock replacing everything else he had felt, Stephen glanced down at his bloodied hands. He took in the sight of Tom on the floor, his head and shoulders propped up against the wall. Stephen didn't know if the blood was Tom's or his own, and he didn't care. Slowly, he turned around to face Belle.

"What are you doing?" she demanded, stepping forward.

Her words broke the spell, and Adam raced over to Tom and pulled him up to a sofa.

Stephen and Belle stared at each other, seemingly oblivious to the activity taking place only a few feet away.

"What were you doing?" she demanded.

His jaw tightened as he remembered. In his mind's eye, he saw his brother, the brother he had been responsible for so many years, wrapped in the embrace of another man. He wasn't sure which he felt more, revulsion or rage —or maybe it was fear.

His nostrils flared. He had raised his brother. He was responsible for how he turned out. And it had been brought home to him more fiercely than he could have imagined how deeply he had failed. Guilt pushed into his mind. But he wouldn't have it. It wasn't his fault, or so he told himself as the anger, thankfully, began to rebuild.

"Get out of my house, Belle," he said slowly, his voice like steel, before turning to his brother. "You, too."

Adam met his hard stare. "Please, Stephen. Let me explain."

"What's there to explain?" he exploded, before visibly regaining control. "We have nothing to talk about." He wouldn't speak his brother's name. "I want you and your . . . friend out of my house."

"Perfect!" Adam cried. "Just perfect! I would hate to think that you would react any other way than as the narrow-minded selfish soul that you are."

Stephen tensed.

"I've tried to talk to you," Adam continued. "I've tried to gain your help." His voice softened. "Why can't you listen? Why can't you at least try to accept me for who I am instead of trying to turn me into who you think I should be? Can't you at least try?"

"Accept this? Like hell I will. It's unnatural, nobody would accept this."

"Belle accepts me! Why can't you!"

With an infinite slowness, Stephen turned deadly eyes on Belle. "You knew?"

"Yes," she said, her chin rising defiantly.

"Why didn't you tell me?"

"It wasn't my story to tell, Stephen. But as long as you know, you seem to forget one very important fact."

"And what is that?" he asked, his face a mask of sardonic rage.

"No matter how you feel about Adam's way of life, he's still your brother."

Stephen stared at her, then at Adam. "Not any longer," he ground out. And with that, he strode from the room.

Belle and Adam watched him go, staring at the empty doorway, each lost in their own thoughts.

"You don't need him, Adam," Tom said from the sofa.

Adam didn't turn away from the door. "But I do. More than you realize." He took a deep breath. "More than I realized. He's the only family I have." He dropped his head to his hands. "I think it's best if you leave."

At length, Tom pushed awkwardly and angrily up from the sofa. At the doorway, Tom turned back and opened his mouth to speak, but Adam cut him off. "Don't say anything else. Just go."

Tom snapped his mouth shut indignantly, then did just that.

The room seemed unnaturally quiet as Adam and Belle stood side by side.

"I suppose you heard all the noise through the wall?"

"No," she whispered. "I didn't know this was going on. I came over because some man is over at my house trying to measure the ballroom for flowers. I came to demand an explanation."

"Ah," he said with a tired sigh, "the party. I guess Stephen never got around to telling you."

"The party?" Belle asked, turning to look at him. "What party?"

Adam still stared at the empty doorway. "The party on St. Valentine's Day. For your birthday."

Her mind reeled. A party. She staggered back, catching herself on the solid back of the sofa.

For her birthday.

CHAPTER
TWENTY-ONE

Saint Valentine's Day. Her birthday had arrived at last.

Papa had already left for his morning chores when Belle woke. He wouldn't be back until close to noon for the midday meal. Time enough to put the finishing touches on her birthday celebration.

Thirteen. Finally. The magic number when she would leave childhood behind, or so her mother had always said.

A piercing sadness shot through her. "Oh, Mama," she murmured into the quiet room.

Even though it was Belle's birthday, she had made a special gift for her father, something she knew he would cherish. She could hardly wait to see the look in his silver-blue eyes when he returned home and pulled the string free from the brown paper-wrapped parcel.

Anticipation left her nearly breathless all morning long as she did her best to clean the house, prepare her special meal, and bake a cake. She couldn't wait to see the look on his face when he entered. She might not be much of a cook, but her gift? He would love it. She was certain.

A smile curled on her lips when she wondered if he would bring her a stick of peppermint. But that hardly mattered. What mattered was that today they would start over, they would start a new life.

Breathing deeply, she put the last touches on the cake before she turned to the task of cleaning up before he came home.

The house was done, the meal simmering in a pot on the stove, the cake on the table. As soon as Belle had finished dressing and all was ready, she felt quite grown up in the dress which she had cut down to fit her from one of her mother's old gowns. She hummed her mother's favorite melody and glided across the room, anticipating the dance she would share with her father.

She danced with an ease born of long days of practice while her father was at work. A royal princess on highly polished hardwood floors couldn't have danced more beautifully than she.

But as the minutes ticked by with no sight or sound of her father, Belle finally sat down on the wooden bench, running her finger along the paper-wrapped parcel that held her father's gift.

It was well past noon when she heard his footsteps on the small front porch. She jumped up from the table as he pushed through the door.

He stopped in the doorway without a word. His craggy face was hard as he took in her newly made gown. Her heart seemed to stop when he didn't move and the smile she had counted on, prayed for, didn't appear.

Blood rushed up her neck to her cheeks. The sound filled her ears. With stilted movements, she hurried to the stove. "Beef stew!" she chimed, forcing cheer.

No response.

"With little baby onions," she added, somewhat desperately. "Your favorite."

He still didn't move, but his pale gray eyes narrowed. Cold air came in behind him, chasing out the warmth. Belle banged the heavy top down on the pot. She rushed to the table. "I know it's my birthday, but . . . I have a present for you."

Still he only stared.

Desperately, frantically, Belle ripped the paper away before she held up the gift. She saw him suck in his breath.

"Madeline," he breathed, staring at the sketch of the woman who looked so much like Belle.

"Yes, Papa. I drew it for you," Belle said, a tiny bud of hope burgeoning in her breast.

Her father slowly lifted his eyes from the drawing until he met her gaze. But what she saw in his eyes was not happiness or love. Her hope died a swift, painful death, because she knew in that instant with a clarity far beyond her mere thirteen years that contrary to what she had believed, everything wasn't going to be all right.

CHAPTER
TWENTY-TWO

Belle paced. Every step she took sent a jolt of pain up her spine. It wasn't that she was really affected by the pain, it was more a cataloguing of it, comparing it to other days. Today was worse.

Her eyes were red, her lacquered hair wild about her face, tossed and curled like a furious black sea.

Tomorrow was her birthday. February fourteenth.

"Please, dear God," she prayed fervently, "let Stephen be wrong. Let my father arrive."

Stopping in the center of the floor, her head fell back. She held her arms out on either side of her body like wings. If only she could fly. Fly away, so fast and far. Like a bird. Not subject to the vagaries of man.

The darkness loomed. Her arms dropped to her sides. For her there was no escape from the bits and pieces of memory, or the missing fragments that threatened in that dark, murky place in her mind.

She hadn't been out of the house in days, had barely left her room. Maeve and Rose brought her meals, trying to coax her out. But Belle ignored them.

She closed her eyes and held herself tightly. The day was nearly at hand. One day before her birthday, with no other sign of her father than the diminishing memory of a man she hadn't seen in seventeen years. How would she survive if he failed to come—this time?

This time she had believed he would come. With all her soul. With all her heart. Her foundation secure. But then she met Stephen, making her doubt, chiseling away at her belief as if it was nothing more than dry, crumbling mortar.

Damn him, her mind cried.

A loud bang sounded through the house. Her eyes snapped open. Hope surged. But then she remembered. The party. No doubt some other workman was down there now, preparing for the huge ball Stephen had Adam arrange.

A ball for her birthday, in the grandest of ballrooms, with a huge crystal chandelier.

"Oh, Papa," she cried, before she bit the length of her finger to keep from screaming out.

She had tried to talk to Stephen, but he wouldn't see her. Neither did he cancel the party. It was as if he had washed his hands of the whole affair. "It's already paid for," a man who appeared to be in charge had told her when she had tried to get him to take all his decorations and invitation lists away and burn them.

It made no sense. It was her house, and short of going to the authorities, she had no way to get all the decorators and caterers and waiters out of the house.

She didn't want a party, she had told the man.

"Sorry, lady," he had replied. "I got my orders."

Walking to the window, her thick leather boot caught on the rug. She caught herself on the window frame with practiced ease. If only she could stop the party, she thought suddenly. It was too early. This wasn't the year, she realized with unexpected clarity. That was it! It was too early. It was too early for her father to arrive.

Hope rushed in, filing the cracks in her compromised

foundation. "Next year," she whispered. "He'll come *next* year. He hasn't had time to learn that I'm here."

Purpose and determination pushed all other emotions aside. She would go over to Stephen's house and demand to see him. She would have this party canceled yet. Then next year, yes, next year, her father would come.

Her step faltered when she thought of Adam. She hadn't seen or spoken to him since that fateful day. She had been so wrapped up in her own problems that she hadn't thought of him. Guilt filled her. How selfish she had been. But she would make it up to him, just as soon as she halted this mad party.

Nathan handed the sheets of paper to Stephen. The men were upstairs in a room that Stephen had begun using. He hadn't returned to his study downstairs since the day he had learned the true nature of his brother. His hand tightened around the pen that he held, strangling it.

"Mr. St. James?"

Stephen dropped the pen and sighed. After a pause, he turned his attention to the papers. He didn't want to read them, had told himself he wouldn't. He didn't want to know what Nathan had learned. But as always, like the moth he had become in regards to Belle, he glanced over first one then another of the pages.

"What about the father?" Stephen asked.

"I haven't found anything yet."

"And no doubt never will," he muttered as he began to read in earnest.

At first he read quickly, dispassionately, but soon he began to slow, returning to the beginning and starting again. He had doubted that she had been married, had thought that she had made it all up. But with the pieces of paper he held in his hands, doubt was extinguished. She *had* been married.

Pain seared through him, though it had nothing to do with jealousy. His pain was born by reading the date of her marriage.

"Is there anything else, sir?" Nathan asked.

Startled, having forgotten the other man, Stephen looked up. "Yes. I mean, no. I mean, I don't need anything else. You can leave."

As Nathan walked from the room, Stephen was dimly aware of the front bell ringing. After a moment, he left the room and came to the top of the stairs where he could see down to the foyer.

The bell rang again, bringing Adam out of the parlor, staggering, just as Nathan reached the front door. Wendell was nowhere in sight when Adam pulled the door open.

"Adam!"

Stephen recoiled at the sound of Belle's voice.

"You poor dear, you look terrible," he heard her add.

Even from this distance, Stephen could see that Adam's eyes were glassy, his smile vacant.

"Thank you," Adam offered with a mocking salute.

"Hello, Mrs. Braxton," Nathan said, tipping his hat before he slipped out the door.

When Nathan stepped out, Belle stepped into the foyer.

"Do come in," Adam said, bowing drunkenly.

"You've been drinking—and too much, based on the looks of you."

"No, m'dear. Not enough. I can still think."

"Adam . . ."

"Don't," he said sharply. "I don't want your pity."

Belle sighed. "Why won't you let anyone help you?"

He turned away from her with a jerk, heading for the stairs. Belle hurried after him.

"Adam—"

But her words were cut off when her boot caught on the thick edge of an Oriental rug. Gasping, she reached out, grabbing, but found nothing more than air. From the top of the stairs, Stephen lurched. But Adam turned back in time, catching Belle in his arms.

Stephen halted his flight, holding on to the railing with force to hold himself back.

"Clumsy old me," Belle said, pushing self-consciously away.

Adam studied her, his eyes clearing slightly, the liquor making his tongue bold. "How did it happen?" he asked simply.

Even from this distance Stephen could see her sharp intake of breath. He waited, his breath held, for her answer.

"How did what happen?" she asked, straightening the bodice of her gown.

"The limp. What happened to make you limp so?"

Looking away, Belle smoothed her skirts. Stephen thought she wouldn't answer. But after a moment, he heard her say, "I was born this way."

The words were a slap. They hardly made sense to Stephen. He thought he must have heard incorrectly.

"Born that way?" Adam probed.

"Yes, Adam. Now, would you be so kind to tell Stephen I am here to see him."

Adam seemed to debate. "He's unavailable, Belle. I'm sorry."

"Ah, his orders, I'm sure."

"Yes," Adam said. "Really, I'm sorry."

Stephen couldn't move. He tried to make sense of what she had said. *Born that way*. His mind filled with the remembered sight of her leg—brutally broken, then never repaired. Looking down at her, his anger, never far, resurfaced. She was lying. Just as she had lied about so many things.

And just then, she looked up and found him.

"Stephen," she breathed.

Adam whirled around to find his brother. Emotions creased Adam's face—hope, sadness, regret, all dashed by despair. After a moment he turned away and disappeared back into the front parlor.

Stephen's jaw clenched and he started to turn away, to return to his new study.

"Stephen!" Belle demanded.

He halted, his back to her.

"Stephen, I need to talk to you."

"Go away, Belle."

"No! We need to talk!"

What was there to say? he wondered. What would she tell him? More lies, undoubtedly. "No, we have no need for talking. There is nothing more to say."

"Maybe for you, but I have plenty to say!"

He snorted. "That doesn't surprise me. But I'm no longer interested in listening."

"Too bad!" she screeched. "You are responsible for that party at my house, and I will not have it. Call it off."

"I would think you'd enjoy a party," he said dispassionately. "But if you don't want it, *you* call it off."

She grit her teeth. "I've tried. But they won't listen to me."

He merely shrugged his shoulders and continued toward his study.

"You arrogant, unfeeling, selfish man! It's my house! Do you hear me. *My* house. And I don't want a party."

He froze. Long months of frustration and anger and uncertainty congealed in his mind. Slowly, menacingly, he turned back to her. His smile was cold. "No, Mrs. Braxton. It's *my* house."

She took a step back, confusion marring her perfect brow. "Your house? That's absurd."

"No absurdity. Simply the truth. I had the contract revoked. On a technicality. In the future, you'd do well to hire better solicitors."

"You're lying!"

"No, Belle. I may be many things, most of which you have taken great pleasure in enumerating these last months, but *I* do not lie."

She stammered and stuttered, before saying, "You can't get away with this! I'll fight you!"

His cold smile fled. "If you do, you'll lose. I'll crush you, Belle, just as I have crushed a thousand others."

Her shoulders came back. "But you won't crush me," she said, the disquiet magically gone from her voice.

His eyes narrowed. "Of course I would."

"No, Stephen. You wouldn't. You would never hurt me. Just as you would never intentionally hurt . . . anyone else."

His anger grew. "You're wrong. I can and I will."

"No, you won't!"

A fact. No doubt.

He stared at her hard, before he turned on his heel and strode into his office angrily. Belle followed, hurrying up the stairs as fast as she could manage. He was standing behind his desk when she finally reached the room.

"Stephen," she said, her breath short.

He wouldn't look at her.

"You said you don't lie, then don't lie to me now. You saved me, Stephen. You won't take away the one thing I've worked so hard for and destroy me now."

Fury, frustration, and cold empty loss riddled his brow as he grabbed up a document, the papers crumpling in his fist. "You're wrong!" The words reverberated against the walls. "It's done. Do you understand? Finished. You are living in *my* house!"

Staring at the document he held extended in his hand, Belle stepped forward. As if taking hold of something deadly, she took the papers and began to read, first once, then again. She pressed her eyes closed. "Why?" she finally asked. "Why did you bother to save me?"

"You betrayed me!"

Her head shot up. "I've never betrayed you!"

"You knew about Adam and didn't tell me."

Anger welled in her breast. "That's not the reason!" she said, her tone seething. "You're doing this because I said I wouldn't be your wife."

"I loved you, as I have never loved anyone else in my life."

"That was your mistake, not mine. I told you all along I had no interest in marriage. All I wanted was to be your friend."

"I don't need friends!"

"Everyone needs friends!"

"Not me! I wanted a wife! Not a friend. Not a paramour! A wife!"

"But I don't want a husband," she whispered, turning away from him.

Stephen could hardly believe the things he was saying, but couldn't help himself, couldn't stop the anger and frustration, and . . . panic that flowed through his veins, thicker than his blood. And like a child, he couldn't seem to stop himself from lashing out again, as if he wanted her to hurt as badly as he was hurting. "I guess the story you told Adam about your leg being something you were born with is about as true as you having been happily married."

She stopped in midstride.

He came around the desk. "I know all about your leg."

Her back was to him, but he saw her flinch.

"Yes, I saw it."

"No," she breathed.

"Yes, the night I . . . saved you, as you are so fond of saying. That is no defect from birth, Blue Belle."

He took her arm and turned her around. "You're a liar, Blue Belle Holly. Admit it. You lied about your leg, just as you've been lying about this father of yours. And while I know now that indeed you were married, I find it hard to believe that it was the happy marriage you have presented."

She tried to break free from his grasp. "Let go of me," she bit out.

Stephen's anger and frustration dissolved, leaving only heart-breaking panic in its wake. "Tell me, Belle. Tell me that you didn't love him. You couldn't have."

"Think what you want," she hissed.

"Good God, Belle. You were married on February the fourteenth."

"I hate you," she ground out.

"Tell me, Belle."

She jerked her arm frantically, but his hand was like a band of iron, holding her captive.

"Did you really love him so much, or was that just a story you told to keep me away?" His voice softened and he watched as her eyes clouded and grew distant. "Tell me. Did you really love him? Could you have possibly loved someone when you were so young? God, Belle, you were married on your thirteenth birthday."

CHAPTER
TWENTY-THREE

WRENVILLE 1877

Belle woke slowly. The first thing she noticed was the unfamiliar surroundings. The next was the pain. Intense, throbbing pain that seemed to come from nowhere specific and, consumed the entirety of her young body.

She tried to move, but the pain seared through her leg. Falling back, she pressed her forearm over her eyes. What had happened to her? she wondered desperately. It was her birthday. Why was she here in this foreign place? The fleeting image of her father's face as he looked at her gift passed through her mind, but nothing else. She remembered nothing else. Nothing. She only felt the pain.

"Where are you, Papa?" she whispered. But the unfamiliar room held no answers.

A noise drew her attention. Moving her arm away, she glanced to the side. Her mouth dropped open in silent protest. The farmer, dressed in a crisp black suit with white shirt and starched collar. The hated farmer, his head and shoulders framed by a mirror which hung on the wall behind him. Dear God, he sat, stiff and unmoving, staring at her without saying a word.

"Farmer Braxton," she whispered, alarmed.

Unmindful of the pain, her head jerked to the other side as she tried to place her surroundings. Fine linens, brocade chairs, gold-gilded picture frames. Nothing, however, was familiar.

When she looked back, he was gone, the mirror empty save for the finely plastered walls reflected from the opposite end of the room.

Had she imagined him? she wondered frantically. Was this all a bad dream? But by then her body throbbed unbearably, and her mind couldn't concentrate, only longed for darkness and sleep—escape. Though just before she sank back down into oblivion, she caught sight of a band of thin gold capturing her finger.

She woke again. She had no idea if she had slept a few minutes or a few days. The room was dark except for a hurricane lamp of finely cut glass that burned low on a small silk-skirted table in the corner. She remembered her dream about the farmer, sitting, staring, and she shuddered. Relief followed quickly—it had been nothing more than a dream, she reassured herself.

But her relief was washed away like a wave on the sand when he walked in, the farmer, a tray held in his hand. Without a word, looking at her only briefly, as if he couldn't bear the sight of her, he set the tray beside the bed. The fine bone china slipped a bit when the tray tilted. He righted the dishes awkwardly.

"What are you doing here?" she whispered, her voice small and scared. "Where's my papa?"

"Eat," he murmured, his face a mask in the shadowy room, then he turned away and left.

She was too scared to eat, though she couldn't put a name to the fear.

Papa, where are you? she wondered frantically. Never in her twelve years, no thirteen, she amended silently, had she ever been so scared. How was it possible for her to be here without her father?

Pieces of unformulated answers began to swirl in her

mind. Her birthday party. The look on her father's face. Alone with the farmer . . . the ring. Unease began to fill her, so she put the thoughts from her mind. She wouldn't think about it—yet—but deep down she knew she was afraid to think about it, afraid what the answers might be. She concentrated on her leg instead.

Pain was her only companion during the passing days. The only person she saw at all, other than the farmer, was an old woman whom Belle had never seen before, who came in to wash her and change the sheets.

One day when the woman was leaving the house, her voice drifted back to Belle as she was lying in the bed, trying to adjust to the pain that was always greater after the woman left.

"She'll never walk again, of that you can be certain," the woman intoned in her scratchy voice.

Shock and, more importantly, fear raced through Belle's body. Couldn't walk? How was that possible? her mind screamed. Surely the woman was talking about someone else. Her leg hurt, yes. But never to walk again? That was impossible. Surely.

Taking a deep breath, Belle lifted the covers, forcing herself up on her elbows, fighting the pain. She had to see, had to know. At the sight that met her eyes, her mind swam. It was all she could do to stay conscious. Her lower leg was black and blue, swollen, looking like a mockery of the one that lay next to it, perfect and white. Even through the swelling and the color, Belle could see that her aching leg was no longer straight.

That was when the despair hit her, tossing her relentlessly against the rocky shore of an unforgiving sea of desperation.

What had happened? How could her leg look as it did? Again, she couldn't remember. She bit her lip, tears springing into her eyes. Hot, burning tears streaked her cheeks, falling down onto her pillow, and it was all she could do not to scream.

Shortly after, the farmer came in, holding an open Bible in his hand as if he had been reading.

"I want to go home," she pleaded through her tears.

"You are home."

Her breath caught. "No! To *my* home," she demanded obstinately, dashing her tears away. "I want to go home . . ." She started to say, home to her father, but something stopped her. The fear of the answer? She didn't know. Instead she finished with, "to sleep in my loft." It was easier to think about the fact that there was no light in this room, no window to the world by day or the heavens at night. "I shouldn't be here. It's not right."

"You're my wife," he stated, snapping his thick, black Bible shut.

Windows and heavens vanished from her mind. "Wife," she breathed, stunned. Though, of course, the thought had been there all along. Thirteen—the magic year. And the ring. "How can that be?"

He looked at her curiously. "You don't remember?"

Honestly she didn't, didn't remember anything other than preparing for her father's return, the sketch, the cake, but nothing else.

She turned her head away from him, refusing to believe, telling herself it was all a bad dream and that soon she would wake and be at home, safe and secure in her own bed. By now the despair that had become a constant companion much as the pain had, was crystallized into something different, though what she couldn't say. She only knew that she had begun to feel differently. Blue Belle Holly had ceased to exist. The little girl who danced in her father's arms across the rough-hewn floorboards of their tiny cabin was gone, extinguished like a fragile yellow flame. And when she turned her head and found finely wrought furniture and expensively woven rugs, she knew it was true. Her mind seemed to shift and change. Old, familiar thoughts took on different hues, became unfamiliar.

And as the days turned into weeks, and the weeks into months, whenever she woke, she woke in the farmer's house, in the farmer's bed.

Wife. Her young budding chest clenched as the word snaked through her head. Her mother had been a wife. Mrs. Wilmont who ran the mercantile was a wife. But they were old. She wasn't. She was supposed to be in school, learning sums, reading books. How could she be a wife? Wives didn't play in the fields or swim in ponds in the spring and summer.

She tried to comprehend, but couldn't, or wouldn't perhaps. And though she didn't know exactly what it was, there was some other hushed something that had to do with being a wife that loomed over her head like a feared monster under her bed, never seen, but there. And she had no one to ask what that something was, no one to talk to. The farmer was never around long enough to ask questions, not that she would have asked him anyway.

Wife. How strange, she began to think dispassionately, her mind sometimes a muddle, as if she swam in cloudy waters. Mrs. Farmer Braxton. The thought brought her up short, clearing her mind. She didn't even know his Christian name. She was the wife of a man she didn't even know.

When he was there, he never touched her, rarely spoke, only stared at her, especially when he thought she was asleep.

Eventually, Belle managed to sit up for a length of

time against the plush pillows. Every now and again, memories of St. Valentine's Day would slip into being, but she always pushed them away. In their place she began to create a fanciful world in her head. She expunged the hazy, partially remembered reality. And as time passed, the fanciful world became indistinguishable from reality, became a new truth which she believed in as surely as she believed that her name was Belle.

Eventually, she managed to swing her legs over the side of the bed, but walking was impossible—just like the old woman had said. Belle fell back against the feather mattress, her legs dangling over the side, and she tried not to cry. She had learned that crying did absolutely no good. Her father still wouldn't be here, and her leg would still be a mess. The tears would burn, but she never let them flow.

Then one day the farmer brought her a hand-carved crutch. The sun was out and had slipped in through the doorway, illuminating the bedroom. In the years her father had worked for the man, Belle had never seen him up close, only from a distance. Since arriving in his home, she had only seen him in the darkened room. In her innocent mind, she had turned him into a hideous monster, scarred and misshapened. But this man was no monster.

His hair was blond, and he looked much younger than she had thought, though still, in her eyes, he was old —probably well into his thirties, she reasoned. Ancient, to her way of thinking. His eyes were blue and his skin smooth. He seemed to grow uncomfortable under her scrutiny. But instead of leaving, he came closer.

Belle's heart lurched and staggered. She shrank back against the pillows. The room had grown hot, and earlier she had pushed the covers to the side. When she reached out to pull them back, he reached out and stayed her hand.

"No," she whispered. She didn't know exactly what she was saying no to, but she said it as instinctively as a squirrel gathered nuts to save itself from winter.

He ignored her. Lowering himself onto the bed, the mattress sank beneath his weight. His movements were awkward, and Belle watched as if everything was happening in slow motion. His eyes scanned the length of her.

She thought she would die. "Please, no."

He only continued to look, though never as low as her leg. And just when he extended his hand and she knew he would touch her, she jerked away and cried out. "No!"

With the movement the covers fell free, leaving her broken leg exposed against the mattress. His extended hand froze. His pale skin blanched, and the strange look that had been in his eyes only moments before vanished, replaced by what Belle could only call revulsion. As if burned, he dropped his hand away.

"I brought this for you to use," he said shortly a second later.

"What for?" she asked, relief mixing with mortification that the sight of her leg was so repelling.

"To walk," he snapped.

"But the old woman—"

"What about her?"

"She said I'd never be able to walk again."

His fair countenance darkened. "She doesn't know what she's talking about. You'll walk again if you will it."

She looked at him, then at the stick, before she held out her hand. Whether she hated him or not, she couldn't afford not to believe him. "Then I will. That way when my father returns, I won't be a burden."

The farmer stiffened. "Your father isn't coming back."

Fear raced through her. "You're lying."

She saw the anger grow, distorting his features, and she forced herself not to be afraid.

"Don't you ever call me a liar!"

"My father is coming back for me," she responded tightly. "He wouldn't leave me here. He wouldn't. He hates you."

His fist crashed against the wall. "Your father isn't coming back for you! You're my wife! Do you understand? Mine, all mine, only mine! Just like the cows in the pasture and the horses in the stable. You are mine." His face was ravaged, his silky blond hair falling in his eyes. "And don't you ever forget it. Mine!" he raged. "Only mine!"

Belle might only have been thirteen years old, but she had aged tremendously since the day she watched her mother's coffin being lowered into the cold, hard earth. Her chin raised a notch and she boldly met his angry gaze. "I am not yours," she whispered vehemently, "and never will be."

Then she turned away and started to cross the floor, one meager step at a time, ignoring the throb of pain in her leg and where the wood bit into her underarm. She would learn to walk with the stick, then once she was strong enough, she would learn to walk without it. She would.

Then she would walk away. Forever. Free to find her father.

CHAPTER
TWENTY-FOUR

"Damn it, Belle," Stephen said, running his hand through his dark hair, "answer me. Did you love him so much?"

Belle's lips pursed into a straight line, her eyes burned and her throat ached. How had she ever thought she would be free? God, she cried silently, she would never be free.

She turned stiffly toward the door, walking with careful steps, afraid that at any moment she would crumble. If she could just make it home. *Home.* The word was a mockery. This home that she had made for her father, the home that he had always said he wanted. She didn't know if she should laugh or scream. She prayed instead. *Please, Papa. Please come home.*

When she reached the front door of Stephen's house, her delicate fingers grasped the brass knob, white against gold, until the door swung free and she was outside.

Stephen followed her, out of his house and down the steps, his hair rippling in the breeze, his loose white sleeves billowing like sails, his angry steps taking him into her house. He spoke to her the whole way. But no matter what he said, she neither spoke nor answered, just walked with determination, he on her heels like a badger. Another time he would have been embarrassed by such a scene. But it wasn't another time.

Once inside, she took the long stairway, slowly, carefully, her hand so white against the stained and polished bannister.

Stephen watched her climb from the foyer, up and around, up and around until she disappeared and he knew she was at the top, in her room, four stories above the earth. He should leave. He knew it. He told himself over and over again.

With a muffled curse, he raced up the stairs two at a time. When he came into her room, breathless, the sight struck him still. He found her standing at the French doors that led out to the balcony, her forehead pressed against the pane, her breath frosting the glass. Desperate and alone. How many times had he found her just like this?

The sight tore at his heart, ripping away his anger— or was it jealousy? he wondered suddenly. He didn't know, didn't have time to determine. She looked like a little lost girl, her blue hair ribbon askew, and he couldn't even see her eyes. But he knew if he could they would be filled with that longing for things he was afraid he would never understand. If only he could. If only she would let him. And he understood then that she was the key to her past. He could search the world, find birth records, marriage records, even records of death, but the inner secrets would have to come from her, from her lips.

"Did you love him so much?" he whispered into the silent room.

The sound of his voice seemed loud in his ears, as if he had screamed the words. Belle appeared not to have heard, or if she did, she clearly didn't care to answer. But he couldn't let it go. "Answer me, Belle. Please. Quit running away—from me, from whatever is in your past. For once give me a straight answer." He hesitated. "Did you love him so much that you'll never be able to love me?"

He saw her body tense, and he could tell that she had closed her eyes. But still no words.

His heart sank. He was fighting a futile battle, banging himself against a rampart of steel that he clearly would never be able to breach. He wanted to scream, to cry, to rage at the frustration and futility of what his life had become. He was out of control, his life was falling apart. First Adam, and now Belle.

Taking a deep breath, defeated, bewildered beneath the pain, he turned to go. And then she spoke.

"I'll be thirty years old tomorrow." Silence. Then, "Did you know that"

"Did I know that you were turning thirty? No. That you were having a birthday? Yes. The party, remember." The party. The party that was supposed to have been the occasion on which they would have announced their impending marriage as well as a means to celebrate the day of her birth. Such a fool he had been.

"Ah, yes" she said, "the infamous party that others are planning in my house, and about which I have no say. That party, you mean?"

Stephen grimaced. "I'm sorry."

She gave a self-deprecating little sigh. "Don't be sorry, Stephen. It doesn't matter. Have a party, don't have a party. I'll turn thirty whether others come to celebrate or not. Birthdays come and go, year after year, bringing hope, then dashing it until I don't know if I'll ever be able to hope again."

"What have you been hoping for, Belle? Tell me, please. For your father? For your husband? For what, Belle?"

She took a deep breath. But the words she provided

had nothing to do with his question. "While I've spent my time hoping all these years, I realize now that life has passed me by."

"Hope? Life passing you by? What are you talking about?" His voice was impassioned as he stepped closer. "I don't know of anyone who seems to live so fully as you."

"*Seems,* I think, is the telling word here. Running away, is more accurate, just as you pointed out only moments before. Activities to command the mind, to fill my time so I don't have to think. And I've been running for years."

He came so close that he could touch her. His fingers longed to caress her arms, pull her back against his heart, hold her tight, and never let her go. "Tell me, Belle," he said, as he finally gave in and touched her, his long, strong fingers curling around her arms, then turning her back. "Tell me what you're running from," he pleaded, looking down into her eyes.

They were no more than scant inches apart. Her head was tilted back, and he watched as her eyes found his lips. Desire surged through him, but it was a deeper desire, a desperate desire to make things right, make her whole.

"Sweet Belle, I want to help you. Only help. You say your life has passed you by, then good. Now you can move on, move on to a better life, one that's full and rich."

She didn't respond, simply stared at his lips, then his jaw and cheeks, before she ran her fingers through his hair.

"A life with me, Belle. As my wife."

Her fleeting smile was haunting. "A wife that you would love and cherish?"

"Of course," he breathed.

"Then love me now, Stephen. Show me how you would cherish me."

This time, he was the one to tense. He wanted her, his body's throbbing response to her demand was proof enough of that. But unlike his body, he wanted answers.

"Please," she whispered. "Don't be bound by questions that have no answers."

"Of course there are answers. You simply don't want to provide them."

"Maybe. Maybe not. Or have you ever thought that perhaps I don't begin to understand the questions, much less know the answers? Did it ever occur to you that there is one indisputable moment in my life when everything changed?" She looked at him closely. "Not so different from you. Your life changed when your parents died."

The words from long ago resurfaced in his mind. *They're never coming home.* It had changed him, irreparably. He knew that. But had it changed him so fundamentally that people saw him differently?

Suddenly he remembered throwing berries out of a tree. Laughing and smiling. Believing in pots of gold and buried treasures.

"The difference," she continued, "is that I have a huge gaping hole in my memory—and as a result, in my life. One day my leg is perfect and straight, the next it's not. I don't remember the incident that changed me. I remember before, then after, but not that moment. It's gone, except for bits and pieces that haunt me at every turn." Her voice grew strained. "If only the rest would disappear, too."

"Oh, Belle—"

"Shhh," she said, pressing one finger to his lips.

"Don't say anything. Please." Then she reached up on tiptoes, her fingers curling in his shirt.

She was so lovely and innocent and fragile that he thought he might break. And it was then that he gave in, the dam giving way, his desire tumbling forth with an intensity that could easily destroy everything in its path.

He pressed his lips to hers. "God," he groaned as he opened his mouth on hers.

His arm wrapped around her shoulders, binding her to him, while his hand came up to caress her cheek, his thumb lining her jaw. His kiss was gentle, loving, though commanding, as if demanding that she return to him all that he felt for her. Though she didn't speak the words, he felt certain that she did return his sentiments, at least that is what he wanted to believe—had to believe. She was there, in his arms, sharing his love.

And in the nearly overwhelming darkness that surrounded them despite the daylight hours, they found each other. Anchoring in the storm.

His hand trailed over her throat, feeling the hard steady pulse of her heart. Opening his mouth on her pulse, he ran the backs of his strong fingers slowly down her collarbone until he came to her breast, so full and lush. He took the weight against the palm of his hand. Her head fell back and she murmured his name.

He longed to feel her rosebud nipples from beneath her velvet gown, to caress them with his tongue, make them rise.

Ignoring shoulds and shouldn'ts, Stephen swept her up in his arms and carried her to the bed. Bracing one knee on the mattress, he lowered her, his body following hers until he was stretched out over her, his hard lean thigh coming to rest between her own. With her arms wrapped around his shoulders, her head flung back, he caressed her body with his lips as he moved the fabric away to touch skin until they each laid together entwined, their clothes tossed aside, forgotten on the floor.

When she tried to cover her leg, he pushed her hands away. "I love you, Belle, all of you." Then he ran his fingers up her arm to her breast, making her forget.

He took one nipple in his mouth, as he had longed to do, laving the bud until she moaned, her back arching to his touch. Her fingers wound their way into his hair.

When he moved between her legs, she raised her knees. He pressed against her sweet opening. She was tight, too tight, he thought fleetingly. But she whimpered, and moved against him, causing him to slide deeper, ceasing all thought. He pushed forward, her back arching, as she tried to take him in. But then he came to a barrier.

Belle Braxton, undeniably, was a virgin.

"Belle," he began, confused.

But Belle only pulled him closer, tears streaming down her cheeks to fall unheeded into the bed. "Love me, Stephen," she repeated, moving against him. "Stop asking questions."

And then he thought no more.

With one strong thrust, he broke through the proof of so much that was wrong. He cried out with sheer, maddening sensation. She quickly muffled her cry of pain against his shoulder. Heat alchemized into desire, then into uncontrolled passion, raging, burning them both in the storm. He moved within her, his lips devouring her body. And just when he heard her cry out and felt her body quiver with its release, he remembered the day he was afraid he had become the moth to her flame. He was no longer afraid. If this was what it was like to burn, then so be it. And just as he thrust one last time, crying out with his own release, he was certain he would never be the same.

Long moments passed before his heart slowed. He could feel hers imitating his own.

"Belle," he murmured, his body still against hers, holding her tight, skin pressed against skin, his eyes oddly burning. He felt so much, but had such inadequate words to explain. Love certainly only scratched the surface of his emotions. But as his heart slowed, and the intensity of the moment passed, other feelings set in. The confusion returned, along with all the questions, and though he knew he should set them aside, he couldn't. "I don't understand. What has your life been before you came here?"

Raising up on his elbows, he looked deep into her eyes. Dark hair lay wild against the light pillow casing. Blue eyes looked back at him, bright against pale skin. But she would not speak. He dropped down and groaned into her shoulder.

Belle felt the vibration of his deep voice down to her soul, rumbling, stirring. Never in her dreams had she imagined that lying with Stephen could fill her with such intensity. But it was more than passion that his intimate touch had awakened in her. Much more. She felt alive as she had never felt before—alive with yearnings that once awakened she was certain would never lie dormant again. Belle felt as if Pandora's Box had been opened, revealing a need for Stephen that went well beyond what deep down she had suspected. And that scared her.

Belle felt as if she might break. And like Adam had wanted so often to do, Belle wanted to talk, tell Stephen all her hopes and fears. But she had seen firsthand how no matter the love Stephen felt for someone, he had shown that his love could not span the valley of difference. He might want her desperately now, but later? What would happen when she couldn't meet his exacting expectations?

But then she caught sight of her favorite overstuffed chair. Pretty and perfect. Repaired. By her dear Stephen. Returned to her only days before. A bud of hope crept into her soul. Maybe he *could* accept her for who she was. Maybe she was wrong, maybe he wouldn't try to fit her into a mold of "the perfect woman," something she could never be. He had seen her leg and had not rejected her. He was here, wasn't he? Sharing a piece of heaven with her like a gift from the gods.

Her mind filled with an excitement and happiness she hadn't felt since she was a child. He loved her. He had said so. And lying there beside him, she knew she loved him, too. It didn't matter that she shouldn't. It didn't matter that he might deter her from her path. She loved him, with all her heart and soul.

She took a deep breath, pulling in the courage to tell him of her feelings, tell him about her husband. But Stephen spoke first, stopping her words.

"Tell me about your past, Belle. I can help. It's not too late for you to start a new life." His dark eyes brightened, the full lips that had caressed her so intimately curved into a smile. "I haven't had a chance to tell you, but I've hired a seamstress to make you a whole new wardrobe, and a French chef to teach you to cook. I even managed to hire Mrs. Walderpole to teach you the finer points of entertaining."

The words she had been on the verge of speaking stuck in her throat. Hope was dashed, again, devastating her. How had she ever believed, even for a second, that he wouldn't want to change her?

Her eyes burning and her throat tight with unshed tears, Belle rolled away, then stood, pain washing through her body.

"What's wrong?" he asked, startled.

She pulled on the velvet dress that lay like a puddle of shimmery color on the floor.

"What did I say?" he demanded, the tone of his voice rising. "I thought you'd be pleased."

Her hair tumbled down her back. She turned back to him, her fingers working the fastenings, her hair swinging out from the sudden movement. "Nothing, Stephen. You said nothing. And I don't need your help, never have, never will."

He stared at her forever, then swung his legs over the side. Standing, he snatched up his pants. Belle could only watch, despair flooding through her. He was so beautiful, she thought, just as she had said that first evening in the Bulfinch House. Only now she knew the extent of his beauty. Chiseled back tapering to slim waist, the hard curve of buttock, suddenly covered by black pants when he pulled them on. Despair rocked her body.

She walked to the French doors that led to the balcony. A few inches of powdery snow covered the ground, a miniature range of mountains rose and fell, running along the balustrade. A gust of wind blew in when she pulled the door open. Staring out, she was unaware of the cold.

"What are you doing?" Stephen demanded. He strode over, his boots pulled on, his shirt nearly buttoned, to shut the door.

"Do you hear them, Stephen?"

His steps faltered. "Do I hear what?"

"The voices."

He looked first at her then out into the cold. "What are you talking about, Belle? Get away from there."

Just when he reached the door, she stepped out, her bare feet leaving imprints in the snow.

"Damn it, Belle. Get back in here!"

Arms extended, she twirled awkwardly.

"Belle!"

His bootprints wiped hers clean, but before he could reach her, she climbed up onto the balustrade. Stephen froze.

"Belle," he said on a harsh intake of breath.

"It's like being on the edge of a canyon, standing up here, high above the street, covered with snow. If I close my eyes, I can make-believe the house fronts are cliffs, and the cobbled street is the rock-strewn bottom."

At the sound of his footstep, she jerked back, her eyes daring him to come nearer. Stephen stopped instantly. After a minute, she relaxed.

"Aren't you going to ask me how in the world I would know what a canyon looks like if I've lived my whole life in Wrenville?"

"I'm going to ask you to come down from there."

Belle only smiled. "When I was a child, in addition to telling me all about Boston, my father told me all about canyons . . . and places far away. He's been to many canyons. All his travels, you know." She looked at him harshly. "He does exist, no matter what you say."

"This isn't the time to get into that, Belle."

"True." The harshness fled. "He says out west you can see forever, and from miles away you can see smoke rise in the air, giving shape to the wind. I love that, the idea of wind made real by paintbrush strokes of white smoke. When he comes for me, I'll travel with him. Did I tell you that?"

"Belle," he said sharply, taking another step forward. Her eyes widened with alarm.

"Come down from there," he said, his steps ceasing.

She looked down at him with a coy smile. "Remember Lucinda?"

"No more stories. Get down from there."

"You remember. The woman who once lived across the street."

A cold, paralyzing fear suddenly snaked through his body. "Belle," he said desperately. "What are you doing?"

She turned slowly to look out over the world. "I wonder if this is what Lucinda felt like, perched on the rim of a canyon like a bird, so free and alive, as if she could fly, breaking away from all that bound her down, just before she plunged?"

"Dear God. Please, Belle, come down from there."

"Do you think it really was the wind, Stephen?" She looked back at him. "Or did she jump?"

With a start, as if the idea startled her, she turned quickly, too quickly, to glance down the four stories to the ground. Her balance, precarious under the best of circumstances, teetered. Her eyes widened, and her hand reached out, trying to grasp at something to save her.

Time hung suspended. Breathlessly, painfully, Stephen watched in horror. His mind worked as if it swam in the churning river mud which coursed down the center of many a canyon. Dread, fear, and despair consumed him. "No!" he roared, forcing his limbs from inaction. With lightning speed he reached out and grabbed the soft flesh of Belle's arm and yanked her to safety.

His eyes blazed first with relief then anger once he saw, not contrition or fear, but humor dancing in her eyes.

"Do you think that was what happened?" she persisted. "That she didn't mean to fall, but there was no one there to save her?"

He couldn't believe it; she had nearly plunged to her death and now she was teasing him. "Damn you!" he roared. "You could have been killed. Doesn't that matter to you?"

She only laughed. "That seems to be the way with me. Always on the edge, always pulled back."

"You *are* crazy!" He released her arm with disdain, anger snapping into irrational rage. "No wonder you were still a virgin. Your husband probably didn't want to have anything to do with you."

Her smile vanished. Her porcelain features turned glacial. Stephen was stunned by the transformation and cursed himself for his stupidity.

"You're right," she said with a venom made more deadly by its proximity to her smile. "My husband didn't want to have anything to do with me, not once he saw my leg. He couldn't tolerate my limp. He couldn't abide the sight of my broken body. My hideously crippled body. I was a freak to him. So, no, I didn't love him. I hated him. You've been pushing me to that admission for days. Are you satisfied? Are you happy that you know? You weren't going to be content until you knew that I didn't love someone else. So I admit it. I hated my husband," she yelled for anyone to hear. "But you can think again if you want me to admit my father's not coming for me, because he is. He is!"

Stephen watched, dumbstruck, unmindful of the cold and snow. The scene sickened him, not because of how Belle was acting, but because he realized, as he stood there in the early February cold, that in his attempts to make her see what he thought she should see, he was pushing her to the limits of her endurance. He still had no idea what her past held. He still had no idea how her leg had been brutally broken. He only knew that she lived in a world not quite of man, and not quite of make-believe, not quite sane and not quite crazy, as she tried to deny the truth of whatever dark past she held, or perhaps just wanted to forget. Since he had met her, he had done nothing more than try to make her remember.

And though he believed that in some recess of her mind she knew that either her father didn't exist at all, or if he did that he wasn't coming for her, something closer to the surface kept those realizations at bay. Or, he hated to admit, for reasons unknown she simply felt compelled to continue to lie to him. The thought seared him. He loved her, as he had loved no one else. And he could think of no way to help her. She had made it clear she wanted nothing from him.

She had asked him to leave her alone, but selfishly he had denied her request. After the soul-shattering lovemaking they had just shared, Stephen didn't know how he could ever let her go. But he realized then, standing coatless in front of her barefooted form on a balcony covered with snow, that he must.

Relentless, gaping loss curled around his heart. But it didn't matter what he felt, he admonished himself. What mattered was Belle. "I'm sorry—about everything. And after the ball tomorrow night for your birthday, I'll leave you alone and you'll never have to see me again."

They stood, staring at each other, their breaths coming in harsh, cold puffs. But neither spoke. Finally, Stephen turned to go. And as he left, he never saw the despair that had returned to her eyes, or the hand that reached out to him, or the words that hung frozen on her lips.

CHAPTER TWENTY-FIVE

Stephen strode angrily through the streets of Boston toward his office, his head down, never giving a thought to taking his carriage despite the frigid weather. He was unaware of the sting of cold on his hands or hatless head; he was only aware of Belle. Belle. Sweet Blue Belle.

Crazy Belle.

God, how could the rumors have proven to be true? his mind raged. But as his steps took him blocks away from her home and the dangerous balustrade levels above the unforgiving cobbled street, he knew it was true. Belle was crazy. She lived in some sort of dream world, waiting for a father who undoubtedly wouldn't arrive.

He pushed from his mind the insidious thoughts that there was more truth to her words than he cared to admit, and that a large part of her problem was him. Thoughts of Adam leaped into his mind—Adam like a ghost drinking himself to death in the room that was once Stephen's study. His heart ached, but he locked it away. Adam no longer existed to him.

The vibration of the elevator seemed to sink to his very bones as the cage rose with frustrating slowness to his office. He felt as if he would scream by the time the door was pulled open on the top floor.

"Mr. St. James!" the receptionist said. "You're here! Mr. Banks is looking for you."

Stephen hardly heard. He walked back to his office,

saying nothing, noticing even less as his mind swirled with images of Belle up on the balustrade like a angel ready to take flight. From him? The fact remained that she had jumped up there after running from him, running from his questions, from his demands that she see her life as he felt certain it was. Why was it so important that he push her to such realizations? he wondered. Selfishness, he thought. Because he was selfish.

And what if he was wrong about her father? What if he had been wrong all along?

He flinched at the thought. No. He couldn't be wrong. He wasn't, or so he tried to tell himself. But he had to admit he'd been wrong about the husband. He could be wrong about the father, too. No. He wasn't wrong. The only way she would be able to get on with her life would be to realize it. If only she would.

"Mr. St. James!"

Stephen's head came up with a start, and he was surprised to find that he stood at a window, looking out over the city. He turned sharply.

"Mr. St. James!" Nathan cried, his always perfectly proper professional demeanor gone. "I found him! I found him!"

Stephen's heart stilled. "Who?" he asked, a pervasive dread washing over him.

"Mrs. Braxton's father!"

His mind rocked with the impact.

"He's alive. And he's here in Boston!"

Stephen's breath caught in his throat. "He's here?"

"Yes! Imagine that. Right here in Boston. Apparently he just arrived."

Stephen's world closed around him, the words echoing in his mind. The foundation of his life—his belief that what he did he did because it was right—crumbling before him.

Dear God, I was wrong.

His mind staggered at the sudden, brutal realization of the truth he could no longer deny.

I was wrong.

First with Adam. Now with Belle.

Not only did Belle's father exist, but the man was here, in Boston, just as she said he would be—just before her birthday, in time for their dance. He realized as well, that in his selfish attempt to make her his, he had tried to destroy her faith in her father so he wouldn't have to compete, and in doing so he had been destroying her.

He turned away angrily, his selfishness nearly overwhelming him.

"He's here, and I—"

"I'm not interested in details," Stephen said sharply. He wanted to be left alone.

"But sir—"

"Just have him at the ball for Belle's birthday." As soon as he said the words, he realized this was an opportunity to set things straight, make things right. An apology of sorts. He would surprise her with the gift of her father in a setting where they could have their long-awaited dance. He almost smiled at the look he knew would curve on her face when she saw her father. But his smile didn't come. In finding the father, he knew with a certainty that he had lost her forever.

"But sir—"

"Just do it!" Stephen snapped. "And keep it quiet. I want it to be a surprise."

Nathan hesitated, before he shrugged his shoulders, then turned and left the office, leaving Stephen alone, staring out over the buildings and streets of Boston, once a city he loved, now simply a series of places where he had spent time with Belle. And he wondered as he stood there how he would ever get over the loss.

The house on Arlington Street glittered like a jewel against the black velvet night. Clouds were rolling in. A storm was predicted—snow and ice, mixed with rain. Hardly the perfect night for a party.

Carriages were lined up as far as the eye could see. The ball had turned into the event of the season. With all the construction that had gone on in the house, Bostonians were eager to see the finished product of the notorious Widow Braxton.

Almost everyone invited knew that they were there to celebrate Belle's birthday. No one there except Stephen and Nathan knew that Belle Braxton's father was the actual gift.

At the top of the stairs just inside the ballroom doors, Stephen stood next to Belle. Dressed in a gown of lavender silk, her porcelain features were a frozen mask. Her body might be next to him, but Stephen knew her mind was far away.

Getting her to attend at all had been next to impossible. "This one last thing, Belle," he had said that morning. "Once it's over . . . I'll sign the house back over to you. Officially. No strings attached."

She had looked at him without speaking. If only she would say that she didn't want the house, that she wanted him. For a moment he thought she would say the words. Instead she had only turned away, leaving him alone in her foyer, workers hurrying about, decorations going up, food being brought in, musicians setting up in the ballroom.

He glanced down at her now. Stunning, he thought.

She was stunning, even though she didn't smile, hadn't smiled all evening. Not even when she had told him he looked devilishly handsome did she smile, nor when she had added, "my pirate-man." His heart raced at the memory, so sweet and poignant, and he wished he could turn back the clock and do things all over again.

Her dark hair was done up in an elegant design of twists and curls, her long, lavender gown skimming against her skin much as he longed to do. He glanced away with a muffled curse. Just as the clock could never be turned back, his hand would never touch her body again.

They had been standing there for a few minutes, though it felt like hours, as guests filtered in. Elden and Louisa Abbot were there, as was the Widow Hathaway, Lewis, and even Clarisse Webster.

"Is Adam coming?" Belle asked.

Her voice startled him, then wrapped around him until he felt as if he would strangle.

"I take it the answer is no." She sighed. "He loves you, Stephen. And just as importantly, he's your brother. Your love should be unconditional."

His family, Stephen thought. But as always the vision of Adam locked in another man's embrace snaked through his mind. It wasn't anger that he felt. Just a sickening dread. It was his fault. He had done everything wrong. If her father hadn't fought for Adam, had let the others take him, Adam wouldn't have turned out as he had. Or if he had been a better example. Or if . . . The possibilities were endless, proof that Stephen had failed miserably in raising Adam. He had failed at filling his father's shoes.

His foundation crumbled even further.

"Oh, Stephen," Belle said softly, looking up at him.

But Stephen only stared forward. With a sigh, Belle turned back to the long line of guests.

"Hello, Mrs. Smythe. How good of you to come," she said like a hostess any fine Boston matron would admire. But as soon as the woman stepped away, Belle gathered her skirts and turned away.

"Where are you going?" Stephen demanded.

"To find Adam."

"You can't leave now. You're the guest of honor."

"Fill in for me."

"How, pray tell, do you expect me to do that?"

He received the first smile of the evening. "Do something crazy," she said, her smile sad and distant. "That should suffice."

And before he could say another word, she slipped out through the doorway, just as another guest greeted Stephen.

As much as she wanted to find Adam, Belle needed to breathe. She hadn't liked standing there, trying to smile as each of the guests passed by. If she didn't escape, at least for a while, she wasn't certain she could survive the night.

She had tried again and again to get Stephen to cancel the party. She hadn't gotten much further than speaking to Nathan and Wendell. Stephen wouldn't see her until that morning, when he had come looking for her to make certain she would attend, and by then it was too late. So the plans for the party had continued forward like a sailboat in a brisk wind.

Belle hurried up the steps to Stephen's house. Wendell let her in.

"Where is Adam?" she asked.

"He isn't here, madam."

Belle groaned. "Has it been bad?" she asked, walking into the parlor to warm her hands by the fire.

Wendell grimaced. "I'm afraid so. And I worry. The younger Mr. St. James is . . . not himself. Though I guess neither is the elder."

Belle concentrated on the fire. "Do you mind if I stay a while, Wendell?"

"No ma'am. In fact, I'll go find you some tea."

Time passed. Sipping tea, Belle watched the flames flicker in the fireplace, mesmerized. Forgetting the party.

"Belle!" Stephen came through the door. "Are you going to return or are you going to stay here all night?"

"Do I have a choice?"

The look on her face dashed whatever remaining hope Stephen had that they might stand a chance together. "We all have choices, Belle," he replied.

"Do we?" She shrugged. "Not always, Stephen."

He stared at her, wishing yet again for answers, but he knew they wouldn't come. "Come on. You have a house full of guests."

They walked back to her house quietly, Stephen catching her protectively when she slipped on the ice. Neither spoke, until eventually Stephen asked, "Was Adam in?"

Belle glanced up at him. "No, he wasn't there."

"Ah," he replied before silence reigned between them once again.

By the time Belle and Stephen returned to her house, the line of carriages waiting to deposit their occupants had diminished. The house was full. Just inside the door, Nathan caught Stephen's arm, pulling him to the side. "He's here," he whispered. "He came in while you were next door."

"Who's here?" Belle asked, her eyes suddenly brightening.

Nathan and Stephen looked at her.

"The pastry chef with your cake," Nathan quickly interjected.

"Oh," she said, then turned away sharply.

The music started up, filling the house, washing over Belle like a teasing caress.

Her father hadn't come.

She was a fool to have believed he would. Yes, a fool, she admonished herself harshly.

She began to hum as Stephen guided her to the ballroom. But humming didn't help. She began to count, slowly, to herself. One to thirty. Then over again.

It was only nine o'clock. From everything she had heard, a ball could last well into the early morning hours. How had she let Stephen talk her into attending? How would she survive? The music. The dancing. All on her birthday. In this house in Boston. Under a huge crystal chandelier. Dear God, she didn't know.

If only she could touch Stephen, ask him to hold her —and she would have given in and done just that, had Clarisse Webster not chosen that moment to join her.

"Belle darling. I believe I just met a relative of yours."

Belle tilted her head in question. "A relative of mine? Here?"

"He bares a striking resemblance to you. Not in hair or eye color, but something about him . . . I was just certain you must be related. Holly was the name."

Belle's mouth went dry. "You met someone named Holly?" she asked, her heart beginning to pound.

"Well, yes. New to town, I believe."

Belle turned sharply toward the crush of guests, hope

rekindled in her blue eyes. Couples danced across the floor in concentric circles, around and around, in time to the music, until suddenly, magically, they cleared.

Displaying one man.

He was tall and large. A burly man out of place in a fine cut of evening clothes. The beard was gone, but the face was undeniable.

Papa! her mind cried. Tears burned at her eyes. He had come. For her birthday. To dance. In the grandest of ballrooms

"There he is," Clarisse stated, pointing at the man.

His smile was the same. The gray eyes just as pale. It was all Belle could do to stand still. She wanted to race to him and throw herself in his arms. But she would wait. She had waited for seventeen long years. She could wait a few minutes more.

Slowly, much too slowly for Belle's pounding heart, the waltz came to an end.

"Mr. Holly," Clarisse called.

The man turned toward them. What little doubt remained, vanished. It was him. *Papa.* Her papa.

But then the couples all around dispersed. And for the first time Belle noticed the woman on his arm. Belle staggered back into Stephen's solid chest. Confusion swirled.

"Mr. Holly," Clarisse called again, waving him over.

The man started forward. Belle's heart hammered; she pressed back into Stephen, as if to escape.

"Miss Webster," the man bellowed, his eyes gray and smiling.

A groan sounded deep in Belle's chest, drawing the man's attention. And then, finally, after a million lifetimes, their eyes met.

His boisterous smile faltered. His steps ceased.

"Madeline," he breathed, his voice barely a whisper, not understood.

But Belle heard, Belle understood as they stood no more than a few feet apart, staring, neither moving.

"Mr. Holly," Clarisse said. "This is Mrs. Hershal Braxton. Mrs. Braxton, Mr. Browning Holly."

Belle didn't speak, only stared. Stephen looked on, his hands secure on her shoulders. Clarisse looked on, her perfectly painted face furrowing in question. Only the young woman on the man's arm seemed unaware of the tension.

"Papa," the girl demanded, "the music is starting again. And you promised me every dance."

Belle's mind staggered and swayed. Her thoughts collided, her life tumbling before her. The room closed in on her, hemming her in, making it hard to breathe. She was unaware of Stephen's hands, which tightened on her shoulders, or of Clarisse's look, which had turned to concern.

"I thought perhaps you were related," Clarisse stated uncertainly.

"Papa!" the girl demanded.

Papa. For a second Belle thought she was caught up in a bad dream, as happened so often at night. Her mind pitched back and forth between Wrenville so many years before, and Boston this night, as she tried to make sense of the unimaginable. But this dream, she knew, was all too real—a reality that made no sense.

Her father. With another daughter.

A sob caught in her throat. How was it possible?

It didn't matter that she hadn't seen her father in seventeen years. It didn't matter that a lifetime in which families could be made as well as broken had passed by. The sight before her still made no sense.

"Related?" The word finally filtered through the dense fog in Belle's mind. She glanced at Clarisse with a start, before she looked back at the man. "No. No, we're not related," she said, her voice laced with an eerie calm. "Another Holly, I'm sure. Now, if you'll excuse me," Belle added, the words carefully enunciated, as if she might get them wrong.

She had to escape, out of this room, so she could breathe. But she knew with a sickening certainty that no matter how far she ran, she would never escape his light gray eyes, or the young girl who had danced in his arms.

Very carefully, trying to breathe, she started to turn away.

"Belle," Stephen began.

"No," she said, her voice catching as she jerked free of his hold.

The small group watched her go. Stephen turned deadly eyes on Browning Holly. "What the hell is going on here?"

Browning didn't seem to hear; he only stared at Belle's receding back, his ruddy complexion turned white.

"Don't leave," Stephen instructed, his gaze slaying him on the spot. "You have some explaining to do." Then he turned toward the door, shock, fear, and dread warring in his breast. Good God, what had he done? he wondered, racing out the front door after Belle.

The skies had opened up. The snow that had covered the ground was rapidly turning to slush under the weight of the rain and ice falling from the heavens like tears of the gods. Wind blew, whipping the elements about at its whim. Stephen raised a forearm to shield his eyes as he searched for Belle in the storm.

"Belle," he shouted, the sound whisked away into the cold, dark night.

Instinct carried him into the Public Gardens, through the spiked wrought iron fence, down the winding paths, until he saw her. Her limp was pronounced, exaggerated by the cold and her flight. He closed the distance that separated them with a few frantic strides.

"Belle," he called through the wind, catching her, then turning her back to him.

Her face was wet and ravaged, blank, as if she didn't recognize him.

"Belle," he repeated, shaking her. "Belle. Talk to me," he cried, freezing rain cascading down his cheeks. "For once, talk to me. Tell me what is happening—tell me what happened."

A deep, ravaged groan welled up in her and she tried to turn away.

He forced her back. "That *was* your father Belle. You know it, and I know it."

The wind whipped her hair from its moorings, casting it adrift in the tempestuous storm. And as she stood there, Stephen watched as her frozen countenance began to crack like the ice on the lagoon the day she had tried to save her scarf.

"Dear God, Belle," he said, his voice a desperate caress. "Tell me what happened."

CHAPTER
TWENTY-SIX

WRENVILLE 1877

Belle stood silently, her dark ringlets curling down her back, the sketch in her hands, her thirteenth birthday cake sitting on the table, dread filling every inch of her being.

No, everything wasn't going to be all right, her young mind reasoned with a clarity well beyond her years. Her father was too quiet as he stared at the painstakingly executed drawing.

"Papa," she said tentatively, her fingers curling around the heavy paper edges, her half-moon nails biting into the dark brown pigment she had used for her mother's hair. "Do you like it?"

He stared at the sketch of his wife for a breathless eternity. Without warning, his fist smashed into the rough-hewn wall. "I can't take this, do you hear me? I can't take this any longer!"

Belle stood dumbstruck as he moved toward the door, his head bowed.

The door was closed, but the curtains over the small window to the side were opened. For the first time, Belle noticed the wagon that waited outside, packed and loaded, a horse she recognized as being from the town livery gnawing impatiently on the bit. Slowly, as if in a dream, her father looked back at her, his pale eyes boring

into her. An uneasy foreboding washed over her, leaving
her weak.

"Papa." She forced the word. "What's happening?"

"Go pack." He picked up an empty satchel she
hadn't notice by the door and thrust it toward her.

"Where are we going?" she asked, the sketch slipping
from her fingers, see-sawing back and forth until it lay
forgotten on the rough hewn floor.

"Go pack."

"But—"

"GO PACK!"

Belle stepped back, away from his harsh words. Her
mind circling frantically, she took the bag he forced on
her and climbed the ladder to her loft. With little thought
for what she put into the satchel, she did as she was told,
before returning to the main floor.

Where were they going? she wondered desperately,
her heart pounding so loudly she could hear nothing else.
How could they leave their home? When the teasing
thought entered her mind that finally they were going to
Boston, to share the life of her father's dreams, the matu-
rity that she had achieved since her mother's death told
her it was nothing so simple.

The crisp afternoon sky was clear. Her father thrust
her coat out to her. With trembling hands, she pulled it
on before he doused the flames in the fire with the bucket
of water she would have used to clean the dishes from the
party. The angry hiss from the hearth filled the house.
Steam billowed up like a thick curtain, and Belle wondered fleetingly if she could hide in it. But the cloud held
no safety as her father stepped out the door. Paralyzed,
Belle could only watch.

"Come on," he snapped back at her, his broad shoulders hunched against the cold.

She clutched her satchel, and hurried outside. He was angry now, she reasoned. If only she could pacify him. But how? "I'm sorry about the drawing, Papa," she said. "I'll never do one again."

But her words held no sway. He continued on, never looking back.

He didn't climb into the wagon, but walked around it, then out of the small yard they called their own. Her dread began to grow and take shape as they walked, Belle clutching the large satchel with both of her small hands, her father walking with determined strides in a direction that could mean only one thing.

They were heading down the road that led to no place but the house of the hated farmer.

"Papa?"

His step never faltered.

"Papa." She tried to keep the quiver of anxiety from her voice, having to run every few steps to keep up, the bag banging against her knees beneath her mother's old dress. "Where are we going?"

Still no answer.

At the fence that surrounded the yard of the farmer's house, Belle halted at the gate. She had to be dreaming. This couldn't be happening to her. But when she blinked, then blinked again, hoping to clear her mind, or awaken herself from this nightmare, the only sight that met her was her father, angry and impatient.

"Quit dallying, girl."

Girl. So uncaring and detached. Her head swam. What happened to Blue, or Blue Belle? Dear God, what had happened? "No, Papa," she stated, her tiny voice quavering.

He turned searing gray eyes on her. He took the few

steps that separated them, grabbed her arm, and pulled her forward.

Every fiber of her being recoiled when she found the farmer waiting on the front porch, a store-bought rocking chair pushed softly by the breeze.

This isn't happening, she chanted to herself, as if when she said it enough she would begin to believe.

"Here she is, Mr. Braxton," her father said curtly. "Just as I said."

Though he stood in the shadows cast by the porch overhang, Belle could tell the farmer's gaze slid over her like she was no better than livestock, a look she couldn't define etching his murky features. Instinctively, she murmured a protest and tried to pull away. Her father held her tight.

When he seemed to have looked his fill, the farmer pulled a small though clearly weighty bag from his coat pocket. After a moment, staring at Belle all the while, he tossed it to her father.

The clink of coins beneath smoothed canvas rattled in her father's hands when he caught it. Stunned, Belle looked on. She tried to formulate thoughts, make sense of the unimaginable, but could come up with nothing more than one thing.

Her father was selling her!

Dropping the satchel, she staggered back and would have fallen if she hadn't caught herself on a neat pile of wood stacked by the porch.

"Papa," she breathed.

He looked up from the bag of coins he held. He stared at her for long drawn out seconds, and for one brief moment Belle thought he would take her into his arms and tell her that truly it was all a bad dream. He dropped his eyes away and shoved the money into his heavy coat pocket instead.

Without so much as a word of love or good-bye, his head lowered, he turned and started away.

"Papa!" she cried, racing after him, clutching his arm. "You can't leave me! You can't leave me here!"

"Go back, girl. You're of a marriageable age," he said tightly.

"I'm thirteen," she cried incredulously.

"As I said, old enough to be married. Now you're his."

It was as if he had slapped her. The words he spoke gave voice to what she had suspected, but to hear them, from her beloved father's lips . . . "Papa, no!" she begged, clutching his arm in a frantic grip.

When she wouldn't let go, he pulled her back to the farmer with a curse. "Have some pride, girl," he bit out, shaking her loose.

Her eyes went wild, her breath short as she stared in shocked disbelief at his receding back. Just when he got to the gate, she felt a staying hand reach out and take hold of her shoulder. She realized with a start of hysteria that it was the farmer.

"No!" she cried, breaking free and racing after her father once again.

This time her father practically dragged her back, his craggy face set against her desperate cries. She hardly noticed the dark rage that was growing on the farmer's face, the tight lips and narrowed eyes. She cared even less. Her father was leaving her, and as evidenced by the packed wagon she had seen sitting outside their house, he was leaving forever.

"Please God, no," she screamed, when the farmer took hold of her arm at the bottom of the steps.

She kicked and cried, her boot heel catching on a thick branch of kindling.

"Stop it," the farmer ground out, doing his best to hold her back.

But Belle was wild, the last year and all its frustrations overwhelming her. The death of her mother, the silence in her once joyous home. And now, the ultimate betrayal of her father. She kicked and screamed for her life, heedless of the angry grip on her arm, mindful only of her father's receding back.

Her heel caught the farmer in the shin and he roared in pain. But when he tried to capture her again, she kicked and clawed like a wild animal, her hair tangling around her face in a web of black. She escaped, but only temporarily before the farmer caught her, dragging her back, her dress tearing, her boots gouging the earth.

"Stop this!" the man raged, his face mottled with red. "Stop this instant!"

Belle kicked out from the ground, catching him off guard and he tumbled backward, into the wood pile.

"Papa, you can't leave me! It's my birthday," she cried, her mind holding on to what she could manage, locking out the rest. Her sobs choked her, her body racked with emotion. "We haven't had our dance," she cried deperately, her tears streaking the dirt that dusted her face. Scrambling up off the ground, Belle ran after her father.

Furious, the farmer roared, pushing up from the pile of wood, his large hand fisting around a thick, swollen branch. "I said stop!" he shouted, striking out.

The wood caught her leg, hard. A sickening crack echoed in the suddenly still afternoon. With his back to them, her father jerked, and his step faltered. He stood frozen in the farmer's yard, his neck taut, his shoulders stiff—but he didn't turn back.

Belle watched, breath held, pleading quietly through her tears. "Come back, Papa. Please come back."

But in the end, he continued on, out of the farmyard, out of her life.

Belle lay in the dirt, the wood falling to the earth by the farmer's side. Dropping her head into her arms, her mind numb to everything but the memory of her father's receding form, she murmured, "Come back, Papa. Please come back. Please come back."

"Papa, please come back."

Tears streaked her cheeks, though this time they weren't mixed with dirt. This time they were streaked with icy rain and snow when she opened her eyes. A cloudy winter sky brooded in the heavens.

Her thoughts shifted and collided when she found not the hated farmer but Stephen hovering over her, his arms holding her protectively. Moments passed in confusion before she finally realized that she wasn't back in Wrenville all those years ago, but in Boston, the story spilling out like the rains from the heavens. The long-suppressed bits of memory that had lurked in the dark murky place in her mind had finally come clear, her moment of undeniable change finally remembered.

At length, she looked into Stephen's eyes and found her pain reflected in their depths. For a moment she drew in a deep breath and closed her eyes, before she opened them again and whispered, "Papa's not coming back."

Stephen stared at her, his hard, dark features etched with pain as the bells of Arlington Street Church tolled the hour in the distance. "No, my love," he said, his voice strained, his tears mixing with the rain. "Your father's not coming back."

CHAPTER
TWENTY-SEVEN

It seemed a horrible replay of the night Stephen had found Belle in the park lying in the mud all those months ago. But tonight he carried her securely in his arms, his shoulder healed—because of her. So many things had changed in his life—all because of her. Sweet Belle. An angel with broken wings, who could no longer fly.

Unlike the last time, Stephen vowed there would be no improprieties. In some strange way it was as if he was being given a second chance to right his wrongs of the night he had acted without honor. His footsteps faltered in the snow when he remembered the party that raged on in her home. But the back door would do fine, and the back set of stairs would allow him to carry the wet and delirious Belle up to her room without being seen.

He banged his boot against the door at the back of the house. Hastings pulled it open in an instant.

"Good God, what's wrong?" the butler demanded.

"We'll need hot water and towels, and a fire."

Stephen didn't hand her away as he had before. He carried her up the servants' staircase, bypassing the ballroom, up to the top floor and her bed. But this time, as the servants scurried about, building up the banked fire and removing her clothes, Stephen not only stepped outside, but he sent Hastings to find a doctor.

Stephen paced the hallway as the doctor and servants saved Belle from the ravages of the cold. If only they could save her from the ravages of her past, he thought, his heavy footsteps echoing in the hall.

The music was still playing below when the doctor came out of Belle's room and joined Stephen in the hallway. "She's just wet and tired. She'll be fine."

"Is she awake?"

"Well, no. But don't worry, she's just resting."

Stephen went to her side. She lay beneath the bed covers. He sat next to her for hours, watching the shadows cast by the fireplace leap across her face. Eventually the music died down, and the guests departed, leaving the house with an eerie quiet, but Belle neither opened her eyes nor reached out to take his hand.

Finally, Stephen went home to change, his clothes still damp. When he returned, Belle lay much as he had left her, and his concern grew to worry.

The doctor returned in the morning. His brow furrowed as he felt her forehead and checked her pulse. Maeve stood next to Hastings in the room, worry creasing her brow.

"There's no reason for her not to be waking up," the doctor said, scratching his head. "Don't understand it. No, don't understand it at all."

Maeve whimpered. Hastings wrapped his arm around her shoulders and murmured something in her ear.

It was much the same for days—Belle never waking, Stephen growing more desperate and frantic by the moment.

"I love you, Belle. More than I dreamed possible." He held her hand to his lips. "Wake up and let me show you how much."

For a second he thought she stirred. But when he looked closer, her eyes were still closed, proving him wrong.

She had told him he had saved her before, if only he could do it again. But how?

It was early on the fifth day when the bedroom door fell back on its hinges. Stephen turned to find Adam standing in the doorway, eyes bloodshot, hair disheveled, clothes badly rumpled, as if he had slept in them for weeks.

The brothers' eyes met and held, then Adam grumbled and looked away. He took unsteady steps forward, his gaze trained on Belle.

"Belle," Adam murmured, sitting on the side of the bed. "Don't do it."

"Do what?" Stephen demanded, his heart leaping into his throat.

Adam cast his brother a scathing look of disdain. "She's giving up."

"What?"

"She has no will to survive."

"How do you know that?" he snapped, his heart lodged. But even he knew the answer. The affinity they shared. Jealousy reared its ugly head.

Adam seemed to sober a bit. "I know it because I have eyes in my head, nothing special," he replied, his tone cold. "I have eyes in my head that allow me to see what people really are."

"Meaning?" Stephen asked, his body stiff, his voice ominous.

But Adam didn't seem to care. "You see what you want to see whether it's there or not. You think you're like Father, but you're not. I may have been young when he died, but I remember him, better than you obviously. He was kind and good, and not judgmental as you are. He didn't expect everyone around him to fit into a mold.

He loved people for who they are. Just as he loved Mama."

Stephen's nostrils flared and his head jerked back as he remembered the times he had thought of his mother as being like Belle. He wanted to turn away, but his brother's words held him captive.

"She was kind and good," Adam continued, his eyes closed as if he could see her in his mind. "But she was outrageous. Everyone said so."

"How could you possibly know such a thing?!"

"Because she told me." Adam's voice softened. "She laughed and loved it. And so did Father."

As much as Stephen wanted to deny Adam's words, he couldn't. Until just recently, he had forgotten so much. So hard had he concentrated on being in control that he had nearly forgotten the fun and the laughter. But how to turn back—how to undo all that he had done?

Still, the answer eluded him.

Adam would know what to do, he thought unexpectedly.

The jealousy grew, but he tamped it down with effort. Just now, there was no room for jealousy.

"You said you wouldn't hurt Belle," Adam sneered. "Look at her. I saw her dash out of the house into the rain with you behind her. I don't know what happened, but I understand enough about you to know that you hurt her deeply, and now she's giving up."

What could he say? Stephen wondered. Could he explain? Blame her father? No. Stephen knew that for very different reasons, he was as guilty as Belle's father. "No matter what you think, I love her. You might share an affinity with Belle, but she is my life." His eyes implored his brother to believe. "And I'll save her, Adam. I will."

Adam's sneer turned to disdain, then he turned on

his heel and left. Stephen watched him go. He started to pace the room, feeling impotent despair over the events he had brought to pass. His mind circled as he tried to come up with answers.

He spoke to her every day as if she were awake, as if she could actually hear him. Dropping down beside Belle, he took her hand in his, kneeling at her side. "How, Belle? How can I make things right?"

Her closed eyes and silence seared him. He had driven a woman whom he loved to the brink of madness, and his brother to the brink of despair, all because he had tried to control everything around him.

He pressed the back of her hand to his cheek. "Please, Belle. You must survive."

Then suddenly he remembered something she had said to him long ago.

I know things about you, and I don't know why.

She had said that to him. Not to Adam. *To him.* At the time, he thought her foolish. But now he had to believe that they *did* share a bond, different from what she shared with Adam, but a bond—a bond that could help him save her.

Suddenly he understood the affinity Belle and Adam shared. There had never been a reason for him to be jealous. It was not a lover's affinity that they shared. Finding Adam in the arm's of another man should have dispelled that notion long ago. He should have realized that they shared a different kind of bond, a bond between two people who were two of a kind, two people whose lives, for reasons beyond their control, would never conform to society's standards. Stephen realized then, as well, that people who stand apart from the crowd are not necessarily insane or depraved.

Like his mother.

Whom his father loved with all his heart.

Understanding struck hard and unyielding. But how, he still wondered, after this realization, could he right his grievous wrongs? Then it came to him in a blaze of light.

"I love you, Belle," he stated with conviction. "And I'm not going to let you give up."

Then he was gone, taking the stairs two at a time to the ground floor. Stephen raced out the front door and to his own house. He found Adam in the study, the decanter of brandy empty by his side, a gun on the table before him. A chill ran down Stephen's spine at the sight.

"I'd like to think the gun is there for decoration," Stephen said, paralyzed in the doorway.

Adam's head jerked back, and Stephen could tell he was trying to focus.

"Ah, brother," Adam said. "Decoration? In the end, perhaps. For now, however, I'm trying to gain the courage to kill myself."

Stephen stepped forward. "I've heard that it doesn't take courage to kill one's self. But it takes courage to live in a world where there are people like me who think they know best, judgmental people who want everyone to live the way they do to prove that their way is correct." He paused. "A better man doesn't need proof. A better man loves unconditionally." His throat ached. "I'd like to be a better man."

Adam looked at his brother, his eyes still trying to focus, but he didn't speak.

"I never told Mother that I loved her," Stephen said. "I won't make the same mistake with you."

"Ah, Stephen," Adam groaned, with a slow shake of his head. "You didn't make a mistake with Mama. She loved you."

Stephen's throat tightened. "But she knew that I chose Father over her. She didn't know that I loved her."

Adam sighed. "Oh, Stephen. Of course she knew." His head dropped back against the chair, his eyes closed in memory. "Don't you think there were times when she wished I was more like Father? But that didn't mean she didn't love me. She loved us both, Stephen, for different reasons, but equally."

Stephen looked at his brother, his throat tight. "Can you ever forgive me?"

Tears surfaced in Adam's eyes.

Stephen dropped down onto his knee. "I'm sorry, Adam. I was wrong to treat you as I have all these years. Tell me what I can do, what I can say to make things right."

A moment passed, then Adam took a deep breath. "You already have," he said, offering his brother a slight smile.

Reaching out, Stephen grabbed Adam's shoulder. "Thank you."

"Enough of this. You need to get back to Belle."

Stephen pushed up and headed for the door, but stopped when Adam spoke again.

"Save her, Stephen."

Without turning back, Stephen pressed his eyes closed before he nodded his head. "I will."

The day was trying to brighten, the sun attempting to shine through the billowing clouds in the sky as Stephen slipped into the belfry of Arlington Street Church. He climbed the stairs, up and around, higher and higher, checking his pocket watch every few steps. At the top he looked out over Boston, and while he stood there, the clouds finally parted and the sun came through. He

turned toward the Public Gardens and the houses that
stood so near, and the room at the top of one on Arlington Street where Belle lay.

He waited, hoping and praying as he had not done in
years. She had to hear. And just when his watch showed
eighteen minutes after three, he pulled on the thick bell
rope as hard as his ample strength would allow.

CHAPTER
TWENTY-EIGHT

Belle stirred at the sound of the bells. She had woken before, off and on, but had never gained the energy to force herself out of bed.

Papa.

The memory of the week before came crashing back like an elevator falling back to earth.

She turned her head to the side, fighting back tears. Taking a deep breath, she tried to assimilate how her life had changed. Other memories, ones she had held securely at bay for so many years now, rushed over her. Her mother, her father, the farmer. Her leg. The gaping hole in the sequence of her life was finally filled.

She thought of the years she had lived with Farmer Braxton before he died. She didn't know if he had ever felt any guilt over what he had done. They had lived together for twelve long years, rarely speaking, she spending most of her time alone in the room with no windows. No friends, no one to talk to. Talking to herself instead, telling herself over and over again that her father would return for her. If she wasn't saying the words out loud, she was thinking them. She realized now that she had come to a point where fact and fiction had blurred. She had come to *believe* her father would return. She had come to depend on it, starting each day with the certainty that this day would be the one, ending each day with the hope that tomorrow would bring him back.

But now the belief, and as a result, the hope—all hope—was gone, destroyed by the very man she had waited for all this time.

Papa.

Her foundation had crumbled, forcing her to accept the fact that her father had walked out of the farmyard to start a new life.

And another daughter had danced in his arms.

Belle pressed her eyes closed, searching for oblivion. But still the bells tolled in the distance, demanding her attention. When finally she opened her eyes and turned her head, the first thing she saw was the grandfather clock against the wall.

Eighteen minutes after three.

Her heart leaped in her chest.

"If you're not stodgy, then prove it by climbing the belfry at Arlington Street Church and ringing the bells."

At eighteen minutes after three.

It seemed a lifetime ago that she had spoken those words to Stephen. Perhaps it was another life where cakes looked like birds and crystal chandeliers looked like teardrops. A time before she knew her father wasn't coming home.

Despite the weakness from days in bed, with her heart lodged in her throat, Belle swung her legs over the side and walked to the French doors that led to the balcony. Stepping out, she was afraid her ears were deceiving her. But the sound rang throughout the Back Bay, loud and distinct, clear and unmistakable.

Bells. At eighteen minutes after three.

Inhaling deeply, she closed her eyes, nearly overwhelmed by emotion—by memories. But this time she didn't hold them back. She let them come. Memories of a child loved, and a child forgotten. Memories of a daughter. Memories of the virgin bride of a man who no longer wanted her.

And her father. How strange, she thought. No longer was he Papa.

While lying in bed, everyone thinking her unconscious, her father had come to her. "Belle," he had whispered from the side of her bed. But she was still too close to unconsciousness at the time, and still too close to despair to respond. He had turned away, had started to go when she heard Stephen enter the room. All was silent for a moment.

"What the devil are you doing here?" Stephen had demanded, his voice low and deadly.

Her father's response still played in her head.

"I didn't know what had happened to her," her father had said quietly.

Then a violent thud and gasp of breath. "Like hell you didn't know," Stephen had ground out, pinning her father to the wall. "I just want to know why. How could you have sold your own daughter?"

Her father had muttered and cursed, until finally he said, "I don't know."

The thud again. "Not good enough. Why, damn you. Tell me why."

"Because!"

Belle had heard the anger rise in the room like a wave of heat.

"Damn it, because. Every day, every day that I looked at her, I was forced to confront how I had failed. I had promised her mother I would be a success. God, how I had failed her. I couldn't take it any longer, and Braxton had always fancied Belle. It seemed the perfect solution." He hesitated. "She was of a marriageable age, after all."

Another thud, harsh and brutal, a deep gasping

breath. "She was a child!" Stephen roared. "A child, damn you. Your own flesh and blood, and you destroyed her!"

"I didn't know, I tell you!"

"You lie! You knew that he crushed her leg and still you left!"

"I was confused," her father whimpered.

"But not too confused to go off and start a new life with the money you made from that heartless transaction. You remarried, had another daughter, then gave her all you had failed to provide to the very child who had paid with her life to provide it for you."

"That's not true!"

"Like hell it isn't. I know everything about you, Browning Holly. You sold one daughter to have another."

"Keep Letty out of this!"

Letty. It was like a slap. A father protecting his daughter. *But what about me?* Belle wanted to scream. *What about me?*

"That's right. Letty," Stephen had raged. "Take Letty back to Philadelphia. You've done enough damage as it is. But remember, I know where to find you now. And if Belle ever wants to see you again or wants anything from you, you can bet I'll find you."

By now Belle could sense her father's tears. Part of her wanted to call to him. But another part of her, a part that was growing stronger, feigned sleep. She couldn't call out to him. Strangely, with the memory of another daughter dancing in his arms, she no longer wanted to dance with him. She wanted her life back. She wanted more.

Stephen. Dear God, she wanted Stephen.

But he had already told her it was over between them. And who could blame him, she added when she recalled her behavior of the last months.

Had she been swept off, or did she jump?

Her own words came back to haunt her. Crazy words, all for some imaginary life she had made up in her head. Stifling the tears that burned behind her eyelids, Belle wondered if she wasn't as crazy as people said she was.

She wanted to scream and cry, yell at the man who had been her father. But she was so tired, so very tired, she only wanted to sleep.

And she had for days, on and off, responding to no one.

Until the bells.

She stepped out onto the balcony, the cold winter air having begun to recede, as had the bells. Gone—the sound swept off on the breeze—as if it had never been.

She strained to hear. But there was nothing. No sound. No bells. She had been wrong.

She went back into her room and eyed the bed. But in spite of what clearly must have been her imagination, telling her the bells were ringing at eighteen minutes after three, she was out of bed, and suddenly she wanted to live. Her father had stolen seventeen years from her; she would not allow him to steal the rest. And while she had lost Stephen, she knew it was time to move on with her life. She would miss him always, but she would be thankful to him, as well. As painful as it had proven to be, he had forced her to see her life for what it truly was.

And she had survived.

She clutched the armoire.

She had survived.

A tiny spark of hope that she had thought forever snuffed out flared to life. She might have imagined the bells, but she wasn't imagining the feeling that began to burgeon in her chest. Hope. She could do anything as long as she had hope.

She walked to a basin filled with water and splashed her face. Resting frequently, she brushed her hair and completed her ablutions. She pulled open the huge armoire that stood against the wall. And just after she had pushed aside the painstakingly made gowns of lavender, pulling on her favorite blue velvet dress instead, she heard it.

Music.

Her hands stilled and her heart raced.

Her favorite waltz, coming up through the walls. The one where she allowed herself to dance.

Was it possible that she hadn't imagined the bells?

Her answer came when the music didn't disappear, only grew louder, proving that she wasn't hearing things. Proving that she wasn't crazy.

Proving that she was being given a second chance.

Her father was her past. Stephen St. James was her future.

With hesitant steps, still partly afraid to believe, she followed the sound, down the stairs, and out the door, until she stepped into Stephen's ballroom.

The music filled the high-ceilinged room. The sun had broken through the clouds. And there she found Wendell standing next to Cook, and Maeve in the crook of Hasting's arm. Rose, swaying happily to the melody. Adam, looking a bit the worse for wear, a half smile soft on his lips.

And Stephen. More handsome than she remembered, taking her breath away, standing so tall and proud, perfect except for the tiny half-moon scar just below his eye.

"Belle," he breathed, his gaze intense. "You came."

A tremulous smile quivered on her lips as she remembered so long ago when she had spoken those very words to him. "You sound surprised."

The intensity in his eyes lightened, and she knew he remembered that day as well. "I'm always surprised when you do anything I ask," he responded, repeating her words.

The music rose, swirling around them. Taking a step forward, he extended his hand. "I thought perhaps, you might accept this dance?"

His deep voice rumbled through the room, wrapping around her. A light, as bold and brazen as that cast by the crystal chandelier, flared to life in the darkness of her soul. That undeniable moment was still there, would always be there, she knew, but just then it mattered a little less.

"Yes," she breathed, "I would love to dance."

Then, taking his hand, she stepped out onto the hardwood floor as regally as a queen, and accepted the dance of her long-held dreams.

EPILOGUE

"Father! Father! Mother's cooking again!"

A nine-year-old boy slid to a halt just inside the doors of Stephen's study. Glancing up from the papers spread out on his desk, Stephen sat back in the leather chair, his smile mixing with a groan. "Are you certain, Trevor?"

"Yes, Father," the boy answered, a big mongrel dog trotting up beside him. "And she's almost done!"

Moments later, Belle sailed into the room, her unruly hair pulled back, her porcelain-white skin highlighted by a rosy glow, a plate covered with baked goods in her delicate hand. "Look what I've made," she chimed, her blue eyes dancing with excitement.

Stephen and his son eyed the items in question. "Cookies," they replied in unison, their amazingly similar features marked with doom. Even the dog, after sniffing the air, lay down on the Aubusson rug and put its paws over its head.

Belle, however, didn't seem to notice. "For my favorite fellows." She turned to her son's cherished pet. "Even you, Godfrey. I've made some shaped like big, fat, juicy bones."

Godfrey made a peculiar sound, then crawled away, escaping the study on Arlington Street. Stephen and Trevor tried to do the same.

"Where is everybody going?" Belle demanded, though a smile lurked in her eyes. "No sooner do I take the cookies out of the oven than Rose has an appointment downtown, Wendell suddenly remembers your evening wear needs to be laid out, and Maeve and Hastings disappear without a word."

"I'll eat your cookies, Mother."

Belle turned back to the doorway to find a little girl with a mass of curly brown hair and the bluest eyes imaginable. "I know you would, sweetness. But first, show your father and brother what you've made."

"Look, Father." Six-year-old Alice St. James extended a plate of her own.

"What is it, love?" he asked, opening his arms to his daughter.

Alice hurried forward. "Cookies! Just like Mother's!"

Trevor and Stephen exchanged a grim glance.

"Just like Mother's?" Trevor asked.

Belle laughed, wrapping her arm around his shoulders. "No. Alice's are edible."

Stephen's, Trevor's, and even Alice's eyes opened wide.

"Don't look at me like that," Belle said with a laugh. "Of course I know my cookies aren't so good. Do you think I haven't noticed that Adam and Tom are the only two people who will eat them?"

Stephen grimaced. "Only because my brother has a stomach of steel, and Tom wouldn't dare offend you in any way, great defender of him that you are."

Belle smiled fondly. "Well, someone has to." Then suddenly, inspiration seemed to strike. "I know, I'll take them over to Adam's."

"Great idea, Mother," Trevor said. "I'll take them right over."

"I wanna go! I wanna go!" Alice exclaimed, bouncing up and down, her cookies flying all over the rug.

In a flash, Godfrey miraculously reappeared to devour the baked goods in a few hasty bites.

"Oh, my Lord. Godfrey!" Belle demanded. "You're going to be sick."

Stephen groaned.

"Trevor, get Godfrey out of here," Belle instructed.

Trevor took hold of Godfrey's collar and began to pull. Alice tried to help.

Stephen shook his head, but a wry smile curved his lips. "I remember thinking long ago that before I met you my life was in order—everything as it should be."

"What do you think now?" Belle asked, turning back to her husband once the children had gone.

He reached out and pulled her close, pressing a desperate kiss to her forehead. "I think that finally, with children running through the house and a mangy dog at their feet, but most of all, with you at my side, my life is truly in order."

"What about the fact that I still can't cook worth a lick, wouldn't know a stylish gown if it jumped up and bit me in the face, or couldn't say the 'proper' thing to save my life?" Her face filled with a mixture of defiance and concern.

At her expression, Stephen's teasing smile faded, his countenance growing fierce. "Especially because of those things. I love you, Belle. Forever. Just as you are."